Sacred Ponies

Caroline Hartman

Red Dobie
P R E S S

Exton, Pennsylvania

First Edition
Library of Congress Control Number: 2014946273
ISBN 978-0-9893871-1-8
ISBN: 0989387119
Published by:
Red Dobie Press
an imprint of Alexemi Publishing
P.O. Box 1266
Exton, PA 19341

www.AlexemiPublishing.com

Cover Design by Bradley Wind, www.bradleywind.com
Please visit the author's website: www.carolinehartman.com

Printed in the United States of America

Sacred Ponies is Dedicated to Two Special Ladies:

My Sister, Joyce Gillespie Gaw
And
My Cousin, Linda Morris Pearson

Part One
The Nebraska Territory 1865   1
1.   Crossed Swords   3
2.   The Chicagoan   10
3.   An Evening to Remember   15
4.   Prairie Oysters   23
5.   Bear Claws   35
6.   The Edge of Civilization   42
7.   The Indian Village   50
8.   Powder River Country, Hunting Ground of the Lakota   58
9.   Blue Moon   64
10. Yellow Bird   75
11. Mary   82
12. Sunset to Sunrise   86
13. Small Pleasures   90
14. French and Indian   95
15. Old Flames   102
16. Buffalo Plaid   112
17. Red Cloud   120
18. A Pony Show   130
19. Tea Leaves and the Sweat Lodge   138
20. Whiskey   146
21. Obsessions   155
22. Words, Words, Words   162
23. Five Hundred Miles   174
24. The Trek   181
25. No Lollygagging   187
26. Face Off   192
27. Canada   196

Part Two

The Indian Academy at Camelann   201

28. Trial by the Fire   203
29. Camelann   213
30. No Coincidences   226
31. The Green-Eyed Monster   238
32. Open House   243
33. Good News, Bad News   248
34. Not as They Seem   258
35. A Bad Penny   267
36. Fort Phil Kearney   278
37. Hearth and Home   283
38. Christmas Gifts   288
39. Cabin Fever   296
40. Dreams and Drums   304
41. Back into the World   309

Part Three

Red Cloud Comes East   313

42. Red Cloud Comes East   315
43. Red Cloud Returns   323
44. From Fire Comes New Life   327

CAST OF CHARACTERS

Daniel Wallace Charteris—Former Union Brigadier General, Co-Owner of Camelann, Brother of Abbey, married to Summer Rose.
Summer Rose McAllister Charteris—Daniel's Wife, Mother of Mac, Gussie, John Alexander, and Lilly.
Abbey Charteris Kincaid Dupree—Daniel's sister, Mother of Alice and Emil.
Hal St. Clair—Former Union Brigadier General, Co-Owner of Camelann, Brother of Emily, married to Fanny.
Fanny—Hal's wife; Mother of Hank and Charlie.
Flora and the Reverend Howard Tuttle—Daniel and Abbey's Mother and her second husband.
Louisa Lenora Charteris—Half-sister of Daniel and Abbey, young daughter of Daniel's father, Louis Charteris and Pearl Mason.
Captain Ed Kincaid—Abbey's First Husband.
Captain Jake Hunt—Ed's friend.
Mary Hathaway—Abbey's Friend, Mother of Laramie Rose.
Lt. Emmett Hathaway—Mary's Husband, Artillery Lieutenant., father of Laramie Rose.
Lt. Colonel Winfried Dietrich—Commanding Officer of Ft. Laramie.
Hilda Dietrich (Dame Dilly)—His wife.

General U.S. Grant and Julia—Commander,
Union Army and his wife.
Lt. General William Sherman—Union General.
Major General Philip Sheridan—Union General.
Lt. Randall— Col. Dietrich's aide.
Master Sgt. Gilley and Georgia—Stationed at Fr. Laramie.

NATIVE AMERICANS
Red Cloud—Headman of the Lakota Sioux.
**Man-Afraid-of-His-Horse, Two-Face
and Spotted-Tail** —Headmen.
Wakanda—Sister of Red Cloud, Shaman of the Lakota Sioux.
Guilliame Emil Thunder Cloud Dupree—Half-breed son of
Wakanda and Nicholas Dupree, brother of Dr. Tilley Dupree,
father of Splashing Rabbit, Alice Fire Cloud, Emil Ruing
Cloud, brother of Walks in the Sun, second husband of Abbey.
Five Stone (Quentin Stone)—Rogue Arapahoe,
self-appointed protector of Abbey.
**Dancing Bird, Walks in the Sun, Morning Star, Sweet
Owl, Happy Moonbeam, Kicking Crane, Big Bear, Crazy
Horse, Fish, Dusty, Hawk, Lobo**—Other Native Americans.
NEIGHBORS
**Ezra and Margie Zimmerman and Mrs.
Helen Love**—Amish Neighbors.
Henry Evers, Wally Saxon—Tenants.

ANIMALS

Chester and Ruby—Daniel's Horses.

Drum—Will's Horse.

Cricket—Abbey's Horse.

Owen—Abbey's Dog.

Otto—Summer's Kitten.

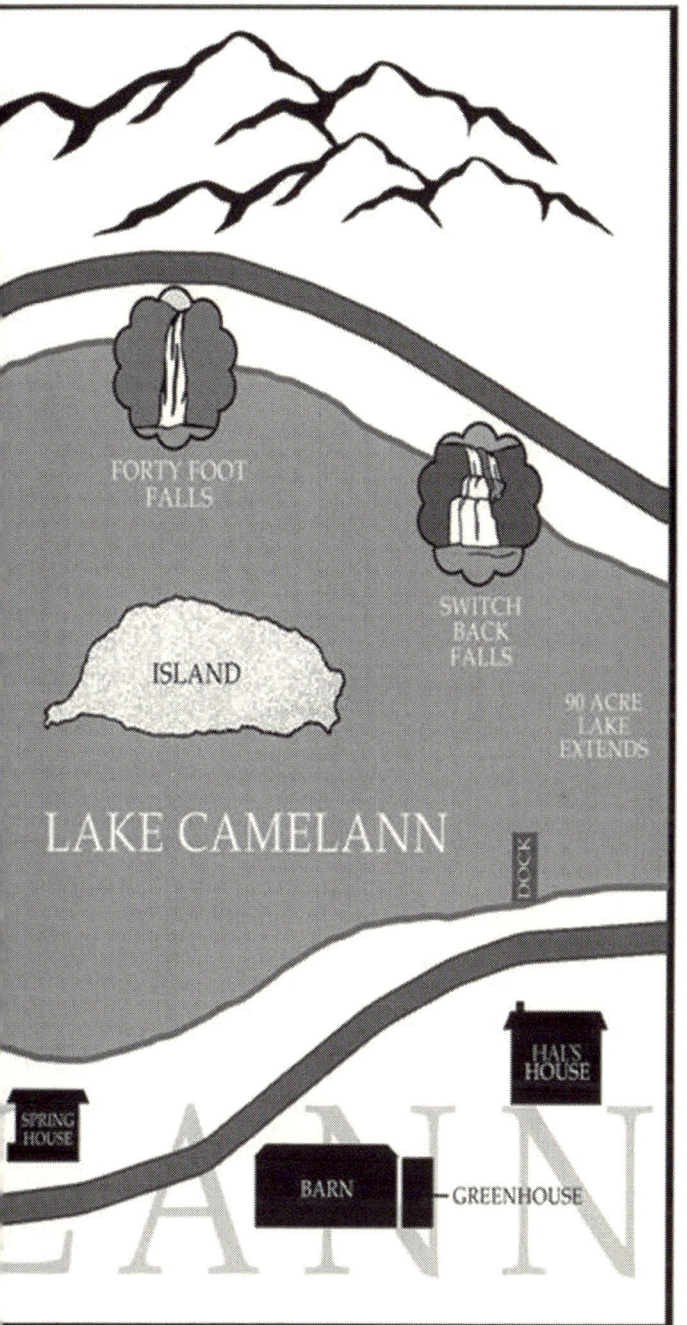

Part One

THE NEBRASKA TERRITORY
1865

"When I was a boy the Sioux owned the world.
The sun rose and set in their lands.
They sent 10,000 horsemen to battle.
Where are the warriors today? Who slew them?
Where are our lands? Who owns them?"
        —SITTING BULL CIRCA 1831-1890

1

CROSSED SWORDS

May 30, 1865

Eighteen-year-old Abbey Charteris stood in the vestibule of
the chapel at West Point fidgeting inside her wedding gown
as if it were lined in horsehair. Her brother, Brigadier General
Daniel Charteris, hero of America's Civil War, stood next to her.
He squeezed her hand. "You'll give yourself a rash if you don't
stand still. Do you want me to call it off? I will. Just say so."

The doors to the chapel swung open and strains of Bach's
Wachet Auf filled the small vestibule, she turned and instantly
calmed. From the side of her mouth, she hissed, "You'd like that,
wouldn't you? You've never cared for Ed, have you?" Bitterness
lingered in her voice.

He gripped her hand hard. He had no good reason to dis-
like him, but Daniel wasn't a big fan of Ed Kincaid. He couldn't
exactly put it into words, just a feeling. Daniel's voice came out
just above a whisper. "It isn't a matter of liking or not liking Ed.
What I object to is where he's taking you." He squeezed her hand
tighter as the chaplain nodded and he nudged his sister into position. "Ft. Laramie is the end of civilization, the frontier."

Even over the music, they both could hear their mother's sobs. He reached over with his right hand and patted her arm. *It's a wonder,* he thought, *she hasn't thrown up. Our mother is bawling like a banshee, our father deserted all of us for a whore and won't even attend his only daughter's wedding, and I'm acting like a pig-headed baboon.* He forced a smile, and Daniel's smile was known to make even grandmothers swoon, "Don't pay any attention to me, Abbey. I just don't like you growing up. What I should do is telegraph General Sheridan to warn the Indians you're coming west."

She reached beneath her bridal bouquet and squeezed his hand. Her face lit up with a smile just like his. Although seven years separated their ages, new acquaintances and old friends mistook them for twins. She was a soft rendition of him: tall, good looking, blond, with pale green eyes, smooth skin, and perfect white teeth. Years ago the knowledge of their parents' selfishness and immaturity bonded their relationship and made them both stronger.

Only two evenings before, on her last night in her childhood home, Danny had sat patiently on the side of her bed, explaining how her life had been irrevocably changed now their father had deserted the family, served their mother divorce papers, and run off with a courtesan. Except Danny, of course, hadn't used the word courtesan. He'd been much blunter.

"Dad isn't coming back, Abbey," he said. "He's given up his career, his bid for a Senate seat, a great deal of money, and us for this *whore*. The house has been sold. Any money the family has managed to hang onto must now go towards taking care of Mother." He'd sighed, his lips drawing tight. "I'm not sure she'll ever recover. Nan Charlotte is taking her to Europe until the gossip dies down, but that might take years. Philadelphia can be brutal." He'd smiled then and looked about her fancy bedroom. Her wedding gown designed by Worth hung on the back of the door. "No more ordering dresses from Paris, Abbey. Ed's an officer, and he'll be able to support you, but it won't be in the style you've always known." He stood; his face colored a little. "Someone, Mother or Summer explained all the birds and bees stuff, right?"

She'd patted his arm and nodded. She knew he'd have been embarrassed, but he would have explained.

He let out a long breath then kissed her cheek, "Phew!" Then he left.

She had sat for a long time motionless on her lace-covered bed, staring at the finery around her. She'd been raised like a princess on the Main Line, had never really wanted for anything. Now, all the trappings of wealth were gone. Daniel was gone, living by choice in the wilderness with Summer Rose and their children. Her father was gone, preferring the whore's company to that of his own children. And her mother, Flora, wasn't here either, not in spirit, anyway.

Her mother's sobs grew louder, resonating through the chapel. Flora had been crying for days, and Abbey suspected that Flora's tears were as much for her daughter as they were for her. Abbey was not only leaving her home, but all that remained of her friends. And she was about to move to one of the most god-awful places on earth: Fort Laramie in the Dakotas. She had no choice. Ed had volunteered.

The music again surged. Abbey leaned her head against Daniel's shoulder. Her throat ached from holding back tears. She whispered, "You said you thought Ed was a good man. What makes a good man?"

From the side of his mouth, he grinned and said, "Big question. Short answer. A good man knows what is right and has the balls to do it."

As Pachelbel's *Canon* surged, Abbey leaned forward, her face so serious. "How will I be able to tell if he's right?"

He dipped his head and lowered his voice. "You'll know. Just ask yourself what would your big brother do?" He looked up and there in a rainbow of sunlight, waited Captain Edward Kincaid, the man who she was about to join in Holy Matrimony. He stood with maybe twenty other people: a handful of family and friends. When their father had run off with the harlot, the Philadelphia debutante crowd had fled like lice off a drowning rat. Only two of Abbey's old clique, Mary Hathaway and Emily St. Clair, had made the trek to West Point for her wedding day.

This wasn't the crowd any of them had envisioned when she planned her wedding, but as she approached the altar everyone stood and smiled. Even her heavily veiled mother rose, though her shoulders still shook.

Emily and Mary, her very best friends, smiled encouragement. They cried, too, because they were about to be separated from each other. Emily was off to Europe right after the reception, along with Abbey's mother and Uncle Hal. Fortunately, Mary was going to Ft. Laramie with Abbey. Mary's husband, Emmett Hathaway, had actually *requested* the transfer. Ed had volunteered, too. Now the war had ended, many of the Union officers Ed had fought alongside from Shiloh to the Shenandoah had planned to join them. They were heading west to protect and supervise the completion of the transcontinental railroad and to quell the Indian unrest.

"It's a wise move for our careers, Abbey," he said. "General Sherman said that completing the cross-continental railroad is the best way to protect America."

"Danny said the same thing." She patted his arm. "A year or two out here, then we'll move back East. How bad can it be?"

Her eyes scanned the chapel, touching on the guests. Union officers in their dress blues dotted the small congregation: her brother, Uncle Hal, Ed Kincaid, a few friends, and his best man,

Jake Hunt—or rather, Captain John Jacob Hunt III. Jake had been Ed's best friend since they'd roomed together their plebe year. Stocky but hard, with dark hair and gray eyes, he was attractive enough in Abbey's opinion—certainly not of her brother or Ed's caliber—but the other girls considered him a catch. Rumor spoke of old money from whaling in his family. He certainly seemed rich. Her friend, Emily St. Clair, though, had broken off with him just before Abbey's wedding, but when Abbey asked her what had happened, Emily had looked teary-eyed at the question.

"I only know he's not for me," she'd said. "Don't worry about me, silly. It's your wedding day."

Jake acted as if Emily meant nothing to him, and Abbey tried not to show how greatly relieved she was by the breakup. Abbey didn't say as much to Ed, but she didn't like Jake. She never had. She wasn't exactly sure why she felt that way, but she often sensed Jake would prefer to drop her into a hole or send her off to play in the nursery so he and Ed could discuss Army business or play poker or drink too much whiskey and horse around. At other times, however, she caught him evaluating her female assets, which made Abbey very uncomfortable and angry. She was happy Emily was on her way to tour the continent, far from Jake. She was also very glad that Captain Jake Hunt would not be at Ft. Laramie with them. Somewhere in mid-Nebraska, he and his men would head north into the Black Hills.

She spotted a couple of men in civilian dress. Her heart for a moment surged but her father had not miraculously materialized at the last minute. She'd known all along that he dared not show his face, but deep down, well, she had hoped.

Tonight she would be leaving everything she'd ever known, and he hadn't even written her a note.

They reached the end of the aisle and stopped in a pool of light from the stained glass windows. Daniel turned toward her and gently folded back her veil. As he bent to kiss her cheek he dabbed at her tears with the end of a starched handkerchief, and the poignancy of his gesture almost made her cry again. He knew she'd be emotional, and he had the foresight to tuck his handkerchief in his sleeve just in case. Her stiff upper lip, the one thing that had maintained her down the aisle, wobbled.

Oh, Danny, you are my hero. I know you're a good man.

Now Daniel turned his sister gently toward Captain Edward Kincaid and gave Ed her hand.

Ed took it. "You look gorgeous, Sunshine," he whispered.

Abbey felt the soothing warmth of his palm through her glove. She longed for today to be over, for the moment when they could slip into their bridal bed. They'd been engaged for ages and had waited so long. But what Abbey wanted more than anything on earth was to fall asleep, safe in his arms, then to wake up still there and still safe. It had been so long since she felt safe.

This longing for security sustained her through their vows, all the way up the long aisle in step with Mendelssohn's *Twelfth Night*, under the crossed swords, and over to the inn for the wedding luncheon, which became a blur of champagne, fruit salad, and tasteless creamed chicken on toast points.

Her father's absence burned a hole in her heart. Couldn't he have at least sent flowers? A note? Unfortunately, she wasn't the only one to notice. Flora kept up her sniffles through the entire luncheon. Thank God for Nan Charlotte, who waved smelling salts under Flora's nose.

Abbey sipped her third glass of champagne and the bubbles tickled her throat, making her giggle. Someone chimed spoons, and someone else slipped another full glass of the bubbly wine into her hand. She turned to Ed and leaned into his burly shoulder, his reassuring arms folded around her, and his sweet face, lit by those smoldering, whiskey-colored eyes, bent toward her for a kiss.

From beneath her lashes she caught Jake Hunt glaring at her, and the raw intensity of his expression startled her. *Why was he staring like that?* The man gave her the creeps. Pulling Ed closer, she kissed him again, trying to forget Jake's scowl. But the kiss only reminded her of the awful truth: she was about to follow this man into the wild Dakota territories. Jake wouldn't be the only unpleasant thing. Fortunately, the champagne smoothed the rough edges, made her stronger. She took another sip, then kissed her husband again. *Glare all you want, Jake Hunt.*

2

THE CHICAGOAN

The morning after her wedding night, Abbey woke to the clacking of the *Chicagoan* as it rumbled around her. Foggy details seeped into her throbbing head, and she moaned into the pillow. Somehow she found and used the bathroom, then stumbled back to bed where she rolled onto her belly and buried her head under the pillow. Stripes of blinding yellow light flashed into the compartment through the shutters and made their way under her pillow, forcing vague memories of last night into focus.

Two things came to mind. First, she awakened alone. Second, she felt no different than yesterday and suspected her virginity was intact.

She and Ed had planned a two-night honeymoon in Saratoga, but the Army had changed Ed's orders at the last moment. Instead of a luxurious hotel room, they now sped west in the rear half of a boxcar—but not just any boxcar. The two top commanders of the United States Army, Generals Sherman and Sheridan—she always got the two of them mixed up in her head—had arranged for the newlyweds to occupy half a private car with its own bathroom, located at the end of the special troop train, giving them some privacy. *Considerate of them,* she thought, though she would have preferred the honeymoon suite in the swank Saratoga hotel. She frowned at the effort of remembering which General was which. Then in a rush, it came back to her. Sherman was the redheaded one; Sheridan was the short one.

The rhythm of the train gave no comfort. Her head pounded, and every joint in her body ached. Even after having brushed her teeth her mouth tasted vile, and nausea lurked in her throat. Scenes she'd rather not remember flashed by, and she cringed at the memory of Mary and Summer Rose helping her out of her wedding dress and into the ghastly flamingo pink peignoir, a gift from Ed's great Aunt Madeline, his only living female relative. Mary and Summer had held the little item up in the dim candle-light and giggled.

"Be thankful it's nighttime," said Mary.

"The color is atrocious," Summer agreed, "and it certainly doesn't cover much. Did you wear something like this on your wedding night, Mary?"

Mary shook her head, her eyes wide and round like an owlet's. "Oh, no! We're Presbyterians. Cotton, a little lace, but nothing like this! It shows *every*thing." She giggled, then covered her mouth when she hiccoughed. Abbey wasn't the only girl to have drunk too much wine. "Emmett would have loved it, though," she said, lowering her eyes. "But he doesn't need much to excite him. I try not to wear anything provocative." She glanced back up at Summer, her voice quivering. "What did you wear?"

Summer's expression lit up as a rush of memories swept through her. She blushed, and before she could remember that Mary had been in love with Daniel before Daniel had even met her, Summer blurted out, "I made a sweet little gown of white lawn embroidered with red roses, but Daniel had me out of my clothes before I had a chance …"

Mary stiffened then looked down at Abbey in the sickening pink froth. In a mad effort to change the subject, she blurted out, "I'm afraid Ed won't have any surprises."

Unfortunately, Ed experienced several surprises, starting with Abbey throwing up all over the hideous pink peignoir the moment he stepped into their compartment. His resourcefulness and kindness made her cry and throw up again, this time dousing his white trousers. Ever the gentleman, he just smiled then found soap and warm water, even a toothbrush. He turned his head as he helped her out of the ghastly confection—saying something about the color being horrible enough to make anyone ill—and into a more practical gown. After that he wrapped her in a cotton blanket and held her while a porter cleaned up the mess. The last memory she had was of snuggling in his arms.

Now she squinted up at him as he entered their compartment, the sun a bright screen behind him. He was clean-shaven, immaculate in his captain's uniform, and balancing a domed oval tray in one hand. He looked happier than he had any right to be.

"I see you're alive," he said.

With some effort, Abbey sat up and fluffed pillows behind her. She still felt queasy, but one corner of her mouth curled. "And still a virgin, a very embarrassed one. I'm so sorry, Eddie. Why didn't you sleep here?"

A boyish grin filled his face. "You sprawled across the entire bed. I didn't have the heart to move you. Jake's cabin had two bunks." He lowered himself and the tray to the bed, a fold-up contraption that consumed most of the compartment. "I thought perhaps we'd address your hangover before turning to such serious matters as what to do about your virginity." He grinned as he uncorked a bottle of ginger ale. "I think this will do you far more

SACRED PONIES

good than anything else." His eyebrows danced as he poured the drink over shaved ice then handed the glass to her. "Little sips."

The fizz in her throat felt wonderful and the ice even better. But when he lifted the silver dome from the tray, uncovering four pieces of toast and a rack of bacon, she blanched. He grinned at her reaction, and she was struck again by the look of him. While Ed might not be as devastatingly handsome as her brother, he possessed a great smile, open and sweet with a twinge of little boy devilment.

"This is for you." He arranged a slice of bacon on half a piece of toast and held it out for her. "I breakfasted with Jake."

She bit her lip skeptically, and he chuckled.

"Trust me. I've had a little experience with hangovers, Sunshine. Just nibbles. You'll feel much better with food in your stomach."

When she'd finished all the ginger ale and half the bacon and toast, he took the tray and set it outside their compartment. When he returned, he arranged himself, still fully dressed in his crisp uniform and gleaming boots, on the edge of the bed. She took a deep breath, inhaling his scent of soap and Bay Rum, and realized with great relief that he'd been right. She did feel better.

He picked up her hand and kissed it. "I have a suggestion, Sunshine. Actually, Jake proposed this. Of course, we'll do whatever you want, but what he recommended makes a lot of sense. Rather than going out and mingling with our fellow officers—and I guarantee you there will be questions and much teasing—Jake suggested you and I just stay here in our compartment. Trust me, my comrades have no manners." He shrugged a light, comfortable lift of those broad shoulders. "We don't have to do anything if you don't want—maybe invite Jake for lunch. I have lots of reading to catch up on."

She squirmed, confused by Ed's apparent lack of enthusiasm to share their bed. "But—

"Don't worry. You can nap, read, watch New York state roll by. We're married, Abbey. There's no hurry. I'm just happy to spend time with you."

The idea of staying in the compartment sounded perfect to Abbey, but there was no way Jake Hunt was joining them for lunch or anything else. By this point, the ginger ale had worked miracles on her aches, and the toast and bacon had calmed her nausea, so she arched her back, pulling the bodice of her modest nightgown tight. Her new husband's eyes flashed, Abbey could tell that even in the demure gown she presented a fetching picture: a mass of wild blonde curls, pale green eyes, skin as fresh as dew on a rose petal. She might resemble Daniel, but Abbey was all girl. Friends envied her, said her complexion seemed pore-less

Laying her head back against the pillows, she stretched and her full breasts pressed against the thin white cotton. Ed's simmering brown eyes focused on them, and he reached over and placed his hand on the outside of the sheet, running it up the long line of her thigh. A bar of sunshine caught his West Point ring, making it shine. She pressed her fingers over Ed's hand and guided it over the sheet, following the slope of her hip and belly to just above where her legs met. Her tongue peeked from between perfect white teeth.

"We don't *have* to do anything," she said smoothly, "but we might. Why don't you take off that uniform? Oh, and check the lock on the door, would you please? I'd like you all to myself."

3

An Evening to Remember

As the train rattled through the rest of New York state, a corner of Pennsylvania, and all of Ohio, they made love. Ed proved a knowledgeable lover, and Abbey an apt and enthusiastic student. They napped in entangled bliss and sent the porter for food twice, and until half a day out of Chicago, the newly married Abbey Kincaid stayed either bundled in a gorgeous green velvet robe, embroidered with lavender and white violets or wrapped in nothing but a sheet. Ed preferred the sheet.

Abbey intercepted two notes from Jake, which she shredded. If Ed noticed, he didn't let on.

The troop train rattled through the night, not stopping at villages, and flashes of light washed over their bodies. On the second night he nuzzled her neck and whispered, "I never imagined marriage would be like this. You're a wonderful surprise."

"What do you mean?"

"The fellows have been giving me advice for weeks. They said you'd be sore and wouldn't like what we did in bed." He chuckled. "How many times now? I haven't hurt you, have I?"

She shook her head and rubbed her hands over his rock hard chest and upper arms. "I love you, and I love what you do to me." She rolled onto her back and let out a long sigh. "We waited so long for this."

He snorted gently. "I had no idea you'd like it." The train plummeted into darkness, and his strong soldier's body pressed her hard to the mattress. "Do you like me to be rough or gentle?"

Her voice was husky. "I like both." She nipped at his shoulder playfully. "Right now, I think gentle."

"Gentle it is. Slow or fast? Most girls like slow."

"Oh, I think I like wild." She giggled. "But slow will do this time. I think my handsome captain has used up all his wild. So tell me … have you slept with many women?"

He giggled as he rained kisses between her breasts to her bellybutton. "What do you think, Sunshine?"

"You certainly seem like you know what you're doing."

He reversed the direction of his kisses.

He started to move. Slowly. "Okay, Sunshine. You asked for slow."

Another town flashed by, and by the light cutting through the shutters she saw his whiskey-colored eyes twinkle. She closed her eyes and smiled.

"You, young lady, are driving me crazy," he whispered, leaning down so his breath tickled her ear. "I need a little help. I think it's a man's natural inclination to go fast. Slow me down. Ask me questions."

She caught on quickly. "What is the capital of Delaware? Spell it, please."

"I know that one. D-o-v-e-r."

"Oh, my God, that feels good." She sucked in a breath, then managed, "New Jersey?"

"T-r-e-n-t-o-n. What will you ask when we run out of states?"

"South America? Europe? Will you last that long?" She groaned slowly. "I don't know if I will. New York?"

"As long as you have questions, I'll last. A-l-b-a-n-y. After Europe?"

She drew in a quick breath. "Oh, my God, Eddie. That is so good. Math? I'm good at math. Are you? Rhode Island?"

"Of course I'm good at math. I'm an engineer. But I'll get bored with math. Saskatchewan."

She chuckled. "Saskatchewan isn't even in the United States."

"Oh, Sunshine." He laughed and kissed her temple. "Do I have to get them right?"

"Can you spell it?"

"S-a-s-k-a-t—"

He spelled it wrong several times—slowly—and when he finally got it right, neither of them cared if he was slow or fast. She thrashed and shook. When her sweat soaked body finally calmed, she curled into a ball and clung to him.

"Where on God's green earth did you learn to do that?" she asked after a few moments.

The train slid to a stop, and he peeked between the shutters, then back at her. He grinned his little boy smile and murmured, "A little east of Gary, Indiana."

"Gary, Indiana?"

"Yeah, Sunshine." He winked. "That's what the sign over the station says."

As they passed into Illinois, Ed was obviously struggling to keep his eyelids open. Still, he ordered baths for both of them, and after long, hot soaks, a short nap, and a bottle of champagne, they dressed for a special dinner hosted by the generals. This was to be their first venture out of their honeymoon cocoon.

AT A STOPOVER in Chicago the generals arranged a small dinner party, inviting half a dozen officers and three wives to dinner at a lakeside hotel. The breeze off the water was balmy, bringing the distant clanging of halyards and buoys, and the occasional shriek of a gull. To the south they could just see the lights of the city, and far out over the lake lightning flashed with heat.

The party ordered from menus, dining by lantern light on one of the many porches. Lake Michigan lapped softly below them. Down on a pavilion near the water a quartet played popular songs and couples danced. Abbey sat between her husband and Jake, and across from Mary and Emmett Hathaway.

Mary and Abbey had been best friend since forever. All their lives they planned to be sisters-in-law, but Summer Rose had ruined that dream when Daniel married her instead of Mary. Mary's marriage to Emmett was definitely done on the rebound, but that meant nothing. Seeing her glowing face across the table now, no one would guess Mary had ever loved anyone other than Emmett Hathaway, the clean-cut, redheaded, blue-eyed, young captain of light artillery. Their marriage seemed made in heaven. Tonight Mary sparkled, she was so beautiful. Renowned for her flawless white skin, she wore a celery green organza dress with capped sleeves and a low oval neckline. Ringlets of her dark, almost black, hair framed her pretty face, and around her slim neck she wore a tight, dark green velvet ribbon with a diamond encircled cameo pinned to it.

For months after Daniel married Summer Rose, Abbey and Mary hated her for destroying their dream. They fantasized about drowning her in the river, poisoning her food, or shoving her under a carriage, but Daniel's wife proved impossible to not like. She ignored their insults and appeared as if she couldn't have cared less about their attempts to exclude her. Through it all she remained poised and beautiful and absolutely crazy about Daniel. Abbey had learned a great deal from Summer Rose about how to behave under duress.

On Mary's other side sat General Sheridan—the short one. He was leaning toward the conversation taking place at the end of the table where General Sherman—the one with red hair— talked with Colonel Dietrich and his wife, Hilda. Hilda Dietrich was known behind her back by the somewhat derogatory name of *Dame Dilly*. Childless, tall, rail thin, and a good deal older than the young wives—at least she *looked* much older—Dame Dilly had attended Smith College and took every opportunity to make sure everyone knew it.

Colonel Winfred Dietrich, "Win" to his friends, was red-faced with immaculate white hair and a neatly trimmed beard. He was to be Emmett and Ed's new commanding officer at Ft. Laramie. He drank like a fish.

Everyone soaked up plenty of champagne, and the men topped that with whiskey, then more wine. Abbey enjoyed flirting with her new husband, whispering to him about returning to Gary, Indiana, but Ed's filters regarding proper behavior diminished with each drink. Long before the first course, he was slurring his words and pointedly eyeing his wife's impressive décolleté—as was every man at the table. Abbey wore a shell pink dress of many layers of lawn, and the scooped neckline had a standup ruffle, giving the illusion a person could peek over it and see her bellybutton. Of course such a feat was impossible, since her lovely breasts blocked the view.

Halfway through the entrée, an inebriated Ed picked up one of his lamb chops and swiped it across his lips, then leaned toward his wife.

"You look just like a little pink lamb chop," he told her, his words punctuated with alcohol-induced snorts and giggles.

"When I get you out of your pretty pink dress, I'm going to start on your little pink toe and gobble up every delectable pink inch."

He devoured the lamb chop with great gusto, keeping his glassy eyes on her. With her face an even brighter shade of pink than her dress, Abbey glanced around surreptitiously; praying no one else understood what erupted from his mouth. Unfortunately, even the people on the next porch looked over.

Mortified, Abbey stiffened her spine and savagely pinched Ed's thigh. That closed his mouth. On her other side, Jake snorted and choked, spitting a mouthful of green peas into his big linen napkin. All she could hope was that some of them went up his nose. She was about to elbow him when Colonel Dietrich, his face glowing as red as if he'd swallowed a stick of dynamite, followed up with an announcement to the entire table.

"Captain Kincaid, if you're not up to it, I'll fuck her for you." He then burped, raked his hungry gaze over her neckline, and said, "I've been thinking about doing just that all evening."

The silence that followed could have been cut and served in a dish. Then, as they all watched, their new commanding officer suddenly fell over and planted his face in his plate. Abbey hoped he drowned in the gravy. Dame Dilly turned a deathly gray, but Abbey knew instinctively that anything she might say to the woman would only aggravate the situation, so she avoided everyone's eyes and asked the stone-faced waiter for a roll.

"And some butter, please," she added sweetly.

General Sheridan nodded to Emmett, and each officer stood and took one of the colonel's arms, hefting Colonel Dietrich to his feet. Mashed potatoes, green peas, and cream gravy stuck to his face and dribbled from his beard as the officers half-carried, half-dragged him to a cab. Based on their efficiency, Abbey sensed this was not a new occurrence. Every eye on every porch followed them, except those of Mrs. Dietrich, who glared at Abbey. She stared as long as she could, then followed her husband.

After she left, Mary reached across the table and squeezed Abbey's fingers. "You handled that beautifully."

Abbey frowned at her husband. He appeared to have sobered up, because now he wouldn't meet her gaze. Jake had left the table and was standing by the railing, blowing his nose.

General Sheridan and Emmett returned just as General Sherman moved from his place at the end of the table and took Jake's seat next to Abbey. He ordered a brandy for everyone at the hushed table, including the girls, then lit a cigar. Gulls, excited by bits of garbage being tossed in the lake, careened overhead while waiters cleared the Dietrichs' debris. As the white-gloved hands served the drinks, the red-haired general, the man whose army burned Atlanta and brought South Carolina to her knees, lowered his chin and surveyed the young officers and their wives.

"This will not become common gossip." He tapped his cigar on the edge of an ashtray and looked directly at each person. "Colonel Dietrich is a hero and one hell of a good Indian fighter, but he shouldn't drink." He took a long pull on his cigar and said, "Though you can hardly blame him, with a wife like his."

A careful chuckle rolled through the men. General Sherman lifted his brandy glass. "I insist we all forget this incident happened. If word of this travels back to Congress, several of our illustrious Senators and congressmen might have conniptions, perhaps strokes." He took Abbey's hand. "All that aside, young lady, please allow me to apologize on behalf of Colonel Dietrich."

Phil Sheridan cleared his throat, then turned to Abbey and effectively changed the subject. "How is your sister-in-law, the sweetheart of the cavalry?"

Abbey smiled. "Summer Rose is happy. And as beautiful as ever. You know they had twin boys in April, don't you? I imagine they are keeping her busy." From the corner of her eye she saw Mary blanch, but even for her friend she couldn't avoid the truth all the time.

Sheridan grunted. "Trust Danny to keep her barefoot and pregnant. She was the best damn horse soldier I ever commanded. Did I ever tell you about Summer Rose, Cump?"

Cump, short for Tecumseh—William Tecumseh Sherman—sighed. "At least twenty times." He shook his head and grinned at Abbey. "You look more like your brother every time I see you. You know, I'm always being compared to my brother, the honorable Senator John Sherman from Ohio. Did you know they call him *The Ohio Icicle*?" He shook his head, looking disgusted. "I hate it. Being compared, that is. Do you mind?"

Abbey settled back in her chair, relieved the ugly incident had been safely tucked away. Now she faced the two heroic generals, feeling confident. General Sherman was next in line to head the entire United States Army, and General Sheridan was next after him. They might have intimidated many, but Abbey had grown up with them sitting as guests around her parents' dining room table in their Washington home. They were good men to know, especially since Colonel Dietrich and his wife, in all probability, were about to make her life more miserable than she could imagine.

She smiled at General Sherman. "I'm used to it, Sir. You would not believe the number of women who became my best friend just so they could cozy up to my brother." She shrugged. "It used to bother me, but I don't mind now. I wish he were with us."

General Sheridan's eyes slid to Jake Hunt, then to Ed, and his smile quirked on one side. "With you here, it's almost as if he is. Don't you agree, Cump?"

4

PRAIRIE OYSTERS

The military train rumbled over a trestle and let loose a long wailing whistle. Since they stopped only briefly for fuel and water they made good time flying through Iowa. Ed cracked one eyelid, and the moonless black sky whirled by the windows. His tongue and teeth felt furry, his stomach queasy. He groaned and pulled a pillow over his face, then reached down and rubbed his thigh. Abbey's pinch still ached, though he supposed he deserved worse.

Truth was, he felt sick all over, and it wasn't just the fault of all the booze or her pinch. A lot of the problem came from the war being fought in his throbbing head. Part of him longed for his old life, but another part raced toward this new adventure of marriage. *I'd better be careful. I might fall in love with my wife.*

He liked watching her do girl things. In the few days of their marriage, he grew to like watching everything about her. Ed's mother had died when he was nine, and he'd spent his childhood in a household of boys, five wild hellions. His father, an army officer, had dragged them all over the southwest, and an uncle and his older brothers served as substitute mothers. Not one of them looked like this gorgeous girl.

He slid his eyes over her profile, feeling a twinge of pride that she was his wife. Even in her prim, high-necked white blouse and simple black skirt, she looked gorgeous. Her breasts were awesome—even Jake, who was not a breast man, agreed there. The thought of them made him wet his lips. Marriage was far better than he ever expected, and that frightened him a little. Liking his new life had never been in the plan.

He eased his naked body upright against the headboard and pulled a sheet over his lower half. Memories of the last two days worked their way into his mind, and desire coursed through him. Good God, he liked how she responded to him. And to think Jake had told him a girl of her class, a debutante, would be fragile. Lord, she was anything but frail.

He married her for several reasons: the first was to enhance his career—having a wife in the Army was almost a necessity. The second was to simplify his life: wives saw to clean laundry, dinner, paying bills, and easy sex. Mostly he had married this girl because Jake said he wanted him married to Daniel Charteris' sister. He said it would help both their careers. He suspected something more, but he did just what Jake asked—as always.

Right from the beginning, when Jake told him to court her, he didn't think much beyond Abbey's looks. The package was pretty spectacular. Few men would complain. After a few dates, he admired her intelligence and sense of humor. She made talking easy.

God, his leg still hurt from where she pinched him. He shook his head. *Why, oh why, did I call her lamb chop?* He shuddered at the thought of facing her sober. She must have heard his movements, for she turned around and grabbed his big toe.

"Up and at 'em, big boy. You and your little *lamb chop* must gird their loins and face Colonel and Dame Dilly. You have twenty minutes. I want to be in that dining car as soon as it opens."

He knew better than to argue, not when she used that tone. His kit lay on the washstand, clean clothes hung on the door; in close to twenty minutes he was shaved and ready.

Last night they had collected their belongings. Now Ed rechecked their tags and set their trunks outside the door. This personal luggage would be loaded onto wagons for the river crossing and for the long trek by horse-drawn wagon across Nebraska to Ft. Kearney then Ft. Laramie. The easy leg of the journey was over.

She was so confident, smiling, and chipper. Guilt for his behavior washed over him. He held the door for her, but as she passed by his arms came up and blocked her progress. "I'm sorry about last night, Sunshine. I will never drink anything stronger than beer again."

She reached up and touched his cheek with gentle fingertips, then planted a sweet, unexpected kiss on his mouth. "Oh, Eddie, neither one of us should ever touch alcohol again."

He couldn't help but return her smile. He'd expected to face a firing squad this morning, and he much preferred this kind of reception.

She took a deep breath then let it out in a gust. "I don't know about you, but I cannot face the Dietrichs without an occasional drink. I wish I had a glass of champagne right now. Better yet, maybe a shot of whiskey. And the Dakotas! Oh Ed! I've heard it's endless miles of nothing except rattlesnakes, buffalo, and savages. Broiling in the summer, freezing in the winter, ten good days a year, someone told me." She closed her eyes for a moment then opened them. He saw a smile dancing within. She ducked under his arm.

"Follow my lead, sweetheart. Your lamb chop is going to return us to the good graces of Colonel and Dame Dilly. Because you know what? Life will be pure hell if I don't do something and do it now."

THEY ENTERED THE dining car two people behind Colonel and Mrs. Dietrich. Brass gaslights on each table flickered and vibrated as the train plowed west. Determined and a wee bit brazen, Abbey walked up to the colonel's table and asked, "May we join you for breakfast?"

Dame Dilly's mouth dropped open. Before any words popped out, Abbey slid into the seat next to the window, opposite Mrs. Dietrich, and pulled Ed in beside her. The colonel's corpulent complexion deepened.

Abbey leaned forward, looking coyly at the two of them as if she were tremendously embarrassed. In a conspiratorial whisper she said, "I must apologize. I drank too much champagne last night and don't remember thanking you for dinner. To be candid, Sir," she confided, her big green eyes blinking prettily, "I don't remember much of anything."

Dame Dilly started to sputter; the wattles of her turkey neck jiggled with outrage. "How dare you patronize …"

Colonel Dietrich's calloused hand touched his wife's wrist, and his West Point ring caught the wedge of light widening in the east. He nodded toward Abbey.

"Apology accepted, my dear." With his hand still patting his wife's wrist, Colonel Dietrich turned to the white-gloved Negro waiter standing at attention. "Captain Kincaid," he said, "Erasmus here makes the perfect Prairie Oyster. May I order one for you? It's a great hair of the dog." The colonel smiled. "Erasmus claims it cures what ails you and erases all memory of the previous night. Right, boy?"

Erasmus flashed big white teeth. "My special recipe, Sir."

"Two then, and perhaps some of those preserved peaches for the ladies. Coffee all around. Make it quick."

Erasmus brought coffee for everyone and peaches for the ladies, then placed two stubby glasses of his version of a sure-fire hangover cure on the table. Ed stared then sniffed at a raw, floating egg which had been carefully dropped into a shot of whiskey. Grated horseradish, smashed anchovy, a witch's brew of secret spices and condiments, and a bloody splash of tomato juice topped the concoction.

The colonel lifted his prairie oyster, staring the yellow yolk square in the eye just before drinking it down. "Cheers."

Ed followed the colonel's lead and was thoroughly relieved when he managed not to toss it up. Abbey cut a peach slice in half and wished the colonel had ordered a prairie oyster for her.

ABBEY FINISHED HER last bite of toast and heard the thumping of the brakeman running across the roof of the car. The iron wheels screeched as the train rolled into Council Bluffs, Iowa, the end of the railroad line. Outside the windows, the sun rose into a gray prairie sky over the sprawling town. Rough wooden buildings spread out from the rail yards, and Abbey could see more sprouting framework in the distance. High on the bluffs new mansions emerged and Abbey remembered Ed saying they were for the Union Pacific executives coming to town. Beyond the yards lay the mighty Missouri River, thick with steamers, barges, and ferries. Beyond the river sat Omaha and the untamed Indian Territory, which the Union Pacific Railroad readied itself to conquer.

With military efficiency, two hundred soldiers detrained, along with at least twice that many horses and mules, followed by wagons, and artillery pieces. Boxcars full of crates and barrels, bags of grain, flour, and cornmeal, bales of hay and straw, as well as supplies from gunpowder to bandages were transferred to covered wagons then packed onto ferries and floated across the Missouri River to the Nebraska Territory. An emigrant train of covered wagons attached itself to the army column and swelled daily.

Travel was slow, but in 1865 crossing Nebraska was much safer than it was even ten years earlier. Then, nearly a third of its travelers succumbed to disease or drowned. Now, even with ferries making the river crossings safer and the U.S. Army engineers demanding sanitary measures, the trip still seemed to take much too long. On a good day they might make fifteen miles, but good days were rare.

Colonel Dietrich procured horses for several of the wives. Mary and Abbey, as officers' wives, had their own wagon, but they usually chose to ride horses. Most of the prairie was stunningly beautiful, full of wild flowers and thousands of birds. Game was plentiful. Once the girls heard and felt the rumble of the buffalo, but they didn't see them.

The two biggest problems they faced were fuel and fresh water. In lieu of trees, the army cooks used precious coal or dried buffalo chips for fuel; too often the only water available was from the Platte, a brackish river which stretched a mile wide and often only two inches deep, all the way across Nebraska. Again, the engineers lectured on how to procure safe water: let it sit in a bucket for at least an hour, allowing the silt to settle, then boil it.

Ft. Kearney, which was the halfway mark between Omaha and Ft. Laramie, frightened the girls. Officers' families were living in hovels made of sod. The further west they traveled, the more Indians they came upon, and the more they realized how far removed they were from the power and protection of the United States Government. The fort commander and his staff reeked of whiskey at 11:00 in the morning, and Colonel Dietrich estimated that at least $35,000 worth of U.S. Army supplies were rotting in dilapidated mud huts. Ft. Kearney might have been grand at one point, but it was in such disrepair that it was an embarrassment to see Old Glory flying over it.

"A dozen squaws with papooses strapped on their backs could capture it," said Colonel Dietrich.

Would Ft. Laramie be like this?

At Scotts Bluff, a cow town near Chimney Rock, the wagon train stopped for a full day for much needed repairs. This was the place where Jake Hunt, along with a troop of fifty or so soldiers, would be cutting off to patrol north toward the Black Hills. Abbey was happy to see him go. She had tried hard to like him. After all he was Ed's friend. But she failed. The man was an arrogant showoff who was always bossy to her. Even worse was the way he constantly criticized Ed. "Good riddance," Abbey muttered under her breath.

A COUPLE OF the Russian women, emigrants from the wagon trains, told her of a decent store nearby where the prices weren't too inflated. Ed went antelope hunting, and Mary didn't feel well, so Abbey rode over by herself. The exercise vented steam. Dame Dilly, just this morning insulted her, and between Dame Dilly and Jake, the peaceful journey across the prairie quickly lost its charm.

She glanced around the town, taking in the sights. A big sign advertised whiskey for $8 a gallon—a bargain. Since they apparently had several hogsheads in stock, the place was crowded. Soldiers, emigrants from the wagon trains, hunters, cowboys, and traders all crowded the street, along with their horses and a small herd of cattle. Off to the side of the store, a small group of Indian women and children gathered, and on a rise behind the buildings, two braves—young teenagers—watched from their perches on spotted ponies.

Abbey was disappointed to see Jake already there. As she dismounted, he rode up to her and scowled at the Indians. "You can be damn sure there's a hundred more up in the hills. I hope to see every goddamn one of them dead." As if just realizing who she was, he frowned and glanced around. "Where's Ed?"

"Hunting."

He dismounted, looped his reins around the post then gripped her upper arms hard. "You rode here by yourself? Where the hell is your head? If the Indians take you, it would take a hundred good men to rescue you."

She stepped back, and though his grip lessened, he still held her firmly. She took a deep breath, picturing the nine inch hatpin her grandmother had given her, tucked away in the blue and yellow hatband of her straw hat, hiding demurely among the fake daisies. She was tempted to pull it out and stick him with it.

"Just out for a little ride," she told him. "I want to pick up some taffy for Ed." *Why am I even answering him?*

Without another word, he further tightened his grip until it hurt and roughly shoved her down the street. She sensed every cavalryman—and there must have been twenty—turning toward her like pigeons pointing into the wind. The Indians, the young boys on ponies, the few drovers, all of them stared at her. She pulled her shawl close. Her feelings vacillated between appreciation for Jake's presence and fury at his manhandling of her. *I really,* she thought, *must buy a knife, maybe a gun.*

He navigated her along the wooden sidewalk, past cattle pens and a bar that reeked of beer and whiskey, past the stagecoach office. Across the street stood the store she planned to visit, sitting like an island in the midst of the River Styx.

Her eyes scanned the town, and she grudgingly admitted a little justification for his anger. In truth, this crossroads was no place for a lone woman. Thick dust and the stink of manure permeated over sweat and blood. Drovers hollered the crudest of expletives, made obscene gestures, offered her money. Over the din, someone fired a pistol and a whip cracked. Jake yanked her to the edge of the sidewalk, and one of the horses in a parked team of six reared in its traces. Two drovers veered out of the way, and one aimed straight toward a very small Indian boy playing on the edge of the boardwalk.

Abbey jerked her arm free, elbowing Jake hard in the ribs, and scooped up the child, settling him on her hip as if she always carried a child there. Instinctively, she wrapped her plaid shawl around him then pressed her cheek to the top of his head. His thick black hair smelled of sun and sage. When he moved his head, his big brown eyes stared up at her, a tear hovering in the corner of one eye. Her heart choked.

Jake moved to take the child from her, chiding her. "Are you crazy? Put that child down. He's filthy, probably has lice. They'd just a soon put a hatchet in your back as appreciate you saving one of their brats."

The little boy's heart raced—she felt it pounding against her own chest—and his small fingers clung to her shawl. She stepped away from Jake, shielding the child with her body, and hurried across the street toward the group of Indian women. She hiked her skirts to her knees as she made her way to them. Jake, right behind her, stepped in a puddle of manure and cursed her, blaming her for his filthy boot.

Abbey paid no attention to him. The child's small hands clutched handfuls of her blouse, and his wet cheek left a big damp spot on her breast. When she approached the group, a young Indian girl came up and gently took the child. She murmured something undistinguishable, but Abbey sensed the gratitude in her low voice. The girl bent forward and smiled at the boy, as Abbey pressed a kiss to his wet cheek; he grabbed at her hand, shaking like a jar of jelly.

Jake latched onto her arm again and dragged her up the steps to the porch of the store and ordered her to not venture back by herself. "If I can't come for you," he said through tight lips, "I'll send that idiot husband of yours. Don't you dare ride back alone."

Abbey was inches from pulling out her hatpin and stabbing him with it when she spotted Dame Dilly watching through the store's front window, a satisfied smirk on her face. Jake caught her glance too, and pulled Abbey off to the side to where only the Indians could see them.

Abbey took a deep breath through her nostrils and hissed through her teeth. "Remove your hands from me, Captain Hunt, and do not *ever* touch me again."

He paid no attention to her request. Instead, he smiled like a satisfied cat—or maybe a snake, if a snake could smile—and grabbed her jaw hard. His yellow leather glove scraped her face and his lips all but grazed her cheek. Very slowly, he enunciated his words. "Someday bitch, you'll beg me to touch you."

Her face and neck flushed instantly scarlet. "Never in a million years will I beg you to do anything," she snarled, "but leave me alone."

His upper lip curled, and for a moment she feared he might come even closer. Raw fear grabbed her, coiled tight around her chest. Sweat trickled between her breasts, down her ribs, and disappeared into the dusty fibers of her blouse. She yanked her head free of his grasp; her eyes went to the little hill where the young braves had stood with their ponies, but they were gone.

Now only one Indian—certainly not a teenager—stood on the mound. He was at least half a head taller than Jake or Ed or anyone on the street, and he held the bridle of the most beautiful horse she'd ever seen. Her gaze swept over the shining black animal, then the man. It would have been difficult not to admire either. The horse was magnificent, as was the warrior. His moccasins laced to his knees, and he wore thrummed leggings and vest, both of creamy doeskin. Beneath the vest, a blue cotton shirt stretched tight over his chest and arms. A long, sheathed knife and a tomahawk hung from his waist, and a woven rope strap, drawn diagonally across his chest, held a rifle to his back. Around his neck hung an elaborate necklace of what she thought might be bear claws, and a burst of red, yellow, and white feathers fluttered on the side of his head. A leather cord held the dark strands of hair from his forehead, but the back hung loose, blowing as black and wild as the horse's mane. Handsome, powerful, a man other men would follow. When his gaze shifted to her, heat rushed from the roots of her hair to her toes, and her knees felt liquid. His eyes, an impossible wintry blue, locked on her.

She'd never seen anything like him. Fascinated, she couldn't look away. He nodded ever so slowly towards her then shifted his attention to Jake. The lines of his face changed, hardening, his hand moved to the hilt of his tomahawk.

Jake's grip loosened. "Don't ride back alone." He turned and walked away.

WILL THUNDER CLOUD pressed his hand against the fringed doeskin of his vest, still stunned. His heart hammered, pounding with an unfamiliar urgency against the cage of his ribs. His legs felt like limp rope.

He watched the girl turn and walk into the store as he ran the scene through his mind again. He saw his son, Rabbit, playing alone on the wooden walkway. The little boy was all he had left of Rain, the wife he had lost to a Crow raiding party. Thunder Cloud's sister, Sun, stood off to the side, giggling with her girl-friends instead of watching his son. She had been careless. He saw it all again: the horse rearing, the drovers wheeling their wag-ons as his small son played nearby, unaware of danger. At the memory, his heart jammed in his throat. He'd been absolutely helpless to save Rabbit. He blamed not only Sun, but himself as well. His attention had shifted between the cavalry column and the girl, then he'd checked back to his son through his bin-oculars, but there was nothing he could have done from such a distance. His son should never have been left alone.

He'd spotted the girl the minute she rode into town. How could he not look at the wild blonde curls, the lush line of her breasts, and the shadow of long thighs beneath her skirt? He noticed, too, the confidence in her shoulders and the way she held her head. He'd spent his winters in Ontario and Quebec with his white father, and he knew white women. He knew right away this one was *crème de la crème* just as he knew the loudmouthed bully who had grabbed her arm was *merde*, not fit to touch her.

His sister, Sun, would be reprimanded for her lack of vigi-lance, though he already knew she felt terrible.

I will follow this woman from a distance, he told himself. Make sure she gets safely back to the Army train. That's the least I can do. Maybe, he thought, maybe then my heart will still.

5

BEAR CLAWS

She didn't wait for either Jake or Ed to come for her. Instead, after shopping, she walked back to her horse, accompanied by two young sergeants from C Company. She bought a bag of penny candy for Ed, and on a whim—which she really couldn't afford—she purchased an entire bolt of large checked, bright yellow cotton. It had been on sale, and after the humiliating encounter with Jake Hunt she needed a little cheering up. The bright cloth and the act of spending a little money helped. She'd find some use for the material eventually—perhaps a skirt. After all, she was the proud owner of a sewing machine, thanks to Danny and Summer's generous wedding gift.

One of the sergeants tied the bolt of material to her saddle, then she stood with the sergeants on the boardwalk as Jake's company formed, admiring their efficiency. The troops were well disciplined, their horses groomed, the soldiers all spit and polish. In a strange way, the commotion of soldiers, ordinary citizens, and Indians brought to mind the pageantry of Sir Walter Scott, and she had a strange feeling that history was in the making.

Ed had apparently given up on the hunting, for she spotted him among the troops as they prepared to ride. He stood near

Jake, directing muleskinners and drovers through the thick swirls of dust, slapping his hat against his leg. Ed put an arm around Jake's shoulders, and Abbey figured Jake must have made a joke, for both men laughed. She frowned, watching the way Ed's arm remained on Jake's shoulder, and an odd, almost frightful uneasiness fluttered in her chest. When Jake turned and spoke to Ed again, an expression of such unmasked delight spread across Ed's face that Abbey caught her breath. An instant later, Jake's gaze met hers, and the man threw his head back and laughed. She stared hard at him, trying to understand, but soldiers on horseback moved and blocked her view. When she next saw Ed he was nowhere near Jake, but her apprehension remained.

After a moment she shook off the unease and became immersed in the pageantry. The horse soldiers, a long mule train of supplies, several wagons, and a huge herd of cattle all positioned themselves to move north. Dust, the noise of braying beasts, creaking wagons and leather, the crack of whips, filled the air along with the musky smells of horse and sweat. In addition to all this excitement, two crusty-looking hunters dressed in filthy red and black plaid shirts rode in with their own string of mules. The animals were loaded with fresh buffalo meat which appeared black from the flies. The crowd stirred as if they could already taste dinner, and after what seemed an eternity, the troop formed into a column and departed toward the Black Hills.

All the while she was in the street Abbey sensed the tall Indian watching her. She glanced over to the hill where he still stood. He was too far away to see his expression, but she felt that same warm flush course through her. The crystal blue eyes staring through Indian features burned into her memory.

Abbey felt a soft pressure against her hand and spun around, but it was only the Indian girl who had taken the child, just a shadow in the crowd. The girl pressed a soft leather bag into Abbey's hand then held a finger to her lips and disappeared. Abbey slipped the bag into the pocket of her skirt then glanced back to the mound. The two teenage braves on their spotted ponies had returned, and neither the warrior nor his horse were anywhere in sight.

THE OFFICERS' MESS was little more than a chuck wagon. At her request, one of the cooks made Abbey two chicken sandwiches and a pot of tea, which she took to Mary and Emmett's wagon. Close to tears, Mary picked at the chicken. Her monthly cycle had started again, and though Abbey reached over and held her friend's hand, she felt helpless. Mary wanted a baby, and it just wasn't happening. She and Emmett had been married over two and a half years, and she'd confided to Abbey more than once that she feared she'd end up a *dried up old biddy like Dame Dilly*.

Abbey found a bottle of brandy and poured a little in each of their cups, which helped to lift their spirits. A little later, Dame Dilly stopped by and noticed the bottle. She glanced at Abbey and scowled.

"They were selling whiskey for $8 a gallon in town," Mrs. Dietrich said, her tone snide. "I suggest you stock up."

Good grief, thought Abbey. She probably thinks I'm a drunkard. In defiance, not giving her any reason to doubt, Abbey added a dollop more to her tea.

As Dame Dilly scuttled away, Abbey whispered to her best friend, "Don't worry. You will never be that ugly or that mean."

LATER, ED FOUND her, and they walked with their horses to the wagon. The teamster had parked it off by itself in the high prairie grass, and once the man had brushed down and fed the horses, Ed sent him off for the evening. Caked in dust and sweat, Ed stripped out of his grass-stained uniform and managed a quick wash and shave. Water was so scarce along the Platte River that a bath was not possible, so Abbey settled for what she called a bird bath. Somewhat clean, they snuggled amid the crates and barrels in the wagon, made love then took a nap.

When she awoke, Abbey pulled on her green velvet robe and picked up their discarded clothing. The pouch from the Indian girl fell out of her dress pocket. Curious, she pulled the little ties and opened the small leather bag, then gasped as a bear claw necklace spilled into her hand. She immediately recognized it as the one the tall Indian had been wearing. The treasure gleamed in the fading sunlight, surprisingly heavy and exquisitely made. Ten highly polished bear claws, each tipped with silver, dangled from a heavy silver cord. Between the claws opaque blue and green beads interspersed with silver ones. It was truly beautiful.

She took the necklace to Ed and told him the entire story, including the part about Jake manhandling her and the ugly things he said. Ed sighed heavily, his eyes soft with empathy. He set down his whiskey flask and took the necklace from her. He weighted it in his hand then gently slipped it about her neck.

"This goes perfect with your eyes and your skin, Sunshine. You have silver earrings, don't you?" His hand cupped her chin, nothing like the rough grip Jake had used. She felt Ed's warm breath on her face and smelled the whiskey in it. "Pay no attention to Jake, Sunshine," he said. "He was nervous about leaving, and I suspect he's a little jealous."

But ever since they'd left the chapel at West Point, Ed had known it was worse than simple jealousy. Every time the two men were on their own, Jake made some biting, derogatory remark about Ed being led around by the ring in his nose—or by his testicles. Jake hated the fact that Ed was married, which was confusing. After all, Jake had been the one who had urged him to marry Abbey. But when it came down to it, what made Jake the angriest was seeing that Ed really enjoyed being with his wife.

Christ, thought Ed. *What am I to do? Damned if I do and damned if I don't.* He tucked a curl behind Abbey's ear, and the smuggest of smiles eased across his face. His lips pressed tenderly against her forehead; his voice came out soft, like puppy breath.

Ed chuckled. "He's green with envy. You're one gorgeous woman, Sunshine. Your body…I've never seen any woman built like you. It makes men sort of crazy. And your skin. It's lush." His eyes sparkled. "And hey, Jake knows you're all mine. Any man would be jealous."

And he knows I am fast becoming all yours, he thought.

She blinked and wiped a speck of dirt off his cheek. "You're biased."

"You bet I am." He grinned and his hands smoothed over her bottom. "Do we have time for …?"

She tried to look shocked, but really, how could she resist? She never did. Besides, it was their honeymoon.

BETWEEN BITES OF bison stew everyone oohed and aahed over her necklace—everyone but Dame Dilly, who treated Abbey to her trademark scowl, as they fixed their plates at the buffet. Colonel Dietrich, only slightly inebriated, fingered the bear claws where they rested on her chest, and Mrs. Dietrich glared furiously at her. As if it were Abbey's fault the woman's husband was such a letch. Ed quickly soothed the jealous beast by removing the necklace and handing it to the colonel so he could inspect it without hovering over Abbey's bosom. No one wanted a repeat of what happened in Chicago.

When they asked how she'd acquired the necklace, she told them most of the story, leaving out the parts about Jake. She didn't mention the tall Indian either, telling the story as if it came from the girl. The colonel huffed at the necklace then handed it to Dennis Gander, one of the hunters who had brought in the buffalo meat. Gander looked down his long nose, inspecting it.

"Next time, let them trample the little bastards. They grow up, you know."

Abbey's nostrils flared. Although Dennis Gander, now haphazardly shaved and wearing a white shirt and black coat, appeared somewhat respectable, he still reeked of unwashed body, raw meat, whiskey, and mule. He held up the necklace and made an announcement to everyone sitting about the fire.

"I saw this exact necklace on Will Thunder Cloud, Red Cloud's nephew. He's the bastard half-breed of Red Cloud's sister and a French Canadian trader. His French name is Guillaume Emile Dupree, and Red Cloud trusts him as a translator. He speaks French, English, Spanish, and half a dozen native languages. Once you see his eyes you won't forget him." He took a deep breath and handed the necklace back to the colonel. "Only blue-eyed Indian I've ever seen. Bronze skin, black hair, and pale eyes, sure enough, he's the devil's spawn. He's a big son of a bitch, too. Rumor has it he's good with a bow and a knife." He narrowed his eyes speculatively at Colonel Dietrich as the colonel handed Ed the necklace. "Will Thunder Cloud's head on a pole would be a great trophy."

The visual impact of such a brutal idea punched Abbey in the stomach. She lost her balance and staggered backwards. Ed caught her and helped her sit on the wide wooden tongue of one of the wagons.

The hunter followed, his yellow stare glued to her. "You saw him, didn't you, girlie?" Dennis Gander said, smiling. A blast of rotten teeth and stale booze hit Abbey. She turned her head to keep from gagging.

Ed paused, his fingers light on Abbey's neck as he fastened the necklace. "That's Mrs. Kincaid, to you, Gander."

The hunter reluctantly stepped back, but not before Abbey caught the look of scorn on his face, mocking her. She reached up instinctively and touched the necklace, and Ed's hand covered hers, warm with reassurance. The heat raced through her again. She didn't know if it came from Ed's hand or the necklace, but she suddenly knew it was important for her to lie. The Indian hating was widespread and vicious.

She shook her head. "Oh, no," she told him, wiping her damp hair back from her face. "I only saw the child and a girl." She managed to paste a winning smile on her face, and although she had no idea how she'd swallow a bite, she said, "I'm just starved for some of your bison, Mr. Gander."

6

THE EDGE OF CIVILIZATION

Before daylight the wagon train stopped near Ft. Laramie, and Emmett and Ed left with their troops. As the last of the troopers faded into the dust, Mary, Abbey, and the other wives stepped onto the dark road that wrapped around the parade ground and looked around their new world. Ft. Laramie stood at the edge of the plains, the gateway to the mountains, and the very edge of civilization. Abbey stared around them in silence. The air held no chill, but the stillness and the beauty sent shivers deep into her bones.

White frame buildings outlined the rectangle, glowing like ghosts in the faint light, and a neat row of cottonwood saplings stood along the road. This wild, beautiful, and forlorn land would be their home for ... how long? When she inhaled, she caught the scents of sweet grass, sage, cedar, and wood smoke; above her a million stars studded the dome of the sky. If she gazed far off into the distant west she could see a mountain with snow still on its crest, looming large and mythical in the starlight.

From the far wilds a wolf's howl pierced the silence. Closer owls hooted. Several of the women shrieked and leaped back when a lone raven darted by them, flying at shoulder height, and Abbey heard whispers of an evil omen. Then the eastern horizon cracked and all talk of unpleasantness vanished with the night. A wide band of light spread like wildfire across the plains, and a ball of fire lifted from the edge of the earth. Soft, admiring sounds escaped the ladies as they watched. Birds by the thousands followed the sun, screeching up from the wetlands and welcoming the day. Abbey looked up and watched the stars wink out. She wished she could fly.

The housing officer, Lt. Radford, very young and prone to blushing, cleared his throat, and Abbey hid a smile. She wondered when he'd last been this close to attractive white women? As their party had moved across the prairie, Abbey had noticed that the six of them drew attention simply because they were female and white, a species rare as some of the birds in these parts.

"This way, ladies," he said, tapping a thick tablet against his knuckles. "I have your housing assignments. Mrs. Dietrich told me you'd be anxious to see your new homes."

He led them to two carriages which took them on a slow tour around the parade ground. Wooden offices and stables, painted white, came into view, and Lt. Radford pointed to a two-story structure. "This is Old Bedlam, the bachelor officer quarters, and those, he indicated single story buildings, are the troops' barracks." He shifted his attention to a row of white cottages. "That is where the married officers live."

"Excuse me," Abbey said, "but I thought a fort would have stockade walls and gates. This garrison is open."

He nodded. "Wood is so scarce it would be extremely difficult to enclose our compound."

BY MIDMORNING, HE had escorted each of the wives to their assigned bungalows. Abbey and Ed's future home was set off by itself, and while none of the officers' quarters were luxurious, theirs was in horrid disrepair.

"Who assigned the cottages?" she asked.

The lieutenant fidgeted and bit his lip as he studied his papers. "I usually do so by rank and date of service; however, Mrs. Dietrich assigned these."

That explains a lot, she thought. Something would have to be done.

When their luggage arrived along with the crates containing their household goods, Abbey requested the drovers leave everything on the porch. Then she asked that all the furniture in the house be brought outside and stacked there as well. Covering her hair with a white kerchief and donning white gloves, she set about inspecting every corner of the house, even going so far as to hoist herself up into the rafters, prodding dark corners with a knitting needle. When she was done, she sat on the porch steps making notes; she then marched across the parade ground to the colonel's office, Lt. Radford close on her heels.

Holding out the once white gloves, she said to Colonel Dietrich, "I need a tent pitched outside our quarters, Sir. They are currently uninhabitable. Mice droppings are everywhere, I suspect there are raccoons in the chimney, and something is thumping around under the porch,"

Colonel Dietrich stared in openmouthed wonder as she took off her kerchief and shook out cobwebs. With a look of disdain, she wiped off her shoulders and stood tall, prepared for battle.

"You must, Sir, have a few troopers you could spare who will assist me in cleaning our quarters. Otherwise I'll hire some Indians and send the bill to General Sherman. You cannot expect anyone to live in such filth." She pulled a thick strand of blonde hair across her face, wrinkled her nose, and sniffed. "Good grief, even my hair smells of mouse urine." Until it's cleaned, we will stay in the tent. Oh, and please make sure it's a large tent. I will also need a bathtub."

The red-faced colonel's Adam's apple bobbed. For a moment she thought he'd sputter out an argument, so she smiled and asked after his wife, reminding him with a pretty smile that his wife's hand was thick in this stew. For a brief moment she felt almost sorry for the man. His wife's paybacks for his regrettable behavior around Abbey would no doubt stretch into eternity. But Abbey was used to getting her way, and she also knew that word of former General Daniel Charteris' sister living in a tent—and taking a bath—on the parade grounds of Ft. Laramie would not sit well with neither General Sherman nor General Sheridan. Probably not General Grant, either.

As the colonel instructed Master Sergeant Gilley to take care of the matter, she handed him the tablet.

"Our cottage," she informed the sergeant, "lacks the following compared to what I observed in the other cottages: a dining room table, silverware, chairs …"

Sergeant Gilley told his wife, who rallied the other wives. With Colonel Dietrich's approval, he saw to acquiring all the furniture and furnishings on her list. Before long, Abbey's home improvement plan turned into a community effort, made all the more enthusiastic because every one of the wives disliked Dame Dilly. The woman butted her nose in everyone's business, instructing the young wives on what to wear, when to bathe, and how. She irritated them to no end with her stream of advice on nurturing children, though she had none of her own.

Someone brought a plate of cookies, someone else a cake. Deviled eggs, little sandwiches, and lemonade materialized. One woman commented that it, "Looks like a Methodist Church Supper," and an impromptu picnic ensued. Two dozen soldiers volunteered, anxious to see young white women, but the sergeant disappointed a few when he chose only one dozen. Half of the soldiers swept, scrubbed, whitewashed, and polished the cottage's interior. The other half washed windows, fixed the roof and the sagging porch, and cleared the weeds from the yard. A resourceful private bagged the raccoons from the chimney and the groundhogs from under the porch. No one knew quite what to do about mouse urine.

Abbey set up her sewing machine under the saplings, and with the help of Georgia Gilley they made curtains from the bolt of yellow checked material, even lining them in plain muslin. She arranged for a couple of Indian laundresses from Hog City to come over with their irons and press the curtains before the soldiers hung them—it wasn't until days later that she learned the laundresses doubled as prostitutes during their off duty hours.

From the Indian women, Abbey purchased baskets as well as colorful rugs and blankets, which added interest and color to her cottage. She also picked a huge bouquet of prairie flowers, which she separated into Mason jars and gave to the wives as a thank you. Dame Dilly came to observe all the activity. Abbey fought hard not to grin. The woman steamed with envy.

AS THE DAY closed Ed stepped into their cottage. Abbey had done something amazing. She had made their quarters a home. Throughout Ed's entire life he'd never had a window with curtains, or flowers and a tablecloth and napkins on the dinner table. Cooking proved somewhat of a struggle for Abbey, but with his and Georgia's help, she improved. Tonight she'd roasted several partridges, served creamed potatoes and fresh peas, cornbread, and an elderberry pie one of the wives offered her. The cornbread was a little crispy around the edges, but Ed assured her it tasted great. He'd complimented her on her foresight of cooking a half dozen partridges. "I am always half-starved."

She smiled back, her eyes full of devilment. "You certainly are!"

Evenings with Abbey enchanted him. He loved sitting on the porch swing with the night noises hovering about them. Some evenings they talked long after taps. She'd lay with her head in his lap, and he'd play with her hair. As he ran his fingers through her curls, he let himself open up and told her how hard his growing up had been.

"We weren't poor, but we had no niceties. Dad just didn't know about such things. We sure didn't have a home, not like what you've made here. When our mother died, my father's brother came and took care of us, which meant he kept us from killing each other. He was only seventeen, but big enough to knock our teeth down our throats. Even he admitted he was a mean son of a bitch with a nice streak."

Ed's smile was unsure, but he figured he might as well finish what he'd started. "Our father wasn't much better. He was a captain after the Mexican War, and he dragged us all over the southwest and the Pacific coast. If he scratched his head, we'd all duck. You wouldn't have liked him at all, Sunshine. He had us spread rushes and straw to cover the floor so he could spit tobacco anywhere he wanted. Every week we'd sweep out that disgusting mess and spread clean rushes. I never once brought a friend home. I buried myself in books and school, which ended up being a good thing. That's what got me to West Point."

He sighed, thinking back. It seemed like so long ago. Another lifetime. "West Point made me want to be a gentleman, taught me table manners, and proper behavior." His fingers skimmed over her petal soft cheek. "Your brother taught me how to actually be one. He taught us what is called Command Presence." He laughed. "At six foot, two, Daniel made it look easy, but we learned. He was the first officer to be kind to either Jake or me. You know, he expected absolute obedience, but he was always fair and kind."

An owl hooted and Ed glanced up, staring into the dark. "Believe it or not," he said, "Jake had a worse growing up than I did. His father was rich, but he was a mean, sick bastard. He buggered his servants and his sons."

Her forehead wrinkled, and she sat up. "You mean, he …"

He nodded, then carefully explained exactly what buggered meant. "Don't ever tell anyone, Sunshine. Jake told me that when he was drunk."

"I won't say a word," she whispered, looking stunned.

"Your brother became a mix of father, big brother, and God to both of us. There's something really amazing about Daniel. Well, you know how damned good-looking he is, but it's much more than that. He walks into a room and everyone stops to look at him. To have someone like him take us into his home, introduce us to Summer Rose…" He shook his head, remembering how thrilling that time had been for him. "She made lunch for us. Huge ham sandwiches, potato salad. We sat at the kitchen table and drank lemonade."

That was the first time in his life Ed could remember feeling like he really was part of something, like he mattered. At times like this he could hardly believe his luck. Now Daniel's little sister was his wife. He was so lucky.

Though he loved what Abbey had done with creating a home for them, he did have mixed feelings about their quarters. Their cottage sat off by itself, nearer to the stables than the other houses. He liked the privacy, but he worried about her being alone when he went on patrol, which was most of the time. So he gave her a pony, a puppy, and a pistol.

The dog cost a quarter and the pony was free. She loved them both, and it didn't take long before the three of them were inseparable. They named the puppy Garry Owen, after the 7th Cavalry's marching song, and called him Owen. The puppy resembled a cream-colored bear cub, and his paws hinted that he just might grow.

The pony was already named Cricket, for he jumped almost as high as one at the sight of a chicken. He'd been mistreated and failed cavalry mount school.

"That damned horse is afraid of its shadow," said Ed in disgust. "No wonder he was free."

Abbey hugged the pony. "Be nice Eddie. He understands what you say, and first of all, he's a pony. A big one, I'll grant you, but he's a pony, not a horse. Second, give me time with him. I think he's experienced some ghastly stuff. He just needs a friend."

As for the pistol, the gunsmith refurbished an old Remington Ed won in a poker game, and he took her out to practice once. Only once. He set up a series of targets in the wetlands near the river, and showed her how to load, hold, and aim it. Then he stepped back and watched in amazement as she blew away every one of his targets.

"Are you as good with rifle?"

She nodded.

"You were born to shoot, Sunshine. Did your brother show you how to handle a gun?"

She let out a noise that hovered between a snort and a laugh—it was neither a pleasant nor a feminine sound. "Daniel? He's lucky to hit the side of a barn. Summer Rose taught me."

7

THE INDIAN VILLAGE

In July Colonel Dietrich took a hundred men north toward the Yellowstone, Ed and Emmett included, with plans to meet up with General Connor and patrol east toward the Big Horn Mountains. They would return before snow, which she learned could possibly start as early as mid-September.

A small company of soldiers, the cooks, the band, the men who kept the fort functioning, and a few guards stayed behind. Lt. Ranford, who was snugly wrapped around Dame Dilly's finger, was left in charge. "You know who is running the fort," Abbey whispered to Mary.

Abbey took the time to work with Cricket, walking around the parade grounds with the pony every morning, letting him get used to the bridle. Owen dutifully followed. Mrs. Dietrich happened to come at the same time to exercise the bay gelding the colonel had left for her.

"You're quite the accomplished horsewoman," she'd say, looking down her narrow nose, then went behind her back and told the other wives that Abbey would never ride properly.

At first, Abbey felt humiliated. And when Mrs. Dietrich asked the girls to help at the Indian School, even though Mary and she had taught in the Friends' School in Philadelphia and knew a little about teaching, Abbey accepted reluctantly. She wanted to work with the children, but she feared Mrs. Dietrich was just setting her up to criticize or perhaps to make herself look good.

After a few moments of self-pity, she decided to take a page from Summer Rose's book. "Insults only hurt when you acknowledge them," her sister-in-law had said. So she ignored Dame Dilly's cutting remarks and concentrated on the children, which was exactly what Abbey needed.

They held classes outdoors a few miles from the fort on the banks of the Laramie River, where some Lakota camped. Fourteen students and almost as many mothers or sisters hovered over their charges. Lakota, English, and French were all spoken, interlaced with the colorful and sometimes crude vocabulary of the mountain men. Words snuck into the language such as *Arkansas Toothpick* for a twelve-inch dagger, *or Du Pont* for gunpowder. Food was *grease and beans* or *grub*. When she turned left she was going *near-side*, and turning right meant she was going *far-side*. Whiskey became *fire-water* or *tangle foot*. A young horse or a well-built woman was a *filly*, and someone *gone Injun* was a white who voluntarily became an Indian.

One of her students was the big-eyed boy she'd rescued at the crossroads. He recognized her right away and ran up and hugged her leg. She fitted him easily onto her hip. "You are growing too fast," she teased. She whipped around, frowning, searching for something. "I need a big rock to put on your head so you can't grow anymore."

He giggled, and she narrowed her eyes at him. "What is your name?"

He said something in Lakota, and she asked for English, which was fair. All the younger Indians spoke quite passable English.

"Splashing Rabbit."

He reached up and yanked one of her yellow curls. Fascinated, he let it loose. When it snapped back into a curl, he belly laughed.

"And how did you get that name?"

He giggled and squirmed out of her arms. As he ran off to the other children, Abbey looked at the Indian girls who also giggled.

She shrugged. "He does have big, rabbit-like eyes."

The Indian girls laughed harder and shook their heads. Finally, Walks in the Sun, the girl who had given her the pouch containing the necklace, explained. "He once tried to catch a bunny by peeing on it."

"What?" Abbey grinned then rolled her eyes. "Splashing Rabbit. I get it. He splashed the rabbit." She shook her head, staring after the boy. "Typical boy."

Walks in the Sun, Abbey learned, was Thunder Cloud's sister. As soon as she heard of their relationship, she had to concentrate on not staring. She wanted to see a resemblance to her brother, but couldn't make it out. Dark-skinned and brown-eyed the boy didn't look like his impressive father either. The boy's mother had been killed in a raid by the Crow shortly after the boy was born. Walks in the Sun, along with her mother, Wakanda, cared for him.

At noon on the first day, Walks in the Sun introduced all the teachers to Wakanda, an elegant woman with thick gray braids who smelled of sage and cedar and moved with the soft grace of a doe. The tribe held Wakanda in great reverence, for she was a medicine woman, a healer. Her name translated into English as Possessing Magical Powers. All the women coveted her silky complexion, and wondered aloud how she kept her skin so smooth in the endless sun and wind. Smiling, Wakanda gave each of the white women a ram's horn filed with a sage and cedar-scented lanolin cream for their hands.

"It keeps your hands soft in winter," she told them. "Use it on your face and neck, too. Anywhere." She inhaled deeply while waving her hand in front of her face. "The aroma is good for your soul."

Wakanda gathered one of the little boys, Sweet Owl, in her arms and cuddled him in her lap. Unlike the other boys, he dressed as a little girl and played with the girls. Wakanda rubbed some of the lanolin on his cheeks then tickled him. She smiled warmly to the circle of women then explained, "He's *winktes*. Very, very special."

Dane Dilly sat on a tramped down mound of grass, winding string in her fingers to demonstrate *Cat's Cradle* to two little girls. She looked at Mary and Abbey, one eyebrow arched with disapproval. "Indians have a very different attitude than we do about men and women who … are confused about their gender."

Mary swallowed hard and avoided looking at anyone. She and Abbey knew about homosexuality, but never discussed the subject. Abbey cleared her throat and wondered if Mary remembered the ugly incident that had happened just before the soldiers left for the Powder River Valley. No one who had been stationed at the fort at that time would ever forget it. A young, homesick corporal—a Jimmy Wright—under the influence of alcohol made a blatant pass toward one of his fellow troopers, who complained to the colonel. Colonel Dietrich immediately ordered the corporal stripped of his chevrons and drummed out of the Army. The quasi-ceremony was held on the parade grounds and done with some ceremony, and it was horrid. Drums actually rolled as his rank was ripped away, and none of the soldiers would look at him. But Abbey had watched the tears run down his young face, and her heart ached for him.

Afterwards, the soldiers took all his clothes and left him only a dress. The next morning they found him in the far reaches of the stable, dead in a pool of blood. He'd slit his throat.

Emmett, Ed, and Abbey walked with Mary back to their quarters. Abbey had bawled with great sucking sobs. She managed to say, "How could they?"

But Ed only shrugged. "Actually he's lucky. During the Revolution they hanged anyone like him and buried him face-down like a criminal or an Indian. On the other hand, our illustrious President Jefferson advocated castrating our effeminate brothers rather than hanging them." He'd quirked a sideways smile. "Thoughtful of him, don't you think?"

Now they sat by the fire, talking with Wakanda and some of the other women, but the joyful mood of being with the children had sobered.

"We believe children like Sweet Owl were born with the *Berdache Spirit*," Wakanda said.

Mrs. Dietrich, still teaching the little girls *Cat's Cradle*, informed them "That's a term the Lakota took from the French." She glanced defensively at the other women. "What? I learned about their heathen attitude before we came here."

Wakanda nodded, ignoring her snide tone. "Here we revere all children. We do not punish or reject them. They're allowed to choose whether they want to stay with their mothers and do women's work or become a warrior. Often they stay close to their mothers until they're young adults and decide to become warriors."

Dame Dilly possessed a way of talking that interlaced a snide laugh with whatever she was saying. She used it now. "These boys can even choose to be one of the wives of a warrior. Can't quite wrap my mind around that…imagine?" Her dark eyes darted to each girl. "Disgusting, isn't it…?" She made a dismissive motion with her hand, and Abbey swallowed hard. The colonel's wife clearly liked mothering the young women, but apparently limits to her sainthood existed. "Girls can also choose to be warriors," she continued. "They are allowed to—as the Indians say—run with the wolves."

Wakanda's expression was serene, her smile soft. "Some *winktes* become shamans, healers … leaders."

Mary spoke then, her voice timid. "But we …" She took a deep breath and looked at Abbey. "Sometimes I wonder if they have the right idea. What if we're wrong? Ever since Emmett told me about this, I've asked God in my prayers which way is right. Should we punish them for how they are born?"

THROUGH THE WARM days of early autumn the white women came to the Indian camp three times a week, teaching the children in the mornings, then sharing lunch around a fire outside the tipis. The children sat in any available lap and the dogs hovered, waiting for a dropped morsel. Abbey always drew a large gathering of children who fingered her golden hair and tugged at the curls. Splashing Rabbit never tired of playing with her hair, and although her scalp ached she never stopped him. After lunch Splashing Rabbit and Sweet Owl crawled into Mary's lap, and their sweet friend, Happy Moonbeam, who constantly fiddled with the red ribbons on her pigtails, joined them. Today Mary read *Goldilocks*, animating the words with her voice and widening her already luminous eyes. Wakanda told stories of the Lakota legends in a mix of English, French, and Lakota.

Wakanda's brother, Red Cloud, occasionally came by to watch the children read in English. He walked among the children with twinkling eyes, giving encouragement and smiling at the white women. Red Cloud was an important leader and warrior. When he walked through their little classes he moved with athletic grace. He spoke some halting English and from watching him, Abbey felt he longed to know more.

One day he stopped by, and the warrior allowed Sweet Owl to pull him down onto the sand in the shade of a cottonwood tree. He was instantly mobbed by children clamoring for a story. Red Cloud pulled the little boy into his lap, and all the children gathered in the dappled light. Sweet Owl, his big eyes unblinking like his namesake's, brought his face close to Red Cloud's, and asked, "Have you ever been frightened?"

"Have I ever been frightened?" A deep chuckle escaped from the bottom of the great warrior's chest, rumbling like distant thunder. "Too many times to count."

As Wakanda softly translated to English, Abbey was distracted by a stealthy movement nearby. Thunder Cloud had dismounted from his magnificent horse and now sat not more than six feet behind her, a little to the side. At the sight of him, a warm flutter started up in Abbey's heart and settled in her belly. She pulled her knees against her chest so she could rest her elbows on them, then squinted surreptitiously at him. She watched him lean back against the lone cottonwood with the delicacy of a cat, settling in to listen to Red Cloud's story.

Thunder Cloud wore walnut brown buckskins trousers adorned with silver studs, and his long black hair lifted in the breeze as spots of sunshine danced over his bare chest. The scent of him reached her, a pleasant mixture of wood smoke, sage, and clean male sweat, but he seemed unaware of her presence. His entire face brightened when Splashing Rabbit approached, and he opened his arms, welcoming his son into his lap.

Red Cloud, the storyteller, ran a hand over Sweet Owl's head. Wakanda's low voice followed with the English translation. "I remember one time as clear as if it happened today. I had become separated from my friends after a battle with the Crows up on the Rosebud." He shook his head sadly. "It was one of those battles where no one wins. My pony had run off, and I was on foot searching for him. Just as the sun set, a fierce storm came upon me. Lightning bolts flashed and thunder roared so close my hair stood on end. I stumbled into a cave. It was as black as a bottomless pit. But when I turned back to look out the entrance the lightning flashed and I saw a big shadow block the opening. Something had followed me into that cave. I didn't know whether it was a grizzly or a friend or a foe. Whatever or whoever it was followed me into that cave and lay down near the entrance."

He grabbed Sweet Owl's arms and gently shook him for effect. "I huddled down in my corner, not daring to move, but shaking all over and afraid to breath. The storm moved on, and the cave became as dark as the blackest night. I never slept, just sat there, shaking. When the sun came up, I could see again. All I could make out was a man sitting near the entrance. Eventually, when the sun rose, I could tell he was a Crow. And then …" he said, grinning as he tapped his long nose, "I sneezed." He chuckled. "Not once, but twice. Great big sneezes. The Crow nearly jumped out of his skin. We sat there, looking at each other, not moving. I was frightened beyond fright, and I know he must have been terrified, too. I didn't know what else to do, so I smiled."

The children all stared at Red Cloud. "What happened?" Sweet Owl asked, sounding awed.

Red Cloud shrugged. "He smiled back and laughed. I laughed, too. Then we stood, and I followed him out of the cave. We waved farewell and went in different directions. When he was gone I took the first deep breath I had taken all night."

From the corner of her eye, Abbey watched Thunder Cloud lead the little boy to his black horse. He lifted Splashing Rabbit up then swung his body onto the huge animal. Abbey forced her eyes to look away. She wanted to approach him, thank him for the necklace, say something … but she stayed where she was.

8

POWDER RIVER COUNTRY, HUNTING GROUND OF THE LAKOTA

From a plateau along the Yellowstone River, Ed paused to survey the country. The horizon seemed wider, the sky bluer, and the grass rolled on forever. Even the air seemed different, crisp and clean, as if it had just swept over the Canadian tundra. Before they'd arrived, Ed had memorized the map, so he knew the Tongue River lay below them. Off to the west was the Rosebud. He felt an unexpected pang and realized he wished Abbey were with him. He wanted to show her this lush country.

The army posts of Ed's childhood were most often on dry, scrabble dirt where little grew, on land no one wanted. He'd never seen anything like the lush grass and it stirred his blood enough to consider leaving the army. The past evening an old mountain man, brittle as old leather and his black dog materialized at their fire. "The grass here," he told Ed, "stays green most of the year."

"First," said the old timer, "there's the early spring run-off, when the snow melts, fills the streams, and feeds the land. Later in June, even July, the high snow melts. The fishing is about as good as I've seen anywhere. Game, too." He ruffled the sleek ears of his dog. "Old Blackie here brings the rabbits around, and I sit on a log an' wait for 'em. Sure, we have the wolves and bears, but for the most part, they're more scairt of me than me them."

The old man directed them toward caves. "Stop and see these old caves, the ones with pictures drawn on the walls. Sometimes old Indians go there to hide or die. Beautiful country."

AT HEART ED was a daydreamer. As a wedding present, his mother's father had given him a sizeable bond, and as he led his men toward the Tongue River, he thought about buying a ranch in this beautiful land, raising cattle and horses. Here he could build a life and a family with Abbey, if she went along with it. He wasn't sure how she'd react to that idea, though. She'd been raised a debutante; he'd visited the Charteris' mansion outside Philly, eaten dinner where seven forks and six spoons were used. Would she like this wild country? Since their wedding they'd talked for hours, but never really discussed life after the army. A bubble of anticipation welled in his throat at the thought of talking his plan over with her. Life with Abbey was more exciting than he ever imagined. He was proud of how she transformed their little cottage and taken her new life in stride, apparently not missing her elegant life. Wherever they ended up it would be an adventure.

CAMELANN, PENNSYLVANIA—DANIEL AND Summer Rose's Home Farm

Daniel Charteris sat at the kitchen table reading Abbey's letter aloud to Summer Rose, who was up to her elbows in flour, making apple pies. In the first six pages of the letter, written in Abbey's economical script, she told her brother and Summer Rose of the train rides, both by rail and by wagon, the new experience of living under U.S. Army discipline, and the details of settling into the fort. She described the towns and the trek across Nebraska and devoted two pages to talking about how she'd acquired the bear claw necklace. She told them all about the complicated relationships where she was living, including the interactions between Mrs. Dietrich and the gossipy army wives, and the boredom. "About the only acceptable pastime is flirting, and Mary and I decided not to participate in such dangerous games."

"Sounds like she's having quite an adventure," Summer Rose said when he paused to peer out the window and check on the twins and Mercy as they played outside in the leaves. Mercy, at twelve or fourteen had come to live with Summer and Daniel after the twins were born. Orphaned by the war, she spoke very little but took excellent care of the twins. Summer turned back to her husband and nodded toward Abbey's letter. "I don't envy her the gossipy or flirty wives, though."

Daniel lifted one eyebrow in mock alarm. "Nor do I."

"Don't give me a smart answer, Daniel. Some army wives are very difficult. Some are truly wonderful and helpful, while others can be as vicious as a rattlesnake." She laughed. "I remember two women who openly lined up their next husband in case their current one was killed."

He looked at her, caught as always by his wife's wisdom and her beauty. He loved her ten times more today than when they married.

"Well?" she asked, pinching a crust. "Is there more?"

He settled back in his chair, crossed his long legs, and continued.

"Ed gave me a dog and a pony before he left. They are great company. I miss Ed very much, but I'm told he should return by Thanksgiving.

Mary and I love teaching at the Indian School the most. We have sixteen students now, and they are making such progress. We teach reading and reading and reading, and some arithmetic. We teach them to read English, and the Lakota women teach Lakota by telling stories, since there is no written Lakota language. Mary and I have started a Lakota Dictionary, spelling words like they sound, but that's not an easy feat.

One of my students is a little boy named Splashing Rabbit, who is the son of Thunder Cloud, the Indian who gave me the bear claw necklace. Thunder Cloud is Wakanda's son.

Relationships and family are as important to the Lakota as they are to you and me. She is the sister of Red Cloud and is a great shaman. The tribe reveres her, and she has been very kind to us.

I find it difficult to believe the barbaric stories I hear about these people. Wakanda introduced us to Red Cloud, and he asked us many questions about the cities in the east.

He wanted to know about schools and churches, and how the whites think. The railroad awes him. He's attentive to the children, and questions them on English words. He is so gentle that sometimes I wonder if the emigrants and the soldiers taught the Indians all the barbaric ways. Our country claims to be Christian, but I think we're more Old Testament. Out here it is an 'eye for an eye'. One German rancher with a large family near the fort has fourteen Indian scalps nailed to the barn door. He tells everyone: 'The scalps announce right up front what to expect if they cross me or touch one of mine with their filthy tomahawks, I show no mercy. Their scalps will be right up there beside the fourteen.'

Our outpost at Ft. Laramie is the sole law over an area bigger than the original thirteen colonies.

And I'm so anxious to see Ed. Even out here at the edge of civilization we're planning on celebrating our nation's first official Thanksgiving, and I hope he returns in time to enjoy it. All of us have worked very hard in the gardens and in preserving the food we've grown.

Summer Rose, if you can spare any flower seeds, I'd appreciate them. I long for a flower garden, and I am starved for a peach. How long does it take to grow a peach tree?

Jake Hunt—remember him?—is returning to Ft. Laramie, which I dread. That's a long story with which I won't bore you. Did you ever learn why he and Emily broke up? Is she back from Europe yet? I'd love to hear from her.

Poor Mary. She wants so terribly to have a child, and it is just not happening. I'd love a child, too. Perhaps soon. Love, Abbey."

Daniel refolded the letter with a sigh, then stood and stretched. He looked out the window, checking on the children and Mercy again then walked behind his wife and wrapped his arms around her.

"She sounds happy, don't you think?" asked Summer Rose.

It was a moment before he answered. When he did, his voice was soft. "I worry about her being halfway across the continent. You and your brother, Jack are not the only ones to revere family. Abbey is my only sibling."

Summer immediately thought of Louisa, the daughter of Daniel's deceased father and his second wife, Pearl. They had just heard of Louie's suicide and the birth of Daniel's little half-sister. Summer knew better than to even mention the child. Daniel didn't acknowledge the girl.

Instead she said, "You have to trust that she can take care of herself."

"I know, but it's difficult. She's not nearly as good with a knife or rifle as you are."

Summer Rose rolled out the crust. "Few people are, darling. When she was here I taught her a little. She was surprisingly good with a rifle. Let's consider sending her a Bowie knife."

"I want to spend some time training her first."

Summer Rose patted one flour-covered hand on Daniel's, which rested on the slight bulge of her belly. "You're right. When you write back, don't tell her we're expecting. Not yet. No sense in making anyone jealous." She twisted to look at him then purposefully smeared flour on his cheek. "You just look at me and I miraculously become with child."

Daniel kissed the side of her neck, chuckling low in his throat. "That's not exactly my recollection of how it works, but I won't tell if you don't."

9

BLUE MOON

The weekend before Thanksgiving, Ed's column marched into Fort Laramie. A coating of snow dusted the ground and crept beneath their collars. The soldiers, shaggy and in need of grooming as much as their horses came bearing gifts: a dozen slain turkeys and several venison carcasses, as well as goods bartered from the Indian tribes in the north.

"Although we shot at least a dozen wolves," Ed said, as he presented a large brown paper and twine wrapped package to Abbey "the wolves followed us."

Half-expecting a bloody wolf pelt, Abbey gingerly touched the bulky package. Out tumbled a full-length doeskin coat, white and pristine. Ed smiled broadly and held it open for her. Never had she seen anything so beautiful. While the doeskin was gorgeous, it was the hood to hem lining of lush sable fur which made the coat warm and rich. Mrs. Dietrich looked green. Ed slid the cloak over Abbey's shoulders and whispered. "This is the prize. I traded it from a small band of Flatheads. Don't let anyone talk you out of it. They will try."

He nodded toward Colonel Dietrich. "While the coat is beautiful, the next thing we found is worth far more." Ed motioned to the soldiers to remove the canvas tarps.

Louder oohs and ahhs came from the wives and resident soldiers as a huge sled, towering twenty feet high, loaded with wood was uncovered. It was enough to provide fuel for much of the winter.

The army cooks took the turkeys and venison and combined them with the abundance of fresh and preserved vegetables grown at the fort. Colonel Dietrich spent hours devising fair distribution charts and directives for proper storage of the wood, and had a small bridge built over a creek to make hauling it easier.

TWO WEEKS AFTER Thanksgiving, Abbey received a long letter from her brother informing her of their father's suicide in Chicago, and the birth of Pearl Mason's daughter, who she claimed was their half-sister, Louie's daughter. They'd named her Louisa Lenore. Abbey read the letter twice, the second time out loud, and Ed watched her reaction to the words. She was sorrowful at the news of her father, but Abbey had already mourned him when he'd left his family, so his death seemed anticlimactic. But Louisa … she told Ed that she didn't know how to feel about a new baby sister. "Daniel," she told Ed, "will never acknowledge her as related to us, so I'll probably never, even see her." "And," she added, "how do we know she is actually our father's child? Her mother was and may well still be a whore."

By the New Year, Abbey wasn't thinking about anyone else's child. She was sure of her pregnancy. The expectant parents were ecstatic. They told no one, mainly to spare Mary heartache, but Abbey did telegraph her brother and Summer Rose who immediately sent a box of baby things: flannel blankets and rattles, little undershirts, sweaters, diapers and diaper pins, handmade booties, and a blank journal to record these momentous times. One of the army wives spotted the baby things and word of her condition spread faster than whooping cough.

Of course, Dame Dilly and Mary heard the news, and while they both were immensely jealous, they graciously congratulated her. When Jake Hunt and his troops returned to Ft. Laramie in late January, Jake too spotted the baby clothes. Unlike the ladies, he wasn't at all gracious. He shocked Abbey by yelling at her, calling her names, and telling her how stupid she was.

He grabbed her upper arm and hissed. "Good lord, woman, where is your head? Giving birth on the edge of the frontier is not only stupid it's dangerous. Major Oliver doesn't know a thing about babies. For Christ's sake, he's a surgeon. He could well be up on the Yellowstone when your time comes."

Jake jerked open the door; a cold wind rushed in. "Not only that but you're endangering Ed's and probably my life, too. Your husband will be thinking about you and not his troops. You've put him in a terrible position." He stomped out the door. "And I'll be worrying about Ed."

Ed knew right away what really provoked Jake's anger. It took no time at all for Jake to maneuver Ed out of the house and over to Old Bedlam, the Bachelor Officers' Quarters, where the usual Saturday night debauchery was in full force. Old Bedlam, an on-post hotel of sorts, jumped with foot-stomping music and ribald revelry as single officers drank, played cards, or danced with the camp followers. Most of those followers were Indian girls, outcasts from the tribe of what the soldiers dubbed Loafers, Indians who hung around the fort.

Jake and Ed shrugged out of their heavy coats, sat at a table, and ordered a bottle of whiskey for each of them. An unattractive, pockmarked Indian girl who couldn't have been more than fifteen draped herself over Jake and whispered into his ear.

As Jake slid his hands inside the girl's blouse, he yelled at Ed. "You idiot! How did you let that happen? They make those French letters to prevent babies, you know. For God's sake, the sutlers sell them." He shook his head, his face growing redder with every word. "You may as well have slipped a noose around your neck. She has you by the balls now. Get rid of it." He glared at Ed and downed two quick shots.

The girl on Jake's lap suddenly jumped and tears filled her eyes, but her nervous smile quickly returned. She kissed Jake's neck. Ed knew what was going on in the girl's head. Jake cowed him, too, though there wasn't any real reason for it. Ed not only was stronger than Jake, he was also taller and bigger and a natural fighter, too. But Jake, like Ed's father and uncle, even his brothers, knew what words to use, what looks intimidated Ed.

"Want me to do it?"

Ed glanced up, confused. "What do you mean?"

"The Indians sell a wicked potion, made from mushrooms or toadstools," Jake said with a shrug. "Dried crow entrails, I don't know. They make a tea that flushes the little bugger away." He motioned toward the Indian girl. "How do you think *they* get rid of unwanted baggage?"

Ed shook his head briefly then stared at the floor. "It would break her heart. I can't do that to her."

"What did you do?" Jake asked, leaning in closer. The look on his face was pure disgust. "Fall in *love* with the princess bitch?"

He hated it when Jake called her princess. Sure, she was a deb-utante, but she didn't deserve such platitudes. There was nothing phony about Abbey. Ed tried to muster his fierceness to defend her, but he failed. In Ed's childhood memory, women were far from revered. Even now, fragmented memories and ugly laughter from his father and uncle came unbidden. "They're only good for one thing. Fucking." He could face down seven hundred Indians, but not Jake Hunt. He poured them both another shot.

"I guess I have."

Jake didn't say anything, only stared at him. The raw hurt on his face hit Ed like a two-by-four. Jake tossed down his shot then grabbed his bottle of whiskey in one hand and the girl in the other, pushing her toward the stairs. Before Ed had married, they'd often taken a woman together. In fact, he knew Jake harbored hopes that Abbey might someday go along with a threesome, but Ed had shot down that idea. He knew what put the fear of God in Jake. "Daniel let me know he held me responsible for her. He'd kill us both."

Jake paused at the top of the stairs and glanced down at him expectantly. "Bring my coat."

Nauseous, Ed picked up his hat, his bottle of booze, and grabbed their coats. Then he followed Jake.

FOR THE SECOND time that month, the moon was full. Tonight it was brilliant in a cloudless indigo sky. The air, though, smelled of snow, a big snow coming from Canada. Ed, more than a little drunk and feeling the heel of all heels walked the compound twice, drinking the little that remained in his bottle, letting the bitter cold work its way into his bones. As drunk as he was, he didn't feel much of anything, nothing except a horrid guilt.

The girl, even at fifteen, was long past any freshness, and the usual wildness with Jake was brutal. When Jake fell asleep, Ed left the girl some money, dressed, and walked out of Old Bedlam. He checked the stables, spoke to the muleskinners and buffalo hunters who gathered around a fire, then drank a couple of shots with them. Later—he wasn't sure how much later—he stumbled back to their cottage and noticed the puppy tied on the porch. That was odd. He knelt and covered the trembling dog with a burlap bag, then cringed at the noises coming from within the house. *What the hell was happening?* He heard a muffled scream, and again the voices and the laughter from his childhood came to him. The cold and the amount of whiskey he'd consumed fumbled his fingers. The wooden latch wouldn't work…

When he finally managed to open the door, Jake was waiting. He smashed the side of Ed's face with an iron skillet then turned away. Ed stumbled into the living room and fell like a stone, barely conscious. Jake slammed the outside door and stormed past him. Through the half-open doorway to the bedroom, he could see Abbey's bare legs on the bed. She was tied face down and Jake, half-naked stood over her. Ed rolled to the side and threw up, then watched from the floor, blood pooling beneath his ear.

Jake turned towards him, grinning manically. He held up Abbey's nine-inch hatpin, making sure Ed could see it. "You should train your princess bitch better," he hissed. "She stuck me with this! Goddamn, did *that* sting." He frowned slightly then shrugged at Ed. "She wouldn't drink the bloody tea."

"No!" Ed whispered, his voice rasping, knowing suddenly what Jake was going to do, but there was nothing he could do. He was absolutely useless.

Jake spread Abbey's legs and plunged the hatpin deep into her. She screamed, and Ed lost consciousness.

HE REGAINED IT along with some sobriety when the cold water hit him.

Jake was nowhere in sight. Abbey or perhaps Jake had untied her, and she stood over him, dressed, still holding the dripping bucket. Her entire body shook with rage. Tears smeared across her cheeks. She looked as if she might kill him. Her eyes were black, nearly swollen shut. Blood dripped from her nose and mouth.

"He told me you've been lovers since West Point. Good God, Ed. It's true, isn't it?" She didn't wait for an answer. "How *could* you? He's insane. He was more jealous than any woman ever was about Danny. He's not about to let you go."

Ed struggled to his feet, trying to clear his head. He was soaked. She pointed the Remington he'd given her at his gut, and although it shook, he knew she wouldn't miss. Her voice dropped dangerously low.

"Slowly slide your gun over here, Ed. I'll shoot you. Trust me. I *want* to shoot you." She sniffed. "He said you both slept with a whore tonight. Is that true?"

Ed dropped his chin against his chest. He deserved this. He deserved worse than this. He' knew what kind of man Jake was, knew what he was capable of doing. And he'd let it all happen.

"I can explain, Sunshine."

She gasped for air, and words gushed from her mouth. "Don't you *dare* Sunshine me." Big tears slid out of her swollen eyes. Her voice was hoarse. The hurt in it sliced down his spine. He wished she would just shoot him.

"What exactly can you *explain*, Ed? I *loved* you. I gave you my heart, my trust. You may as well have stomped on my heart." She motioned with the gun for him to back up. "I knew from the beginning there was something I didn't like about Jake Hunt. In a million years I would never have dreamed he was your lover. And you took a whore together? Just thinking of that makes me ill. That is *disgusting*."

She wiped her face on her sleeve, smearing the material with her blood. "He's jealous of me, jealous like a woman, only worse. He's *sick*, Ed. How *could* you? What am I supposed to do? The thought of you touching him makes me want to vomit."

Tears ran through residues of blood on her face and she shook. *I'm so sorry, Abbey.* "I broke it off with him tonight. It's over."

"*Over? Now* it's over?" she shrieked. "Shouldn't you have thought of that before you married me? Dragged me out to this godforsaken nowhere? Perhaps you could have told me you liked men?"

She tried to narrow her eyes, but Ed could see it hurt her to do so. "He tried to rape me, Ed. How's that feel, knowing that? Your lover tried to rape your wife, tied me up and beat me. But he didn't want a woman. To be explicit, scrawny, tough, Jake Hunt couldn't get his equipment working. He's *pathetic*."

She hiccoughed and used her arm to wipe more blood off her face, but more trickled from her nose. "He did what he did to me so it would hurt *you*." She laughed with no humor and tears poured in a sudden flood from her eyes. "In case you're curious, it worked. Every inch of me hurts. You think my face looks bad? My body looks far worse. I can barely walk. He tried to destroy my baby. He said you knew he was going to kill it, because you didn't have the guts to do it yourself." She shook her head. "Where *were* you? That's why you didn't come home? Isn't it?"

She started packing, stuffing her clothes and the baby's into a haversack, pointing the Remington at him every time he moved. Sobbing and shaking between breaths, she picked up his pistol, shook out the bullets then shoved them and the gun into the haversack.

"I can't stay here."

Ed didn't think he could hate himself any more than he already did, but the next words out of his mouth proved him wrong. "You won't tell anyone will you? You know …"

She sucked in a big breath, nodding. Her voice lowered to a croaking whisper. "I know, Eddie. I remember what they did to that boy. I can't watch them do that to you. You're West Point, an officer…if I thought they'd treat you decent, I'd run to the colonel, but no, I know what they'd do. They'd make sure one of them or the Indians kill the two of you. No, I can't stay here."

Her voice broke again and her arms sagged at her sides. Tears streaked her face and shudders coursed through her. "You told him every detail from our marriage bed, didn't you? What I liked. How *could* you? That hurt more than the blows, the—" She was sobbing hard now. "I *loved* you, Ed. I gave you all my heart, my innocence. I *trusted* you."

Calmness swept over her and she wiped her face again. Her shoulders slumped and she looked smaller, even more defeated. "Goddammit, Ed. I could kill you. It'd be so easy. But ... but I care." She gasped a breath. "Stupid, stupid me. Why, I don't know? I can't stand for them to hurt you."

He started to move, but her eyes hardened and she cocked the gun. "Don't you dare come near me. I know where to aim. I may still care for you, but that doesn't mean you can ever touch me again. The thought of you touching me sickens me."

His voice was little more than a whisper. "Where will you go?"

"That is none of your concern. You have no say over me any-more." She waved the gun in the air. "He tried to convince me that Danny was part of this ... this ..." She shook her head, but her eyes stayed on him, tears streaming down her face. "He said you only married me because I looked like Daniel, that you were in love with my brother, not me. He wanted me to telegraph Danny and get him out here. I spit in his face. I know my brother. He'd never—"

Ed was crying now, wishing he could die. How could he have done this to her? "If you believe nothing else, Abbey, know I love only you. It never had anything to do with your brother. Jake ... he was the one who wanted him. From the day he met Daniel, he was obsessed with him."

"I should shoot you."

The wind picked up and howled around the little house. Owen whined and scratched at the door. With a sudden chill Ed realized the life he built was over. Gone.

"Do it, Abbey."

She shook her head, then picked up the hooded fur cloak and slipped it on. "Too easy. Take off your boots and pants, Ed. Your underwear, too." When he hesitated, she motioned with the gun. "Trust me, no one will hear a gunshot way down here."

With shaking hands, he shed his clothing then grabbed a blanket and wrapped it around his lower body, feeling indescribably ashamed. With an effort, she leaned down and picked up the bundle, then threw it all in the fireplace. The clothing hissed and steamed, filling the cottage with white smoke. Shocked, Ed rushed to rescue them.

"Why did you do that? Christ, those boots cost a month's pay."

She fired a shot into the ceiling, and he froze midstride. "You'd better worry about a lot more than the price of your boots," she hissed. "My parents bankrupted the family trying to get out of their marriage. I don't have any money, but by God, I'll find a way to end our marriage. Before you even think about doing anything rash, consider what I could tell a court. Danny's a lawyer. So is Hal. He's one of the best in the country. They'll help me—if one of them doesn't kill you first."

He wiped the mucus from his face on the blanket and stared at the fire. Flames licked at his boots. "I'm sorry, Abbey," he said, his voice raspy. "I don't know how to fight Jake. I never did. I don't know if I can, even now."

She didn't speak, and he couldn't look at her. The fire caught the stripe on his trousers and flared bright then died.

She picked up the haversack and hoisted it on her shoulder. "Whatever you do," she finally said, "keep Jake away from me.

Tell that bastard if he comes after me, I will tell. Everything. I never want to see either him or you again."

Then she slipped out the door—along with every good thing he'd ever possessed.

10

YELLOW BIRD

Under her breath she muttered every swear word she ever heard, the profane and the obscene. She untied Owen; he followed her to the stable where she saddled Cricket and strapped on the saddlebags, fitting Owen into one. She stopped at Mary's house and tucked a note under her door. Fear of Jake and what he might do to her baby motivated her to not linger, despite the sharp smell of snow. Jake had warned her not to leave the house, threatened to hunt her down and kill her if she disobeyed. But Abbey wasn't about to stay here and let him follow through on any of his threats.

As she remounted the pony, she heard music and revelry spilling from Old Bedlam. The smell of roasted buffalo meat came to her from the fires of the muleskinners and hunters. Everyone and everything seemed very far away. Loneliness and fear knifed through her, keeping the pain at bay. Her tears froze on her lashes.

The high moon silvered the landscape, and she could see the vacated Indian camp, the wind whipped and whistled through the sparse lodge pole pines and scattered the dry ashes of the dead fires. She remembered Splashing Rabbit telling her about their winter camp—up, up, up and over the mountain, then down, down, down—so she had a vague idea of where to go.

"What choice do I have?" she wondered out loud. "And Wakanda invited both me and Mary to visit their winter camp. Where else can I go?" *Funny,* she thought, *as she pointed Cricket toward the mountains, I trust the heathen savages more than my own kind.*

THE CRAMPS STARTED with the first snowflakes. A fierce, hungry fear enveloped her, made her heart fill her chest. But she couldn't acknowledge it. Staying clear-headed and determined was her objective. Fear might just get her killed. She lowered her head and urged Cricket onward.

She'd heard tales of experienced trappers wandering in circles in snowstorms, only to be found frozen in the spring. And now she'd heard the wolves, not all that far away. She checked her pocket to make sure the Remington was still there then went over her options. The snow might end by morning. If she could lie down the cramping might ease. The important thing was to protect her child.

A little way up the mountain she came upon a sheltered area surrounded by boulders and an overhang of pines. She gathered fallen branches and wove a nest of boughs. The dry needles and cones made great kindling, so she started a small fire and curled up beside it. The sable coat kept the wind at bay, and Owen cuddled tight against her belly, giving her warmth and comfort. Cricket lay down in a protected niche like a big dog, further blocking the wind.

After a while the cramping eased, but Abbey's head felt as if it might split open. She hurt in so many places she hoped she might die as she fell asleep. And under all the pain, the foundation of her world crumbled. So much of what she believed had been shattered.

Will Dupree rode Drum, leading two packhorses piled high with furs. He caught a whiff of smoke from her fire then picked up her scent. Enroute to his village from the Big Horn, he approached from downwind, whispering to her pony, feeding him sugar cubes. He crouched near the sleeping bundle and the puppy emerged from his nest, wagging his tail. Will petted him and the dog licked his fingers. When Will added fuel to the fire, the lump didn't move, and he leaned in closer to understand why. Even with the bruising and swelling of her face he recognized her. And he smelled the blood. He knew women, but sensed the scent came from more than her cycle. Without touching her, he knew a fever raged.

After he unpacked his animals, he took a big, well-cured black bear skin, one he planned to keep for himself, and wrapped her tight, like a papoose. She moaned but didn't awaken, and even while he warmed water and made coffee, bacon, and toasted bread, she slept. He sat beside her, wiped her face with the tepid water, and cleaned the crusted blood from her upper lip and ear. Very gently, he leaned her against the stack of furs. She stirred a little and ate a few bites of toast. She sipped at the coffee but her eyes refused to stay open.

As she slumped down to sleep, her fingers touched the bear claw necklace, then his cheek. He understood she recognized him and felt better; he did not want to frighten her. He covered her again and ate a little of the food.

A light snow fell, and she kept shivering. Her pony rose and stood in the lee of Drum and the packhorses. Will covered each horse with a buffalo hide. He removed his tomahawk and knife, wrapped them loosely with his rifle, in a skin then tucked her Remington and the other pistol inside the bundle. He carefully opened the bearskin and tightly curled his body around her shaking form. The puppy whined, and he pulled the little dog into their cocoon.

The moon peeked out of the clouds every once in a while, and the snow floated down in silver dollar-sized flakes. Because of the shelter she had chosen, little snow fell on them.

A stillness brought to mind the interior of an empty church, dawn came with a sunless sunrise. The world remained dim and gray and silent, and they stayed warm in the bearskin, dozing. The cloud cover increased, and snow floated like gossamer curtains outside the protective pine branches. She eventually woke, and because she couldn't stand alone, he helped her hobble outside their campsite to relieve her bladder. He turned his back but helped her balance when she squatted, then she suddenly jerked and cried out. Blood and worse stained the snow, unavoidable proof of what happened.

"No," she sobbed, struggling to stand. "No!"

She bent double and cried, cutting the silent morning with deep, shuddering sobs that tore at his heart. She lay limp in his arms when he carried her to the fire then laid her gently back into the warm bed. As she lay there quiet but shaking, he melted more snow and dipped soft cloths in the warmed water, and cleaned her as the bleeding and the cramps continued. He packed cloths between her legs, even inside her. She turned her face away from him; her body jerked with silent tears. He wrapped snow in a cloth and dabbed at her face and hands, always mindful of bruises. Eventually she sipped water and nibbled a piece of bacon before falling back to sleep. When her breathing settled, he went off by himself.

⚬❧

HE RETURNED MUCH later, though Abbey had no idea how long he'd been gone. She could tell from the stillness around her that twilight was near. He built up the fire and bundled the three of them again in the bearskin. They slept. Never had she felt so warm or so safe. Owen snored.

Later the smell of coffee and Owen's wiggles woke her. She emerged from the cocoon, shedding some of the bearskin as she sat up. The small fire warmed the air, and the backdrop of boulders and pines, heavy with snow, gave the illusion of a cave. Cricket and the other horses stood nearby, each draped with a buffalo robe and munching contentedly from feedbags.

Her gaze went to the tall Indian with blue eyes sitting a few feet away. He was watching her, and when their eyes met he nodded to her.

"I'm Will Thunder Cloud Dupree," he said as he handed her coffee. Of course she knew who he was, but she'd never before heard him speak. She hadn't expected the French accent then she remembered hearing that his father had been a French trader. "Call me Will." One side of his mouth curled up. "I know you're Abbey from the fort. My son, Splashing Rabbit, named you ZiZi. That's short for Yellow Bird. He's talked of little else all autumn. I think you have a serious admirer."

He held out one hand, and she shook it, seeing the situation through a haze. How odd it seemed, meeting this way. He'd cleaned her up as if she were a baby, seeing parts of her no one except her mother had ever seen, and now he acted so nonchalant. His blue eyes with such white whites were so out of place with his dark skin.

As if he read her mind, he pointed to his eyes. "From my white father… and perhaps a few other white grandfathers or grandmothers somewhere along the line. I'm far from pure blooded which my uncle, Red Cloud reminds me all the time." He stood and went to his pack. When he returned to the fire, she watched him thread a rope through the belt loops of a pair of heavy denim trousers. "Put these on. You'll be warmer. Do you need help?"

How ridiculous, she thought, to feel shy after all that happened. She shook her head and felt heat flood her cheeks.

"I think I can manage." She hesitated then took a deep breath. "Thank you, Will Thunder Cloud. Thank you for everything you have done for me. Call me Abbey—though ZiZi does have a certain charm."

He nodded and set about cleaning up breakfast, then went off by himself again. Deep in the bearskin, Abbey wriggled carefully out of her skirts and into the trousers, which were sufficiently large enough that she was able to take one of her petticoats and wedge it up between her legs to soak up any more blood. She rolled up the long trouser legs and tucked them around her boots, then stared at the blood-soaked skirts she'd set to the side. Every time she thought about the baby a knot twisted around her heart. She fought the tears lurking behind her eyes.

When he returned he crouched next to her. "I'll call you Abbey Yellow Bird," he said.

For some reason, the words brought her comfort.

"We'll rest today," he said, "then I'll take you to my mother's tipi. It's a rough ride, but we'll take it slow. Come. I want to show you something."

He stretched out his hand and led her to the place in the snow where she lost the baby. He'd built a small pyramid of stones which stood about waist high. She could see the places nearby where he'd cleared snow to find the rocks. She glanced at him, and he surprised her again by taking her hand.

"I was raised a Jesuit," he told her then bowed his head.

"*The Lord is my shepherd; I shall not want. He maketh me to lie down in green pastures; he leadeth me beside still water*s."

Her voice joined his in a whisper. "*He restoreth my soul;*

"He leadeth me in the paths of righteousness; for his names sake. Yea though I walk through the Valley of the Shadow of Death, I fear no evil for thou are with me…"

Weak from crying through the impromptu service, she slumped against him. He supported her back to their nest and heated more coffee. When she was calm, he motioned to her black eyes and the lacerations.

"Who did this to you? Your husband?"

She shook her head. "No. His friend."

"The captain in Scotts Bluffs?"

She nodded.

"I remember." The eyes hardened to blue ice. "I never forget a face."

11

MARY

Mary's hands trembled as she held Abbey's note.

"Dear Mary,

I'm hurt and afraid. I need to get away. Do not blame Ed. He's not at fault. I'm going to visit Wakanda. She gave us both an open invitation. I will send word that I am okay.

Love, Abbey"

The back of the paper was smeared with dried blood. Mary's hand still trembled as she studied the words for the tenth time. She didn't know what to do. Earlier Emmett had been summoned to Headquarters because a prostitute had been found dead, strangled, behind Old Bedlam—and *oh goodness*, gossip and rumor flew like a tornado. Was a murderer loose on the post? When she went to Ed's house, he didn't answer his door. Owen didn't bark. What was worse was when she checked the stable and found not only Cricket's stall empty, but a smear of blood on the gate. Mrs. Dietrich, who happened to be feeding her horse, came over. "You look as if you've been crying again. Mary, you must pull yourself together. The colonel doesn't like whining. Please try, Mary, not to whimper in front of him." She touched Mary's chin. "It makes your skin all blotchy."

Mary fiddled with a coat button and sucked in a shudder and handed the note to the woman.

Mrs. Dietrich read it twice and frowned. "Good Lord Almighty," she muttered. Deep lines twisted around her mouth as she refolded the paper then buried it deep in her jacket pocket. "I'll show this to Winnie. Don't say anything to anyone. You know how awful the gossip can be around here."

Mary opened her mouth to speak, but Dame Dilly petted her shoulder and arched her left eyebrow. "Poor Abbey's been acting strange ever since she received that necklace. Don't you think so?"

Mary knew very well Mrs. Dietrich wasn't concerned with Abbey. Instead, Dame Dilly was putting words into Abbey's mouth. Her only thought was with her husband's reputation as a commander. Out here in the middle of nowhere, with no place to go, Saturday nights were a trial, but last night was particularly worrisome with the discovery of a dead prostitute. The post boiled with gossip. Rogue Indians were nothing to fear compared to Army wives.

"Go home, dear child," Dame Dilly said. As she turned and left the stable, she called over her shoulder, "I'll take care of this. Go home and take a nap."

Mary, speechless, watched Mrs. Dietrich's retreating back. The woman scurried up the hill like a cat with a prized mouse.

"Don't worry?" Mary muttered, furious at herself for having shown her the letter. "You crazy old bat. Of course I'll worry." She bunched her fists at her sides. "Don't you dare make Abbey look bad."

Mary ran from the stable to her house and dug into the hidden trove of money her mother sent her. She had quite a bit. Then she headed to the telegraph office. She'd wired her parents twice before: when she'd first arrived and at Christmas. The new technology was one of the few things that made being stationed here in this godforsaken hole bearable. She already had the telegram composed in her head when she entered the office. She prayed the lines were in order.

TO
DANIEL CHARTERIS
CAMELLANN
MORGAN'S CORNER
ADAMS COUNTY PENNSYLVANIA STOP
ABBEY HURT AND IN DANGER STOP RAN OFF TO THE INDIANS STOP COME AT ONCE STOP MARY HATHAWAY

Summer Rose received the telegram in Pennsylvania that evening. Mr. Graves, the one-armed stationmaster in Morgan's Corner, drove the buckboard out to her, and she read it immediately. She forwarded it to Chicago where Daniel and Hal, his law partner, were advising on a case involving the Union Pacific Railroad. When the telegram reached Daniel the next morning, he and Hal St. Clair were meeting with General Sheridan and General Grenville Dunn about Union Pacific infringement.

"Captain Kincaid's wife? She's your sister? I haven't met her," mumbled General Dunn. His voice came out as if he stored marbles alongside his molars. "But I just read a report about *him*." He ruffled through some papers. "General Conner commended him. Said he handled himself very well in battle." He took a deep breath. "This telegram emphasizes my point, gentlemen. We must clear out the hostiles. They're dangerous, and commerce demands we keep our people safe."

General Sheridan cleared his throat. "Excuse me, General Dunn, but the telegram says she ran off *to* the Indians. It doesn't say she was abducted." He stood and turned to Daniel. "The fastest way is by train to Fremont. That's the end of the line."

General Dunn also stood. "I apologize, Mr. Charteris. Until the Indian problem is settled we won't have a transcontinental railroad. These barbarians are killing Americans. We need to do something."

General Sheridan pulled his lips tight, looking frustrated. "Right now my concern is sending Daniel on his way." He looked away from Dunn, concentrating on Daniel. "My aide will set you up with horses and vouchers for feed across Nebraska. Hope you're in shape for a long ride." He shook his head with regret. "Wish I were going with you."

Hal St. Clair also stood, his eyes dark with concern for Abbey. He'd known her all his life, watched her grow up. "Don't worry about business, here, Danny. I'll carry on."

Before boarding the Union Pacific in Chicago, Daniel telegraphed Summer Rose, told her where he was headed and promised to keep her informed. The railroad now pushed past Council Bluffs since Abbey traveled on it. Now it continued through Omaha and into Fremont, Nebraska. As promised, when Daniel arrived, General Sheridan had a string of four good horses waiting.

12

SUNSET TO SUNRISE

Will Thunder Cloud caught four sizeable trout in the mountain stream, filleted, and fried them with bacon and onions, and made Johnny cakes from cornmeal he carried in his pack. He fixed Abbey's portion on the only plate he possessed and ate his meal directly from the skillet. She used the fork, he the knife. Ravenous, she fought the urge to slurp up the trout in her fingers. Never had food tasted so good.

The snow stopped. The crisp air hurt to breathe. When she finished the trout, she leaned back against the pile of furs and laid her hand on her stomach.

"That was wonderful. Thank you."

He took her plate, scraped the bones in the fire, and gave Owen their crumbs. He'd already fed the horses and watered them while he fished. Now he topped off their coffee and sat beside her on the bearskin, both of them resting their backs against the piles of furs. Owen lay between them, looking content.

"You picked a good campsite, Abbey Yellow Bird," said Will.

He handed her his binoculars and pointed east to where two rivers joined. Birds by the tens of thousands were landing on the water, their cries and the roar of their wings sounding like applause even from far away. Hawks, eagles, and raptors she couldn't name soared by on updrafts. The setting sun silvered the rivers, and the fires at the fort flickered beyond. Through the binoculars the soldiers looked no bigger than bugs, and the fort resembled a child's plaything. She smiled a little at the thought.

"I feel very humbled and safe," she said softly. She reached up and touched the bear claw necklace. "I never thanked you for this beautiful necklace. I didn't do anything to deserve such a valuable gift, but I treasure it. Thank you."

He picked up her hand and pressed it flat between his palms. "You deserve the necklace and my eternal gratitude. I was too far away, stuck on the hillside watching my son through these." He lowered her hand and held up the binoculars. "I expected to see him die then you like an angel saved him."

IN FREMONT, NEBRASKA, Daniel looked up to the swaying sign, Alfred J. Jenner, Outfitter, est. 1864. He walked about the store and pulled down from the shelves rugged western clothes: two each of shirts, socks, and sweaters made of top grade wool, and heavy denim trousers. He also bought a wide-brimmed hat and tooled leather boots with two-inch heels, which would be useful on a long ride. When the bespectacled proprietor, Alfred Jenner, heard where Daniel was headed, he talked him into a thigh length leather jacket lined in sheared wool.

"You'll want warm gloves, too." At Daniel's nod, Alfred Jenner added lined leather gloves to the growing stack of merchandise on the counter.

"How soon before I run into hostile Indians?" asked Daniel, indicating a Henry rifle.

Mr. Jenner handed over the rifle. "You might not run into any. Not all Indians are hostile. Most are just trying to survive the winter like we are. The Army destroyed their winter stores, and too often the emigrants shoot on sight. No wonder they hate us." He narrowed his eyes, squinting critically at Daniel's blond hair. "You might want to consider a short haircut before you venture out, though. Yellow hair is prized. No sense in tempting them."

Daniel didn't respond but picked out a Belgium-made double-barreled shotgun with barrels made of Damascus steel, as well as ammunition for both guns and for his Smith and Wesson. He added everything to the goods on the counter then waited as Mr. Jenner went to get him an oiled slicker, two Hudson Bay blankets, a mess kit, a waterproof pouch of matches, and minimal food and coffee.

"What are you doing about the horses?"

Daniel tapped his pocket. "I have an army map and vouchers signed by General Sheridan. I'll need several bags of oats." He sighed. "Where's that barber?"

Mr. Jenner chuckled. "Not far. And he's not busy." He motioned to the chair in the corner. "I'm the barber too. Why don't you change first? Want to take your old things?"

"Would you keep them here? I don't want the extra weight."

IT WAS FEBRUARY, and it was cold, and it was a trip Daniel would remember all his life. February began the great North American bird migration, during which Sandhill Cranes, ducks, geese, and other water birds of amazing variety darkened the sky and made their way from Mexico or Central America, perhaps even South

America, to the Arctic. Millions of birds settled in along the rich wetlands of the Platte to rest after their long flights. Every evening when Daniel stopped to rest and replenish the horses and himself, he made sure he camped on a rise overlooking the Platte so he could watch and listen to the roar of birds as they roosted. It meant he could awaken to the amazing migration.

13

SMALL PLEASURES

Abbey awoke the next morning just as Will emerged from the woods. She noticed, first, the distinct smell of soap, then saw that his hair was wet and frosted. "You bathed? Where?"

He glanced over his shoulder. "In the stream."

"It must have been freezing."

He nodded and gave his half smile, flashing his white teeth. "It was."

She stood abruptly, grabbing her bag. *If he can, I can.* "Show me, please." He stood with his back to her as she stripped and plunged into the water, taking perhaps the fastest bath ever. She knew without any doubt that he wouldn't turn, wouldn't invade her privacy. She trusted him. Besides, he'd already seen most parts of her. With lightning speed she soaped and scrubbed her body, washed her hair. Even at that speed, by the time she stood behind him wiping her body dry, she was numb to the bone.

She fumbled in her bag, pulling out clean underwear along with a clean shirt and sweater. Because of her bruises she hadn't worn a corset, and she discovered she liked the freedom. She pulled the trousers back on, then fresh socks and her boots. With a towel wrapped about her hair they returned to their camp, she burned the bloodied petticoat then buried herself deep in her fur coat, huddling close to the fire as she dried her hair. Somehow being clean made her feel a hundred times better.

He crouched close to her and studied her face. "*Bien*," he said softly, nodding with satisfaction. "The swelling has gone down. Do you still bleed?"

She shook her head and heat rose in her cheeks. White men never asked such questions.

"Can you ride?"

She nodded.

"Good. We will leave after breakfast." He nodded toward the fort. "*Il est temps.* They sent out search parties today. We must go." He reached up and touched one of her curls, pulling it like his son always did then let it snap back. He grinned, his odd eyes sparkling.

"*Incroyable*," he said. "Amazing. Splashing Rabbit told us, but I didn't believe him."

DANIEL ROTATED THE four horses every two hours and made good time, but Nebraska was big. The long ride gave him plenty of time to go over what he already knew. From Mary's telegram, he understood Abbey had not been abducted by the Indians, but she'd gone to them. What happened to her? Why had she run to the Indians? In the back of his mind he remembered Abbey's last letter, tried to recall what she'd said, and came up with the one mention she made of Jake Hunt. *Jake Hunt—remember him?—is returning to Ft. Laramie, which I dread. The story is long and I won't bore you with it. Did you ever learn why he and Emily broke up?*

What happened? Even if Jake had done something untoward, surely Abbey could have put a stop to that. Abbey was no shrinking violet. He couldn't imagine anyone groping her and receiving less than a black eye. General Sheridan had told Daniel the story about Colonel Dietrich's rude comment to Abbey at that fateful dinner when he ended up falling face first into his plate. At Daniel's shocked expression, General Sheridan only gave him a wry smile then complimented Abbey's poise.

Perhaps the colonel had made a pass. After all, Dietrich was her husband's commanding officer, and—poised or not—Abbey was only nineteen. Daniel knew well the problems attractive women encountered at outposts where men hadn't seen a white woman in months. Years of proper decorum often were not enough. Being as big as he was, he rescued his Summer Rose many times, but some men still evolved into idiots around a well put together woman, especially when alcohol was added to the mix.

Daniel had no idea what happened, but he foresaw nothing but problems. And then there was Mary, his old girlfriend. She'd contacted him, which was the right thing to do. Now he just hoped to God she wasn't a problem.

MARY FELT NAUSEOUS with anxiety. She hated being chastised. Dame Dilly and Emmett both yelled at her for sending the telegram—in fact, Mrs. Dietrich shoved her face so close to Mary's she could smell her face powder. *I wonder if she knows the pores in her nose are huge?*

"Now her brother's on his way!" Mrs. Dietrich squawked. "General Sheridan telegraphed Win with that bit of news. Oh, why did you have to telegraph him? If this costs my husband a star, I'll … I'll make sure your husband is never promoted." Her face contorted. "You'll never again have a decent duty station."

❧

EMMETT'S EXPLANATION WAS calmer. "Daniel retired from the army at the end of the war; however, he'd been a brigadier general and a hero. And he still has the ear of Sheridan. Colonel Dietrich doesn't want Daniel privy to some of the shenanigans that go on around here."

Mary's face twisted into a puzzle. "What do you mean?" she asked as she slid some molasses cookies she'd made that morning and a few apples into a paper bag for him.

Emmett took the bag, removed a cookie, retightened the bag then put the remainder in his saddlebag. He bit into the cookie. "Uhmm... molasses, my favorite. Thanks." He bent his head and kissed her gently on the lips. "For one thing, sweetheart, even a dead prostitute is serious evidence. Then there's the late night drinking parties the Colonel hosts, the gambling. Don't go repeating any of that." He smiled a little. "We're in enough trouble, as it is."

"Oh, I'm so sorry, Emmett, but I had to," Mary cried, wringing her hands. "No one cared what happened to Abbey, and it just isn't right. Dame Dilly wanted to hush it, as if our Abbey did something wrong. There was blood on Abbey's note, and I saw a big smear in the stable near Cricket's stall. And more on their porch. Something terrible must have happened for her to run off like that. Where's Ed? Is he out looking for her? Will we find his body next?" She took a shuddering breath and her shoulders drooped. "Could she really stop you from being promoted?"

He shrugged easily, then hugged her. "Don't you worry. I have a West Point education. I'm an engineer. I can work somewhere. This really is an untidy mess, though. You stay in our quarters while I'm gone."

"I'm so—"

He bent his head and kissed her forehead. "—and honey, it's not your fault. Ed's gone after Jake Hunt," he said as he pulled on one of his heavy gloves. "The colonel thinks Jake may have killed the prostitute. Someone saw him out of uniform riding off with the buffalo hunters. In my opinion, Jake's always been a wild card. I wouldn't be surprised if he did something to Abbey." He glanced at Mary's terrified face then cleared his throat. "I mean scared her, maybe."

He hoisted his saddlebags onto his shoulders and stood tall. "I'm checking the trails west, just in case she went that way. I'll be gone all day, maybe overnight." He touched his wife's cheek gently. "Let's hope your girlfriend has a *bona fide* reason to run off, or she's going to be in big trouble, creating all this hullaba-loo, costing Uncle Sam money. Good Lord, she could cause an Indian war with all this mess."

Mary stiffened her spine. "Abbey doesn't scare easily or run without cause. You should know that about her."

"Well, just pray she's okay and had a good reason." Leaning down and despite his saddlebags, he gathered Mary into a tight hug and kissed her. His bright red hair fell over his forehead. He frowned, feigning anger. "Now, don't go falling in love with your old boyfriend while he's here. Remember you're married to me."

14

FRENCH AND INDIAN

The mountains were shrouded in a thick mist and a light snow fell, which Will told her was a good thing. She attempted to ride Cricket, but he proved too skittish for the slippery trail. Will pulled her up behind him on Drum then led Cricket with the pack horses. She clung to the back of Will's saddle and leaned her cheek against his back.

They came to a breach in the trees and looked down the mountain at an ant-like line of mounted infantrymen leaving the fort.

"More than likely they cannot see us from this distance, and the snow will cover our tracks." He turned and held his finger along his nose. "And I'll smell them a mile away. My big nose is good for something."

The words slipped out before she could think. "I like your nose. Makes your face look distinguished."

He laughed, a rich rumble from deep in his chest. She felt the vibrations against her cheek and closed her eyes, smiling. Their faces were inches apart.

"You know, you are the first person to ever compliment my nose. Wait until I tell my mother."

AFTER ONLY A half day of travel, Abbey realized she never would have made it through the mountains by herself, and she never would have found the winter camp either. It was well hidden; she had been foolish to even try. But what else could she have done? There were no emigrant trains to join, and she wouldn't dare go to that German rancher with the fourteen scalps nailed to his barn door. And, staying at the fort was out of the question. Someone would have seen her swollen face and asked questions. After all that had happened, she couldn't even think of looking at Ed, let alone staying in the same house with him. Above all, the possibility that she might see Jake terrified her.

They arrived at a mountain spring and a small pool. Will eased Drum to a halt and slid effortlessly to the ground then held out his hands and easily swung her down, holding on to her waist. After the long ride her legs were jelly. He led her to a big rock and held her steady until she settled. Then he saw to the horses, made a quick fire, and started coffee before she dared stand on her own. Eventually she felt better, and she slowly walked to the pool to wash her hands.

Back at the fire he reached into his pack and produced hard tack and cheese with salty strips of dried meat, then set them on a cloth with his big knife.

"You're very resourceful."

He nodded, smiling. "*Oui*. That is my Indian side. Help yourself. "

Will was a good-looking man. Abbey's eyes traced over the thickness of his black eyelashes and the sharp planes of his face, landing on those disarming blue eyes. She picked up a cracker and a piece of cheese, handed it to him, then fixed a bite for herself.

"Are you more Indian or French?" she asked.

He blew on his coffee, thinking. "I suppose that depends where I am, who I am with." He pointed his cup at her. "With a pretty lady, I hope my French side steps forward to charm her. On the other hand," he added, his eyes twinkling, "if a bear sneaks up behind her, let us hope my Indian side materializes."

Without warning, he jumped to his feet, grabbed his tomahawk, and scanned the trees. Abbey jerked, then looked behind and around her. Owen, startled, sat up, and barked.

"Where?" Abbey cried.

He laughed. "No bear. I'm teasing you. *Je m'excuse*. I can be French again." He reached over and petted Owen, making a fierce noise in his throat. "Growl if you smell a bear. So will I."

When they'd finished with the food, he packed up everything including Owen, dampened down the fire, and remounted. After he swung her up behind him, he reached back and pulled her arms so they wrapped around his waist.

"Hang on tight. The going is rough from now on." He turned his head to the side so she could see his smiling profile. "And besides, both the French and the Indian sides of me like the feel of your arms on me."

HIGH ON DRUM and safe behind Will, Abbey breathed in the crisp air and surveyed the winter landscape. Here higher in the mountains, trees grew thick. A long row of spruce, almost bent to the ground and arched over the trail; the bushes beside the path brimmed with small birds gobbling their fill of red berries. In most places the wind cleared the trail of all but a scant dusting of snow; in other places, however, it came up to the horses' knees. Hawks and eagles circled above, and below, Will pointed out tracks of deer, badgers, and rabbits. He even nodded his head toward the unexpected sight of a wolf drinking from one of the little rivulets that had popped out of nowhere and bubbled down the mountain.

"The animals seek out running water. Most is frozen," he told her, "Watch out for the wolves."

That night they camped beside a mountain stream with ice forming along its banks. Will tied the horses and they pawed the snow to expose a little grass. A fine mist crept up around them as Will built a fire, and Abbey foraged for firewood. Will quickly snared a rabbit, and she collected watercress then made biscuits from his supplies. They settled beside the fire in a contented silence, smelling the cooking food. After dinner, she cleaned the utensils while he repacked their gear, blanketed the horses, and built up the fire.

He held up a deck of cards. "Faro? We'll use sticks for chips,"

Memories of childhood marathon sessions of faro with Daniel, Hal, and Mary came to mind. She nodded, and they sat with the bearskin tucked around their legs. Owen burrowed between them. The firelight reflected on their faces, lighting their expressions, bringing warmth to the bitter night. Abbey found herself laughing and enjoying herself for the first time since … well, she couldn't recall. After Jake's brutal attack and the loss of her child, she never thought she could smile again. Outside the circle of firelight, owls hooted and frozen branches creaked, sometime popping under the weight of ice and snow. In the distance, a mountain lion screeched, frightening the horses, but Will quieted them with his hands and voice. As the moon rose in the clear night sky, the wind shifted from the north. When it was too cold to play cards any longer, Will banked the fire, and they crawled into the bearskin, snug with Owen between them.

How odd, thought Abbey. But it feels so right for her to sleep side by side with this stranger—this dark-skinned, half-breed Indian. She couldn't imagine what her mother might think, but that no longer seemed to matter. What mattered was that she felt safe.

A clump of snow fell from the trees, and bright stars winked down at her. Will pointed to a little patch of sky. "See there? Your child watches over you."

She found comfort in his words, but tears filled her eyes, and her vision grew fuzzy, her throat thickened. He touched her cheek, and she felt his warm breath tickle her face.

"I didn't mean to make you cry."

Biting her lip to hold back a sob, she shook her head and hugged Owen, then wiped away the wetness on her cheeks before it could freeze.

"It's okay. Tears help."

They lay in silence a while longer, neither of them speaking. *Isn't he supposed to be a savage?* Abbey thought. *Shouldn't he want to ravish me, take my scalp?* She blinked up at the stars, feeling lost. *My world is upside down. How do I know who to trust? How do I know which star is my child?*

Owen let out a settling breath and snuggled closer.

"Pick any one you want." Will's voice was soft and calm as the velvet black sky.

Abbey turned her head toward him. "How did you know my thoughts?"

His warm hand touched her shoulder, the pressure of his arm solid against her own. She resisted the unaccountable urge to curl her body into his. He said, "It's just that way with some people. You and me, we don't need a lot of words."

Sometime during the night the dog moved, and Abbey awoke to find herself half under Will. His warm hand rested on her waist, his breath tickled her cheek. She couldn't move; she felt paralyzed. But it wasn't from fear. She was amazed to discover her body desired him, responded to him. Heat rushed to her face. *Good grief, I'm no better than an alley cat, one of those loose girls at school—or God forbid—a whore.*

She lay without moving, feigning sleep, aware of every breath he took. The beat of his heart joined hers, and the heat of him enveloped her. Deep inside she burned with desire. A while later, his weight eased from her, and he moved his hand to her cheek and kissed her there, soft and tender. Again Abbey fought to urge to press her body tight to his. It was not a kiss one might give to a child, nor one she'd forget.

Late the next afternoon they arrived in the winter camp. Ponies grazed by the stream, fires produced cooking meat, and children helped their mothers stretch large hides over enormous racks. Several wind chimes lent a mystical air and purple clouds streaked the winter sky. Blue smoke from the fires twined with the mist and curled around the tipis. An owl hooted a haunted greeting and drums echoed through the mountain hollows.

Three young braves stepped forward to take the horses. Will Thunder Cloud dismounted then helped Abbey down, holding her arm, keeping her balanced. When she was steady, he motioned to the guards then led her past his people and toward two lodges set off by themselves. Every eye in the camp seemed to follow them. Will stooped and picked up Owen, then tightened his arm around Abbey's shoulder.

As they moved through the gathering crowd, he whispered, "Keep your eyes straight ahead."

Incomprehensible relief filled Abbey when she spotted Wakanda walking toward them. The three of them embraced, and for quite a long time Will spoke in quiet Lakota to his mother, who then took Abbey's hand. Abbey was reluctant to let go of

Will. Leaving him frightened her. But Wakanda's smile felt kind and gentle, and the empathy in her eyes helped ease her fear as Will's hand slipped away.

Embers glowed from the small fire, casting orange and red light on the curved interior walls. Wakanda took Abbey's coat and helped her lie on a small pallet. When Abbey was comfortable, the shaman sat beside her and they hugged again. Both women shed tears then Wakanda wiped Abbey's face with a warm cloth. After tucking a wool blanket around her, Wakanda lit a dry branch. She fanned the smoke throughout the lodge then added it to the fire. Before long the warm air inside the conical tent grew both strong and soothing with the scents of sage and cedar.

15

OLD FLAMES

At first light and *in* the midst of a snow squall Daniel arrived at Ft. Laramie. He crossed Nebraska in four days and had lost at least twenty pounds. After seeing to his horses, he checked into the Bachelor Officers' Quarters and managed a real bath in near scalding water. He shaved and donned the new clothes from Jenner's store and talked the cook into making him a plate of bacon, toast, and eggs, which he wolfed down. Towering over every soldier on the post in his two-inch heels, he went looking for the post commandant. The snow had ended and now the sun on the brilliant white caused him to squint.

Word of his presence arrived before he did. Colonel and Mrs. Dietrich, who he had met years ago in Washington, graciously welcomed him to their home. Mrs. Dietrich handed him an envelope.

"We received a message slipped into the U.S. Army mailbag from Red Cloud's sister," she said. "Abbey is safe and wants to remain with the hostiles over the winter. Your sister doesn't want to see anyone, and she has Red Cloud's protection."

Daniel read the note, consciously keeping any expression from his face. He refolded the paper, slid it into the envelope, and handed it back.

"Is it possible to get a message to her? I believe Abbey would see me." He frowned. "And, where's Ed? I have a few questions for him."

Colonel Dietrich walked to a cabinet and withdrew a full bottle of whiskey. He pulled out his pocket knife and started to uncork the bottle.

"Someone smacked him across the face with an iron skillet," Colonel Dietrich said. "Knocked him out. He thinks it might have been Jake Hunt. When Captain Kincaid awoke, his wife was gone, along with her horse and her dog. One of the Indian laundresses saw her leave alone. Captain Kincaid took a couple of men out to look for Captain Hunt."

"May I speak with Mary or Emmett?"

"Emmett's leading a patrol west to find your sister. Isn't that right, Win?" Mrs. Dietrich asked with a tight smile. "I'll send for Mary. May I fix you some breakfast?"

Daniel shook his head. "No, thank you."

The colonel held up the bottle and let out a loud breath. "General Charteris, you may want to prepare yourself. Your sister's more than likely gone Injun. It happens. Some good-looking brave comes along, sweet talks her." He shrugged. "Maybe her husband mistreated her. It's lonesome out here. He's gone on patrol for months at a time. Being an army wife is not easy." He nodded to his wife, one eyebrow lifted. "Who knows what goes on? Can I interest you in a shot of whiskey?"

Daniel stood. "No, thank you, Sir. I want to speak with Mary as soon as possible. If you'll excuse me, I know my way around an army post. I think I can find the Married Officers' Quarters."

He picked up his hat, smiled his best smile, and nodded to Mrs. Dietrich.

He stepped out of their house and into the street, his eyes again adjusting to the sun on snow. Rather than focus on how much he wanted to break Colonel Dietrich's jaw, Daniel spent a moment remembering Mary. For a short time they'd thought themselves in love. He knew now that what he felt for Mary was nowhere near love. They'd grown up together in Philly during those golden years before the war, affluent children of the establishment. Their mothers had plotted their marriage since they were toddlers, but he'd never really noticed Mary until the Christmas Ball in 1862—just months after the slaughter at Antietam when they all knew how real this war had become. He found himself under the mistletoe kissing this delightful little dark-eyed friend of his sister. Mary was a couple of years older than Abbey, and over the next few months they had heated up to long, deep kisses and heavy breathing. They were all but engaged.

Then he'd met Summer Rose, and *poof!* Any feelings he might have harbored for Mary evaporated like mist in the morning sun. Suddenly he was married to the love of his life, Mary was married to Emmett Hathaway, and the war was boiling hot. Almost as swiftly, the war ended and he was the proud father of twin boys with another baby on the way. To make it even more wonderful, he was still so in love with Summer Rose he physically ached for her. It wasn't just in a-man-wants-a-woman-way, either. He longed to hear her voice; even just the sound of her whistling as she fed the twins, cooked, did chores around the house. The thought of walking into a room and catching a hint of her scent tightened his throat and almost brought tears to eyes.

How had Mary fared, now that she was married to Emmett? What had Abbey said in her letter? Poor Mary. She wants so terribly to have a child, and it is just not happening. I'd love a child, too. Perhaps soon.

MARY MUST HAVE spotted him from her front window, for she came running up the path without her coat with eddies of snow swirling around her and threw herself into his arms. He picked her up and swung her around, unexpectedly happy to see someone from home. It seemed perfectly natural to keep his arm around her as they walked back to her cottage. Once inside the Hathaway bungalow, Mary took his coat and hat, hung them near the door, placed his gloves on the hearth, and led him to the big chair by the fire.

"Let me fix some tea." She shivered, rubbing her hands together. "I need some even if you don't. If I recall correctly, you never seemed to mind the cold."

She came back in a few minutes with a tea tray, equipped with a Royal Doulton tea service, a quilted tea cozy, and a plate of cookies. She placed the tray on a little table before the fire then let the tea steep beneath the bright yellow cozy made to look like a calico chicken.

"Thank you for your telegram," he said when she'd finally sat down. "Do you know what happened? Her last letter sounded so—"

Mary held a lump of sugar in miniature silver tongs and waved it over his cup. "Two?"

He nodded. "—Happy."

She poured the tea and handed him the cup, then offered molasses cookies. He declined. Formalities concluded, Mary began to talk.

"She was ecstatic about the baby. So was Ed. They tried to keep it a secret, but then your wife sent the baby things." The crackling fire and spoons rattling in teacups filled the brief silence. Her lower lip wobbled slightly.

"Colonel and Mrs. Dietrich showed me a note from Red Cloud's sister telling us that Abbey's safe, but she doesn't want to see anyone," Daniel said.

Mary pressed her hand against her chest and let out a big sigh. Her eyes glistened with tears. "Oh, thank God! I didn't know they'd heard from Wakanda. Oh yes, Abbey's safe with them. She works with the children, you know, and they're fascinated with her hair." Her eyes widened, and she took a restorative gulp of tea. "Now, Emmett would say that is not a good thing, considering they collect scalps—especially brightly colored ones—but I think she's probably safer there than here."

Daniel restrained his urge to jump at her words. He lifted an eyebrow.

She held the cup to warm her hands and leaned towards Daniel, looking secretive. She lowered her voice. "Oh, Emmett doesn't like Jake Hunt. Neither do I. He thinks Jake might have done something to scare Abbey, and he's pretty sure it was Jake who killed the prostitute. Either him or the buffalo hunters …" She took another sip. "They'll find a way to blame an Indian, though. They always do."

Daniel didn't quell his words this time. "A dead prostitute?"

Her cup rattled as she nestled it into its saucer. "Oh, they didn't tell you? Saturday night, the night Abbey disappeared, they found an Indian girl dead behind the BOQ. She'd been strangled and last seen sitting at a table in *Bedlam* with Jake and Ed. One of the guards remembered seeing Jake later, out of uniform, leaving with the buffalo hunters. He hasn't returned, and they're considering him a deserter. Ed is looking for Jake, and Emmett's looking for Abbey. I … I don't know why Ed didn't go after Abbey."

She frowned. "Emmett said the colonel insisted that he be the one to look for her."

Daniel set his jaw. "Is the Indian Camp far?"

Mary nodded. "But maybe someone could meet you part way. Come with me. I have an idea."

Daniel helped Mary into her brown wool coat and donned his jacket while she tied the ribbons of an ugly bonnet; she picked up a muff made of red fox. Outside, she led Daniel along freshly shoveled walks and through the parade ground to where a few Indian women sold their wares. The wind whipped the fine snow into a frenzy, and Daniel shivered inside his coat. He'd spent most of his army career in the Blue Ridge Mountains of Virginia and had thought the winters there were cold. In comparison, Virginia was paradise. *What a godforsaken place this is to be stationed,* he thought.

"We'll just send a message on our own," said Mary, stopping by two Indian women who were sitting on a red and green blanket, displaying baskets, blankets, and beadwork.

He could tell she knew the women well by the way she leaned toward them and touched their arms, their shoulders. The women giggled, glanced at him, and giggled again.

"I know them from the Indian School, and I bought many of their wares." Now she asked about their children and introduced Daniel. The women snickered and jabbered in Lakota, pointing at Daniel.

"They can tell you're Abbey's brother," Mary said, smiling.

When Daniel pulled out paper to write a note, Mary touched his hand and shook her head. One Indian woman looked from side to side to make sure no one else watched, then reached among the many layers of blankets and sneaked out the edge of a mirror. She whispered to Mary, who translated. "A signal is much faster."

ABBEY SLEPT FOR several hours. The following morning, after she ate scrambled eggs wrapped in cornbread, Wakanda led her to a sweat lodge where Walks in the Sun and Morning Star stripped down to nothing but blankets. The four women sat for a long time in the hot steam; Abbey told them a little of what happened at the fort, for her body spoke of the beating. But she couldn't talk, not even in the dark intimacy of the sweat lodge, about losing the baby or of Ed's betrayal. She suspected Wakanda knew just about everything; she and her son had talked, and, after all, she was a shaman. But Abbey's hurt was too fresh to share.

When Wakanda deemed them sufficiently sweated, the Indian women doused each other in clean water and wrapped up in fresh blankets. On the way to Wakanda's lodge, they gathered baskets of snow and once in the shaman's tipi they rubbed her skin with it. Wakanda noted each bruise and cut, saying something in Lakota. They then scrubbed her gently with coarse lava rock until she glowed pink; they then massaged her, always moving their hands from Abbey's head to her hands or feet so the bad spirits would leave her body. Wakanda chanted while the young women anointed her skin with the sage and cedar-scented lanolin cream. When she sniffed curiously, Wakanda explained.

"These are sacred herbs. They cleanse the spirit and help you to heal. Sage will release the dark thoughts that trouble your mind. Cedar is our guardian. Its strength will chase away the bad spirits."

When the Indian girls finished the massage, Abbey's muscles felt deliciously limp; certain spots ached, but nothing like before. Outside the tipi, birds clustered and squawked as though trying to claw and peck through the hides. Inside the Indian girls fluttered about Abbey and insisted she wear a beautiful dress made of fringed doeskin. It had been cured to a creamy white and decorated with indigo-dyed porcupine quills and silver studs. The material settled on Abbey like a glove, the soft hide gentle on her tender skin. When she was dressed, the women slipped beaded moccasins lined with fur on her feet. They combed and braided Abbey's hair, tucking in red and yellow feathers. When Abbey asked, they told her red and yellow were the good luck colors of the Lakota. Silver beads, to match those on her bear claw necklace, fastened her braids. She rested on a pallet beside Wakanda's fire, and late that afternoon Thunder Cloud came to his mother's tipi with his friend, Kicking Crane. Thunder Cloud's sister, Walks with the Sun, and her friend, Morning Star, joined them. On their heels came Splashing Rabbit, Sweet Owl, and five other small children. They all sat cross-legged around the shaman's fire, dressed in their finest, their dark eyes shining.

Thunder Cloud sat next to Abbey and touched her hand, giving her his half smile. He spoke in Lakota to his mother then translated for Abbey, telling her the whereabouts of both Jake and Ed. Then he told her about a man who had just arrived at the fort, claiming to be her brother.

Her heart raced with hope. "Daniel!"

"Can you describe him?"

"Well, he's big. Tall. With hair like mine. They say he looks like me. How on earth …" Her eyes widened. "Mary must have telegraphed him."

Will nodded. "I will ride down and speak to him. Give me the answers to questions only he can answer. Do you want to see him?"

Her hands fluttered about her throat. Her words had difficulty getting out as horrid wave of homesickness swept over her. "Oh, yes. More than anyone else in the world."

His mother threw another handful of dried sage on the fire and chanted, then knelt before the two of them. Distant drums picked up the rhythm of her chant. Wakanda said something in Lakota to Will, who took Abbey's hand and held it. The shaman again chanted something Abbey didn't understand. Again more dried powders made the fire flare and sputter. Everyone in the circle looked at

Abbey and smiled: Will squeezed her hand, her stomach clench. Something akin to fear circled around her heart. The girls and the children fanned the smoke toward their faces and breathed deeply. Will, too, waved smoke toward both of them. He then lifted her palm face up and kissed it. His lips were warm and moist.

Her heart raced. "What . . ."

His finger brushed along the curve of her cheek. "We're married," he whispered. "Hush, Abbey Yellow Bird. The elders demanded we do so. Unmarried, the old women would have sold you to the Crow." He gave that half smile again. "Trust me. Even being married to me is better than being sold to the Crow." He offered her a cup; she smelled whiskey. She took it in both hands and gulped it down.

Will chuckled. The smooth skin over his cheekbones colored a pale pink, "We were to share that." A hint of a smile lingered in his voice.

Without a word, his mother refilled the cup. He took a sip then held it to her lips, for when she lifted her hands, they shook. She sucked in a deep breath, terrified. No matter how she felt, she knew enough not to insult him. She understood she owed him her life.

"I'd be honored to be your wife, but I'm already married."

Wakanda made a slicing motion with her hand and let loose a long string of Lakota.

Abbey whispered. "What did she say?"

Will looked at their joined hands then met her eyes. "You wouldn't understand the words, but she ended your white marriage."

Abbey swallowed hard. "Will they hurt Ed?"

Anger flashed in his eyes. "When they find him, yes. He led the charge that killed many of our people. I would kill him just for how he treated you. For not protecting you."

Tears welled in her eyes. "Ask them not to. I don't ever want to see him again, but I don't want him harmed."

Wakanda made a guttural sound in her throat and whipped her hand back and forth, muttering *Witko Tho Ke!,* which Abbey had already learned meant "crazy."

Will stood then knelt before Abbey, still holding her hand. "I'll send word that Kincaid is just to be captured not harmed, but many of us would like to know how he allowed such a thing to happen to you." He folded her fingers carefully and squeezed her knuckles, then planted a kiss there. "*Je suis ton ami,* Abbey Yellow Bird. I am your friend. I will not harm you." He kissed his own fingertips then pressed them to her lips. "Now I shall see this man who claims to be your brother."

Her gaze followed him as he moved about the tipi, locking onto the golden-brown skin of his hands, smooth and bronze. His presence filled the tipi for he glowed with strength, and she wondered vaguely if someone had scrubbed him with lava rock and snow? Was he bronze all over? Color heated her cheeks, and she sniffed the familiar scent of sage and cedar on him, but then again, everything smelled that way here.

He smiled that little half smile again, and she suddenly remembered how he knew her words without her saying them. He winked as he pulled her to her feet. Not for the first time, she noticed the muscles in his forearms and felt his strength.

When she stood beside him, he stooped to whisper near her ear. "No matter how hard you try, Abbey Yellow Bird, you'll never look like an Indian." He planted a quick kiss on the top of her head. "There are no blond Indians."

Without missing a beat she replied. "I was under the illusion there were no blue eyed ones either."

16

BUFFALO PLAID

Kicking Crane, Big Bear, and Crazy Horse, all on horseback, took turns observing the bison hunters through Thunder Cloud's binoculars. Although the Indians were bundled in buck-skins and shaggy winter buffalo robes, the snow stung.

The hunters made no effort to hide themselves, which was impossible anyway. Two wore bright red buffalo plaid shirts; the third wore a thrummed buckskin coat. Even from a half-mile away, they all smelled fierce: filthy bodies, rotten teeth, bad meat. "They need a two-day sweat," said Big Bear.

Each hunter carried an accurate rifle. Three of them could mow down a big section of the herd, so many buffalo that they hired rogue Indians—men even their own tribes feared—as muleskinners to collect the hides.

"What does the army pay for hides now?" Kicking Crane asked nodding toward the growing wagonload of bloody hides.

"Not the Army," said Crazy Horse. "A company in Kansas pays $3.00 for a raw hide and a quarter for a tongue. The whites think smoked tongue is delicious."

Kicking Crane snorted and shook his head. "They're crazy. I like the liver. Raw."

Crazy Horse nodded. "Me too."

He aimed the binoculars at the three soldiers, who, at a distance, followed the hunters. Crazy Horse and the others were under Red Cloud's orders to do nothing but observe. Otherwise, he could have picked them all off like shooting ducks. All white men are careless. *Lucky the Crow aren't tracking them*, thought Crazy Horse. They'd turn the herd and run them down.

The second night there was no moon and Crazy Horse, shadowing the soldiers, watched Fringed Jacket sneak up and shoot the captain. Crazy Horse could tell he'd only winged the soldier on purpose. The bullet just ripped open his left arm and nicked his side. Crazy Horse could easily have killed him. He suspected Fringed Jacket's intention was to send the soldiers back to the fort, but the white men didn't go. One of the other soldiers bandaged the captain's arm and side and continued to follow the hunters.

WHILE THE SUN was bright, the native women who had sent the mirrored message for Mary received a return signal, telling them to wait at the foot of Mt. Laramie. Someone would find them.

Daniel sat on a downed tree with Mary and the two Indian women, who didn't appear to speak much English. He had tried to talk Mary into staying home, but was not successful. As they waited, Mary told him how heartbroken she was because she hadn't conceived. And that discussion led to her telling him way more than he wanted to know.

"I don't know if it's my fault or Emmett's," she said. "I don't know if we do it wrong or not enough or too much—I heard too often makes it less potent—but I'll tell you, Daniel, I'm about ready to take some hapless soldier into the bushes." She stood and turned around, watching his reaction. "I haven't lost my girl-ish figure, have I?"

Daniel ears burned; he was very glad of the darkness.

She cleared her throat expecting an answer.

"Mary, you're as lovely as you were at sixteen, even lovelier. I'm sure it will work out for you and Emmett. I understand it can take time."

She watched him with a look of great intensity, and he just kept on talking, hoping that at least it would keep her quiet. "Summer Rose and I ... well, she's my heart and my soul, you know. The mother of my sons, and she's expecting our third ..."

He watched a tide of jealousy, green as bile, fill her, forcing big tears from her eyes, and he felt bad for letting his mouth run off. Daniel glanced at the Indian women. They didn't acknowledge they understood a word, but their eyes told a different story. He wished Mary hadn't come. If there was any way he could send Mary back to the fort, he would, but she wasn't about to go. Right now he'd give a twenty dollar gold piece just to have her quit crying.

The weather turned grimmer; becoming the kind he disliked the most: cold, raw, and wet. The temperature hovered just above freezing, the moisture fluctuating between ice and rain. The heavy gray sky seemed to press down on them, and he couldn't help but think the colonel's whiskey sure would taste good right about now. He shivered and stamped his feet, trying to keep the numbness from his toes. The four of them huddled under the dripping pines along with their two horses, waiting for the Indian women to roast an antelope he'd shot. It was enough food for a dozen people and was taking forever to cook. He poured another cup of coffee and motioned to Mary, but she shook her head when he offered some to her. Too late, he remembered she only liked tea.

One of the Indian women suddenly twitched alert, which gave Daniel a little warning. A breath later a tall, broad-shouldered

Indian with a rifle materialized on the edge of the circle of light. He wore leather boots like Daniel's, well-worn denim trousers, and a wool shirt, topped off with an almost white jacket of doe-skin and an army-issue oilskin. He nodded to the two women and to Mary, who had jumped to her feet with surprise. Daniel stood slowly, observing the Indian. There were not many men he could look straight in the eye. This man he could, especially since they both wore boots with two-inch heels.

He noticed the strange blue eyes within the dark face and sharp cheekbones; he hoped the man could speak English. He extended his hand. "I'm Daniel Charteris, Mrs. Kincaid's brother."

The big Indian took his hand, allowing the rifle to slide to his back. "Pleased to meet you. I'm Will Thunder Cloud Dupree. Call me Will."

Relieved to hear Will's French accent, Daniel motioned toward the coffee pot and the Indian women rushed to fix a cup. The big Indian's eyes shifted from Daniel to Mary. When it was offered, Will declined the antelope, but he nodded his thanks for the coffee. He took the cup and crouched in front of the fire, holding it to warm his hands.

"Abbey gave me two questions to ask, to make sure you are who you say you are," he said. "What was the name of her first pony?"

Daniel didn't like that he called her Abbey, but he hid his reaction. "Cinnamon."

Will's eyes narrowed with interest. "She broke a bone when she was four. What was it?"

Daniel held up his left pinkie and wiggled it.

Will nodded apparently satisfied. Then he looked at the three women. "Even though it is late, we'll leave soon. The trail is very slippery and dangerous, especially in the dark. I suggest the women return to the fort."

The Indian women started to gather their things, but Mary set her jaw. "I'm not about to abandon my friend."

Will pointed his finger at her and spoke with no hint of a smile. "Understand, then. No crying. If you cry or complain, I may cut out your tongue."

Mary froze. Daniel looked away; knowing he should say something protective for Mary's sake, but he didn't for his first priority was finding Abbey. He would do nothing to jeopardize her safety, and he sensed the Indian wasn't serious. And the truth of the matter was he felt immense gratitude for demanding Mary's silence. *Why didn't I think of something like that?*

WAKANDA LED ABBEY to an obviously new tipi right next to hers. She kissed Abbey's cheeks, then left. Alone, Abbey stepped inside the tipi and looked around. Immediately, her heart raced, and she needed to concentrate on breathing. Furs hung on the rounded walls, and layers of buffalo hides covered the ground. Smoke curled up from a small, fragrant fire. In the middle of the tipi sat the bearskin on which she and Will had slept with Owen.

Outside of the tipi children giggled, then someone opened the fly. Owen bounded to her, licking her face then sniffing every crevice of the tipi. Was this to be her home? With Owen? And Will? Fingering the bear claw necklace, she sat cross-legged near the fire, pulling the bearskin snugly around her. Owen curled up in her lap.

She stared at the flames, letting herself sink into a daze. Without warning, Jake's face loomed over her like a genie from a magic lantern. She gasped and closed her eyes, hating her fear. Even the memory of him took her breath away. When she'd refused to drink his despicable tea, he started roughing her up, slapping her, shoving her, jabbing her. She had fought back, but he made short work of her efforts with a couple of hard blows which sent her spinning across the room. She expected him to rape her when he tied her to the bed, and he tried. But nothing could have prepared her for the shock she felt when he told her about his relationship with Ed.

She shuddered at the memory and hugged Owen tight to her chest. "The minute he told me," she said to the puppy, "I knew it was true. I saw how Ed looked at him, but I just wouldn't let myself understand what it meant."

Tears slid down her cheeks, and she tasted the salt. Her voice came out raspy and low. "I loved him so much, Owen. I did. Ed was my whole life, my dreams. And then he went with Jake and a whore! How could he do such a thing?" She rubbed her cheek against Owen's thick fur, wiping tears on his soft coat. Owen whimpered softly, as if he understood every word she said. She took a deep, shuddering breath. "I trusted him. And then … then he let Jake destroy my baby." The tears erupted into sobs now, and they wouldn't stop.

"How could I have been so blind?"

DANIEL KNEW MANY natives, but no one like Will. He was surprised to find this Indian had a sense of humor.

When Emmett spotted their party, he fired his sidearm twice. The Indian watched warily, keeping Emmett in the sites of his rifle, but when he neared, Mary slipped from behind Daniel and ran, sliding across the snow, to him.

Will lowered his rifle. "Her husband?"

Daniel nodded.

Will smiled his half smile and lowered the rifle. "*Ah bien.* Lucky you and lucky me."

Daniel frowned at him, confused, but Will only chuckled softly. "You won't have to bed her," he whispered, "and I won't have to cut out her tongue." He shrugged. "The Indian women told me a great deal." Obviously, the Indian women understood English very well.

They made coffee and camped for a short rest at the same little waterfall where Will and Abbey stopped on their trip up the mountain. When they asked, Emmett explained, "I ran into the Indian women. They told me about Abbey's brother. I sent my men back to the fort." He nodded to Daniel. "Glad I did." He pointed to Will's horse.

Daniel nodded. "I was admiring him earlier. I've never seen anything like him." Drum's mane and tail were long and curlier than a woman's hair, as if it had been crimped with a curling iron. The rest of his thick black fur, even the inside of his ears, was as curly as Persian lamb. When he asked about it, Will explained.

"These animals, they are *sacré*—sacred to the Lakota Sioux. We breed them. They come in all colors, but Drum is a rare black. In the spring he will shed his curls, even his mane and tail. He will be smooth-coated in the warm months. We treasure these horses, and so do the Crow. They raid our horses all the time." He chuckled. "We steal them back."

"Aren't you breeding horses at Camelann?" Emmett asked Daniel. He glanced at Will. "Daniel owns a big farm in Pennsylvania. Twelve thousand acres, isn't it?"

"With my wife and my law partner."

Emmett whistled. "That is one hell of a lot of land. Must be God's country."

The fire popped, but none of the men flinched. Will reached to the side for a piece of wood and tossed it in, raising more sparks. "Abbey told me you're a lawyer?"

There he goes again, thought Daniel, *calling her Abbey*. He still didn't like it, but by now he suspected this man wasn't any ordinary Indian.

"I'm a lawyer who wants to be a farmer. Our law practice pays the bills. I'd like nothing better than to stay home with Summer Rose and breed babies and horses."

Emmett gazed sadly at his sleeping wife. "She wants a baby. Every month she makes herself ill with disappointment."

Daniel and Will exchanged a quiet glance. Daniel suspected Will had listened to their conversations before he made his presence known at the campfire. More than likely, he too had heard more than either of them needed to know about her disappointments.

Will refilled his coffee cup. "I understand how she must feel. Children are most precious to us." He looked at Daniel. "Your sister saved my son's life."

Daniel looked up, and Will told the story of what had happened at Scotts Bluff.

"Doesn't surprise me," Daniel said with a smile. He shook his head. "Our fearless Abbey." His smile faded. "What happened to have her run away from the fort? Run to you?"

Will's blue eyes drilled into Daniel, and both his look and his voice turned cold. "She didn't run to me. She ran away because she was raped and beaten. I found her. She lost the child."

Daniel felt the ground shift beneath him. He'd had no clue. *Abbey!* How could this have happened to his little sister?

"God Almighty," he managed. "How is she now?"

"Healing. Slowly. She's with my mother in her tipi." He narrowed his eyes at the men. "She took a fierce beating."

"Did Ed—"

Will interrupted. "It wasn't her husband who hurt her, though I hold no respect for him. He allowed it to happen. It was his friend, the one who struts around like a rooster."

Both men nodded. "Jake Hunt."

17

RED CLOUD

In the morning the cold rain stopped, but before they could start out they needed the sun to rise high enough to melt a little of the ice on the trail. While they waited they drank coffee and Will introduced them to *galettes:* dough wrapped around a stick and baked in the fire.

Even after the ice began to melt, the descent was treacherous. Mary rode on her husband's rust-colored gelding, and the men walked, leading their horses. After noon the ice lessened, and they made better time.

As they travelled, braves hidden in the folds of the mountain announced their progress, and echoes of their greetings bounced off the rocks. Each guard held a rifle and made sure the white men noticed.

The cluster of tipis finally came into view and Daniel saw that the encampment, unlike what he'd read of the summer gatherings, was small, maybe twenty lodges. Smoke pressed close to the earth, winding around the tipis like a soft gray muffler. The camp bordered a mountain stream fed by a spring, and only the sound of the bubbling water greeted them as they walked by several fires. He wasn't surprised at the cool reception, considering he and Emmett were armed white men, and Emmett was still in his uniform. A few dogs came up to sniff, and Will quietly warned them not to make eye contact with the dogs. Young boys, not yet teens, came to take their horses, and Mary slid off the gelding. Older boys took their saddlebags and moved toward Emmett and Daniel's guns, but Will held up his hand to stop them.

He led them uphill to his mother's lodge. Once there, Wakanda nodded to the two men, then motioned for the boys to put the gear inside a smaller tipi as she hurried to Mary. Several children were already there, clamoring around Mary and hugging her. Daniel couldn't help thinking she looked like a brown hen with a cluster of chicks beneath her wings.

Wakanda scooted the children away and led the little party further along the path to a new tipi. Abbey must have heard the commotion, because she ducked beneath the fly and ran to her brother and hugged him tight. Daniel's embrace was just as fierce. After a moment he pulled back so he could study the damage Jake Hunt had done to her beautiful face, and his blood boiled. All these awful cuts and bruises—and that was *after* the Indians had been helping her to heal. He hated to think what the original damage looked like. He glanced at Will, who silently studied them both, and gave an almost imperceptible nod of thanks.

Will took Abbey's hand and led them inside her tipi where they all sat around the fire. Daniel sat on her other side, pointedly glaring at Will's hand holding hers. Daniel knew she had tales to tell, couldn't wait to tell him, because he recognized Abbey's expressionless face. After all, it was a reflection of his. She slid her other hand into Daniel's and squeezed it, and he saw relief in her eyes. *Daniel's here,* they seemed to sing. *All will be well.*

Morning Star and Walks in the Sun entered then, their arms filled with platters of roasted meat and colorful vegetables wrapped in thin corn shells. Very young girls carried in an urn of water with pots of steaming coffee and Meadow Tea, and food was passed around, filling bowls and cups. Everyone ate then wiped their hands on damp cloths provided by the small children. When they were done, Wakanda flashed her dark eyes and spoke softly in Lakota, directing the children to take away the dishes and cloths. As they left, she stood and threw more wood and herbs on the fire.

The skins hanging over the doorway parted, and three warriors entered. Without a word, they sat across from Abbey, and Daniel sat straighter. No introductions were needed. Even he recognized Red Cloud from a drawing published in *Harper's Weekly*. The deference with which he was greeted, how he carried himself, and his elaborately embroidered coat and distinctive ornaments further announced his importance. He wore many colorful necklaces, feathers and a breastplate made from long, thin, highly polished bones from a buffalo's hump. They rattled with every move he made.

Thunder Cloud made introductions anyway. "Two Face, Man-Afraid-of-His-Horse, and Red Cloud, meet General Charteris and Captain Hathaway. You already know the young women from the school."

Daniel could tell the headmen were well aware of who everyone was. Man-Afraid-of-His-Horse, a great leader in his own right, withdrew a long pipe of clay from inside his clothing. After some ceremony of lighting it, he passed it around to all the men, and the astringent odor permeated the lodge. When the pipe returned to Red Cloud, he spoke.

His bone breastplate rattled as he nodded to Daniel. "Welcome, General Charteris."

Daniel spoke slowly to Red Cloud, his tone low. Will translated. "Thank you for your hospitality to my sister, to me, and

Lieutenant Hathaway and his wife. Sir, I'm honored to be here."
His eyes lingered on each leader then returned to Red Cloud. "I
am no longer a soldier. I work as an attorney, a lawyer." He lifted
Abbey's hand. "I come as her brother. Please call me Daniel."
His face turned to Emmett. "His rank is confusing. During our
Great War he was a captain, but since then he's been demoted
to a lieutenant." He smiled. "He's still the ranking officer here."

Red Cloud glanced at the men on either side of him then
he grinned and spoke in Lakota. Will again translated. "They
say lawyers or attorneys are even more dangerous than soldiers.
Their weapons are words."

He nodded to Abbey. "Your sister caused quite a stir. Our
braves gambled for her scalp, and the old women wanted to sell
her to the Crow. The old women are very serious. A young, unat-
tached woman makes them jumpy." His voice was melodious,
warm, and carried a hint of humor. "The old men made noises
about how they'd like your sister's moccasins beside their sleeping mat." He flapped his hand as if swatting flies. "Makes the old
women crazy."

He paused and closed his eyes for a moment. The smoke
from the pipe twisted up in front of his face. When he opened
his eyes again, they were warm. "My sister and her family have
grown to care for Yellow Bird. To protect her, she is now married to Will Thunder Cloud, my nephew."

Daniel stared, unable to speak. When he felt Abbey weakly
squeeze his hand, he realized his grip was probably cutting off
her circulation. He relaxed as much as he could and looked at
Abbey in disbelief. *Wasn't she already married to Ed? Had Ed died?*

Red Cloud went on to explain, with Wakanda, Will Thunder
Cloud's mother translating, of how Thunder Cloud had found
Abbey, about the loss of her child, and her condition when Will
found her.

"She was bleeding heavily, nearly unconscious. Many men would have left her for wolf meat. Thunder Cloud cared for her as if she were his sister, maybe his daughter." He smiled broadly. "Now we welcome her to our tribe as his wife, now a woman of my family."

Shock gave way to profound gratitude, and Daniel blinked back tears. He reached behind his sister and touched Will's shoulder, nodding to Wakanda and all the Indians.

"Thank you."

Red Cloud missed nothing. Now Will translated. "Her former husband tracks the buffalo hunters, who have already killed three hundred buffalo, maybe more. They take just the hides, sometimes the tongues, leaving the rest for the vultures and coyotes. The stench will fill our nostrils for months, and bleached bones will cover the plains for years. Soon," he said, his voice dripping with sarcasm, "we won't have enough scavengers to handle the feast."

He looked at Emmett, frowning. His tone hardened. "How much does the army pay for a buffalo hide? More than for a scalp? We know what your people intend. Destroy the buffalo, destroy the Lakota. The men who send out the buffalo killers asked me to sign a treaty. What kind of treaty would come from those who want to starve my people?" The flames of the fire flashed red on their faces. He crossed his arms over his chest, rattling the bone breastplate. "I was born a Lakota, I have lived as a Lakota, and I will die a Lakota." He narrowed his eyes, skeptical. "Do you know about treaties?"

But Red Cloud didn't wait for an answer. He held up his hands to keep everyone quiet, and his eyes slowly surveyed the group. A blast of wind shook the tipi, interrupting the moment.

He nodded to Daniel, Emmett, and Mary. "You are our guests. I ask the gentlemen to sit with our council tomorrow, speak with us, and tell us what your leaders want. Many lesser headmen have touched the pen to sign the treaty." He nodded to the men beside him. "But they want our marks. I do not trust them."

He angled his head toward Thunder Cloud. "Rest tonight. Stay here with my nephew and Yellow Bird. Wakanda will see to your needs."

Sweat slickened Abbey's palm against Daniel's, but she didn't speak. Owen chose that moment to squirm out of her lap and circle behind all the Indians, sniffing them. Red Cloud grabbed the puppy and held him by the scruff of the neck.

"Ah! A gift? Dinner?"

Abbey cried out, but Red Cloud roared with laughter. His eyes twinkled. "Fear not, Yellow Bird. I like to tease pretty girls." He walked around the fire and handed Abbey the puppy, who wriggled happily back into her arms. "Besides, dog doesn't taste good. No, you and yours will not come to harm, Abbey Yellow Bird. You are now my family." He glanced at Daniel, then back to Abbey. "I would trust Thunder Cloud with my life," he told Daniel gently. "Trust him with your sister."

After Red Cloud and the other headmen left, everyone stood and stretched. Wakanda set several *gras lamps*—little buffalo tallow-filled tubs with a piece of rag as a wick—along the dark edges of the lodge. The lamp lights flickered and threw shadows on the curved walls. She added pine logs to the fire then handed out beautifully embroidered buffalo robes. Each had been painstakingly scraped and cured with buffalo brains to make the leather pliable on one side while still warm with shaggy fur on the other side.

Daniel rolled a robe around his body and sank down beside his sister. Will crouched and scooped up both the bearskin and

Owen, then patted the fur as if inviting Abbey to sit there. The silence between them spoke loudly. Abbey looked from her brother to Will, then down at her hands. "I want you to hear what happened in my words," she told them. She looked at Will. "You know some of this."

She nodded to her brother. "I first encountered Will in Scotts Bluff. Ed went hunting, Mary was ill. I rode by myself to the town, which infuriated Jake. He marched me down the main street as if I were a murderer on my way to the gallows." She told him about saving Splashing Rabbit, and finally voiced the vague uneasiness she experienced seeing Jake and Ed together.

She released a deep breath. "I saw how Ed and Jake looked at each other and didn't understand. I was crazy in love with Ed. I … I thought we were happy." She swept her hands over her face, wiping tears from her bruised cheeks. "At the time," she grimaced, "I knew such friendships existed but I didn't realize what they entailed. Not until months later when Jake explained explicitly what it was about."

Daniel reached over and petted her arm. He didn't know what to say.

Then she got to the night months later, after Jake returned, when she'd been beaten and betrayed. She skipped some of the uglier parts—she said something about Jake and her hatpin, but still couldn't verbalize exactly what Jake had done. Her shudders and shaking hands spoke volumes. Daniel looked ill with helplessness.

She sucked in another deep breath. "Ed and Jake have been lovers for years." She blinked through tears at Daniel, her expression desolate. "Just saying those words makes me ill. I can't understand it." Her voice broke and she gave a little heartbreaking shift to her shoulders. "My life crumbled. I think Ed knew Jake wanted to destroy my baby. I suspect Jake must have hinted at it beforehand, because Ed didn't come back to the house that night. When Jake tied me to the bed, I prayed for Ed to return ... but he didn't. Knowing all this, knowing that he allowed Jake to hurt me destroyed my feelings toward Ed."

Daniel's hands bunched into tight fists. He knew of homosexuals. He wasn't naïve, but he never dreamed his sister would need to contend with them. He thought of Ed, of how he'd abandoned his wife, left her in the hands of a monster, and his nails bit into his palms. *I will kill the man,* he vowed. *I will kill them both.*

"I cannot forgive him for that," Abbey said softly, "but I understand his fear that his fellow officers might kill him if I asked for help. Jake made me very aware of what they would do."

She looks tired. So tired. As if she had heard his thought, Abbey stretched out on her belly and elbows, hugging Owen. Will came around and covered her with the bearskin, sliding it under her and smoothing it over her back, then sat beside her. She smiled up at him and Daniel fought back a sudden flare of anger. But he didn't hide it fast enough. He knew she'd seen it.

"I know what you're thinking, Danny. Everything has turned upside down. Everything has changed. What you have to understand is that all of this left a big emptiness inside me. I had nowhere to go. I trusted no one. I was scared to death and all by myself."

She glanced toward the side of the tipi where Emmett and Mary slept. "I couldn't tell even them for fear they'd report Ed. I did think of going to the emigrant trains, but none were nearby, and I didn't have a rifle. I vomited at the thought of Jake finding me." She let out a big shuddering breath. "Just the thought of him touching me sets me to shaking."

She dropped her head into her hands and he saw how the sun had baked her pale skin to a smooth golden brown. She'd become tougher out here, his little sister. But no one could expect her to be that tough. When she looked up again, the exhaustion in her face was twisted with pain.

"And I didn't want to see Ed. I loved him—with all my heart—and maybe a small part of me still loves him. But part of me wants to kill him. He threw me to the wolves and left me to die. How can I ever forgive that?"

Daniel shook his head, but he couldn't speak.

She sighed. "There's something else, Danny. Something I'm kind of afraid to say out loud, but it's true. I've discovered something about me lately. You see, down at the very core of who I am, I don't like white people."

Daniel frowned, but said nothing. During the war he'd often felt ashamed to be part of the same species that enslaved black people.

Abbey slipped her hand into Will's. "I hate how they drummed that poor corporal out of the military for being different. I hate Dame Dilly's hypocrisy, how she pretended to be my friend then talked about me behind my back. I detest her husband's lust and how he treated me, and I hate the way he treated the Negro waiter on the train. Good Lord, I hate the smell of hunters and muleskinners. I hate Jake and Ed, and I even hate the Indian prostitutes because they've become part of the white world." She puffed out a breath. "And let me tell you, hate takes enormous amounts of energy.

"Remember our lives in Philly, Danny? I believed in love and marriage, in happy endings. Yes, Daddy made Mother cry, but I was so stupid. It never occurred to me that a husband might hurt his wife. Daddy didn't do that. You don't." Her voice broke. "So I clung to the fairytales. I was such a dolt. I saw you and Summer." She turned to Will. "They are about the happiest couple on earth. I wanted what they had. You saw me. I was a mess. Jake beat me with his belt buckle and did unspeakable things to kill my baby. And Ed did nothing, nothing to help me. The loss of my child left me empty. Then I thought of Wakanda and her kindness. So here I am."

She reached out and squeezed Will's hand. "Daniel, know this. Will Thunder Cloud could not have been kinder to me. Thank heaven he found me. I owe him my life."

One little *gras lamp* flickered, another winked out. The wind howled and shook the tipi, and the small fire cast their faces in orange-red light. Daniel touched Abbey's hand then looked at the big man sitting beside her.

"For what it's worth, I give you both my blessing. But there are a lot of possible repercussions of a marriage between men and women of different races. Will, your family seems okay with it, but to be candid, I'm not sure how I feel about mixed blood. In the East eyebrows will be raised and doors slammed in your faces. Have you considered children? Have you read the newspapers?" He turned to Abbey. "And there *is* the problem of Ed, you know. Despite everything, I'm sure Ed considers you're still his wife."

"Daniel," she said, giving him a gentle smile, "you worry too much. I am not back East. I'm in the middle of the Indian Territory, so where would I get my hands on a newspaper? Right now I just want to stay warm. And feel safe." She reached over and touched Will's hand again and smiled. "The dog sleeps between us, anyway." She cleared her throat. "And Ed? Well, no one knows where he is. Crazy Horse thinks he's dead and vows to kill him if he isn't."

18

A PONY SHOW

Will wanted warmth, too, and while he never had any intention of consummating their marriage right away—and certainly not beside her brother, he wanted her. What healthy man wouldn't? *But it must be mutual,* a rational part of his mind said. *Marriage isn't all under the bearskin. Marriage is in bright sunlight. I am not just choosing a woman for myself. A wife will be Rabbit's mother, Wakanda's daughter, a member of my tribe. And then there is my French family. To them, I am mixed blood. He had enough problems with Catholics and Protestants. He remembered arguments with his French/ Catholic* Grand-Père *about the One True Faith and he'd concluded they all looked for reasons to argue.*

One hand petted Owen, the other rubbed her back—making sure his hand stayed on her back. When he felt her relax into deep sleep, he slumbered as well, sleeping sound and warm inside the bearskin until the dog moved. A draft of icy air shot into their nest, and he spooned tight against Abbey. Inside the tipi the darkness was thick, and inside the bearskin he was surrounded by her. Her scent, her soft breath, her sweet bottom pressed against his thighs, her warm feet tangled with his own. He resisted a sudden urge to ease off her dress and leggings and run his hands all over her soft skin. He wanted to kiss her with his whole body, not just a little peck on top of her head.

From just about the first moment he saw her, the day when she saved Splashing Rabbit, he wanted her. That day in Scotts Bluff his heart had swelled in gratitude for her courage and admiration of her beauty. He watched her scoop up his son and march across the street, her skirts hiked to her knees, dodging horses and teamsters. Nothing would stop her. And Good Lord, even with his heart beating like a war drum at the safety of his son, desire had risen in him like a geyser. He wanted her then, and he wanted her now.

Within the bearskin, she turned in her sleep and arched her back, then leaned into him. She snuggled her face into the crook of his neck, and he felt her heartbeat, strong and steady. *I'm no saint,* he thought as desire swamped him. She made an odd, clacking noise with her tongue, and he knew she was still asleep. He meant to just brush his mouth against hers, but somehow his lips lingered and hers melted into his. The kiss deepened to something tender and sweet, like warm chocolate, then catapulted to raw desire, swishing like a shooting star to every nerve in his body. Still asleep, she moaned and pressed into him.

Something cold touched the back of his neck and he froze, visualizing her brother's pistol, then recognized Owen's whimper. Reluctantly, Will pulled away from Abbey and let the dog snuggle between them. Owen licked his neck.

In the lowest of voices he whispered, "I know, Owen. Someday I will thank you. But not tonight. Right now I'm wishing Red Cloud had served you for dinner."

He fell back asleep, but not for long. Just as the day lightened, sending streaks of sunlight streaming through the smoke vent, the children crept into Yellow Bird's tipi like fox kits, and no one was about to sleep any longer. The children twittered as they carried in urns of coffee and Meadow Tea. Wakanda came with them, bringing with her a basket of delicious-smelling hot yeast rolls, dishes of dark honey still in the beeswax, bowls of jerky mixed with dried cherries and nuts.

Wakanda clapped her hands, interrupting the children's talk. "The little ones have been asking for Mary since long before the sun came up. I grew tired of listening to their chatter so I brought them here."

As the sleepers stretched and yawned, then went outside to the latrines, Wakanda opened the vents and added fuel to the fire. Will looked down at Abbey as she and Mary snuggled back in the bearskin, holding hands like little girls. Now that all the secrets had been revealed, their easy rapport seemed to have returned.

WAKANDA STOOD, HER smile warm. "We have a surprise for everyone. Do what you need to do to prepare for a short ride. Dress warm and bring robes to sit on. We will be gone most of the day. All the ponies are saddled and wait just outside."

The weather was as good as late winter in the mountains gets: hot sun, little wind, and clear skies. Hints of spring abounded. Abbey noticed the sap showing red in the fine tree branches, and more birds than usual seemed to flutter about. She stooped and picked a tiny bouquet of yellow, white, and lavender flowers peeking out from the crevices in the rocks, then tucked them in her hair. She felt grateful for the day and felt herself healing, in body and heart.

Both Will and Daniel asked Abbey to ride behind them, but wise Wakanda, anticipating exactly this, saddled Cricket herself and urged Abbey to ride by herself. The small children, though they were all excellent riders, were tucked onto adult laps, and as they rode through the camp, Indian children, men, and women with papooses joined them, either on horseback or walking alongside. Abbey noticed that every male was armed with bows and arrows as well as rifles. Most wore sheathed daggers and tomahawks on their belts.

In a canyon they came upon a *remuda* holding at least forty of the sacred ponies. "Pony," in this case, proved to be an agnomen, for many of the animals stood fifteen hans and higher. In essence they were both horses and ponies. None had the hang dog demeanor that some Indian horses possess, and all were fuzzy as wooly bears, their manes and tails crimped and unbelievably thick.

The two teenage boys, Lobo and Hawk, took charge. Everyone dismounted, and the ponies and horses ridden from the camp were rounded up and led away. Then the boys brought two of the mature sacred horses out of the pen, both brown and white paints and so close in looks they may have been twins. Other boys led more curly-haired horses to out of the way nooks in the hills.

Nature had provided an amphitheater. Red Cloud and the headmen draped in beautifully embroidered robes took seats on a high ledge, and other families followed suit, fitting themselves into the hillside. On a slight rise with a good view, Will Thunder Cloud spread a buffalo robe for Abbey, his mother, Mary, and several of the children. He spread another, and invited Daniel and Emmett to join them. He took a seat beside the men, smiling with anticipation.

"You're in for a show few white people ever see," he told them. He pointed to the young boys who, despite the cold, had stripped to just breechclouts. Their horses wore only an Indian bridle and a neck rope. "Since they were five years of age these boys have been working with their pony. At night they sleep with a rawhide string connected from their wrist to the bridle. They practice with their horses until they can start or stop them with a verbal command, and they guide and manipulate the horses with just their knees." He lifted his eyebrows toward Daniel, who looked skeptical. "Just wait. You seldom see an Indian thrown from a pony."

Wakanda, chanting in a low voice, carried a small pottery urn toward the boys. Smoke from the bowl wafted around the boys and horses as she blessed them. When she completed the ritual, Wakanda returned to the rocks; the boys rode off to the left. They galloped back and each boy dropped so he hung upright on either side of his mount, then bounced back and remounted from each side. Holding on by only a heel, the boys, still moving at great speed, slid under the horse's belly or around the broad neck, then bounced to the ground and back onto the horse, then again to the other side. Even more impressive was when the boys did the feats in unison. They rode out of view then came thundering back, standing on the backs of their ponies, balancing one behind the other, with a foot on each animal. The ponies maintained a fast gait while the boys kept up their show: turning around, standing on one foot, jumping from one horse to the other. It was amazing horsemanship.

Mary leaned forward. "Should we teach this to Dame Dilly?" she whispered.

Abbey reached back and squeezed her hand. A few days ago she never would have imagined being happy again. Now she cheered and laughed like a child as the braves rode by at a gallop.

In a low voice she asked Will, "Is Drum trained this well?"

Will chuckled. "He is, but I am not. I lived in Quebec with my father and missed much of the early training."

Every time she spoke with Will she learned more and became more intrigued by him. She cocked her head to one side, fingering the flowers in her hair, hoping for more insight.

He raised his eyebrows and took her hand, squeezing it gently. He smiled that half smile she was coming to like very much, then rested back on one elbow. "There's much you don't know about me, Abbey Yellow Bird. I spent two days in Philadelphia once." He smiled at her surprise, then tugged a stray hair from between her lips. "Did you sleep well last night?"

She blinked and returned the squeeze. "Yes. Not one bad dream."

From the corner of her eye, she saw Daniel frown. She imagined Will noticed, too. She knew Daniel disapproved, and she knew every argument, but she could do nothing about his objections.

Will tightened his grip on her hand and sat up. "Here comes the parade."

Drawn to Abbey and Mary, as well as to Will's commentary, a few more children crowded onto the buffalo robe. Just as five horses and riders, all in full war paint and regalia, passed in front of them, the children tucked themselves into adult laps. The acrobatic riders had impressed them all with their expert horsemanship; however these men on the painted warhorses were true warriors. They had painted and dressed themselves and their mounts in elaborately embroidered blankets and bridles.

"This show is just a small glimpse of what used to be," Will said, sweeping his arms along the parade route. "Imagine the summer gatherings when tens of thousands came. The last such get-together was held about ten years ago. Then lodges dotted the plains as far as you could see. Thousands of warriors gathered and paraded along the avenues between the lodges, all dressed and painted."

"The paint tells a story, doesn't it?" Daniel asked.

Will nodded, keeping his eyes on the spectacle before them. "The warrior paints his horse in the same patterns and colors he uses on his own face and body, and the horse carries a message meant to show his owner's accomplishments and thus intimidate the enemy." He pointed out marks painted on several of the horses. "Some marks are used by all the Sioux, but each tribe has its own totems. The rectangle means the rider led a war party. Red handprints are a Lakota sign that indicates killings made in hand-to-hand combat. The Crow uses white handprints."

Will rested his hand on Abbey's shoulder leaning close to her, ignoring her brother's stiffness. Abbey, fascinated, stared at each pony as he spoke. "What about those? The short horizontal lines, one above the other on the horse's front legs and muzzle?"

"Those are coup marks, which represent a brave or reckless deed." Will laughed. "Much like any teenager bragging."

He gestured to a powerful-looking roan. "The white hoof tracks marching along her flanks indicate a successful horse raid. We don't have any today, but if you see blotchy or abstract shaped marks, those speak of a horse painted in mourning for the death of his master."

He pointed to the third horse. "Notice the long, zigzag lines are lightning. They speed the warrior into battle. Red or white circles around the eyes enhance the horse's vision."

Abbey gestured toward the last horse in line. His owner had tied up his tail and braided golden eagle feathers into his mane. "He's beautiful. Does it mean anything?"

Will nodded. "He's ready for war."

LATER THAT DAY, Red Cloud and Will drew Daniel off by himself. When they asked Daniel what he thought of their sacred ponies, he noticed Will had moved so that he stood downhill a bit, as if he didn't want to tower over Red Cloud. So Daniel did the same. Will nodded toward Emmett, a few feet away.

"The redhead tells me you trained and led cavalry during your war. Is that so?" asked Red Cloud through Will's translation.

Daniel nodded to Red Cloud. "I did. And we had some impressive riders, but nothing like what I've seen today. I really like your ponies, too. How is their endurance?"

Red Cloud nodded, seemingly impressed with Daniel's question. Here was a fellow warrior and horseman.

"Twice that of any horse you have," Will translated. "Would you be interested in owning some?"

The question took Daniel by surprise, and a glorious image of these beautiful animals running in Camelann filled his mind. "I would," he said without hesitation. "I'd buy every one of them if I knew how to get them back to Pennsylvania."

Red Cloud nodded, showing no expression. "If we could arrange that, how many would you want?"

"How many are you willing to part with?"

"Maybe ten? Twenty? Would you want twenty?"

Excitement surged through Daniel. "I'll take as many as you are willing to part with if I can get them to the railroad, and, of course, if I can afford the price."

Red Cloud turned toward the herd. "Let me think about those questions. Do you have a map?"

Daniel nodded.

"*Bien.* Bring the map with you to the Council Meeting."

19

TEA LEAVES AND THE SWEAT LODGE

Wakanda scooted all children and adults from her tipi, all except Mary and Abbey. Just before they stepped inside, Abbey looked up to the streaks of rose and orange slashing the bellies of the overhead clouds; the air smelled moist with a hint of warmth and the scent of slow roasting meat. A shiver slipped down her spine.

Wakanda stood in the doorway, her hand pressed to the small of her son's back. "You, take the white men to Bird's tipi, then to the sweat lodge. These young women will stay with me. They need to rest."

Will raised his eyebrows, but did as told.

Wakanda directed Mary and Abbey to sit on pallets while she rooted through what Abbey thought must be her pharmacy. Hundreds of waxed paper envelopes and small jars were organized in skin bags and in a valise-sized wooden chest with dozens of tiny drawers. As Abbey watched, Wakanda selected dried leaves and powders, mixed them in a little earthenware bowl then steeped them in steaming water. She rattled a string of bones over the pot, chanting, and tossing selected powders into the fire, which then flared purple and blue. Several times, she stirred the brew, saying more chants, waving feathers through the smoke. When she finished, she ladled the dark, scalding liquid into cups. Abbey stared curiously into hers and noticed a few leaves had settled into the bottom.

Ignoring Mary's wary expression, Wakanda took her hand and smiled gently. "The children adore you, and you love them. Yet, you have none of your own." Mary squeezed her eyes shut, unsuccessfully holding back tears, but Wakanda held a finger to her lips. "Shush, sweet girl. I will give you little bundles already made up, and they will help. Every evening drink a cup of this special tea." She held up an admonishing finger. "If your handsome red-haired lieutenant drinks a cup with you, it works even better. Regardless, you drink the tea then bed your husband. Every night."

Mary's smile faded and she took a careful sip. "Every night? What if he doesn't…?"

Wakanda grinned and touched Mary's cheek. "Trust me. He will. You'll soon have a papoose." She giggled and lowered her eyes, a very youthful gesture for the gray-haired woman. "The tea makes husbands happy." She shrugged. "Makes happy wives as well."

"This tea mends wombs." Wakanda said, touching Abbey's shoulder. "You lost a child and your body needs to recover. The tea I give you heals wombs. And hearts, too. Every day you must drink two cups. Tell me, have you rid yourself of the man who didn't protect you? The one who makes you cry?"

Abbey frowned, puzzled. How did Wakanda know she cried over Ed?

"The children heard you" Wakanda smiled. "Little happens here that I don't eventually learn. Now you must banish him from your mind." She petted Abbey's arm. "You have a big strong husband now—a good man."

As Wakanda had directed, Daniel and Emmett followed Will to his great aunt's lodge. Dancing Bird, who the children of the tribe affectionately called Bird, was a sister of Red Cloud and Wakanda's father. Small, delicate, with skin like crinkled paper, Bird's head was topped with downy white hair. She resembled a cross between a dried apple doll and a gosling. In this land of the great migrations, Daniel saw her as a small gray heron, and thought how suitable her name was. When he approached, she sat him before her fire. He didn't move as she pressed his shoulders then softly ran her hands over his face and head, humming and making clucking noises.

Will explained. "Her sight is limited. She's seeing you with her hands."

Daniel nodded. He only met one blind person before, and remembered that woman using her hands to see. Bird outlined his face with her cool fingertips, lingering on his dimples and mouth. When she was done she patted his head and his shoulders, murmuring something.

Will translated with a smile. "Big man. Good teeth. And she likes your smile."

Bird made an equal fuss over Emmett, checking his scalp, his eyelashes. She sniffed at his hair and asked Will a question.

"She wanted to know if your hair is red," said Will.

She gave them cups of whiskey and buffalo stew laced with buffalo-berries, and made with onions, turnips, wild garlic, and sweet potatoes. She served them cornbread with bowls of honey, dried cherries and plums. When they had eaten their fill, Will provided the white men with loincloths. Daniel and Emmett exchanged a dubious look.

"For the sweat lodge," Will explained. "This is what we wear."

Emmett shrugged, and they both shed their clothing. Bird gathered up their things as they left.

Of simple design and built low to the ground, the sweat lodge consisted of buffalo hides fit snuggly over an oval framed structure. A medicine man stood outside, minding the fire, heating the special rocks. When the stones were hot enough, using a rake and a wooden bowl, he maneuvered a number of heavy stones to a shallow pit inside the lodge. Will ushered everyone inside, and as the men seated themselves, dippers of water were dropped onto the special hot rocks. A great hissing erupted and white steam filled the small enclosure.

They weren't alone in the sweat lodge. Through the cloud of near-scalding steam Daniel recognized Red Cloud, Man-Afraid-of-His-Horse, Big Bear, and Two Face. He counted four other young men. They sat shoulder-to-shoulder and hip-to-hip on woven mats, and like the Main Line Railroad west of Philly, no one spoke. Daniel almost chuckled to himself thinking of the diversity in this great country of his. In his mind's eye he pictured Philadelphia businessmen riding the Main Line in loin clouts.

It was a strange feeling, but Daniel wasn't about to run from it. Everyone else seemed content with the sweat dripping from their faces—even Emmett. Daniel felt a river of sweat course down his spine, even drip from his fingertips. Eventually, he allowed himself to sink into the sensation, his body to soften with the heat. Four times the elder replaced the hot rocks and added more sizzling water, intensifying the heat so it felt difficult to breathe.

After what felt like several hours, the elder chanted something in Lakota, and Two Face got up and left, followed by all the others. Whooping as the sudden chill hit his nearly naked body, Will dove into a large snow bank, and the white men followed. They rolled like horses, scratching their backs in the snow, welcoming the cold. Invigorated and clean to the bone, Daniel howled like the rest of them.

Will handed them wool blankets to wrap around their bodies before returning to Bird's lodge, and when they arrived they saw she'd taken the dirty clothing and laid out clean things from their packs. She'd brushed Emmett's uniform, but held up Daniel's dirty trousers with something resembling disdain, mumbling and shaking her head.

Will snorted. "She likes you. She will see that your clothes are cleaned." He smiled and asked. "Do you charm everyone?"

Daniel bent and kissed the old woman's forehead. "I try."

As night descended, with the mountains black against the stars, the men walked into the long council hut and sat around another fire. Wind chimes, the sound of water falling, and distant drumbeats joined the cacophony of the birds as they roosted.

Man-Afraid-of-His-Horse passed the clay pipe in silence. Once it made its way around the circle, Will introduced Daniel and Emmett to everyone else. A few of the men spoke English and made an effort to do so; however, Will quickly translated anything said in Lakota to English or vice versa.

Red Cloud's deep voice rattled his bone breastplate. "The soldiers and agents want us to come to Ft. Laramie and sign a treaty. I've asked for only two things. I want no forts on the Bozeman Trail and no whites traveling through our hunting ground." He touched the side of his head. "Do they think my head is empty? My braves report army wagons loaded with lumber heading toward the Bozeman." He pointed his chin toward Daniel and Emmett. "Even a papoose would understand. Wagons loaded with lumber on the trail to Montana? I know what they are doing." He gestured to Daniel. "Did you bring your map?"

Daniel tugged it from his shirt and Red Cloud motioned for him to come closer. Two men shifted their position with a jangle of polished bone plates, making room for him to open the map. It was of the Dakota and Nebraska Territories, depicting the country from the Arkansas River to Canada, and west to the mountains.

Will and Emmett stepped forward and each held up the sides of the map. Daniel sat beside the leader and pointed to places familiar to them and Will translated into Lakota: the Black Hills, the Yellowstone, and the Big Horn, then he drew his finger along the Laramie, the Platte, and the string of rivers that flowed north into the Yellowstone River. From the looks on the Indians' faces, he could tell they caught on quickly.

As soon as Red Cloud pointed out their hunting grounds, Daniel knew the United States Government would never return it to the Lakota. They might pretend to, but they would never leave it alone. Daniel met Will's eyes and knew he understood, too.

"When you go to the fort, allow me to accompany you." Daniel said to the leaders. "I have experience, and I'll read every word of the treaty to you, explain what you don't understand. Will Thunder Cloud can translate."

"How would we pay you?" asked Two Face, his chin lifted with suspicion.

Daniel held up his hand. "You've already paid me by saving my sister." He shook his head. He couldn't keep quiet about this. "Listen, I'm sorry, but I know without even reading the treaty they will not stay away from your hunting grounds. The railroad—you've seen the iron horses on the iron rails—." He pointed to eastern Nebraska then swept his hand across the map from right to left. "They want it to cross the entire country with the iron tracks, right through your hunting grounds. You do not have the men or the horses to stop them."

Red Cloud turned to one of the others, and they spoke quickly. Will's eyes flitted between them, and he gave Daniel a brief shake of his head. Daniel understood. But how could he explain it? How could he tell them of the cities in the east, or the ships crossing the Atlantic, already filled with emigrants?

"If you fight them, more white men will come. More than you can imagine. And many more soldiers. If you kill them all, they will send more." He shook his head and held Red Cloud's stare, wanting to make his point. "You have an opportunity here. They want your land, and one way or another, they will get it. Let me help you make a good deal."

Red Cloud was silent. He took a long pull from the pipe and offered it around again. "A good deal? I don't want them on our land, but I will listen. Tell me, what is a good deal?"

"A good deal is when you get the most you can from them. When you win."

As the men rose to leave the Council Lodge, Red Cloud motioned for Will and Daniel to follow him. They walked along a path and stopped at an overlook where a rising moon drenched silver onto the plains spreading north and east.

"What do you see happening to my people?" he asked softly with Will translating. "Because I feel your people want to wipe the Lakota from the face of the earth."

Daniel took a long time to answer. He knew history, and he knew human nature, and he knew Red Cloud was no fool. He nodded to Will, trusting his translating skills.

"I'm no soothsayer," he finally said, "but I know some of our people would like to destroy yours. But many would not. My law partner and I own twelve thousand acres in Pennsylvania. It's just a little patch of land compared to your tribe's hunting ground of millions of acres, but the land is rich, gorgeous earth, and it belongs to us. It's ours and ours alone, and I'd fight to the death to preserve it for my children and their children. So would my partner and my wife.

"There are men in both our worlds like the buffalo hunters," Daniel continued, his expression tight, and Will nodded as he translated. "There are men who shoot for sport or profit, men, who think only of themselves, leaving offal and bones for those who follow."

Red Cloud turned, and the three men strolled toward the village.

"My sister, Wakanda, has visions and reads the future," the great man said. "She sees a long war coming, one of many wars lasting many years. It will begin soon, and I will win the first war, but the hostilities will continue. We will lose the big war, the one that matters. The white men will round us up like horses into a huge corral, and our children will be thin, hungry, and sickly. Many will die. The snow will turn red with our blood, and the mothers will cry and slash themselves; the hearts of the old men and women will break. The white man will cut our children's hair, dress them in white men's clothing, not allow them to speak our language. The stories will be forgotten."

He stopped, the skin of his brow creased with confusion and concern. The pain in his eyes made Daniel wish he could turn away. "The children will not know who they are. My sister tells me we must school the children, teach them the ways of the white people, but she also says we must not lose our heritage. How can we do such a thing?"

Will said goodnight to his uncle. "You two are doing well without me translating. I promised Abbey a short walk to the overlook. I will see you later, Daniel."

20

WHISKEY

Red Cloud walked Daniel to Wakanda's lodge then bid him goodnight. As he turned to leave, he rested his hand on Daniel's shoulder and said something in Lakota to his sister. She nodded, and Red Cloud left.

Inside Wakanda's lodge, a welcoming fire and *gras lamps* flickered, lighting the dark recesses. The shaman glanced at Daniel as he released a shuddering breath. She could tell his conversation with Red Cloud and Will weighed on his heart.

"The others went for a moonlight walk," she said, then yawned. "They promised not to stay out too late. Would you like a whiskey? I imagine you have a great deal to think about."

Daniel nodded. "I would like that very much." He eased himself to the ground and looked up flashing his easy smile "Will you join me? Summer Rose tells me not to drink alone."

Wakanda smiled. "You love her a great deal, don't you?"

Daniel nodded and noticed her lips curled into a half smile, one very much like her son's. "I do."

He watched her fill two sizeable cups with what smelled like decent whiskey, then nodded thanks as she handed him a cup.

"Red Cloud told me of your predictions, your visions," he said.

She seated herself on a mat across the fire from him and bundled an ornate buffalo robe around her body. The fire reflected on her face, and he marveled at the smoothness of her skin. Wakanda, like her son, was very handsome. Now, she poked at the fire with a stick then took a sip from her cup. "I fear a dark, dark, time awaits my people," she said. "And I worry for our people. Survival is all important, but I want more. I am greedy. I want the Lakota language, the stories, the ways of our people to live forever. I want the children to learn to live in a white world—and my visions tell me it *will* be a white world. Our children need to be educated in your ways. I believe education is the best way to prepare them for your world but still keep their heritage."

Daniel swallowed, letting the burn of the whiskey ease his tension. "My wife's family believes very much as you do. Education of their children was of primary importance. Summer Rose was educated at home and has a far better education than I do. Her brothers all attended college. If her parents had lived she would have attended college, too. In our world mostly the sons are educated, but all of Summer Rose and my children—boys and girls—will get as much schooling as they are capable of getting."

"Did you go to college?"

He nodded. "I went to military school, which is a college emphasizing soldiering skills. I graduated with a degree in engineering."

She stirred the fire. "I sent Will to Quebec with his father." She sighed, an again ancient, aching sound. "It broke my heart to send him away. He was only seven, but I wanted him educated. His father saw to it. Every winter I sent him with the traders, and when he was old enough he too studied engineering at McGill University in Montreal. But there is no place here where I can send the children of the tribe."

She took another sip of the whiskey, and her mouth curled into Will's half smile. "Will's father was generous with his son, but he will not spend money on our Indian children. I would not ask that of him."

She fanned the cup, sniffing the whiskey scent then her eyebrows shot up when she remembered something. "Oh! Red Cloud suggested you might want a woman for the night. I can arrange a girl."

Daniel choked and felt his face flush. The Lakota's relaxed attitude toward sex unnerved him. "Thank you, but I'm a one-woman man."

Wakanda nodded and brushed a few strands of loose hair behind her ear. "You and my brother have much in common. Red Cloud is—how did you put it?—a one-woman man, too. Many of our warriors take several wives, and that usually leads to trouble. Pretty Face is Red Cloud's only wife."

"And Will? Is your son a one-woman man?" Daniel asked carefully. The thought of Abbey married to an Indian was difficult enough to digest. Imagining her married to an Indian with several wives was impossible.

She grinned. "I hope so. You know Will was married before, yes? The mother of Splashing Rabbit was killed in a Crow raid three years ago. Will's father, the Frenchman, is a one-woman man."

Daniel lifted an eyebrow, waiting for more.

Wakanda chuckled. "You don't miss much, do you?" She took a swallow of her drink. "Will's father wanted to marry me and offered, but I chose to stay with my people. Nicholas has married since then and has another family."

Daniel took a deep breath and let it out through his nose. "I have another question for you. I've been told by informed white men that Indians cannot handle alcohol. Yet you and Will do.

I've never seen Red Cloud drink spirits, but the other headmen act okay with it. Why would they tell us this?" Wakanda sighed again. "Like white men, some Indian men drink too much, abuse alcohol, some don't." She shrugged "I do know too some of our braves are like children. They don't have any discipline or self-control. They're unworldly."

Daniel nodded. "Some white men have that tendency, too." He pulled out his pocket watch.

Wakanda yawned. "Here, let me refill your cup." She stood, graceful as a long-legged crane. "She's very safe. Will cares for her."

Daniel held out his cup and grimaced. "I know. That's what worries me."

MARY HAD SUGGESTED the walk, and Abbey had agreed whole-heartedly. The weather seemed more early spring than late winter. The moonlight cut shadows as sharp as if made with a razor. Will insisted Owen not come with them, and he tied the dog inside Abbey's lodge.

"The bears are waking up," he explained. "He'd make a nice morsel for a hungry bear."

Will guided the girls and Emmett up a path to an overlook which took their breath away. The moonlight stretched and melted into the night, creating a black and silver quilt of hills, streams, and rolling plains.

Abbey stepped near the edge of the overlook, then backed up and leaned close to him. "It looks dangerous."

Will pulled her close, draping his buffalo robe around them both. He flashed a mock serious expression. "All the more reason, my dear, to stay close to me."

She snuggled into his warmth and added. "… said the big bad wolf. How do you know that story?"

As they moved along the path, she loosened her hair from the restrictive braids and shook it out. It felt almost sinfully good.

"You know already that when I was seven, my mother sent me to live with my father during the winters." His hand combed through her hair. "While I was there, my stepmother read us all the fairytales."

"Us?"

"My father has another family. I have two younger half-sisters and a half-brother, and a very generous stepmother. From the time I turned seven until well into my twenties, I lived in their home in Quebec City during the winters and returned to the tribe every summer." He smiled. "Some look down on half-breeds. I see it as a gift. With my upbringing, I now have a foot in both worlds. My father is a prosperous fur trader, and he wanted to marry my mother, but she chose to stay with our people. Since my mother is Red Cloud's sister, both men educated me, taught me the ways of their worlds. I consider myself very fortunate. All my life I've been influenced by brilliant men and strong women."

She stopped. "Was your wife strong?" Before he could answer she looked away, shocked at her own bluntness. "I'm sorry. If you're not ready to talk about her, you don't have to answer."

Mary and Emmett, walking ahead of them, spread their robe in a protected niche near an indentation of rocks which had obviously been used as a fire pit. They paused their conversation and gathered wood, pinecones, and sticks to light a fire. Will spread the buffalo robe he'd wrapped around his shoulders and knelt on it. As the fire flared, he offered his hand to Abbey.

"I don't mind. I can speak of Splashing Rabbit's mother. We were very young and happy. She taught me much of the way of the Lakota." He narrowed his eyes, thinking. "Was she strong? She was strong willed, perhaps even too strong willed."

"What do you mean?"

"When the Crow took Rain In Her Hair, she fought back. If she hadn't, she might have lived. I believe that sometimes it takes more strength to know when not to fight. Do you remember the story Red Cloud told Sweet Owl at the Indian school? The one about hiding in the cave with the Crow warrior? A wise man knows when not to fight. Rain never learned that lesson."

He leaned back and tilted his head to the stars. He pulled her loosely to his chest and touched her hair and smiled.

"Now, it's my turn for a question. You are obviously not a maiden. Did your husband make you happy when he touched you?"

She let out a deep breath and puffed the hair out of her eyes. "Your question is tougher than mine."

He smiled and lifted her hand and kissed the back of it. "It is. I ask because I want to make love to you." His gentle smile broke into a grin. "And we *are* married."

Heat rushed through Abbey, but she made a great effort to hide her reaction and act nonchalant. She didn't know what to expect from this man and the idea of marriage still confused her. Avoiding the question, she gazed up to the bowl of the sky, the stars so thick they seemed a silver swirl of light.

He touched her chin and looked into her eyes. His intensity seemed alive, coiled, exhilarating. "You haven't answered my question."

Her voice wouldn't work at first, and when it did it came out almost as deep as his. "He did. He taught me a lot. I think that's why I was so surprised and hurt to learn … he liked men." Her voice caught and he touched her hand. Grateful for the darkness, she continued. "I never thought I'd want to make love with anyone else, but ..." Her voice wavered, and her cheeks flooded. "I like you..." She let loose a nervous giggle. "I'm blushing, and I don't know why. I'm not really a shy person. I just find it difficult to talk about ..."

He rolled toward her and outlined her face with his little finger. His hand came to rest on her throat, his arm pressed between her breasts, and his long black hair brushed against her cheek.

"You don't need to talk, Abbey Yellow Bird. Just listen. I'm aware that you have had a difficult time. Your face still shows bruises, and I realize you must feel tricked into this marriage."

She looked away, embarrassed that he'd read her so well. But it was true. She'd had no say in any of this.

"It's all right," he assured her, drawing her gaze back to him. "I will not ask you to do anything you don't want to do." He smiled his dazzling smile. "I warn you however, I will do my best to make you want me."

She felt his warm breath on her lips and the sensation tingled all the way to her toes.

"Even bruised you are more beautiful than any woman I have known. Any man would want you," he said quietly. He looked across the fire to where Emmett and Mary lay entwined and lowered his voice further. "I've longed to kiss you since I first saw you in Scott's Bluff."

Her hair now fell in a riot of curls. His fingers combed gently through the strands, teasing every nerve in her scalp, then came to rest on the bear claw necklace. Holding her gaze with his own, he cupped her slender neck and kissed her lips, bringing her alive with sweet nibbling kisses.

The tension left her in a rush, and she molded into him, fitting her body into his hollows. He sighed deeply and pulled away from her, looking down into her eyes. "Good Lord, Abbey, I want you. All of you."

He glanced over to Emmett and Mary, who were too interested in each other to peek over the fire. When she smiled at him, he cautiously spread her fur-lined cloak and reached beneath the fringed hem of her blouse. She wore nothing beneath the silky doeskin, and his hand inched over her skin until he found her bare breasts, the nipples already pointed. She couldn't stop the sigh from escaping through her lips, and he eased her underneath him. With his kisses lighting sparks through her body, Abbey melted, feeling like a puddle of honey. From down the mountain came the slow sound of drums, far slower than her heart's own beat.

Suddenly he rolled away and sat up, leaving her to feel strangely alone. Then she realized his intention and watched, fascinated. From his shirt he withdrew a big white handkerchief, brilliantly white in the moonlight then watched him slide a short knife from his boot. He pulled her up to sit beside him, leaving the fur cloak wrapped around their legs.

She'd read about what he intended, and felt a tinge of fear when he lifted her left hand. With a swift and precise movement, he cut a cross on the inside of her wrist then did the same to his right. Twining their fingers together, he raised their hands sending a stream of crimson blood running down their arms. He pressed his lips to the bloody stream then bound their arms together.

"The ancients married this way, and now we, are of one blood, one heart," he whispered. "When you are ready we shall become one body and one soul."

He kissed her tenderly, and she tasted the salt and metal of their blood. He wiped her mouth, then his own, and held the bloodied cloth between them. The drums seemed closer, louder, and the evening breeze stirred the fire, shifting it. Sparks flew toward the heavens. He pointed to a shooting star, and she instantly thought of her lost child.

She took his free hand and kissed his palm, then spread it flat over her heart. Every cell in her body felt a rush of warmth.

"I want you, too," she whispered. "I like your touch, and I don't fear you. But I don't know if I'm ready. Do you ... do you understand? Can you?"

He pulled her close, kissing her temple, her cheek, and she ducked behind him as Mary and Emmett began to stir on the far side of the fire.

"*Bien sûr, ma petite.* I understand," he said, then chuckled. "And I no doubt deserve all this waiting. I surprised you with the marriage, and I apologize for that, but the old women were plotting to sell you. One old crone had already sent messages to some Crow renegades. I can wait a little longer, Abbey Yellow Bird. My brain understands perfectly. It is my body, I am afraid, which is impatient." He flexed one bicep, winking. "I am not, sweet girl, made of granite."

He kissed her again, a long passionate kiss full of hope and fire, their hands still bound between them.

"I promise, ZiZi," he whispered. His rough palm brushed her cheek, then pushed loose strands of hair behind her ear, and came to rest on her slender throat. "I will never hurt you or allow anyone to harm you. I will protect you—and our children—with my life. Always."

21

OBSESSIONS

Abbey stood with Wakanda on the same overlook where she and Will had built the fire the previous night, where their blood had mingled, where they almost made love. She watched the contingent of Oglala warriors make their way down the steep trail with her friends, and fought back tears. Mary and Emmett turned and waved, then her brother. Finally Will Thunder Cloud did the same. Her heart about ripped through her chest.

Drums and *hau kolas,* greetings from the guards, echoed through the mountains while eagles and hawks circled and soared high overhead. The smell of pine smoke permeated the mist. Abbey's attention lingered on the backs of her brother and Will Thunder Cloud as they maneuvered their mounts down the winding trail. Tall and similarly proportioned, with broad shoulders and deep chests, the men were as alike in shape and size as matching salt and pepper shakers. *And about as different in temperament as the two spices.*

Her body and mind wilted with exhaustion from the assault of emotions hurling through her. Just the thought of last night sent a hot, exciting flush through her. She knew she wanted Will physically, but was there more? Did she love Will Thunder

Cloud? A voice inside her head told her that she *could* love this man. In some ways, she already did. No one, not her parents, not even Daniel, had ever been as kind to her as Will had been. Tears threatened at the back of her throat when she thought of how he'd helped her when she lost the baby, helped her with the bleeding. Then he'd built the cairn … she pictured it in her mind and the tears rose to her eyes. He looked back over his shoulder and his smile enchanted her even from a distance. She glanced at his mother, shrugged, and blew him a kiss.

Even from a distance his smile warmed her. *Do I love Will Thunder Cloud? I thought I loved Ed and look what happened with him? And Ed knew all the right moves. He taught me a lot, taught me what I thought was love. I thought our marriage was made in heaven. How could I have been so blind? How can I ever trust my judgment again? Am I losing my mind?*

She wiped the salty wetness from her cheek and wondered if he was bronze all over, then blushed at her thinking. But she couldn't get the picture out of her head.

As the small band rounded a bend, Wakanda's hand brushed against her arm. "Let's make some tea. We'll talk. I'll tell you of his father." Color spilled over her high cheekbones and Abbey's face flushed too. She just remembered Will's mother was a shaman. More than likely she'd just read all Abbey's thoughts.

JAKE HUNT WHISTLED as the image of Daniel Charteris filled the circle made by the binocular lenses. No longer in uniform, the former Union general, even a little fuzzy, looked too good to be true. Two of the rogue Indians looked over, and Five Stone, the ugly one with pointy black teeth, grinned knowingly, and outrageous anger consumed Jake. Ever since he first encountered the magnificent, half-naked Colonel Charteris, a nascent obsession had stirred. Daniel Charteris would be his. Damn if that big Indian would figure that out and sneer at him.

Now, Jake shook his head and came back to the present. He followed Red Cloud's band with his glasses until the trail branched toward the fort then turned his mount toward the prairie.

A firm in Kansas paid $3.00 for every raw buffalo hide, and a quarter for a tongue. In the East smoked buffalo tongue had become the rage. So every buffalo they killed brought in $3.25. They could each easily kill a minimum of two hundred beasts a day. Such a harvest tallied to $650 per man per day. Damn better pay than what a U.S. Army Officer received.

Expenses were minimal. They'd killed so many buffalo the hunters hired a small band of half-starved rogue_natives, some Bruléss, some Arapaho, some who had never seen a blonde woman, men from the far North to skin the hundreds of carcasses splattered about the plains. Even well fed now, the renegades frightened the white hunters. Led by Five Stone, whose immense body and hideous face glared at the whites with such malice, he frightened even Jake.

Jake turned and looked up to Mt. Laramie. They must have left the princess bitch in the winter camp while the men headed to the fort. He smiled. Would Ed try to rescue her? He'd lost track of Ed but he didn't care. Abbey's spineless husband wasn't in the best of shape to rescue anyone. The Arapahoe killed Ed's two soldiers and wanted to take Ed's scalp, too, but Jake stopped them, not because of any residual feeling, but rather because he wanted Ed to suffer and, he liked the idea of Ed being a spectator when he took the princess' brother.

If you want to catch a fish, put the bait on the hook, Jake thought. *I'll send the renegades after her. That should scare the spit out of her. If they behave themselves I'll promise them a piece of her.* He shuddered. He'd seen what savages did to white women. Even Jake couldn't imagine what this six-and-a-half-foot giant with legs like tree stumps would do to a girl like Abbey. He imagined Abbey, all that blonde hair and those long legs, so like her brother.

THE FOG, THICK as stew, hid Ed as he followed the Arapahoe. Amazed that he'd been able to keep up on foot, he hunkered down in the stand of cattails and scouted the area. Cold mud soaked him, and every breath hurt like a son of a bitch. He rested his rifle across his legs and clutched at his side. Fresh blood oozed onto the rags poor Pvt. James had used to bandage it. Yesterday these devils killed both James and Harding. He found them scalped and mutilated. The heathens believed some nonsense about making their enemies helpless in the next life by carving up their bodies in death. Usually this was woman's work, but the braves knew how as well. He didn't like to leave James and Harding to the crows and the coyotes, but with only one useful arm, he had little choice. Besides, he overheard Jake instructing the heathen to find Abbey and bring her back to the muleskinner's camp. He couldn't allow that to happen.

Ed stilled himself. Even injured, he was good at sitting like a rock in the cold mud. He peered out between the thick stalks, watching. He smelled booze and figured Five Stone and his bucks must have uncorked a bottle. Ed breathed deeply, wishing he could have a swig. Some liquid courage would serve him well right now. Cold to the bone, shaking, the only thing keeping him upright was the thought of Abbey.

Why? He kept asking himself, *why didn't I stop Jake? I knew what he was going to attempt.*

The Arapahoe moved closer; Ed didn't budge. They make one hell of a lot of noise, he thought. A breeze rattled the dry cattail stalks; he took advantage of the diversion and slid half a yard over. From his new perch, he surveyed the camp through the fog. Smoke from several fires hindered his visibility, but when he squinted he counted eighteen tipis. He was sure there were more. Young boys led a few ponies through the camp, and half-dozen children ran from one conical tent to another, oblivious. Dogs barked, and he strained for a better view. Was that Owen? The dog looked like Owen, but he'd almost doubled in size.

The smell of baking cornbread drifted over him, and his stomach growled.

He heard then saw the tomahawk slice through the fog. It flew end over end, the deadly weapon swooshing by and catching one Arapahoe at the base of his skull, almost severing his head. Ed cringed and slid deeper into the mud. He heard yells as more Indians joined the fracas.

He eased up a little, cringing as his knees straightened. Through fresh shoots of this year's cattails, he made out a ferocious fight in the fog. He recognized the attacking Lakota, led by Crazy Horse, as they chased off the six remaining Arapahoe. Three of the renegades lay in a bloody heap. Crazy Horse's handiwork he was sure. Crazy Horse scared Ed half to death.

Ed crouched, hiding and watching. Patience had always been his strong suit, and it paid off now. His gaze followed the familiar-looking dog, and he was right. Owen led him right to her. He watched the dog wiggle beneath the hides at the back of the one tipi set off by itself. When the camp calmed down, rested in the afternoon, he crawled from the cattails to her lodge, and slid through the spot where the dog had entered.

Abbey, bent over the fire browning slices of mush, muffled a scream. Wakanda drew her skinning knife. When the dog ran up and licked his face, Abbey recognized the unshaven, emaciated, and filthy man. With a cry, she went to him and cradled his head in her lap, barely preventing Wakanda from slicing his throat.

"It's Ed! He's hurt terribly. Help me, please."

Wakanda held her knife in her teeth and disarmed him, then helped Abbey drag him closer to the fire. The shaman opened his army coat, stiff with blood, and saw the extent of his injuries. She smelled his wounds and let out a disgusted grunt.

"I'd be doing him a favor. He's wolf meat."

Ed reeked of sickness. Abbey eased him out of his wet things and dripped warm water over the crusted rags stuck on his arm and side.

"Do you have something to help him?" she asked Wakanda as she wrapped him in a blanket.

The shaman nodded reluctantly. "For his pain, yes." In a sudden movement she grabbed Ed's forearm and smacked his cheek. "I saw what you allowed to be done to her. You touch her again, and I will peel the skin inch by inch off your body. Slowly. And if you allow one of those monsters near her, you'll wish you were dead." To Abbey, she said, "I'll be back in a moment."

When she returned, she brought her medicine chest and applied a heavy, umber-colored ointment to Ed's wounds then both women bandaged his side and his arm.

"The arm is full of poison," she whispered to Abbey. "It should be amputated."

Wakanda selected herbs and powders from her trove of envelopes, stirring and brewing a pungent tea. Abbey spooned it to Ed.

"You look much better," he said, his voice hoarse. He reached for her hand. "How are you?"

She shook loose his grip. "I lost my baby." She still could not bring herself to say *our baby*. "You know what Jake did?"

He took her hand again, and squeezed it. He nodded. "I couldn't stop him. I'm so sorry."

"Liar," she said, jerking back her hand, again. "Why didn't you come home earlier? I heard what he said, and I know what you did that night."

Ed had no response. The tea and his tortured body weakened him, and he fell asleep almost immediately.

Wakanda made a guttural sound as if she were about to spit. Angrily, she picked up his discarded clothing, sorting out his uniform.

"Rid yourself of this useless no good. She stood, holding the garments at arm's length as if they were vermin. "These smell of cowardice. I'll burn them outside and bring over fresh things, though he deserves nothing."

Wakanda paused at the entry, her eyes narrowed. Abbey could see her indecision. It was Wakanda's nature to nurture, but she wanted to protect Abbey, not Ed.

"Keep giving him the tea if he awakens," she said, then shook her head. She grabbed at her knife. "He's not worth trying to save, Yellow Bird."

22

WORDS, WORDS, WORDS

T he mist thickened as the contingent of Indians and whites
made their way down the mountain, so thick the steep and
slick path was barely discernible; a misstep could send any of
them into oblivion. No one spoke, no noise except a hoof against
rock, the crunch of gravel. The pitch of the mountain leveled.
They could hear the racing water, but not see the river then suddenly the white frame buildings of Ft. Laramie loomed out of
the soup. Emmett turned and signaled Daniel and Will with a
slight movement of his head, and urged his mount forward. Will
and Daniel immediately flanked Mary's borrowed mount to protect her. The tack on the Indian ponies was made with no metal,
so except for the occasional horse noises, the creaking of leather,
and the snapping and crackling of the enormous United States
flag flying overhead, the fort stood silent as a primal cave.

Mary admired her husband, now looking quite military, as
he led them around the parade field then halted in front of
Headquarters. Dirty snow lay along the north side of the buildings, but she also noticed crocuses and snowdrops sprouting at
the edge of the cottonwoods. And like the little buds, front doors
along Officers' Row began to click open as women stepped onto

their stoops, children huddled within their mothers' skirts. Every eye seemed to site on her. Mary smelled coffee and bacon, heard pots banging from the mess tent.

Dame Dilly stepped onto her porch, and Mary sent up a silent prayer, asking for strength to deal with this horrid woman. She didn't know if she could ever forgive her for attempting to discredit Abbey.

Last night, as she lay in Emmett's arms, he kissed her and whispered: "You're too trusting, darling. Some people are truly evil. I suspect Dame Dilly is. Don't even consider forgiving her, and never trust her."

She snuggled close to him. "But I was taught to turn the other cheek."

He giggled and grabbed her bottom pulling her tight against him and whispered. "Then expect to get whacked."

Thoughts of Dame Dilly melted away as Mary remembered his hands and his kisses as he made love to her. After just one night of drinking the tea, Emmett seemed like a new husband. He said it had everything to do with her attitude, not the tea. But Mary knew it was the tea. He had wanted her again in the middle of the night.

Now with a heart full of tenderness, she watched Emmett dismount and march up the Headquarters stairs where he saluted Sgt. Gilley then moved inside. After a couple of minutes he returned to the porch and nodded to Red Cloud, motioning for him and his warriors to dismount. Young Lt. Radford, with his ever-present clutch of papers, stepped onto the porch and waited while the party assembled.

Daniel and Will stepped forward with the three headmen. A trickle of fear coursed through Mary when Will went to follow the chiefs inside the building, and Lt. Radford barred his way. Daniel glared down at the lieutenant. He might not be a general any longer, but he had not forgotten how to act like one. He stretched to his full height and his big hand took the roll of paper from the lieutenant's grip without any resistance. It made Mary smile, seeing Daniel's confidence and the lieutenant's lack of it. She could tell Daniel wanted to either conk him over the head with his papers or sail them out over the parade grounds. Instead, he rapped it lightly against the other man's knuckles and nodded to her husband.

She looked over to calm, easy-going, Emmett, smiled and winked. He wasn't a general, but he was hers and he was wonderful.

"We're expected. He's the translator," said Daniel nodding to Will; he handed back the papers. "Trust me, we all need him."

Mr. T.E. Bradford from the Office of Indian Affairs in Washington had known all along that something must be done. The Peace Party waved their Bibles, demanding fair treatment of the aborigines, proclaiming the Indians to be misunderstood and harmless children. The other half of Congress shook their swords and chanted: "*The only good Indian is a dead Indian.*" To that end, someone at the top in the army put in motion a scorched earth policy and ordered the slaughter of the buffalo. "*Their food, shelter, their clothing, all comes from the beasts. If we destroy the buffalo, the Indian will die out like the Wooly Mammoth. Then you can cover the plains with cattle.*"

Meanwhile nothing was done. The cost to the government was mindboggling. Simply transporting General Grenville Dunn's supplies was edging toward two million a month, the railroad was going nowhere, nothing was moving along the Bozeman Trail. The freight haulers, the stage coaches, the wagon trains, even the trading posts, everyone hollered.

A peace treaty had been ratified, and some government-employed nincompoops managed to get a number of insignificant chiefs to sign it. Several of these signers, motivated by the wagonloads of trinkets and molasses, never set foot on the Powder River hunting grounds. Not one real war headman ever considered signing this treaty.

At the same time, hostilities were so dangerous that no traders or half-breeds would venture forth to even ask Red Cloud or Man-Afraid-of-His-Horse to come in. When T. E. Bradford had first come out to Ft. Laramie, the experienced Indian men tried to talk sense to him, but he wouldn't listen.

So when Lieutenant Emmett Hathaway walked into Ft. Laramie's Headquarters, announcing Red Cloud, Man-Afraid-of-His-Horse, and Two Face were outside, T. E. Bradford felt his prayers had been answered.

Mr. Bradford kept them waiting a half hour while he touched up his shave and changed his collar. He took even more time arranging the treaty and pen. The other, lesser chiefs had put their mark where they'd been told to sign; however, he knew Red Cloud and Man-Afraid-of-His-Horse weren't molasses-and-trinket chiefs. Red Cloud nodded to Will, who introduced himself and Daniel to Mr. Bradford, then motioned to the three empty chairs.

"We'll need some time to read this," Will said.

For some unfathomable reason not enough chairs had been provided. *Why would they need chairs*, thought Mr. Bradford as he directed a couple privates to fetch more. *What were they going to do, sit and read the treaty?* Indians couldn't read. So another half hour elapsed while chairs were brought over from 'Old Bedlam' and arranged.

Finally seated, Daniel read and Will translated every word and explained the convoluted passages. When the clause which spoke of roads being cut through the Powder River Country was read, the three headmen balked.

Mr. Bradford attempted to explain that the word *roads* actually meant just one road, which already existed: the Bozeman Trail.

"I realize this can be confusing," he explained, speaking loud and slow. "You see, the road expands to about a dozen trails, but they all go the same place, so it's really only one road."

Red Cloud frowned at the man as if he were crazy. Daniel mumbled something to Will, who spewed words in rapid Lakota. Red Cloud stood carefully, then spoke to Will in Lakota. Will translated Red Cloud's words, "That is the problem. We will not tolerate any roads. Hear me: No roads through the Powder River Territory—no white men in our hunting ground."

T.E. Bradford's Peace Treaty remained unsigned. Red Cloud and his party rode out of the fort and back to the mountains. Red Cloud had one thing left to arrange before he moved his camp north to the Powder River Country.

WILL KNEW IMMEDIATELY the identity of the injured white man lying beside Abbey's fire. The rank smell of river mud and sickness, the emaciation, the clay-colored complexion did not hide the identity of this lump of rags. Will looked to Abbey then to his mother. Both women shrugged. He tamped down the urge to slit the man's throat. "His injuries?" he asked Abbey.

Abbey jerked her shoulders and looked up. She heard the anger low in his voice.

He noticed her wet eyes.

"Wolf meat," muttered his mother.

Will touched Abbey's arm, then stepped outside the tipi. He sent a boy for Crazy Horse, who had handled himself well in recent raids. Although Abbey's former husband looked as if a ten-year-old could manage him, Will wanted someone formidable, and no one appeared more formidable than Crazy Horse. When the warrior arrived, Will spoke to Wakanda, Crazy Horse, and Abbey, "He must go. He led a company at Tongue Creek. His life won't be worth a puff of air if the tribe learns he is here."

He motioned to Crazy Horse. Together the two big men poured the injured man into his damp uniform which Wakanda had not yet burned.

Crazy Horse, whose fierceness increased when he smiled, grinned and drew a finger across his own throat. "He must have snuck in with the *merdé* who came up earlier." He touched his knife. "Want me to …?"

They both noticed Abbey jerk. Ed noticed, too.

Will shook his head and spoke in Lakota. "I know that would be easier," he said to Crazy Horse. "Wait until the tribe is settled for the night, then take him down the mountain and head him toward the fort."

Abbey gasped. She'd picked up enough Lakota to understand. She said, "No, no. They'll kill him."

Will shrugged. His mother made a guttural throat noise and spat out a string of Lakota. Crazy Horse tied Ed's arms to a thick stick and secured his upper body, jerking the rawhide tight then led him outside. Abbey went to follow, but Will stopped her in the doorway. He looked over the top of her head toward Ed, who glanced back as he ducked out the door

"Do you still love him?"

She buried her face against his chest. "No, no. How could I? It's just that … at the fort they are so unfair. They'll hurt him, probably kill him."

Will touched her cheek, hearing the impossible sympathy in her voice, and he nodded, looking back at Ed. "At times death is a blessing."

Will picked up Ed's haversack and rifle and left the tent. When he returned, he told Abbey, "Crazy Horse will take him to the caves along the Yellowstone River. A number of outcasts, Indian and white, live there. If he's tough enough, he can recoup his strength. If not ...."

"I stuffed some jerky and bread in his sack, and some ammunition. Crazy Horse will leave him a gun. He can decide where he wants to go." He couldn't help curling his upper lip. The situation disgusted him. "I fear I will regret not killing him."

He told Wakanda that Red Cloud and Daniel Charteris waited in her tent. When Abbey rose to follow her, he held her by the shoulders, as if he were about to shake her. Instead he wiped away the tears from her cheeks.

"I'm a patient man, *chérie*. But understand me. He abandoned you. He allowed his friend to hurt you and kill your baby. You are no longer his wife. You are *my* wife." He held up his wrist and matched his scar to hers, then kissed her with both tenderness and passion. He smiled and tweaked her nose and arched an eyebrow.

Again, they didn't need words. She understood what he meant. And she nodded, the pain fading from her eyes.

WAKANDA FED THE fire some fresh logs and her mixture of herbs then lit the *gras lamps*. When Will, Abbey, and Daniel were seated, she passed around cups of whiskey. Red Cloud declined and asked for water. She also prepared a small platter of biscuits spread with wild plum jam.

Red Cloud removed his heavy war bonnet of eagle feathers with a sigh, then asked his sister for a cloth to wipe his hands. "I feel dirty after today."

Daniel empathized. He took a cloth from her, too. So did Will. Their visit to Ft. Laramie sickened them.

They wiped their hands and faces then set the cloths aside. Red Cloud spoke. "Daniel Charteris, I have something I must say. Wakanda, Thunder Cloud, and I have discussed this, and many of our tribe also are aware of what I have in mind. Please listen until I'm finished."

He took a deep breath, then looked directly at Daniel and smiled. Wakanda softly translated. "Remember your word, *deal?* I like the word. We have a *deal* to offer you." His eyes twinkled, and Daniel felt a tingle of … unease? Excitement? He sensed no anger in the headman's voice, but there was something there. He heard it.

"You have admired our Sacred Ponies, as anyone would. The Lakota have at least a thousand horses up in the hills, but the sacred ponies are our wealth. One of them is worth maybe twenty to thirty of our other horses. We value them. You are a good horseman. Right away you recognized they were special."

"Thank you. They are beautiful animals."

Red Cloud's eyes never left Daniel's face. He took a sip of water and bobbed his head. "I am also a good judge of men, Daniel. From the moment I met you, I admired you." He nodded toward Wakanda. "You're good with horses and men, and I know men will follow you." He paused and looked around the group, taking in their expressions. "You think, too." He tapped his temple. "Not many men or women think beyond the moment. You do."

The corner of Daniel's blond moustache curled up. He had noticed that.

"And white men leave a trail of blood. You haven't done that. Yet. You even came all this way for your sister, who we have grown to love."

Before Daniel could speak, Red Cloud grinned again and his narrow eyes danced. "We like, too, that you have a big farm in

Penn-syl-van-ia. I realize it is just an insignificant twelve thousand acres," he said, emphasizing Daniel's own words, "but you have land. The Lakota have decided. We will give you, at no cost, thirty-two of our best curly-haired ponies, our sacred ponies. You may take your pick. We will help you get them to the railhead."

Daniel worked hard to keep his face expressionless. His emotions vacillated from wariness to exhilaration.

Red Cloud held up one hand. Will translated. "Wait. Nothing is free, right Daniel?"

Here it comes, thought Daniel. What is it really going to cost?

"What we would like in return is for you to take sixteen of our children with the ponies to Pennsylvania. You will keep the children there until the coming war is over." The smile was gone from his face. "You agree, don't you, that we will come to war?"

Daniel took a sharp intake of breath and nodded. He understood as sure as he knew his name that the Plains were about to erupt into a war as bloody as the shaman's premonitions. The Indians could well be annihilated.

He understood, too, the ramifications of what Red Cloud was proposing. By doing this, Red Cloud was entrusting the future of his tribe to him. The enormity of the responsibility slammed down on him, took any possibility of words away. *To whom would I entrust my sons if their world suddenly became unsafe?* He couldn't answer the question.

Red Cloud continued. "Yellow Bird, Thunder Cloud, and Wakanda will go with you. They will stay in Pennsylvania and nurture the children. Four of our older children will also go with you: the two boys who ride so well, Wakanda's daughter, Walks in the Sun, and her friend, Morning Star. All the parents have agreed and are relieved their children will be safe. Crazy Horse, Kicking Crane, Big Bear, Fish, and Dusty will go as far as the train to help with the horses." He motioned to Wakanda and she refilled the glasses. "You understand what we are attempting?"

Daniel nodded and sighed deeply, but didn't answer immediately. Mulling Red Cloud's words over, he stood and paced in a circle around the fire. After a few minutes he nodded again.

"I see your intentions. You want to keep your beliefs and your values, your way of life alive through the children. The ponies are only an enticement for me and a decoy for what is really happening. Transporting thirty-two horses with my Indian helpers will not lift too many eyebrows now that it's spring and the horses will be smooth-coated and ordinary looking. But it will be enough to distract the whites that we are moving these children across the country."

He nodded to Wakanda, already seeing Summer Rose's smile in his mind. "We have room at Camelann to house and care for them. We'll need to construct some buildings, but we have all summer and autumn. We'll educate the children like you suggested, Wakanda, in the ways of the whites. Will Thunder Cloud, you, and the older children will be there to pass on the Oglala-Lakota heritage, to ensure their education includes that world, too."

He hesitated then chuckled lightly. "I went off to school when I was twelve. They gave me a uniform, chopped off my hair, threw out a bunch of rules, whacked me if I didn't obey. At one point I was so homesick, I ran a fever. I was very ill. During the war, the Army doctors called such an illness Nostalgia, and several soldiers died from it. These children you're sending with us are what? Six? Eight?"

Wakanda nodded. "Splashing Rabbit is four."

Daniel smiled with reassurance. "We will work hard to keep the children safe from this sickness and any other illnesses. We'll go slowly with any changes. Have them pack small treasures. Also as an army officer I learned ways such as cleanliness and sanitation to prevent fever. My wife and her family taught me to value children above all else. They are our blood, our hearts, our future."

Red Cloud nodded with contentment. "I knew I was right to choose you."

Daniel looked at the headman, slightly embarrassed. "Trust me, Red Cloud, I am nothing without my Summer Rose. Before I met her I was a heartless, stupid ..." he chuckled. "Just ask Abbey."

Abbey looked around the group and smiled. "That's only a little bit true. You've always been a good man, Daniel. Summer smoothed your rough edges."

Red Cloud grinned. "I understand this."

Now that Daniel had weighed all the questions and answers in his mind, his heart practically did a cartwheel. "Your proposal," he told Red Cloud, "is sound. In fact, it's brilliant." He motioned to his sister, Will, and Wakanda. "And we make a good team."

"And your wife?"

"I guarantee she will love this." His mind flew, scouting for possible problems and solutions. "Getting to the train concerns me. I made it across Nebraska in four days, but we cannot repeat that with twenty-some people and a herd of horses. The children can all ride, can't they? The horses are broken, correct?"

Everyone nodded.

Daniel stopped pacing and stared at his sister. "What do you think, Abbey?" He wasn't hiding the excitement in his voice.

"I think we can do it." She smiled at Will then slid her gaze around the tipi, meeting everyone's eyes. "You'll love Summer Rose, and Camelann is the perfect place to keep the children safe." She slipped her fingers into Wakanda's hand. "I like that we will be able to keep the Lakota ways safe, too."

Red Cloud lifted his elaborate war bonnet of eagle feathers and rose, groaning like an old man. "Today I feel ancient, and I am not yet fifty winters. Thank you." He shook hands with Daniel then took Abbey and Will's hands in his. He inspected their wrists. "Together you make a strong team. The Lakota will survive."

❦

THAT NIGHT THE drums beat to a frenzy. Abbey and Will sat alone in her tipi. Abbey felt strangely awkward. They had so seldom been totally alone.

Will sat by the fire behind her and rested his chin on her shoulder, his hands on her waist. Except for the dark red coals in the fire, darkness filled the tipi. "Your heart is racing, ZiZi. Am I so frightening?" He laughed softly. "I still have all my clothes on. I won't force you to do anything you don't want to do."

She lowered her eyes and relaxed against the hard surface of his chest, feeling warm and small inside his arms.

"Kicking Crane and Big Bear are standing guard. They even took Owen. No one will bother us." She heard the smile in his voice. "If we just go to sleep by the fire, no one will know but us."

She tucked her head against his shoulder. "You are too kind and too patient."

The fire shifted and flared; he pulled to the side so she could see the teasing glint in his eyes. "Well, if you insist, I'll take off my shirt. Have you seen my chest? All the ladies like my chest. I have many scars."

"Oh, Will." She chuckled. "If you take off your shirt, then I'll probably take off mine."

His black eyebrows danced. "Then we will be in trouble." He bent his head and kissed her neck, sending shivers through her body. "*Ah, my ZiZi*. You are by far the most beautiful woman I have ever known."

She turned all the way around so they were face to face, then unlaced the cords at the top his shirt, then slowly pulled it off. She spread her palms on his hard chest. "Your skin is on fire."

"*Oui*. I am on fire for you, Madame Guillaume Emil Thunder Cloud Dupree, my ZiZi, my golden girl."

23

FIVE HUNDRED MILES

In the morning, heavy clouds hid the sun and almost touched the mountain. Campfires and torches lent a pink cast to the gray, and the odor of tar permeated the busy campsite as parents carried flares, ready to walk with their offspring as they made their way down the mountain. Will, Daniel, and Red Cloud, all on horseback, stood on an outcrop of rock, overlooking the gathering procession of children, ponies, and supplies.

Will had dragged himself away from Abbey's warmth long before light. They'd slept little, but he felt renewed. On rising, he'd sent Kicking Crane and Bear to take the extra ponies ahead and to reconnoiter the trail, along with the teenage boys. The older girls, Wakanda, and Abbey positioned themselves at intervals among the single file of mounted children. The two other braves, Spotted Fish and Dusty, followed, protecting the rear of the column.

Over the scent of smoke and horse, Will smelled thawing earth, green shoots, another renewal over and above the one he'd experienced last night. His gaze sought out his blonde wife and found her in the midst of the children. Memories flooded him, and a soft warmth flushed every inch of his skin. He'd forgotten what it felt like to make love to a woman for whom he cared deeply. The tenderness, the joy, the ecstasy had consumed him, brought to life long forgotten memories in a wild tangle of happiness.

Most of the supplies and three tipis had been loaded on the spare horses. They fitted small items on the backs of the children's ponies. Wakanda knew to pack tight and light. She had told Daniel, "We'll hunt and forage for most of our food." He marveled at how all the details had come together in just two days. Pairing horses and children, gathering minimal supplies, finalizing decisions, it all fell into place thanks to Wakanda's brilliant preparations. Daniel joked, saying she'd have made an excellent army sergeant, perhaps a general. Both he and Will suspected she had been planning this cross-country trek for some time.

Daniel nudged his horse toward Red Cloud and handed him an envelope. "Come to Camelann," he urged. "That's the address where you can reach us as well as some stamps. Have the French priest help you compose a letter. You can mail it from the trading post. We will watch the newspapers, and I'll make sure the children write to their families. I'll write to you as well, and the priest can translate."

He held up the map. "When I get to the railhead, I'll send this back with Crazy Horse." He stretched out his hand to Red Cloud, who grasped it. "In a year you'll be able to board the train near here, and travel all the way to Camelann. I'll arrange passage. Tell me what you need and I'll send tickets."

He felt Red Cloud's grip tighten as the momentousness of their departure descended on both of them.

"We'll build a good school. I promise. When peace returns, so will your children. They'll be ready to educate their brothers and sisters." The headman's face was set, holding in strong emotions Daniel could only imagine. "Red Cloud, you have honored me. Thank you for your trust."

Red Cloud's elaborate war bonnet bowed in acknowledge-
ment. Each one of those eagle feathers represented a battle in
which he'd fought, but Daniel knew this could be the most difficult one. Red Cloud had already said his goodbyes to the children, kissing every forehead, giving each child an eagle feather
and a smooth stone to hold as amulets in the small pouches they
wore at their waists.

Red Cloud nodded and gripped Daniel's shoulder. "Go
quickly. The children and their parents are close to tears. Do not
prolong their pain."

Daniel understood. He could hear the thickness in Red
Cloud's voice. He nudged his new mare forward. Ruby, selected
from the pool of sacred ponies, was a big roan with a silver-gold
mane and tail, and sturdy enough to carry his big frame across
Nebraska. All the sacred ponies had been painstakingly groomed
to remove their curly coats and make them appear to be nothing more than ordinary horses. All of their party, too, walked a
fine line, not advertising either the ponies' value or the children's
heritage. And yet, when it came to the children, they weren't hiding anything, either. Daniel agreed with Will, Red Cloud, and
Wakanda: in no way should the children's Indian identity be com-
promised. The children wore moccasins, buckskin trousers or
skirts, and various colorful cotton shirts under black wool sweaters. Their hair remained long, but was now tightly braided.

At Will's suggestion they truncated the Indian names. "My
long Indian names made me different in Quebec. In a new world
it's best not to stand out." White Hawk became Hawk, Thunder
Cloud, Cloud. Morning Star was now just Star. Despite this, they
understood the importance of not giving them American names.
It was another way they took pride in their Indian heritage.

During a brief meeting, Red Cloud and Man-Afraid-of-his-
Horse directed them to veer north and travel along the Middle

Loup River, where water, game, and grazing would be more plentiful.

"The name *Loup,*" Will told them, "comes from the French translation of the Pawnee word *skidi*, name of the local branch of the Pawnee tribe, which means Wolf."

The children thought travel along the Loup or Wolf River sounded much more exciting than travelling along the boring Platte River.

"Will we see wolves?"

"Let's hope not."

Will's fingers lingered on his son's cheek, marveling at how Rabbit's skin was even softer than Abbey's. His mind flashed to last night, and he smiled all the way to his toes. Again his eyes searched the milling crowd and found her. She glanced up as if he'd called her name, and their eyes locked for a breath.

He bent and kissed his son's head. The children looked at this journey as a grand adventure. The adults all prayed it would be only that. "It *will* be one," Will had confided to Abbey, "if we don't run into fierce thunderstorms or tornados, if those bloodthirsty renegades don't find us, if we find plenty of water, if the rivers don't flood, if the children stay healthy, if … if … if … "

A MIST, JUST enough to slick the trail, accompanied them down the mountain. As they neared the cairn, Will asked Daniel to follow him. In silence they moved through the file of children on ponies and their parents, who still walked beside them, carrying the flares. Will and Daniel joined Abbey when she moved from the trail into the clearing where she'd lost the child. She dismounted beside the small stone pyramid and touched her brother's boot.

"This is where Will buried the baby. Thank you for coming with us." she said quietly. "It helps… helps me say goodbye."

Will brought her saddlebags over, and she reached inside. Yesterday, Abbey had taken a shovel into the forest. Now she withdrew clumps of fern, snowdrops, coltsfoot, liverwort, blue bells, and some nameless yellow flowers.

Daniel tucked his gloves in his belt and stooped beside her. The earth was cold, just thawing. Will dug a little hole, she planted the ferns and wildflowers they'd gathered, and Daniel tamped down the dirt. As he crouched beside her, Daniel felt her shudder, and sudden, unexpected visions of his own small sons lying still and cold in the ground threatened to overwhelm him. The sadness was wrenching. To know, too, that Jake and Ed, men he trusted, had done this, fed his anger. How hard it must have been for her, alone and frightened in the middle of a strange land, to lose her child. He sensed Will on the other side of her, saw his large hands touch her knee.

Daniel cleared his throat, but his voice still hitched as it came out. "Do you know if the baby was a boy or a girl?"

Will shook his head. "Couldn't tell."

Abbey swallowed a small sob. "I named the baby, Kip, thinking it could be a boy's or a girl's name. I hope you don't mind."

She told Will yesterday that Kip was the name Summer Rose had used during the war when she'd disguised herself as a boy. The name was dear to Daniel and Summer. "I'm honored. I'm sure Rosie will be, too. Thank you for including me."

They stood, and Will kissed her cheek before helping her mount. As he passed her the reins, his hand ran possessively down her thigh. Daniel noticed their intimacy, but instead of his earlier sense of unease, he felt immeasurable gratitude that at least they had each other. As the men mounted, the horses' breath steamed the air. Their stomping and snorting and the scolding from the overhead jays, were the only sounds.

JAKE HUNT STOOD a short distance away with Dennis Gander, the buffalo hunter, and Five Stone, his chief skinner. No one spoke. The immense Indian stood beside the riders and horses, his thick shoulders level with animals' withers, his arms and legs bound with ropes of muscles. Rather than buckskin trousers, the attire of the other Indians, he wore just a loincloth and a vest, seemingly impervious to the cold. Knives and two tomahawks hung from his belt, a musket was slung across his back, and from his saddle hung a bow and a quiver of arrows. His skull was plucked except for a topknot with three eagle feathers twisted in the dark hair. His upper arms were crisscrossed with fresh scars, as was his face. *He looks more beast than human,* Jake thought. He only tolerated Five Stone because he spoke English and seemed in control of his band.

He motioned for the skinner to come forward. Five Stone grunted when Jake pointed out Abbey and Daniel through the binoculars. "He's riding the big roan with the silver mane. She's on a spotted pony. Eventually, I want both of them. For now, while I take the buffalo hunters and follow the bison, I want you to stick to these two like a wolf to raw meat. If they change direction, send a brave to me. We'll be back." He handed Five Stone his binoculars. "Keep a distance. Remember: alive and healthy." He grinned. "I'm saving Goldilocks for you. I'll let you give her a poke before we sell her." Jake grinned. "The hair between her legs is gold. Ever see anything like that?"

The big Indian didn't respond.

THE PARTING HAD been difficult. At first, the children managed better than their parents, who sobbed and pulled their hair at the separations. The children, at the last minute, turned in their saddles, holding their arms aloft for their mothers. The crying could be heard long after the rear of the column dipped over a hill. Fourteen of the sixteen children ranged in age from six to nine, and they each rode their own pony. The two youngest children, Rabbit and Owl, hitched along with adults.

Plump little Happy, chewing on the end of one red ribbon, was the first to start sobbing. Soon Rain and Wren joined the fray. Before they all started wailing, Will nudged Drum toward Happy and Rain then led them on their ponies on a mad gallop over the prairie. Hawk took another two, then Lobo took two, then Abbey pitched in, exercising the children, diverting their attention from the sadness.

FIVE STONE WATCHED through the hunter's glasses. The blonde girl fascinated him. Her breasts were awesome: big handfuls. He wanted to see them naked.

He panned the binoculars. Two big men filled the lenses. One rode a powerful black horse, the other a big roan. He'd take either horse, but he especially wanted the black one. The scalp of the rider on the black horse would be a coveted trophy, too. He also liked the rifle the roan's owner carried. In his head he made a list of what he wanted in their order of importance. He smiled, showing his small black fox teeth. First, the girl ...

24

THE TREK

Generals Phil Sheridan and Grenville Dunn sat on the rear platform of the train as it slowed toward the end of the line in Fremont, Nebraska. Dunn was about to resign his commission with the United States Army and become the Union Pacific's Chief Engineer, a job Generals Grant, Sherman, and Sheridan had wholeheartedly urged him to take.

"You know, General Sheridan, there are some things I'll miss about the army." He threw his head back and looked up at the bunting, strung across the rear of the train, then let out a long breath. "But," he held up and shook open a piece of paper, "it won't be receiving telegrams like the one from the commander at Ft. Laramie. Seems your friend, Charteris, created quite a stir out there. He was a brigadier? You'd think he'd be more loyal."

Phil Sheridan knocked the ash off his cigar. "Quit bellyaching, Grenville. You like the money and the privileges. That's some house you're building up on the bluffs. As to former Brigadier General Charteris, I promoted him right before Lee surrendered. Is he being cantankerous? Doesn't surprise me one iota. He could have been a Regular Army captain, but he chose to resign. What has he done now?"

"I wish you'd have stuck him in the front lines?"

Phil laughed. "I fleetingly considered doing so." He motioned the waiter to refresh their drinks. He knew he'd already drunk way too much whiskey and his tongue was wagging, way out of control, but he ignored that warning voice in his head. "You ever meet his wife?"

Grenville took a long sip of his fresh drink and shook his head. "I heard she was quite the looker, built like a brick ... Tell me about her."

Phil sat back and again knocked the ash off his cigar. "Ah, Summer Rose. I fancied myself in love with her for a couple weeks. Pretty as a painting, sweet as her name, and could handle a knife better than anyone I ever met, man or woman. I knew her father, admired him."

"What prevented you from ...?"

Phil took another drink. "I don't rightly know. I suppose I liked him, too, and I'm glad I didn't. I've been invited to stay at Camelann the next time I go east. Mark my words, Grenville, you should make an effort to know them. I'll introduce you to Summer Rose and you'll see what I mean. Difficult to explain."

Lieutenant Downey, Sheridan's handsome young aide, stepped onto the platform. "Excuse me gentlemen. We're about to pull into Fremont. May I remove those glasses?"

In unison, the generals drained them and handed them over.

"When do you plan to go east?"

Phil Sheridan shrugged. "Every once in a while you should show up in Washington. Let the politicians know you're alive." He stood and stretched. So did General Dunn.

"Speaking of being alive, I'll tell you what, General Sheridan. We have to get serious about exterminating the natives. If you can believe it, your golden boy, Charteris apparently helped Red

Cloud decide *not* to sign the treaty. He brought a translator and sat in Headquarters at Ft. Laramie and read the whole damn treaty to the natives—took over two hours. Colonel Dietrich must have been close to apoplexy."

From his mouth came an odd noise like marbles clicking. "If we can't round those heathens up and keep them in one place, we'd best eradicate the entire kit and caboodle." He narrowed his eyes. "I ordered General Conner to kill every, male Indian eleven or older. Between you and me, I'd like to make that *every* Indian, period. President Johnson has the backbone of a dead fish. Why can't we have someone like Jackson when we need him?

"Now tell me about her."

THE PONIES AND children rode four days without any untoward incidents. Even the weather cooperated. Daniel was making a good connection with Ruby, constantly running his hand through her thick silver mane. He talked to her continually telling her what he was doing, what he expected of her, and always, he let her know who was boss. Every once in a while, he reached forward and fed her a sugar cube.

Will pulled Drum parallel to Ruby. "Sounds as if you think she understands every word you say."

Daniel grinned. "She does, don't you, girl?"

The horse whinnied, and Daniel winked at Rabbit, who was perched on his father's lap. "She's a quick learner. Almost as smart as you are." He frowned up at a bank of tin-colored clouds sailing toward them. "Should we break soon?"

Will turned and studied the western horizon. He knew very well the swiftness with which storms could race across the plains.

"There are some hills a few miles ahead," he said. "Let's try for there. They'll give us some protection. I don't like the look of that sky. Where's Abbey?"

Rabbit pointed toward the river. "She went with Grammie and Star to dig tubers."

Daniel nodded to Will. They both knew exactly where she was. Tubers, which were remarkably similar to potatoes, grew in the banks along the Loup. It was dirty work, but the children loved them roasted in the coals of the cooking fires. The women often rode ahead, found a likely riverbank, then dug and collected the vegetables. If they had enough time they'd sneak a quick swim in the river.

"You find them. I'll ride along the line and speed everyone along," said Daniel. He looked at Rabbit. "Want to ride with me?" Rabbit immediately stretched out his arms. All the children loved a ride on Big Ruby.

WILL HAD NO trouble finding the women. With the heat so oppressive, he was tempted to join them, but the ominous black clouds moved faster. Distant thunder rumbled. He dismounted and pointed to the horizon, motioning the women out of the water. His mother and Star climbed out in their soaked cotton shifts and quickly slipped into doeskin dresses, strapping baskets of tubers to their ponies. Indian women knew how to move in a rush.

His wife, however, appeared to be entirely naked, and apparently had other things on her mind. He couldn't help but grin. If he didn't know better, he'd suspect her goal was to drive him crazy.

He pulled loose his blanket, unfurling it with a snap as he walked toward the shoreline. She rose from the water like Botticelli's Venus. She took his breath away. When she stepped into his arms he kissed her. The contrast of her warm mouth and her cold, wet skin sparked an electric current between them that matched the display in the sky. "It is still daylight," he said.

"I was so dirty. No one was around."

The wind picked up and thunder cracked even closer; the sky rumbled. Will stepped back and held the blanket for her while she scrambled into her clothes, then watched her run her fingers through her hair and mount Scout. He strapped her basket of tubers to the horse, then pulled her down to him and kissed her sweetly.

A ferocious crack of lightning ripped open the sky. He looked up to see the big Indian watching them from the hillside. How much had he seen? Will touched his rifle and for a moment considered shooting him. *Good Lord*, he thought, *I'm acting like someone out of the Old Testament..*

From the corner of his eye, he saw Crazy Horse signal the mounted column of children to ride faster. The sky opened sending torrents of rain and stinging hail down on them. Daniel, the other braves, everyone picked up speed as wild spears of lightning, one after another, struck the hills. Will mounted Drum and motioned Abbey to race to the children. Just then Happy Moonbeam's white pony lost his footing and skidded down the hill. Happy rolled in front of the herd of horses. To reach her was suicide. Five Stone dove into the mayhem, and clutched her to his chest. Wrapping his body around her, he hunched into the ground. When the ponies passed, Will reached them. Five Stone, lay face down, his enormous body curled around the little girl. Bloodied head to foot, he didn't move. Abbey rushed to them and took Happy, who miraculously was just frightened. Daniel came over and after a quick survey of the unconscious Indian gave a thumbs-up.

The storm rumbled off as the little band cheered. Soon though, with their usual efficiency, the gang rubbed down the horses, started fires, and set about making supper. Daniel and Will carefully helped Five Stone to Wakanda's fire where the women gave him a buffalo robe, then took his soaked things, and cleaned his wounds. Wakanda fumbled among her wax paper envelopes and concocted a tea which she further laced with whiskey.

She handed Abbey a cup. "Spoon some to the big fellow. He's awakening. Happy, wipe his brow with a cool cloth. Gentle girl." She moved his head to a pillow next to Abbey.

After making rounds and counting heads, Daniel came over and introduced himself. He touched Five Stone's shoulder. "Thank you, Five Stone. All the children are safe. Your bravery is greatly appreciated."

Five Stone started to get up, Daniel shook his head. "Rest here tonight."

Crazy Horse came by and thanked him. When Happy fell asleep, Abbey took over mopping his brow and spooning the broth to him

25

No Lollygagging

By morning the storm disappeared, and although the grass took on a lush green color and sun poured onto the hills, both the children and adults awoke grumbling and complaining. The children knew the routine and led their ponies through the tall grass, down to the water. Their presence alerted a long skein of cranes which erupted from the wetlands, making a racket. Reacting to the noise, several flocks of colorful waterfowl took flight as far as the eye could see. While the animals watered and fed, the children walked upstream, above where the fowl and horses dirtied the water. There they washed their hands and faces, and brushed their teeth. Abbey had provided toothbrushes and tooth powder, and the children cared for their teeth religiously. With their morning ablutions completed, they sought higher ground gathering near Wakanda.

Wakanda reached into her basket and passed out pemmican bars made of buffalo jerky, dried plums, and nuts, all held together with dark molasses and brown sugar. The women checked each of the children's saddles and packs, tucking an extra pemmican bar for a mid-morning snack and made sure their water bladders were full.

Wakanda spoke to the men. "The children slept in wet blankets. They're exhausted and need to rest. I ache. We all need to rest."

But Daniel and Will stuck to their gut feelings. "We go. Thanks to Five Stone, we haven't lost a child or a horse yet," said Daniel. "I will only feel safe when we are on the train."

"Their clothing and blankets are still soaked. They're wet to the bone. They need to rest."

"So?" Will surveyed the clear sky. "Tie the blankets over the backs of the horses. Their clothing will be dry within an hour. We cannot afford lollygagging."

Abbey snickered. "Lollygagging? Where did you learn that word? It's not French."

"Trust me. It was very popular with my French father. He did not tolerate lollygagging." His blue eyes sparkled. "Therefore, I do not tolerate lollygagging. Not even from my beautiful wife."

He nodded to Five Stone who was dressed and eating breakfast. "Look at our hero. He must hurt all over. A herd of horses ran over him. He's not lollygagging."

Every day, Daniel liked Will more. He appreciated his sense of humor and his moral support, and he liked how he treated Abbey. That Indian blood ran in his veins still concerned him, but now the reasons were entirely different. He tucked those concerns in a back part of his mind.

Abbey kept up her arguments until Daniel finally glanced at Will, who nodded reluctantly. Neither he nor Will had planned to tell the women their news, but it appeared they had to do just that.

Daniel motioned with his eyes for all of them to move out of earshot of the children. "Ease up, Abbey. We need to keep moving because at least six rogue Indians are following us. They stay just out of sight, but Fish and Dusty know right where they are. They're renegades, young bucks who their own people won't even tolerate. They're looking for blood. They want our horses, our women, our children, and our scalps. Remember our first priority is protecting these children."

"Also," said Will, "Crazy Horse spotted Jake with his buffalo hunters a few miles back. He may be just following the herd, but he seems to be sticking close to us, too. I don't trust him."

TWO UNEVENTFUL DAYS passed, though Crazy Horse and his braves kept a careful watch on the Arapahoe and Jake. Then late on the third night, Meadow became violently ill, vomiting and suffering with diarrhea at the same time. The child doubled over in pain, then begged Abbey to help her to the river. They had no sooner stepped beyond the perimeter when a lariat snapped around Abbey's shoulders. She screamed and so did Meadow. The entire camp jolted awake; Wakanda lit a flare exposing a terrible scene. Jake Hunt on a huge flat rock stood behind Abbey. He held her hand behind her back and tossed a paper-wrapped rock to Daniel. Several fierce-looking Indians stood behind them.

Daniel went for the rock while Crazy Horse and Bear melted into the night. Will moved beside Daniel and saw his hands shake as he unfolded the paper. Then he stood beside him, reading the note.

Daniel Charteris: You know who and what I want. Fair exchange: you for her—otherwise the savages get her. Their tongues have been hanging out for days. Come right now! Mine has been hanging out for years. J. J. Hunt III

A drum pounded like a dirge, and on a large flat rock a huge bonfire ignited with a flash of turpentine. Terror grabbed Will and Daniel when they saw Abbey silhouetted against the flames, half-sitting, half-sprawled on the rock, her wrists tethered to Jake's. From a ledge behind her, Jake jerked the rawhide like a puppet master. He then jumped to the rock, kicking her feet out from under her, and forced her to her knees. Clamped his knees around her shoulders, he held a knife to her throat. Also clearly visible were the savages, chanting and gyrating in a hellish dance around her.

Every cell in Will's body burst into action with nowhere to go. Breathing deeply, he slowed his heartbeat and heard Abbey's brother instruct Kicking Crane and Wakanda to take the children, to keep them safe, to stay close to the river.

At the same time he directed Hawk. "Stay here with our horses—Ruby, Drum, Scout, and yours. We need you to be brave."

Will heard Daniel's strong voice, heard his steady words, but he also saw the fear in his eyes. Will stripped to his waist and turned to Daniel, grabbing his wrist roughly and pulling him down to the riverbed.

"W-what are you doing?" asked Daniel.

"This is Indian fighting," Will growled. "It's dirty. My kind of fight. Take off your shirt. Tie it around your waist. Give the bastard a taste of what he wants."

The drum continued its dirge. Will reached down and grabbed a handful of wet clay, using what little firelight he could to see, then drew slash marks across Daniel's cheekbones. He chuckled. "If you plucked your face and chest like a good Indian this would be much easier." He bent and scooped up more clay. "Turn around."

Daniel felt the wet clay, but didn't ask. He trusted Will.

"Now they will know what a great warrior you are. Our size will intimidate them, too."

Daniel said nothing as Will used clay to mark his face and bared torso.

"I'm putting a circle around your left eye which will give you clear vision," Will said, "and coup marks down your arms to denote bravery. This is a lightning spear on your chest for speed, and many marks of horseshoes for all the battles you've fought."

He then marked his own face and arms. As they stepped up the bank, Wakanda quickly painted half of both their faces with dark red clay. She then handed Will his rifle and extra ammunition and a bow, along with a quiver of arrows, then kissed her son. She took Daniel's shirt and handed him his rifle and pistol and fitted two razor sharp stilettos, encased in leather sheaths, into the sides of his boots. She stood on her toes and planted a kiss on his cheek, too, as she tied his shirt around his waist.

"We'll take the children and the ponies and stay along the river."

As they approached the fire, Daniel eyed Will. "You sure as hell look fierce." He nodded toward the bow. "How accurate are you with that?"

Will pointed to the fire where Abbey was. "Know first, Daniel, I will kill her before I let them have her." He nodded to the dancers. "At this distance I am as accurate as I am with a rifle. I use it because sometimes it's wise to be quiet." He withdrew an arrow and nodded toward the hill. "There are six Arapahoe. Crazy Horse and Bear are on your far left. I smell their tobacco and wet clay. They're painted, and they'll follow your lead."

They worked quietly in the darkness, preparing. Will braced a hand on Daniel's shoulder. "You're the decoy. Approach Jake from my left," said Will. "Step into the light. You're good with words. Goad him into cutting her free. Once she's loose I'll pick them off like ducks. When she's in the darkness, man, you run— run like hell for the horses. "

26

FACE OFF

Daniel walked into the circle of light, yoking his rifle across his shoulders, sucking in his gut. The drum stopped. Every hard muscle in Daniel's chest and arms swelled. The twenty pounds he'd lost on the ride showed in the taut ripples of his abdomen, the power of his shoulders. He hoped he looked fierce. God knew he didn't feel it.

Abbey screamed when Jake's knife scraped her neck, but Jake didn't seem to notice. He was cocking his head from side to side, evaluating Daniel.

"My, my, aren't you all prettied up for our rendezvous. Red becomes you, *mon ami*." He laughed and yanked Abbey's hair, wrapping a hank of it around his wrist, so he could see her face. "Huh. You two really do look alike." His fist loosened and her hair covered her face. "Glad to see you aren't prolonging the inevitable, *mon general*." He made a crude gesture with his mouth and tongue. "Goddamn, Danny—you don't mind that I call you Danny, do you? I was so jealous when your friends called you Danny. And well, Danny, you still look incredible."

Daniel straightened his spine, hating the smug tone of Jake's voice, his words. He was not naïve of such overtures. His father made sure he learned to fight young, to protect himself, and his size while it enticed, it also intimidated most. "Call me anything you want, Jakey. Just keep the exchange honorable."

His voice roared. "Let my sister go. Haven't you done enough to her? Killed her unborn child? Beat her almost to death?"

Jake shook his head. "Seems to me you aren't in much of a bargaining position, Danny-boy. I hold all the cards." He waved his pistol toward the savages then quickly aimed it back at Abbey. He leaned close with his mouth spitting saliva across her face. "They're all heated up for you, Babycakes." He licked his lips then turned to Daniel. "They'll be disappointed if they don't get her. Disappointed savages are wicked. Ever see what a white girl looks like after a whole tribe fucks her?" He laughed. It was a dark, crazy noise. He turned to Daniel. "Wanna watch? I think I'd like to watch you watch."

An arrow swished out of the night and found its mark in front of Abbey.

It was Daniel's turn to shake his head. He and Will had agreed. They'd kill her before allowing those heathens to have her. Would either of them have the courage, though? He didn't know?

"Abbey's health is the only thing keeping you alive. Watch yourself, Jakey. I know you hold a couple cards." Daniel grinned. "But I hold aces. You are surrounded. If anything happens to her, you are dead. Let's keep this clean. You gave me your word, and I understand honor ranks up there with God at West Point."

Daniel had attended Pennsylvania Military College in Chester, Pennsylvania. It was a fine school, but not the prestigious Academy, as Jake and Ed had always reminded him. He twisted his voice and laughed, knowing he sounded fearless, wishing he felt the same way. "Or has our mighty fortress on the Hudson lowered her standards? Isn't your motto, *Duty, Honor, Country*?"

He eased down his rifle and visualized the blades in the side of his boots then the Smith and Wesson shoved in the back of his belt. From the edges of his vision he watched the Indian's eyes dart from Jake to Abbey. The big Indian looked about to pounce.

"You have my word," he said. Inside his head, he knew that a lie. He'd kill Jake at the drop of a hat. "You can do anything you want with me, Jakey, and I'll do whatever you demand. But first, free her."

Jake grabbed her face from behind, pressing the knife tight against the cartilage of her throat. Daniel heard him whisper, "Are you jealous, Babycakes? Jealous because I want your brother more than you? Maybe you should have treated me nicer."

Jake laughed maniacally then reached down and sliced open her leather blouse. Her breasts spilled out, and she jerked in reaction. Five Stone lurched for her, but Jake fired at the renegade's feet.

Daniel's voice cracked. It occurred to him that perhaps they had an ally in Five Stone. Was the big Indian attempting to protect her? To Jake he yelled. "It's me you want. Free her."

Jake cut the rawhide binding her wrists, and Abbey's shaking fingers yanked the sliced sections of her blouse together. She sat frozen, wide-eyed, with Jake still pressing the blade to her throat. Keeping the knife steady, he pulled her to her feet.

Daniel sat with his hands on his knees, as non-threatening as he could manage. His voice stayed low, calm, too. "That-a-boy, Jakey. You know it's me you want. Let her go. Otherwise, nothing will happen. You'll be glad you did. I know what you want. You have my word of honor, you'll like it."

The muscles in Jake's neck clenched and he shoved Abbey hard toward Daniel. She fell and slid toward him, scraping her throat and cheek. Five Stone went for her again, but an arrow ripped into the dirt at the Indian's feet.

Daniel stretched out his arm, took her hand, and whispered. "Will's at the bottom of the hill. Walk until you're out of the light, then run like hell. Follow the stream. You'll find Hawk holding Scout."

She nodded, reluctant to release his hand.

It didn't matter for Abbey had no time to run. The moment Daniel released her hand, Five Stone pounced. In one athletic movement he plucked her out of the night like an eagle snags a fish from the lake and tucked her under his massive arm. *Good Lord*, thought Daniel, *he doesn't look real. He's a monster.*

And the giant with his other long arm swung his tomahawk and cut off Jake's head. With Jake's mouth in a silent scream the bloody head rolled toward Daniel who fell back on his elbows. Abbey fainted. Silence reigned on the entire hill.

Five Stone retrieved his tomahawk, his legs planted like tree trunks, and pointed the weapon at Will. "Bring up your black horse and," he looked at Daniel, "and his rifle. You want her alive do exactly as I say."

He jerked Abbey higher against his huge shoulder. "Bring her horse and a blanket for her." He walked over to Daniel. With no warning he brought down his gigantic foot on Daniel's s shoulder. Bones snapped. Daniel screamed. Five Stone bent and removed the stilettos from Daniel's boots and the Smith and Wesson from his belt. He threw the weapons into the night. Will Thunder Cloud, frozen in fear for Abbey's life met Five Stone's demands. He brought up Drum and Scout. He held out the robe for Abbey and two wool blankets, but the Indian shook the tomahawk toward him. No one spoke. Five Stone easily mounted, placing the limp girl in front of him He took the rifle and blankets from Will, then leading Scout he turned Drum, dramatically making the horse rear, and headed due north with all the aplomb of a medieval knight.

Will's voice rang loud and true. "Stay alive Abbey. I will find you."

27

CANADA

The rogue Indians and hunters' crew evaporated into the night. Daniel, in spite of the pain, reminded them all of their first priority: "The children. We must protect them."

He looked at Will. "We'll get Abbey. Keep your head." Will brought Wakanda and the horses up to the hill where she set Daniel's collarbone and shoulder, which took some time. The collarbone was broken and his shoulder out of joint. No one spoke. The pain pulled him into a limp, helpless, heap. He wasn't beaten, but he knew he needed to heal. Wakanda took over as the leader and cut to the quick. "You cannot follow your sister. I'm sending Will."

She handed her son a heavy coat and a bag of supplies. She glanced to Daniel. "I'm giving him Ruby."

Daniel nodded. He groaned a little as he lifted his head toward Wakanda and Will. His words came out in painful stutters. "Send any telegrams directly to Camelann._We should board the train in two days and be in Camelann four days from now." With his good hand he took Will's. "Take my map—we'll mail one to Red Cloud—and take one of the Indians with you. I'd send Crazy Horse, but I want him to protect the children." He paused and looked around the group. "The children are our first priority. Don't do anything foolish, Will Thunder Cloud. I need you. Abbey's tough. She'll have Five Stone eating out of her hand."

FIVE STONE DIDN'T quite eat out of her hand, for she slept for two days, slept as if catatonic. Five Stone worried about her. He believed in omens. Could this be one? He feared his lust for the girl brought the bad luck. Would his desire kill her? He'd possessed few women in his lifetime, maybe five, mostly because of his size, but also his shyness. He knew if he did what he wanted to do to them, he'd hurt them. He had killed the first woman he'd taken.

On the second night the air turned chilly and brilliant golden and blue lights lit the northern sky. She continued to sleep. He rode all night with the girl rolled up in the buffalo robe; he attached her like a bandolier across his chest. He could feel her heartbeat. Her heat kept him warm, and he liked knowing she was still alive. He liked, too, the horse and the rifle.

In the morning she still slept, he shot and ate a rabbit raw. The girl woke for a moment, looked at the raw meat and blood in his mouth, stumbled into some bushes, came out, and curled up in the blanket. He tied his wrist to hers and they both slept. That night they crossed into Canada. Columbine and wildflowers might be sprouting in the Dakotas, but Canada was cold, the earth stone hard.

DANIEL DICTATED A note to Wakanda and Lobo took it to Alfred Jenner, the Fremont Outfitter who returned with Lobo. He checked out Daniel's shoulder and complimented Wakanda on her setting of the joint and the bandaging. He cut Daniel's hair and shaved him then helped him into clean clothes. Alfred stayed the night. He and Wakanda gave Daniel hypodermic needles of morphine throughout the night.

In the morning, he set up shop on a large rock near the river, and all the boys— except Owl, who still preferred dresses and long hair—waited their turn.

When the haircuts were finished, Daniel managed to eat a little oatmeal with molasses. The nausea was gone and with the morphine the pain was manageable. Wakanda told him his pain wasn't as bad as childbirth. He didn't believe her. The children bunched their ponies around him as if they were protecting their leader. Will had taken Ruby; the giant had taken Drum and Scout. Wakanda led the children in prayer for Will and Abbey's safety. The children looked at their leaders wide-eyed and insisted they include Ruby, Drum, and Scout in the prayers.

Daniel was still embarrassed that he'd laid there like a helpless heifer and allowed Five Stone to kill Jake, take Abbey, and stomp on his shoulder. In all honesty, he'd been flabbergasted, stunned, in shock, over Jake's head rolling toward him. During the war a decapitated soldier's head had shed blood and teeth all over him, but somehow this was worse, perhaps because although he hated Jake Hunt, he knew him. The rolling head with the silent scream-ing mouth wouldn't leave his mind's eye.

Only Wakanda had kept her head, so to speak, spewing orders like a commanding general. After she'd sent Will on Ruby with Big Bear to follow Five Stone and Abbey, she pulled off miracle after miracle. First, she picked up Jake's head by his hair and carried it over to his body. To Fish and Dusty she said, "Dig two holes. Put the head in one, the body in another. Keep them apart and bury them over there." She pointed to the river. "I don't want to see them again. Next, she fixed up Daniel, setting his shoulder, no easy feat, then pulling morphine and a hypodermic needle out of her bag. The needle in use during the war was new to Wakanda. The doctor at the fort had given it to her. However, unsure of how much to give him, the morphine all but knocked the big man out.

Now, she gathered the children and led them to Daniel, who looked at each little face. The children stared at him, wide-eyed and open-mouthed. They had never seen him look so sick or so helpless. He was truly a hero. The giant had stomped on him and he still lived.

He spoke to them now. "We have warned you the *ska*—white people—will stare at you and point, perhaps make hurtful comments. Tomorrow you will ride into town, but when you reach the train, you'll dismount and lead your pony up the ramp. When you see the *ska*, watch them from the edge of your vision. Don't meet their eyes. There will be times later on when you will be able to, but it will not be tomorrow. Just keep your pony calm and ignore any mean thing anyone says to you. Your job tomorrow is to keep your pony calm.

"On the train, each animal has its own stall," he said, "and you will stay with your pony. Later, when the train starts chugging and the ponies get used to the train, you can move about, but until we are underway, stay with them. Talk to them. You understand what is happening, but they don't. We are off on a grand adventure, but your pony has no idea. Talk to him, rub him behind the ears. Keep him clean. That's important. Tell him how green Pennsylvania will be, how beautiful, with lots of big rivers and big trees, and acres of green grass. Your voice calms him."

Wakanda smiled. "We'll be right there with you."

THE NEXT DAY a few horses spooked as they were led up the ramp, but one of the adults always stepped in and helped. Carrot enticements worked wonders, as did sugar cubes. As expected, two drunken wranglers hurled insults at the children, but glares from Crazy Horse and Daniel quashed any further remarks. Even with his arm in a sling his presence was formidable. Alfred had sold Daniel a brand new Winchester rifle. One-handed, he fired it into the air. And no one could out stare Crazy Horse. In little under an hour, all were on board. Goodbyes to the warriors were tearful but brave. Crazy Horse shook Daniel's good arm. Daniel hugged him.

The day grew hot and gray; the humidity became oppressive as storm clouds threatened, so they opened the long sliding doors of the three boxcars. The children climbed on the gates of the stalls and waved farewell to their home as the train slowly headed east. Alfred Jenner walked through the cars on the slow moving train and hugged each child and assured them all he'd send telegrams with any news of Abbey and Will, Ruby, Drum, and Scout.

The horses received their feedbags. Alfred sent along boxed lunches for the humans. Splashing Rabbit went to sit with his grandmother and inspected the wonders in his box: sandwiches, cookies, an apple, and a wooden clown with a large hooked nose and a wooden circle attached by a string to the clown. Rabbit spent hours attempting to hook the circle on the nose. Happy found a doll with red ribbons in her hair in her box. Owen went from child to child searching for Abbey and begging tidbits from the children.

Daniel finally slept in the fresh straw which smelled sweet, mixed with the sage and cedar scents Wakanda had used to bless their three railroad cars.

Part Two

The Indian Academy at Camelann

All we wanted was peace and to be left alone.
CRAZY HORSE, CA 1842-1877

28

TRIAL BY THE FIRE

The morphine helped. Daniel slept a lot. That he stayed awake at all amazed Wakanda.

She spent a long time composing a telegram to Summer Rose. When Daniel did awaken she read it to him; they made a few changes. She knew Daniel's wife was due to deliver a baby any day now and did not want to surprise a pregnant white woman. However, from what Daniel had told her of his wife, she knew Summer was tough. So she held little back, telling Summer Rose about the herd of ponies and school of children accompanying them, of Daniel's injuries. She did not tell of Abbey's marriage to Will or of her abduction. Just the description of Five Stone might send a white woman into labor. She posted the telegram from Toledo, Ohio.

TWELVE HUNDRED MILES north and west of Toledo just across the Canadian-United States border, Abbey awoke, cocooned in the snow-covered buffalo robe. She felt the tug of the rawhide attached to her wrist and knew Five Stone was awake and she feared what he might want. She couldn't sleep, even fake sleep, any longer. Her mind whirled.

Abbey was not naïve. Since she was thirteen, men had wanted her. Some just looked like sick puppy dogs, others had whispered what they wanted, and a few had pulled her into a dark room and tried. Never, though, someone like Five Stone.

Can I fake it? A voice in her head told her to just submit. Will had yelled, *Stay Alive!* To submit, however, wasn't in her makeup. An involuntary shudder coursed through her at the picture in her mind of her captor. Was it rape if she didn't fight him? What was it then? Could she pretend to like his touch? A low voice in her head said, *You don't have to like it. Keep your eyes closed. Your mouth, too.*

Another jerk tugged her arm. She eased up toward the light suddenly aware of how yeasty she smelled. How long had it been since she washed? Her body must be filthy. The fresh air felt like sunshine after a storm. Five Stone knelt beside her face and stroked her hair. He smiled. His little black fox teeth nauseated her.

He thought she was just sick when she ran toward the cover of the tall grass. She threw up and then relieved her bladder then returned to the robe. A small fire roasted two partridges. At least they smelled good. He handed her a cup of water. She drank greedily.

She'd always been good at small talk. Debutantes learn such skills. Now, her mind burrowed for subjects. Thank God he spoke English. "Does your name come from the story of David?" she asked.

He nodded and smiled again, showing his black pointy teeth. She studied the scars on his face and this time she didn't run.

"I always loved that story. Five small stones slew Goliath," she said.

He nodded. "I liked the story, too. I took *Five Stone* as my name. I first heard the story in the Christian School in Detroit. I'm pleased you know it. Few know that part—the stones in David's pouch. They just saw me as the evil giant."

He cut off a thick piece of the partridge breast, juicy and sizzling; he held it by the wing, allowing it to cool, then handed it to her. "Eat. You need nourishment."

She ended up eating an entire partridge.

AT MORGAN'S CORNER, Wakanda met Summer, who was every bit as beautiful and gracious as Daniel and Abbey had said. Nothing seemed to disarm her. She squeezed Wakanda's hand. "Thank you for your telegram." She motioned toward two men with a farm wagon. "Henry and Walter were my bodyguards during the war. They are devoted to Daniel."

Now, the two men gently helped Daniel onto the seat. He absolutely refused to be treated like an invalid. "I insist, Wally, I can sit up beside my wife." He glanced at the ticket window. He knew the station master's wife, Martha Graves, would be watching. He murmured. "Don't let that witch see me weak."

Summer looked at Wakanda, not wanting to usurp her authority. Somehow the two women understood each other. She nodded to Wally and Henry. "I'll drive. Find a couple of horses and help guide the ponies."

Although she was huge and cumbersome with the baby, she greeted each of the children, introducing herself as Daniel's wife, telling them to call her Summer. "I have two small boys. You'll love Camelann." She made a big fuss over Owen and asked the name of each pony, which along with the children's names she somehow remembered. Soon, a string of children followed her. Happy Moonbeam with her very dirty red ribbons jiggling slipped her hand into Summer's.

Suddenly, she noticed Abbey was missing. "Where is Abbey?"

Wakanda put her arm around Summer. She whispered. "I think she's okay. Once you're in the wagon with Daniel, ask him. We don't want to upset the children."

In the wagon, after a long kiss which had the children snickering, Daniel put his good arm on her shoulder. In a low voice, he told her all that had happened, everything from Ed and Jake's homosexuality, how Abbey had lost the baby and run to the Indians, and how Will, a blue-eyed half-breed, Wakanda's son, had saved her. "They married. He's a good man, Summer. I'm proud to call him my brother. If anyone can find Abbey, it will be him. He knows the country; his father's a French Canadian trader. I telegraphed General Sheridan and asked him to give Will and his father any assistance. He sent out patrols from Ft. Buford which is on the Dakota-Canadian border."

"You don't seem overly worried about Abbey."

He sighed deeply. "I am sick with worry, but I've done all I can do." He motioned to his sling. "I would have slowed everyone down, but," he shrugged, "I cannot do anything more. I have to trust. And, I vowed to bring the children here."

She leaned her head against his good shoulder.

"Will and I planned to kill her rather than allow the Indian to take her, but I couldn't do it. I guess Will couldn't either. Five Stone, her abductor, he's a giant, ugliest son of a bitch I've ever seen. He is infatuated with her. I watched how he looked at her. If she can stand his attention, she'll live. That's the last thing Will yelled to her. Stay alive!"

Her voice came out soft. "I never told anyone, but when my parents and brothers died, that was my creed. *Stay alive. Stay alive. Stay alive.* I had to live for them. Live because they couldn't."

Summer clicked the reins and changed the subject. "Where are Ed and Jake? I never trusted Jake. And Ed...I know I sound trite...I always thought she could do better. Ed was nice looking, but he had no substance. The trouble is that after the war not many men, let alone good men, were left."

He sighed deeply. "Ed's hiding out in a cave up on the Yellowstone. Jake is dead." He told her about the decapitation. He knew she was tough as a keg of nails.

They rounded a bend and through the fog emerged the outlines of the high arched bridge. Beyond the bridge smoke curled from the chimney of home, a huge lake sprawled behind it, pewter-colored today because of the cloud cover. Behind the lake lay the mountains. Tears filled Daniel's eyes. He took off his hat and slapped the dampness out of it, then wiped his eyes with his sleeve. Summer reached over and kissed him, long and passionately. The children giggled.

Summer pointed to the bridge. There was Mercy, riding Chester, with two small boys, Gus and Mac perched in front of her, waving. Chester, his warhorse during the war, must have caught Daniel's scent. The big horse whinnied, shook his head, and trotted to his master. The boys held onto his mane. Henry and Wally lifted them down to Daniel.

Five Stone had devised a lean-to of pine boughs and the blankets against the trees. Abbey crawled around the fire and under the back drop and leaned against the tree. "Thank you. I was starved."

Five Stone sat outside the lean-to blocking the wind. He nodded and smiled. "I've never seen anyone sleep like you did."

"I've always done that—slept—when I am frightened." She shrugged.

He sniffed the air. "Are you frightened of me, Little One?"

She nodded and lowered her head. "I know I smell fierce. I need a sweat lodge." She secretly hoped her filthy body might repel him.

He brought over a tin of water and set it in the coals. Although the air held a hint of spring, the cold was bitter. From his pack he pulled out towels, soap, and a comb. He smiled again. Bathe, I would like to watch." He pointed to the soap and towel. "That's the best I can do."

She sensed what he wanted. When she lived in Red Cloud's camp, a Sioux woman held by the Crow told of how her captor protected her because he grew fond of her. So she prayed for strength, and when the water steamed she stood. With all the nonchalance she could muster, she stripped to the waist. Her skin immediately turned to gooseflesh, her nipples to hard points, but she took her time washing her face, her arms. She spent the longest time on her breasts, soaping, rinsing, and drying them. Five Stone never moved, just stared. As she finished, he motioned for her to remove her trousers. She tried to do it slowly, imagining how a seductress might strip, but she was frozen, a mound of goose bumps. Again she soaped, rinsed, and dried her long legs, her feet, her nether parts, acting as if she always disrobed in front of strange giant Indians. His attention kept returning to the blonde patch between her legs.

Finally, Five Stone stood and held out one of the red Hudson Bay blankets and wrapped her in it. He helped her to sit on the far side of the fire inside the lean-to. He tucked her feet inside the blanket.

He then stripped and washed himself. He was quite a sight to see. He was enormous everywhere, his erection was as large as that of a horse. She recalled from somewhere that the Czarina of Russia, Catherine the Great, had slept with a horse. *Why would anyone do such a thing? She must have been insane.*

WHILE WALLY AND Henry directed the horses to the large pasture on the east side of the lake, Summer Rose spread a blanket near the shore. With great difficulty—she was very pregnant and he was extremely awkward because of his injured shoulder—Daniel plopped down beside her, leaning down on his good elbow and fitting his head on what little lap the baby wasn't using. A number of children crowded near them. He made a big fuss of patting and kissing Summer's belly, doing so very properly. And then he kissed her mouth very passionately.

The children giggled. He knew Indian children were not shy. He laid with his head on her lap while she made a list of things they would need, asking the children for suggestions: a milk cow, maybe two, a cook, another Amish girl to help in the kitchen, a large table for the porch.

"We have tipis and blankets. Can we have fresh bread and chicken eggs? Cow's butter?" asked Rabbit.

Daniel requested Lobo to bring his saddlebag. From it he withdrew and handed her a sheaf of papers, rough sketches of a dormitory and schoolrooms.

STILL NAKED, FIVE Stone crawled into the lean-to. His tomahawk, knives, and the rifle lay within reach. He opened a tin of what immediately she recognized as bear grease. The smell could awaken the dead. *Why,* she thought, *did I bathe?*

As if reading her mind, he said, "This will keep you warm and is good for your skin. You'll get used to the smell."

She doubted that.

First, he coated himself, everywhere, with the grease. When he laid her down and removed the blanket, she closed her eyes, and thought about sitting on the hillside with Will, of playing faro. The red blanket was warm against her skin, the air freezing. His big hand, surprisingly smooth and gentle, first coated her back, her bottom, and her legs. He turned her over and did the same to the front of her, spending a great deal of time on her breasts then he spread her legs and worked the grease there.

She stiffened.

"Hush, Little One. I will not harm you. Stay warm."

Again, he tucked the blanket around her and petted her hair. "Thank you for showing me the yellow hair between your legs. I didn't know such a thing could be.

She concentrated on the memory of Will.

WILL THUNDER CLOUD halted to rest the horses. Ruby was exhausted. At dawn a skein of geese squawked overhead and awakened him. He wondered if Abbey could see the same geese? Big Bear had made camp in the lee of a huge rock and built a fire. He made coffee and roasted sausages from the pack Wakanda had thrust at them. He looked up again at another V of geese.

A "V" OF geese awakened them. Five Stone could see she was crying. He touched the scars where Will had cut her wrist so their blood mingled. "Is this from your first husband?"

"No. Will made those. My first husband was spineless."

Five Stone nodded. "Tell me about him." He was interested and wondered how any man would leave this woman.

Abbey started talking and the story of her marriage to Ed tumbled out, how she gave him her heart and her body, how he allowed his friend to beat her, the loss of her baby, how Will helped her, built the cairn.

Five Stone's eyes grew wet and he nodded. "Will Thunder Cloud is a good husband?"

She nodded and cried harder.

He rubbed more bear grease on her arm. "Is he a good father?"

She told of Splashing Rabbit. "He is devoted to his son. His first wife was killed by the Crow."

He stood, still naked. His head bent under the lean-to. The cold obviously didn't faze him. He took her hand, fastening the red blanket tight around her and led her to the edge of the hill where they could look down to the Dakota Territory. He handed her his binoculars and nodded. When she peered through them, she could see Will and Bear packing their horses. She couldn't help but wonder if she'd ever see Will again. Tears ran down her face.

"Your clothes and moccasins are by the fire. Get dressed."

When she returned, he brought up Scout and wrapped the bright red blanket around her shoulders again. He smiled slightly. "Go slow. The trail is rough." As he hoisted her into the saddle he added, "You'll not forget me. Now go to your husband before I change my mind and keep you."

As she lifted the reins, her hands began to shake and the corner of her mouth quivered. She wanted to thank him for not raping her, but to do such a thing seemed wrong. Words just didn't come to mind. She reached out quickly touching the side of his face, then nudged Scout down the trail and didn't look back.

THEY WERE JUST specks on the Dakota landscape when Five Stone pulled on his moccasins and buckskins. He packed up Drum and doused the fire then headed first east through Saskatchewan then southeast skirting Lake Superior. He walked leading the horse. He was in no hurry.

29

CAMELANN

Hours later in their familiar bed, Daniel settled the quilt over them and spooned his body around his wife. Clean, shaved, well fed, and somewhat sated, he kissed her shoulder.

"I almost forgot how soft your skin is. I missed you terribly," he whispered, nuzzling into her neck. "I wouldn't even allow myself to think of you, or I'd ache with wanting. There was no way I could not touch you tonight, and once I did, I could not stop. I need you like I need air.

"And ... I want you again," he whispered. He ran his good hand down her shoulder to her belly and received a powerful yet reassuring kick from the baby. He pulled his hand back quickly as if the blow had hurt. "Good Grief. Do you think he's angry with me?"

Summer, giggling a little, turned and kissed his cheek. "I'm sure he or she is furious. You not only woke the baby, but he or she's had me all to himself or herself for the past six weeks." Her body trembling with suppressed laughter. "Wakanda—by the way, I love her—she told me to be sure to bed you tonight, and she gave me tea made from raspberry leaves. Apparently both are Lakota methods to speed the baby's birth."

She reached up and stroked his jaw, ran her fingers down his neck to the shoulder that was not bandaged. "I needed you as much as you needed me, but this time maybe I'll settle for a backrub." She wiggled the baby into a soft pocket of the feather mattress and felt her husband's hand, warm and solid, knead the small of her back. "Oh, that feels heavenly. Daniel, how on earth did you convince Flora and Howie to move to Jack's cabin?"

His big hand smoothed down the sides of her hips, her thighs, and back up. "I told Howie the ducks don't go up to that end of the lake." His hands drifted over her buttocks and to her flanks, just skimming the sides of her breasts.

"But they do."

He lifted her hair and kissed the back of her neck, then pressed long, heated kisses down the cleft of her spine. "I know. When he complains, I'll tell him I was mistaken. By then let's hope they like the privacy or perhaps they'll go back to Scotland."

Summer murmured. "Do that again. It is so good to have you home. Don't count on them returning to Scotland. Flora wants to be around the grandchildren, and Howie is a Presbyterian minister. He'd like to build a church here."

Daniel groaned. "What if I don't want a church on Camelann? When did they get married?"

"About six months ago in Scotland. Cousin Elsie gave them steamship tickets to America for a wedding present."

Daniel chuckled. "That says a lot. Are they broke?"

"She is your mother, Daniel. I'm happy she's not sobbing like she did at Abbey's wedding. In fact, it seems odd she isn't."

With his good hand he pulled her close. "I haven't figured that out yet. Why isn't she bawling? I just want Will and Abbey, when they get here, to stay in the guest cottage. It's perfect—close to us, but separate. I know they need to be near the Indian children, but I think this will be their first time in a real bed with any semblance of privacy."

She snuggled against him. "You sound so sure Abbey will be rescued."

"I have to think like that. You know, as soon as my shoulder heals I will go after them. I feel as if he's the brother I've always wanted.

"And I doubt Five Stone will hurt Abbey, at least not kill her. And Will… "

His arm tightened around her. "I want you to get to know him. It's like…"

She turned to her other side and ran her hands across his shoulder, down his chest then the sleek line of his ribs.

"Your hand keeps wandering," she purred. "No, don't stop. I like what you're doing. Good Lord, that feels wonderful."

"He or she will hate me."

"Ah, perhaps. But I will love you."

DANIEL WEARING HIS dark green bathrobe walked toward the kitchen door. Two naked toddlers perched on his good arm.

He nodded to Mercy. "Stay away from the windows over-looking the lake," I'm taking the twins skinny-dipping. We all need a good scrub."

Mercy ran from the room, a horrified expression on her face. Orphaned by the war, Mercy had cared for the twins since they were born, but she was painfully shy. Her communication was limited to nods, shrugs, and one-syllable words. Summer caught up with the girl and put an arm around her shoulder and kissed her cheek with affection. That's as close as she dared get to Mercy. Otherwise, the girl would jerk away. She was like that with Irene, too. Irene Wood was the nurse who first found Mercy lying in her murdered mother's arms. She'd matched the orphaned girl to Summer and Daniel to help with the twins.

Summer said, "Just ignore him. He's excited to see his boys again, and I suppose he wants a warm bath. I know his shoulder hurts a great deal. You know how warm the lake is. Help me fix this basket of biscuits, and we'll walk over to the Indian Camp." She nudged Mercy toward the kitchen. Once there, she covered a tray of golden biscuit sandwiches with a slightly dampened towel and left them warming on the shelf above the stove for Daniel and the twins. Mercy took the basket of treats.

The forest vibrated with birdsong and the hum of bees and bugs. Overhead the hawks screeched and wheeled through the labyrinth of greenery. As they crested the hill, the scent of wood smoke and the sound of laughter reached them. By the tipis three figures sat on a buffalo robe, and Summer Rose had to squint to make out the little group. When she did, she smiled in surprise. Her mother-in-law, coiffed to perfection and holding a mint green parasol, sat next to Wakanda, sipping tea and licking her fingers, savoring one of Wakanda's molasses buns. Daniel's mother wore beautiful beadwork slippers and a headband. And—wonder of wonders—Howie was in the process of feeding a bottle of milk to a newborn foal. The animal lay like a dog along his leg, happily suckling as if Howie were its mother.

"I thought you sneezed near horses," Summer Rose said as they approached. She nodded a hello to Daniel's mother and Wakanda.

Howie beamed. "I must tell you, Summer dear, I woke in the middle of the night and realized I had not sneezed or wheezed once, not *once*, mind you. Not even amid all those new horses yesterday. This must be an omen from God. I woke Flora, and we moseyed out here first thing to see if it could be true."

He lifted his chin to Wakanda for he had his hands full with the bottle and the foal. "Now look at me! Her mama doesn't have any milk, so we're bottle-feeding this wee one. Isn't he a rare beauty?" He ran a hand along the colt's flank. "Wakanda tells us these particular horses don't cause sneezing and wheezing. You've no idea how this changes my life. I need to speak with your husband, Summer darling, about buying this little fellow and another so I can ride right away."

Summer nodded and Mercy handed the basket of biscuits to Wakanda. As Summer leaned down beside the foal, she ran a hand along his spine. "You're gorgeous." The colt was a rich chestnut color with a flaxen-colored hairbrush of a mane, a matching wispy tail, and a blond star smack in the middle of his forehead. "He is," Summer agreed as she stood. "And he—"

A sharp pain ripped through her so hard she doubled over and grabbed Mercy's arm. Water gushed from her, and she stood helpless, looking aghast at the spreading moisture at her feet. Wakanda and Flora knew what was happening and helped her inside the tipi and onto a pallet.

"Where's Daniel?" asked Flora. "I'll send one of the Indian girls for him." She stood in the tipi's entrance, directing.

Wakanda placed an arm about Daniel's mother. "*Merci*, Mrs. Tuttle, send Hawk or Lobo. They're very fast in the canoe. Tell them the baby's coming. Please start a fresh pot of water to boil and bring in my medicine chest." She smiled placidly at Howie, whose face glowed scarlet against his ginger hair. "Just keep feeding the foal, Sir."

She stepped back inside the tipi, closed the fly, and opened the top vents. She lit a thick bunch of sage and cedar and waved it around the tipi.

"Daniel told me your doctor is away," she said. "I can help with the baby if you would like."

BY THE TIME Daniel arrived, carrying his socks and boots, and wearing dark trousers and a loose white cotton shirt, Summer Rose was dressed in a white robe provided by Wakanda, her hair was fixed in a tight braid.

Wakanda nodded to Flora, her manner discouraging any argument "Please keep the small children entertained with stories or games. You can tell them I'm here, but keep them out of the tipi."

She turned to Daniel. "Your wife wants you here, and no, we don't have time to go back to the house. The baby is ready."

Daniel winked at Summer Rose, feigning confidence. He'd delivered countless foals, but the birth of his child…

Summer took his hand and pressed it to her belly. "Lie beside me, Daniel."

He did, and she pointed to the top of the tipi. "Look up. The light is magical. With the sunlight coming through the buffalo hide it's like looking out from inside amber, all golden and magical. And ancient."

Wakanda hummed in a singsong voice and waved her burning sage. Daniel and Summer Rose heard the children's shouts and laughter, and felt the ponies' hooves pounding the earth. The scent of the lake and grass snuck under the walls of buffalo hides and mixed with the sage and cedar.

"Just hold me, love," Summer whispered. "I feel as if all time is hovering right here."

An hour later, a big baby boy lay wrapped and snug in his mother's arms. Wakanda had helped Summer Rose bathe and dress in a clean gown. She looked beautiful. Daniel leaned on his good side and studied his new son, then stretched and kissed his wife.

"Our third son, thank you." He gave her a little smile. "That seemed almost effortless. Much easier than the last time. Was it?"

A tiny smile curled on her lips, and she reached up to touch his cheek "Easier, but not effortless," she assured him. "After all, it was only one baby this time."

She nodded toward Wakanda, who busied herself cleaning up the area, putting away bottles, rummaging through her medicine chest, folding clothes. "Maybe it was Wakanda, or perhaps this place, but this time was calmer, more spiritual. I'm not sure how, but I felt the spirits of my mother and grandmothers surrounding me, welcoming the baby, even the spirits of women from way, way back, women who I've never met." She bent close to Daniel and whispered. "Did you see anything?"

He frowned, looking unsure. "I didn't see anything, nothing like a ghost. But I know what you mean. There was something … something almost unearthly here, something ethereal." He shivered. "If they were spirits, they were kind ones." He ran a finger over his new son's cheek, his eyes crinkled. "Just look at him. Isn't he perfect?"

She nodded. Their new son was beautiful: smooth-skinned, even featured, and flaxen-haired like his father, like the mane of the colt Howie was nurturing. The twins had been red-faced and wrinkled at birth, but this child looked as if his journey into this world had been easy.

Wakanda stooped beside them. "Stay here and rest. Everyone is clamoring to see him, especially your mother, Daniel." She smiled at the baby. "He's beautiful. What's his name?"

They had spent no time discussing names, but Summer Rose already knew what it was. "John Alexander Charteris," she said, not a shred of hesitation or doubt in her voice.

Daniel looked surprised. "Where did that come from?"

"I have no idea, but as he was born I heard the name inside my head. It's the name he wants. I like it."

Daniel lifted the baby from his wife's arms and kissed the smooth forehead. He'd forgotten how tiny the twins had been at birth. For a moment he just held his son, absorbing his sweet baby smell, studying the tiny creases below his eyes, feeling his heartbeat, which thudded like a steady tiny tattoo of a drum against Daniel's fingertips.

"John Alexander Charteris," he said quietly. "I like your choice of names. In fact, I like everything about you."

Daniel took him outside the tipi and briefly introduced his new son to those waiting, but he returned quickly to his wife, placing the baby beside her. Summer Rose spent the afternoon relaxing, napping, and preparing to nurse the baby. Curious little faces kept peeking through the fly, hoping for an invitation, so eventually Wakanda helped Summer dress and shuffled outside to the buffalo robe. She sat in the dappled shade holding court with her new son, introducing him to his brothers. All the children at the camp marched by, and word of the birth flowed through the community. Now, armed with an excuse to come over to check out rumors about the mysterious happenings at Camelann, a few neighbors arrived, bearing food and gifts for the baby. Huge curiosities tagged after them.

DANIEL WASN'T ALTOGETHER surprised when an impromptu dinner evolved, overseen by Margie Zimmerman, and Wakanda. Once the news was out, folks would want to learn the particulars of not only the new baby but also the emerging Indian village and school. He understood. He also understood they weren't all going to be too pleased with the plan or him.

Ezra and Margie Zimmerman, long time members of the Amish community, lived on the nearest farm and had known Summer Rose all her life. Ezra had built the coffins for her parents and brothers; Margie had been like a second mother to Summer Rose during those horrible months after her family died.

After dinner a few neighbors left, but the children, both white and Indian, played hide and seek and chased fireflies. Wakanda walked about, refilling coffee cups, offering cookies.

Wally and Rachel Saxon, tenets, stayed. Wally and Ezra argued about everything. Summer suspected they both simply liked to argue.

Around nightfall, Lew Graves, the stationmaster who lost his arm in the war, drove his buckboard into the Indian Village. He handed Daniel a telegram, and Daniel, although he wanted to rip it open, casually put it in his shirt pocket. He knew better. Lew's wife, Martha, was the county's chief gossip. Daniel didn't want Lew telling Martha how he ripped open the telegram and jumped for joy or not. He led Lew over to Summer and the new baby. Wally handed Lew a mug of beer.

The night sky filled with a canopy of stars, and the men and women segregated themselves onto separate sides of the fire. Daniel sat near Ezra and Wally. The women gravitated toward the new mother and baby.

Daniel removed his hat and swiped his forehead with his sleeve. It was time to get to business.

"We're going to need a barn—a big one—as soon as possible. But before that I'd like to start work on a two-story building, which can serve as a dormitory upstairs with classrooms downstairs. I've made some sketches." He nodded to Wally and Ezra. "For the Indian School."

Howie and Daniel's mother had already offered a generous amount for the colt. They'd even hinted at buying some ground situated on a hill away from the lake, with a good view of the bridge-—away from the ducks—for their own cottage and a church. Daniel wasn't positive how he felt about living in such close proximity to his mother, but he certainly couldn't say no.

Ezra fumbled about, lighting his pipe and finally settled back. He nodded toward the women. "No offense, but I have to tell you some folks are not too happy about Indians living here. They especially fear the Sioux."

Daniel looked around the group, rubbing his knuckles along his moustache. "What are they saying?"

Ezra looked uncomfortable. His eyes swept Wakanda, Lobo and Hawk, the Indian children. He huffed on his pipe, finally achieving a robust glow. "Understand, this is not my opinion. But others are saying they aren't citizens. They're afraid they'll be murdered in their beds. And they're wondering how you, Daniel, a former general, could bring savages into our midst." He held up his hands. "Remember, I'm just the messenger."

Daniel bristled, even though he knew this would come up. "These children are innocents, Ezra. For Goodness' sake, they're only six to nine years old. Two of them are only four. The teenagers ... well, you couldn't find nicer youngsters." He shook his head, looking exasperated, and nodded toward Wakanda. "This gracious Indian woman isn't about to murder anyone. She is Red Cloud's sister. Her son, Will Thunder Cloud, translated for the treaties." He motioned toward the darkening mountains, toward Gettysburg. "How quickly people forget what we fought *for: Four score and seven years ago our fathers brought forth on this continent a new nation, conceived in liberty, and dedicated to the proposition that all men are created equal.'* Our government just gave the Negros citizenship, but not the Native Americans? Makes no sense."

He took a deep breath and let it out slowly. "I can tell you, I'm going to see what I can do to change such legislation, but first—will you build for us? I can get someone else, but I'd rather have you."

Ezra didn't have a chance to answer. Wally Saxon leaned forward. Still in his twenties, extremely intense and slightly scruffy, he'd been a private under Daniel's command during the war and one of Summer's bodyguards. Devoted to all the Charteris, he usually accepted Daniel's views without any opposition. Not this time.

"My oldest brother's family, Sir, homesteaded to Colorado in '64. His neighbors were murdered and mutilated by the savages. They stole the babies. You know they carry spears with scalps hanging on them? They sew fringes of the women's hair, their braids on their saddle blankets."

Summer Rose looked over. The muscles along Daniel's jaw tensed as if he were about to chomp down and tear meat from a bone. Raw.

"I know what you're talking about," he said quietly. "The story ran in the papers for weeks. Is your brother's family okay? "

Wally nodded. "The neighbors were killed."

"Five adults were killed." Daniel slowly surveyed the group. "The U.S. Army retaliated by wiping out an Indian village of four to five hundred Sioux, more than half of them women and children." He lowered his voice making sure the children couldn't hear. "They bashed in the brains of the children, bayoneted babies in arms, burned their lodges, confiscated their supplies, and ran off their horses and mules."

Point made, Daniel calmed his voice, but there was still well-contained fury in it. "Such things make bad blood all around.

Trust me Wally, every Plains Indian has a reason to want a white man's scalp."

For a moment, the only sounds came from the crackling of the fire and the steady croaking of the peepers.

Daniel spoke again, his voice low and steady. "That's why we brought the children here. Our intention is to educate the children so they can return to their villages and school the next generation. Change is rolling right across this country in the wake of the transcontinental railroad. Full out war with the Indians is coming, too. Will Thunder Cloud, Wakanda's son is coming to live here on Camelann. He and I both believe that only through knowledge can we break this vicious cycle of revenge and retaliation."

He stood, walked around the fire then knelt before his wife. She placed the new baby in the crook of his good arm.

"Say our John Alexander was kidnapped by the Lakota and taken into their tribe. I cannot imagine the heartbreak. Would I want my beliefs erased from my son? Would I want him to be taught only the language of the Lakota?

"No, I wouldn't.

"Yes, I'd like him to learn to handle a horse like the Indian boys do, to cure beautiful hides like Wakanda does, to live off the land, to track like only an Indian can. I'd want him to learn the Indian ways, but I'd want him to keep his white heritage and knowledge. We're attempting to do just that: allow these children to keep their Indian ways, but learn ours."

Summer Rose stood, and he returned the baby to her. He picked up two lanterns in one of his big hands, handing one to Lobo and one to Hawk. He smiled at the few people still on the shore. "It's been a long day for my wife and sons. Me too. I'm going to take my family home now. Wally, I want you to keep an open mind. We'll talk more tomorrow."

He clamped a cheroot between his teeth and lit a taper from the hot embers and waved to those still sitting around the fire. Lobo helped Summer and the baby into one canoe, Hawk helped Mercy and the twins into the other. Daniel, cumbersome in his sling, sat on the floor of the canoe and leaned against Summer's knee. Lobo shoved off and paddled them toward home.

ONCE OUT OF sight of the fire, Daniel lit his cheroot with the taper and opened the telegram. It was from Alfred Jenner. Carefully worded so not to disclose unnecessary information, it read:

GIRL SAFE WITH WILL STOP BOARDING AT FREMONT TOMORROW STOP GOD BLESS

He bent double and with his good arm hugged his wife and baby then threw his head back and looked up to the stars. He read the telegram aloud. Lobo lifted the paddle and shouted a "Yahoo!"

30

NO COINCIDENCES

Summer stood at the kitchen sink watching in the distance as Will and Abbey walked along the lakeshore. The trees along the water now in full leaf fluttered in the breeze as hawks circled above. Behind them the frame of the chapel silhouetted against the woods. Will and Abbey held hands, she leaned into his arm, he kissed her cheek and hugged her. Outwardly, they appeared, as happy as if Five Stone had never come into their lives.

Summer knew better though. She sensed Abbey's fears. Just this morning Abbey had sat across from her, her hands twisted. "No one, not even Will, believes me. Five Stone did not molest me."

Summer reached across the table and petted Abbey's arm. "I won't lie to you Abbey. People are talking. They know what happens to captives. They've seen and heard of how they're treated." Summer let loose a nervous chuckle. "And, trust me, everyone suspects and is watching your waistline."

Abbey hugged Otto, Summer's newest kitten, a blue-eyed, gray puff of fur, tight to her chest. "Well, to make matters more interesting. I am pregnant with Will's child. Everyone will be watching my waistline for the wrong reason. Please, Summer, just make sure Danny knows."

The kitten jerked out of Abbey's lap and walked across the table. Summer swooped him up, clutching him to her chest. The kitten's eyes were as blue as Will's. "I've found it does no good to worry ahead of time. Maybe the baby will have blue eyes and all your troubles will vanish."

Abbey wrung her hands. "As hard as I might try, I cannot imagine giving birth to a baby that wasn't my husband's."

Summer stood and lowered Otto to the floor. Anger welled in her chest. She cleared the tea things and turned her back to Abbey. As she filled the dishpan with hot water, Otto wrapped about her ankles. *Little do you know sweetheart,* she thought. *You do not have a patent on bad luck. I've had my share of rotten luck, too.*

She thought of her own anguish when the twins were born, one twin was Daniel's son and one was Hal's. Thoughts whirled in her head. *You think you have problems sweetheart, try giving birth to the son of your husband's best friend.* She remembered and fought back tears. *One sweet little twin, all blond, was the spitting image of Daniel; the other twin's bottom was stamped with a birthmark—a wild goose—identical to the one on Hal's backside. The damn goose loudly announced my infidelity to Daniel. Don't cry to me, about bad luck.*

Ray had explained the unique phenomena of super-fecundation also known as dual paternity of twins. In other words, twins who were fathered by two men. Such things happened in the barnyard to cats and goats, and it happened to people, as well. When Daniel was presumed hanged and dead, during the war, Summer, heartbroken and drunk, slept with Hal. He did seduce her, but obviously she must have participated. Daniel found them naked in bed and his wild temper snapped. He ended up raping her.

Neither of them was at all proud of their behavior, but the result had been Gussie. Now in her mind, she pictured their dark-haired, blue-eyed boy. What would she or Daniel do without sweet little Gus? Knowing the truth, deciding to not tell anyone of her unfaithfulness or Daniel's rage, they made the decision to protect Gussie with all their resources. Forgiveness cemented their marriage, drew them closer together, and made them aware of something more important than their selfishness.

Now, Summer whipped her head around. She rarely lost her temper, and while she didn't lose it now, she didn't mince words. "Quit feeling sorry for yourself, Abbey. Go out and bring in the wash. There is a mound of mending to do. Busy hands will ease your worry. You are being very selfish. You and Will are having a baby. For God's sake, rejoice! A year ago you'd have sold your eye teeth to be with child."

THE WEATHER HELD all summer, long beautiful days and just enough rain. Everyone worked from sunrise to sunset and often into the night, tending the fields, the vegetable gardens, and the horses. The preparation of breakfast, lunch, and dinner for two dozen people consumed enormous amounts of time. By July, Summer Rose hired Mrs. Helena Love, an Amish woman from Margie's church, to cook for the entire compound.

Mrs. Love, a round, pink grandmother, always in white apron and cap with ties hanging loose, knew how to cook. Every Saturday morning she made apple cider doughnuts. The aroma snuck clear across the lake. Everyone took an eleven o'clock morning break, which they called *elevensies,* and made their way to the door of Summer Rose's kitchen. Adults and children gathered on the back porch, the steps, the stonewall by the lake, and on the grass.

"Thank heaven she only does this once a week," said Summer, as she sunk her teeth into a doughnut, "or I'd never lose this weight I gained with Johnnie."

Her big strong husband came up behind her and kissed her neck. His shoulder had healed and, except for some impairment of his range of motion and mysterious aches when storms approached, it worked fine. He bent and kissed her cheek, whispering. "Don't lose too much. You look pretty good right now." He had trouble keeping his hands off her.

THE AMISH CARPENTERS finished the frames for the horse barn, the dormitory-schoolroom, and Howie's chapel in no time. Daniel and Hal hired any competent hands they could find for the haying and harvesting, and to help expand the pasture fence on the east side of the lake. Hal put to work all the Indian boys six years old or older. Some of the girls helped too.

As the interior of the school-dormitory took form, Abbey, Summer Rose, and Wakanda ordered furniture and linens, kitchen utensils, dishes, and silverware. "I have a little money from my grandparents," Summer Rose told the women. "I want this school to be a first-class operation. We can make clothes for the children, but I want new furniture and bedding, new blankets, sheets, towels, dishes, and glasses. "The children must be so proud of their school, proud enough to send their children here."

"They won't be pampered little brats, though," said Abbey. The three women spent hours in Summer Rose's kitchen devising a fair chore chart for the children's help in cooking, cleaning, and laundry duties. It might not be a huge school, but it was going to be the best Indian school in the country, one the first students could brag about to their grandchildren.

Summer and Abbey rode to Chambersburg with Wakanda, and the Tuttles where they talked to professors at the college about books, maps, and supplies for the classrooms. One of the ministers donated a box of leather bound New Testaments, one for each of the students. Howie proved invaluable, for he had been ordained a Presbyterian minister in Edinburgh. He spoke the language of the church, and while Daniel, Abbey, and Will insisted the school be nondenominational, it followed the beliefs and tenets of the Protestant form of Christianity.

Before the school was ready, the women held classes outside every morning. Howie started each session with a scripture reading and a prayer. At first, the women just taught reading, writing, and arithmetic, though they planned a heavier curriculum come September. Summer opened her own library up to the older children, allowing them to sit on the porch or in her living room and read every afternoon. After just a week of this practice, Summer Rose told Daniel, "I feel so bad asking them to leave. They don't want to stop reading. Isn't that wonderful? Do you think I could let them stay later?"

"Absolutely not," he said, as he spooned against her and removed her nightgown. "We need a little time for us."

UNSOLICITED CONTRIBUTIONS CAME from surprising sources: the Amish families contributed generously in both food and time. The abundance of the Lancaster Valley followed Mrs. Love to their door. Checks arrived from old Philadelphia friends of Flora, Nan Charlotte and her Scottish relatives, Hal and Daniel's fellow officers from the war, and Philadelphia lawyers. Incredibly, Amelia and Harvey St. Clair—the senior partner in the law firm—bought an entire estate library at auction and donated it to the school. A month later a friend of Amelia's donated a piano.

During one of the impromptu doughnut breaks, they were surprised by the arrival of a carriage, top heavy with trunks and cases. It pulled up to the house, the horses covered with lather and churning up clouds of dust. Abbey screeched with excitement when she recognized Hal's wife, Fanny St. Clair, their small sons, and Hal's sister, Emily, who was one of Abbey's best friends.

From the opposite side of the carriage emerged a distinguished gentleman, tall and handsome with graying hair, dressed impeccably in white stock and a tailored suit of rich dark brown wool. A gold chain and fob stretched across his vest. He looked European and remarkably familiar. Next to him stood a pretty, raven-haired girl about the same age as Emily and Abbey.

Will surprised everyone when he stepped forward, smiling, and embraced them both. "What a surprise!" he whispered, then turned to his wife. "Abbey," he said, "I'm pleased to present my father, Nicholas Dupree, and my half-sister, Tilley." He smiled at the lanky, black-haired girl with the slanted blue eyes. "Do you still go by Tilley or do you prefer Matilda now? And how on earth are you here?"

"I'm still Tilley to my friends," she said, as Abbey swept her into a big hug. "Oh, I am so pleased to meet you, Abbey. Emily St. Clair and I were lab partners at the *Ècole de Médecine* in Paris, and when Will wrote and told me of your marriage, I told Emily." She laughed. "And over the course of a few weeks we discovered we were talking about the same Camelann and the same Abbey! We were ecstatic. We were already best friends, so now we're sort of related. Her grandfather invited Daddy and me to a dinner party, and everyone got along, so we traveled out here together."

It took some sorting out as introductions were made all around. The carriage took time to unload, and decisions were made regarding sleeping arrangements. Stories of how they'd all met and became friends, the school, and the sacred ponies were retold many times, and became more elaborate with each bottle of wine. They learned Emily and Tilley had a further bond. They both studied medicine at the *Ècole de Médecine* in Paris and planned to practice medicine in America, which was an almost unheard of ambition for a female.

Mrs. Love produced a delicious lunch of barbequed sausages on rolls and roasted corn, all served under the trees down by the lake.

Whether it was the wine, the gorgeous weather, or simply common interests and stories, the group slid into an easy rapport. Will and Hal had a wealth of stories, and everyone enjoyed teasing Daniel, who was a good sport. The women fluttered around the children like birds at a feeder. They were having so much fun chatting that no one missed Wakanda or the Tuttles until Abbey went to ask her mother-in-law something and couldn't find her.

"Do you think they went over to the tipis?"

For speed, Abbey and Will took the canoe to the tipis, and there they found Wakanda, Nicolas Dupree, and the Tuttles leaning against the fence, watching the sacred ponies. Will's father had removed his jacket and stood casually with one foot on the bottom rail of the fence. From a distance, and in that stance, the resemblance between father and son stunned Abbey. Wakanda, small and beautiful beside him, waved.

Will stopped at the tipi to collect two saddles and a handful of carrots, and Wakanda slapped his hand. "Put those back. They are for soup."

He bent his head and kissed his mother's cheek. "You use saddles in soup? No wonder no one likes your soup." He ducked, laughing, when she smacked his shoulder, then left the saddles on the fence. From the pasture he brought Ruby and a chestnut they'd dubbed Remy—short for Remington, because he was the color of a rifle stock. After some effort involving much bribery with carrots and sugar cubes, both horses were saddled, and Will gave his father a leg up onto Ruby. Will mounted Remy, then took the Henry rifle his mother handed to him.

"We hear mountain lions every night," she reminded him.

"Thanks." Will bent and kissed her cheek, then Abbey's. "I want to show my father the herd and Camelann. I'll see you back at the house. We shouldn't be more than an hour." He reined Remy into a dance then clucked his tongue regretfully at Howie. "I promise. Riding lessons next week."

Abbey, Wakanda, and the Tuttles watched the men settle their mounts into a walk, then cut down the road toward Forty Foot Falls. Howie shook his head. "Wish I could ride like your husband."

Flora studied both the figures on horseback. They wore practically identical white shirts, dark pants, riding boots, and wide brimmed hats. "Mr. Dupree is handling Ruby beautifully," she said as the men stretched the horses into an easy canter. "From a distance, I can barely tell them apart."

EVERYONE SITTING AT the tables heard a shot. Daniel and Hal immediately looked at each other. They knew the shot came from a rifle not a shotgun, which, this time of year made little sense. They didn't want to alarm anyone so remained silent. But as the party continued, Daniel quietly slipped away, riding Chester toward the falls. When he rode back in, he wasn't alone.

It was Rabbit who first spotted them. "There's blood all over Granddad's shirt!" he yelled.

Will's father rode between his son and Daniel, and Hal, on foot, caught him as he slid from Ruby. Will dismounted, while

Daniel took the reins. Will joined Hal and Lobo. They formed a stretcher with their arms and headed toward the house, carrying Nicholas Dupree.

Tilley ran to her father while Emily barked orders to clear the kitchen table, set water to boil, and find clean rags. Summer Rose and Wakanda did her bidding like a well-trained team. Abbey brought Emily's medical bag, then scooted everyone unnecessary out of the way.

Hens in the chicken yard never scrambled faster. Mrs. Love helped Emily into a fresh apron, tying the sash behind her back as the girl scrubbed her hands and arms with good lye soap and near scalding water. Hollering over her shoulder, Emily told everyone within earshot, "They taught us cleanliness is most important, didn't they, Tilley? Scrub, scrub, scrub until it hurts."

WHILE THE WOMEN and Will clustered around the house, Daniel and Hal instructed Hawk and Lobo to guard the road. They took the horses and rode toward the falls in search of unfamiliar tracks.

Emily St. Clair, slender with reddish-brown hair and freckles, possessed sure, gentle hands and a firm confidence, and she knew her patient well. She would be handling this surgery, not Tilley.

"I'm afraid I must ruin your shirt, Mr. Dupree," said Emily, snipping through Egyptian cotton and the undershirt beneath it. "Let's see where this bullet settled."

After gently cleaning his chest and a thorough look with fingers and eyes, she said, "You, Sir, are a most lucky man. The bullet is in a very good spot, well clear of your heart and lungs." She smiled brightly. "And I have chloroform. None of this biting a leather strap while I dig in your chest."

As she talked, Emily handed Summer needles and thread to boil, then kept up an easy chatter. "After the war our Yankee surgeons conferred with their Confederate counterparts. They discovered the Southern wounded fared better than the Northern boys."

Using tongs she laid out instruments on a clean towel. "Can you guess why? They did simply because the rebels ran out of all medical supplies. Instead of thread for stitching, they took hair from their horses' tails and in order to soften the coarse hair, they boiled it, unknowingly sanitizing the thread."

Emily pointed her chin toward her bag. "See the mask? Who feels confident enough to hold it steady and not faint while I probe?"

Nicholas Dupree touched Wakanda's hand. "No one is steadier than Wakanda."

Emily nodded. "Scrub you hands like I do." She took a moment to rewash her hands then set up the gauze in the ether mask and instructed Wakanda on how to operate the flow from the small bottle of chloroform. "Be careful not to inhale the fumes," she said quietly, "or we'll find you on the floor. Only our friend here needs to be asleep. You don't faint at the sight of blood, do you?"

Nicholas' hand came up again and set on Wakanda's arm. He smiled, gazing into Wakanda's eyes. "Never."

DANIEL AND HAL returned from their search. They found nothing so now they waited with the women. When Nicholas awoke from the successful surgery, the men fashioned a stretcher from a door and moved Nicolas to Hal's house. It suited the situation much better than any other of the houses, for it possessed two large first floor guestrooms. Emily and Tilley could share one and watch over the patient in the other.

Because of the attack, Wakanda and the Indian children brought blankets to sleep on Daniel and Summer's porch. Fortunately, the weather remained clear. As the night settled, Daniel again questioned Will on exactly what happened. Will, still shaken, believed the shot had come from the far side of Switchback Falls. He figured his father had been mistaken for him. "Whoever shot my father thought it was me."

Will, Daniel, and the older boys worked in shifts guarding and patrolling the perimeter. They found no tracks near either falls.

The following morning before Mrs. Love's arrival, Ezra, Wally Saxon, and Henry Evers dismounted at the hitching post. Henry Evers, another tenet, had also served under Daniel during the war. They'd heard of the ambush, and both Wally and Henry offered to take shifts of guard duty. Ezra said the men of the Amish community would also take shifts. Today, being Sunday, they would ask at their church for any reports of strangers.

ON MONDAY A letter, postmarked Ft. Laramie, from Mary arrived.

My dearest Abbey,

I'm mailing this to your brother's address in hope he knows where you are. I pray my letter finds you and yours happy and safe. Bizarre rumors are floating around here of Daniel and Will herding a troop of horses across Nebraska. You must tell me about this—if you can— when you write. You know how Ft. Laramie thrives on gossip. If they don't get their daily feed of it, they make it up.

Dame Dilly asked me to pack up your cottage and send the trunk to your brother's house in Camelann. That will go by freight so it will take longer than this letter. Someday I hope to see Camelann. Everyone who knows of Camelann speaks of it as a Garden of Eden. General Sheridan was there. He called it Paradise.

I'm now in possession of an adorable pony named Cricket. One of the Indian women walked into the fort with him. He's a favorite of the wives here.

I started to write that you couldn't imagine the things Dame Dilly has done, but I bet you could guess. I took down all those curtains you made—the ones made of big yellow checks—washed them, and had the laundresses iron them. They were all ready to put in your trunk when Mrs. Dietrich came and took them. Lo and behold, guess where they are now hanging? Take a wild stab. She also took that big Indian rug you bought. She said it would cost too much to ship it. It's now in her dining room along with your curtains. Can you believe the nerve of that woman? And that's not the worst of what she'd done. I truly believe she is evil.

I have the very best news in the world. We are finally expecting a baby! I'm six months along, and I just started showing so I had to tell people. We are both so excited I could barely keep from smiling. I know she must be horribly jealous, but what Dame Dilly did was more than mean. You can imagine how red-faced I am even to write this. She hinted to other officers' wives that the baby might be blond and green-eyed because, if you count back, the baby was conceived about the time Daniel was here. That rumor spread faster than wildfire. I cannot quit crying over it. Can you believe she's so evil? The gossip reached sweet Emmett, and I think he might half believe it. If I have a green-eyed baby, it might just break his heart. Not one person in my family has green eyes. I'm not sure about Emmett's family. I wouldn't dare ask him. Oh that woman! How she could take something that made me so happy then make it so horrible, I'll never understand.

Good Lord, I cannot wait to get out of here. Colonel Dietrich has promised to send us East after the baby is born. He's requested a new artillery officer, and if all happens when it should, we will be home about Christmas. It cannot come soon enough. I am excited about the baby, but Dame Dilly's taken most of the joy out of it.

Write, dear Abbey, stay well, and pray for me.

Love, Mary

P.S. Her insinuations are absolutely not true. I tried to tell a few of the wives about the tea, and they just laughed at me.

31

THE GREEN-EYED MONSTER

Daniel stuck the letter in his pocket, his expression tight. "Thank you for showing me this, Abbey." He sighed and shook his head. "You know, I've been the object of gossip most of my life. Most times I can just shrug it off, but not this time. I'll have to show this to Summer."

Abbey started to say something, but he interrupted her. "We don't hide anything from each other."

He waited until evening while she was nursing the baby in their bedroom. He brought over the candle, careful not to splash any wax on Johnnie, and gave her the letter. He sat on the little love seat beside her and pretended to read the paper, but secretly watched her through his lashes as she read. When she finished, she folded it and handed it back to him, but didn't say anything. She finished nursing, changed the baby's diaper then returned him to the cradle.

When she settled beside him again, she said, "Poor Mary. If she has a green-eyed baby, all hell is going to break loose. There is a chance, you know, she could have a green-eyed baby. I'm not saying—er—you're involved. I know that isn't true. But Mary's been out there in that godforsaken place all by herself ..."

She shimmied out of her dress, down to her shift. "Emmett would be humiliated. I can see how he would be upset by this rumor. I don't even know this woman and I'm furious with her. Our Mary is all alone with those silly women who apparently don't have enough to do. We need to help her."

"But—"

"No buts, darling. This Dame Dilly, or whatever her name is, has set up a very dangerous situation for Mary. Mary's a very nice girl, and I can see how you almost married her. Let's invite her here. That's the only solution." In a deft move, she dropped her shift and pulled on her nightgown without exposing an inch of flesh above her knees, even though Daniel was watching carefully. "You telegraph General Sheridan and arrange the train and an escort. I'll wire Mary tomorrow. The telegram has to come from me—your wife. If I do such a thing it will take an enormous lot of wind out of that infuriating woman's sails. Tomorrow, will you help me compose a very succinct telegram to Dame What's-Her-Name?"

She shook her head, obviously angry. "If the baby is green-eyed, we'll have time to think of something long before Emmett or that wicked woman sees the baby. What do you think?"

Speechless, Daniel just sat there like a rock, staring at his wife. In a million years he never would have expected this reaction. Then again, Summer Rose never did think like most people.

"Where will she stay? We're a little full, and we're not a maternity hospital."

She giggled. "Perhaps we are. We have Emily and Tilley and Wakanda to deliver and care for the babies. She can stay with your mother and Howie. There are two extra bedrooms in Jack's cottage. Your mother always liked Mary, didn't she? If I recall she was very upset you didn't marry her. And, Mary will be such a help with the children." She reached behind her and loosened her braid, running her fingers through the dark strands. "They remember her and ask for her every now and then. Speaking of the children, are they still sleeping on the porch?"

He removed his shirt and sat on the edge of the bed to take off his boots. "The Indian children? They went back to the tipis. Wally and Henry are patrolling tonight." He puffed out a breath. "Thank God. I'm exhausted. I can barely keep my eyes open."

She threw her hair forward, running her hands through the tangles then tossed it back, a sly smile on her face. "Our Johnnie is sound asleep. Are you too tired to sneak out for a swim with me? Maybe you could wash my hair? After all, Mercy is right across the hall in the boys' room. She can watch all three children."

Every cell in his body woke up. "You can't get pregnant yet, can you?"

Her dark eyebrows wiggled. "Oh, no. I'm safe. I'm nursing."

TWO WEEKS LATER, on a rainy Tuesday morning Summer took the buggy into town to meet Mary Hathaway's train. She insisted on going alone. As she and Mary hugged under Summer Rose's umbrella, Mr. Lewis Graves, the stationmaster, directed a couple of teenage boys to carry Mary's trunks to the buggy. He held the umbrella with his good arm while the two women climbed into the carriage. He shook off most of the water from the umbrella, folded it, and handed it through the window. Water dripped off his visor, and the moisture fogged his wire-rimmed glasses.

"Lots of goings on out there at Camelann, Mrs. Charteris. People are talking. Tell me," he said, "what are you doing with all those savages? And I heard a man was shot? And my wife, she says she's sending a lot of flour out there to your place."

Summer Rose's face heated up, and she forced a smile. "This town thrives on gossip, doesn't it Mr. Graves? I assure you, they are not savages. All but four are children." She snapped the reins and hollered out the window. "In a few weeks we'll be hosting an Open House. You and Mrs. Graves be sure to come and see for yourselves."

She turned to Mary. "Amazing, isn't it? Gossip, gossip, gossip. The world thrives on gossip. Now. How are *you?*"

Mary burst into tears and pressed her hand against Summer Rose's arm. "I cannot begin to tell you how happy I am to be here. When I received your telegram, I just plunked down on the bench and cried. I bawled my head off. Emmett thought I'd finally lost my mind. He sends his thanks, too. He was concerned for my safety. A number of the wives are leaving. The Indians …"

She dabbed at her eyes with a sorry looking handkerchief that needed a good soak and time to bleach in the sun. Summer Rose pulled a large snowy one from her pocket and handed it to Mary.

"Thank you." Mary blew her nose. "And your telegram to Mrs. Dietrich … do you know, she *apologized* to me? No one has *ever* known her to apologize."

Summer Rose removed her glove and took Mary's hand. "When Daniel showed me your letter to Abbey, I knew you couldn't stay there." Her eyes dropped to Mary's swollen midsection. "All that tension cannot be good for the baby. Or you."

Mary reddened from her hairline to her collar. "They showed you my letter? You didn't believe any of that … did you?"

Summer Rose chuckled. "You mean that stuff about Daniel? That green-eyed baby balderdash? Heavens to Betsy! You may have a green-eyed baby, Mary, but I know it won't have anything to do with Daniel." She squeezed Mary's hand. "You cannot imagine the rumors that have reached my ears about Daniel since we've been together. If I believed any of them, why, I wouldn't have any fingernails. I warn all young girls: beware of marrying a good-looking man."

"Fingernails?"

Summer Rose giggled. "Mary, if I ever caught anyone trying to steal my Daniel, I'd scratch her eyes out." She wiggled her well-manicured nails and pointed to the left. "Enough such talk. Around this bend you will see in the distance the bridge my father and brothers built." She patted her heart. "Every time I see it I think of the sacrifice they made. They gave their lives for our country. Doesn't this banter about the color of an unborn baby's eyes seem trite? And beyond that … is Camelann."

The sun popped out and the rain stopped in that moment, and Camelann, the lake, the waterfalls, and the cottages nestled among the trees, spread before them in all its beauty.

"Oh my God. I may never leave."

32

OPEN HOUSE

Daniel's mother stood in his kitchen polishing silver forks and spoons. "Danny, do you remember where my silver tea service went? I do wish we could use it. It makes such an impression, don't you think?"

He shrugged. *More than likely*, he thought, *it was sold when we auctioned all the furnishings to fund your divorce.* "Don't fret, Mother, if we used a silver tea service around here, people would think we were putting on airs."

"And someone might steal it," mumbled Mrs. Love as she dropped another batch of doughnuts in the deep fat.

They decided to hold a late afternoon tea to introduce the community to the children and dedicate the school. Sharp shadows from the two story white building and the creosoted wooden fences cut across the green grass. A United States flag snapped against the brilliant August sky. The building sat not far from Forty Foot Falls, providing a clear view of the lake as well as the cluster of cottages and docks dotting the far shore. Beyond that they could see the horse pastures and mountains. The enormous horse barn—still under construction—stretched along the new road between the school and the houses.

Every dish, glass, cup, fork, and spoon in the community had been pressed into service, all set up on white linen-covered tables situated just outside the dormitory entrance. Mrs. Love's doughnuts, cookies, and cakes sat among offerings of pies and confections from the other women. The teenage Indian girls served coffee, tea, and lemonade, and Daniel and Will primed a keg of beer in a tub of ice. The women visited and gossiped; the men stood next to the fence admiring the horses. Indian and white children all played on the grass with Owen and the farm dogs.

Everyone came dressed to the nines, from brand new John Alexander to Mrs. Waters, the ancient postmistress. The Indian children wore matching sweaters, buckskin, and moccasins, the men donned white shirts and jackets; the ladies wore pastels or calico dresses and straw hats. Wakanda, dressed in full Indian regalia, sat outside the tipi with Will's father, who still wore a sling. The men removed their jackets and hung them on the fence. A baseball game started with the Reverend Tuttle pitching. Earlier, he'd given a short, appropriate sermon dedicating the school. He, also, offered prayers blessing their endeavor.

While most people were enjoying the goodies, Hawk and Lobo, barefoot and shirtless, came down the road riding the matching paints. When they neared the school, they stood on the horses' rumps and put on an amazing show. No one looked anywhere else for the next hour. When they finished, Summer Rose introduced Will Thunder Cloud, his father Nicholas Dupree, Wakanda, and Flora to the crowd. Will brought out a white pony and proceeded to paint him, explaining all the colors and symbols. When he was finished with the horse, he painted a couple of the Indian children's faces, explaining as he did so what the symbols meant. He offered to paint the white children's faces, and was met by such enthusiasm that he enlisted the help of Sun and Star.

The women had hung clotheslines and displayed Wakanda's beautiful buffalo robes and beadwork alongside a few Amish quilts made by Mrs. Love's family. When several people made offers to purchase the robes, Daniel explained they weren't for sale for the simple reason that buffalo hides were scarce because of the United States Government policy of killing the buffalo.

"Not long ago herds numbered forty million, now only thousands are left. I'd like to start breeding them, too. Again, the problem is getting the animals here."

Summer gave a tour of the dormitory, showing off the large, airy sleeping rooms—one for boys and one for girls—with a dozen dark wooden bureaus and a dozen beds in each room. The girls' beds had been made up with snowy white sheets and rich red blankets, and the boys' beds were similar with navy blue blankets, giving a patriotic flavor to the rooms. Two classrooms, study rooms, the dining room, and kitchen were on the first floor. She even impressed the guests by demonstrating the hot and cold running water and flush toilets.

Mrs. Graves looked Will up and down. In an incredulous voice, she asked, "Indians don't go to colleges, do they? Where on earth would they go?"

"Montreal. McGill University," Will said. "I'm not the first Indian to attend college, you know. Dartmouth was founded to educate Indians. Some of Harvard's first graduates were Indians. We plan for a number of these children to attend college."

"You're joking. I thought you meant to train them in a trade," said one of the mountain men who stood by the fence.

"Certainly not the girls?" asked Mrs. Graves.

Daniel used his grin. "Be careful what you say in this crowd, Martha." His pale green eyes flashed toward Emily and Tilley. "These two women are studying to be doctors. They already spent a year in Paris at the *Ècole de Médecine*. My sister and Mary

Hathaway are trained teachers. Summer Rose doesn't have a degree, but her parents educated her as well. Trust me. She's a lot more educated than I am. All of us here believe that only through education will we level the playing field."

Otis Dodd, one of the mountain people who lived across the ridge near Ft. Littleton, cleared his throat. Daniel and Summer Rose referred to him as the Bird Man because of the willow branch birdcage he'd constructed for about thirty finches, which he kept on his front porch.

"Aye, might be good to educate 'em, but why here? They come from Nebraska or someplace out west, right? Educate 'em there."

Daniel had never liked Otis. He swallowed hard, contemplating how to answer him civilly. But it was Summer Rose who spoke up first.

"Mr. Dodd, this land we're sitting on right this minute at one time belonged to the native Americans. Ezra has shown me hundreds of arrowheads he's found while plowing. Our forefathers, God bless them, ran off the natives. A grandmother from this valley told the story of an Indian who walked into her house, scaring her half to death. She was ironing and she threw the hot iron at him. I guess she scared him for he never came back. His tribe just left, moved west."

Otis looked at her as if she were crazy. "Did he not have a deed?'

Nickolas Dupree spoke in his deep bass voice. "I come from a family of French *coureur des bois*, traders and smugglers who cared not a hoot about laws or deeds. We go back a long way, to the time of Nicolette and Radisson and Champlain. The Indians moved west because the Europeans depleted the herds and the beaver. I often think of what a true paradise this land must have been before we came. We took this land from them, Mr.

Dodd. To answer your question, no. They didn't know English or French law."

"Their loss," said Otis. He spit a plug of tobacco toward the school.

Before tomahawks and rifles could be locked into place, Daniel stood and nodded to Will, who came to stand beside him. "Thank you all for coming. I imagine you, like we, have chores and animals to attend."

He purposely bumped Otis, and a silver spoon slid from his weathered vest. Daniel glared down at him. "Do I need to hold you by your ankles and shake you?"

Otis shrugged, flashed a wry smile, and withdrew all of his heist, which was considerable. He dropped everything onto a pile in the grass. "Can't blame a man for trying."

33

GOOD NEWS, BAD NEWS

Good news came in huge waves. Tilley and Emily were accepted into the Women's Medical College of Philadelphia, which had been opened in 1861 by Ann Preston, the first woman to receive a medical degree in the United States. The college offered medical and surgical care of women by women, expanded clinical experience for the college's students, and provided training for nurses. Being accepted there was a dream-come-true.

Of course, their parents worried about their safety and how Philadelphia society would view them. That young, unmarried women, studied the anatomy of the human body ruined their innocence. Nice girls, the ones entering the marriage market, just didn't know such things. Respectable Philadelphia families wanted nothing to do with such women. After much talk, Hal and Fanny found them an apartment half a block from the school, in a respectable doctor's house. Emily's parents furnished it, setting the girls up with everything they could possibly need. Nicholas Dupree imported a housekeeper from Montreal, Mrs. Montour, who cleaned, cooked, and also served as a duenna.

The Indian School at Camelann flourished. The children bloomed with the benefits of good nutrition and healthy surroundings, and they blossomed with knowledge. Abbey taught reading, writing, and spelling to the sixteen younger children. Mary came in the afternoon and told stories and taught rhetoric, grammar and English literature to the older children. Summer taught map reading, geography, and history plus piano to the older children, which included Mercy.

Just spending time with Wakanda enhanced all the children's knowledge. Wakanda told Lakota stories and taught some French, mostly using songs and simple sentences. She also taught tracking and Lakota skills such as curing hides, cooking, and drying foods.

Mrs. Tuttle taught proper table manners. "I don't care Miss Happy Moonbeam if you always ate with your fingers. East of the Mississippi, I advise you to use silverware."

Will taught arithmetic, advanced mathematics, and astronomy, and—of course—Daniel and Will taught hippology, the study of horses.

Howie proved an apt pupil.

WAKANDA AND WILL made an Indian drum, and Wakanda invited the women and girls of Camelann, Indian, white, and Amish, to participate in the Birthing of the Drum Ceremony. The eclectic group of women from Happy Moonbeam and Sweet Owl, who still wanted to stay with the women despite his gender, to Mrs. Love and her daughters, gathered, sitting in a semi-circle around the roaring bonfire and the new drum which rested in the center of the semi-circle between the women and the fire.

The lake stretched as a backdrop to the fire, and the men and non-participating neighbors sat on a hillside behind the women. A fat moon spread silver across the lake. Wakanda had instructed the women to all wear flouncy long skirts

Will and Bear started an ancient four beat rhythm on old hand drums. First, in voices as soft as kittens purring, the Indian men chanted along with the rhythm then the women and children joined. Wakanda and the teenage girls stood and swayed moving their hips in a circle to swish their skirts. The little Indian girls followed then Mrs. Love, the Amish girls, Abbey and Summer Rose joined the swaying women as Wakanda slowly led them over the new drum where each woman squatted pretending to give birth. The beat of the rhythm increased, the purring gradually grew to a low growl, then to a whirling frenzy. At a crescendo the women collapsed. For a long time they lay in the silver light until Wakanda rose and stretched her arms toward the moon. Sweet Flower Moon Drum.

A VERY PREGNANT Mary, growing fat and happy, glowed with good health.

One last piece of good news—though she was hesitant to call it exactly that—was Summer Rose was pregnant—their fourth child. "Every time he looks at me, I become with child. Am I going to have a baby *every* year?"

Wakanda, in a rare fit of laughter, said between snorts, "I doubt, Miss Summer Rose, that Daniel looking at you has anything to do with your condition."

Daniel, who came around the corner just then, tried to keep a straight face. He said, "I beg to differ, Wakanda. It has everything to with my looking at her." He snuck an arm around his wife's waist and pulled her close against him. "You snap back so fast, I can't keep my eyes or hands off you."

BAD NEWS CAME in long letters.

From Ft. Laramie, Emmett in his neat penmanship wrote:

"My dear Mary,

The tribes have gathered under Red Cloud. He's now the top leader, and he is whopping angry. He's determined to keep the Bozeman Trail closed, and I'm afraid his work is cut out for him, because back about mid-May Colonel Henry Carrington marched in with the 700 men of the 2nd Battalion, 18th U.S. Infantry Regiment with orders to build two more forts north of Ft. Reno. With him came Pope's 3rd Battalion, who are to man the forts. The Army has blatantly lied to all the tribes.

Man-Afraid-Of-His-Horse slipped into second in command, which I don't think he minds. At least two thousand warriors under Red Cloud's command, harass the forts along the Bozeman. Fort Phil Kearney is completed—12 acres surrounded by stockade.

We are constantly on alert. I am so happy you are safe in Pennsylvania. This is no place for a woman with child. The walls of Old Bedlam vibrate every Saturday night, and Ft. Laramie still resonates with gossip. I heard talk of Abbey living with Will. Tell them not to come back here. The ladies say Abbey went native, and they don't like it. And above all else give my thanks again to Summer Rose and Daniel for taking such good care of you. I hope to join you by Thanksgiving or at the latest by Christmas. Take good care of my son.

Love, Emmett"

Major General Phil Sheridan wrote a much shorter missive to Summer and Daniel.

"General Dunn and I will be in the area of Camelann about mid-October. Would this be a convenient time for a visit?"

Summer Rose rolled her eyes, and Daniel understood why. Johnnie was finally sleeping through the night and was now in his own crib in the nursery, so she wasn't quite as exhausted, but the thought of more houseguests did not excite her. Fortunately, she told him, Flora and Howie had improved tenfold with Daniel's presence. And now that Mary lived out at the Tuttles' cottage, she and Flora entertained each other. Tilley and Emily had moved into their Philadelphia apartment, and Will's father had returned to Canada. She suggested to Daniel that perhaps Hal and Fanny would host the generals. After all, their cottage was larger and more elegant. They had those two first floor guestrooms and indoor plumbing.

As it turned out Hal and Fanny were more than happy to host the new Chief Engineer for the Union Pacific Railroad as well as General Phil Sheridan. Dollar signs sparkled in Hal's eyes.

"Business, Danny. Mustn't forget we need clients to stay in business."

THE GENERALS ARRIVED on a glorious Friday around noon, along with former Sgt. Sully McBride, a bear of a man who took care of the horses and the generals' luggage. Daniel assumed he also served as a bodyguard, perhaps even a body servant to General Dunn. He never said much, seldom smiled, and stayed out of the way. Daniel did notice how he constantly watched Abbey and Will.

The air, heady as wine, smelled of autumn, welcomed the men. The trees dazzled in peak color, and the views and the reflection in the lake took away one's breath. The buildings, the barns, and the grounds sparkled. After a simple lunch served on the wooden table down by the water, Hal and Daniel led the generals on a tour of the lake and school. They spent a lot of time with the horses.

Saturday before sunrise, Hal, Daniel, Sully, and the generals went fowling, first ducks and geese, then pheasants and grouse. Guns boomed all morning.

"Does someone eat all this?" Sheridan asked.

"Oh, yes," said Daniel. "We'll send it over to the school and they'll have a feast. Twenty growing children eat a great deal, you know. We save the feathers, too. We have bags of down in the barn for pillows and feather beds. I think my wife sells the excess to a pillow maker." Remembering her pheasant feather, he added. "The fancy ones she sells to Maude Simpson who uses them for hats." He was proud of Summer's husbandry. He added, "Summer manages a tight ship. We don't waste much of anything."

The general shook his head. "How in the hell did you ever get involved with feathers and babysitting a bunch of Indian brats, Danny? Here we are, trying to eliminate them, and you're educating them. I thought you were a warrior, not a teacher."

To keep his hand from clenching at the general's tone, Daniel stood beside Chester and ran his fingers through the flaxen mane. He was grateful Will had opted not to come. Ever since Daniel had lived in the Lakota camp, spent time with the children, become close friends with Will and his mother, the slights and insults showered on the native Americans bothered him, perhaps even more than it did the Indians themselves.

"Don't get me started, gentlemen," he said, "or we could have our own little war right here. While we both have lost an unaccountable numbers of friends, I don't approve of how the army or our government treats the Indians. Now I'm sure you think I'm out of my mind with this school, but I assure you I am doing the right thing. We've had letters from several groups around the country who want to follow our lead and educate the children."

Both generals made ugly noises. Sully spit.

Daniel fed Chester a sugar cube. "You know I went out to Ft. Laramie when Abbey was forced to run off to the Indians. Well, I ended up staying in the Indian camp. I sat in a sweat lodge with

Red Cloud, Man-Afraid-Of–His-Horse, Spotted Tail, and Crazy Horse. Let me tell you: to sit half-naked in a sweat lodge with your enemies erases a lot of misconceptions. Will Dupree is Red Cloud's nephew, Wakanda, the headmistress at our school, is Red Cloud's sister. They translated for me." He smiled, remembering. "You should really talk with them. They are intelligent, kind people who treasure their children. Children are the heart of the Sioux nation. The only hope of the survival of the red race is education, and when these children mature they can return to their tribe and educate the next generation."

Daniel lifted his shotgun, sighted, and bagged the last pheasant of the day. "Gentlemen, Mrs. Love, our cook, makes delicious apple cider doughnuts every Saturday morning. You don't want to miss those. The children all flock to our backyard for them. Come and talk to them and to Will and Wakanda. You may be surprised. So you know, I've corresponded with President Johnson and General Grant, who hopefully will be our next president. They both approve highly of what we are attempting."

General Sheridan snorted as he mounted his horse. He lit a cigar and clamped it between his teeth, then glared down at Daniel. "Gossip is rampant in Army circles about your sister and that big Indian living as man and wife. Some say she's pregnant. How are you allowing that? I thought she was a nice girl, married that West Pointer."

Daniel spent some time tightening his stirrups. Finally, he said, "Not anymore. Ed died up on the Yellowstone River. Abbey and Will married." He squinted at the general. "Trust me on this, Phil, Will Dupree is a much better man than Ed ever was."

Grenville Dunn, a man of slight build who the Indians had dubbed 'Hawk Eye' or 'Level Eye' because of his surveying equipment, shook his head. Dunn had two prime ambitions, and everyone knew them. The first was to build railroads, and if that meant annihilating the Indians, so be it. The second was to make a fortune. Again, if that meant running over anyone, so be it.

"I'm not so sure about Captain Ed Kincaid's demise, Daniel. Reports have come in that he's living along the Yellowstone, a recluse of sorts, one-armed and half-blind. That, I believe," he said through a dark smile, "would make your sister a bigamist. I'm afraid, Sir, her reputation in army circles is quite tarnished."

Daniel's head jerked around; color drained from his face. Could his sister be in worse trouble? The Establishment considered her still married to Ed Kincaid, who just might be alive. In reality, Abbey did live with Will Thunder Cloud, a half-breed Sioux-French Canadian, as his wife. The Sioux Nation had married them and recently she was abducted by Five Stone, a renegade Arapaho, and held captive. Abbey claimed her captor had not molested her, but everyone knew what happened to captive white women. All eyes watched her waistline.

"By God," Daniel growled. "Someone should put a stop to those rumors. Ed Kincaid is dead." He glared at Dunn, who stepped back. "She's no bigamist."

He stepped closer to Dunn; their faces were inches apart. "If Ed, by some miracle, shows up he should be hanged for desertion. Let's put these rumors to rest, shall we? He abandoned my sister to the likes of Jake Hunt who beat her so terribly she lost her child. To top it off, Jake Hunt and Ed have been carrying on a love affair, even after Ed and she married." He nodded, feeling good about letting all this into the open "You heard me. They'd been—whatever you call it—queer, fairies, ever since they roomed together at West Point. That son of a bitch had better not crawl out from under a rock anywhere where I can find him."

"Whoa, Danny!" Hal said, his voice unsure. "I thought you had that temper under control."

"Not where Ed Kincaid is concerned. It's one thing to be homosexual. If he's bent in that direction, it has nothing to do with me. However, to carry on the affair after marrying my sister then threaten to kill her if she told anyone, to give her no choice but to run to the natives? By God, I'm still furious. Always will be. People say she ran after Will, which is not true. Abbey didn't even know him. She ran to the Indian camp because she had nowhere else to go. She wouldn't be alive today if Will Dupree hadn't found her."

The men all stared at Daniel, and he gave it right back. Then Grenville Dunn jammed one foot in the stirrup and looked up at the saddle. "By damn, I smell those doughnuts."

IN THE CAVES north of the Yellowstone, Ed Kincaid sat in the sun at the mouth of his cave. He counted himself fortunate. First, he was alive. He'd found a roomy, east-facing cave with plenty of timber and water nearby. Secondly, an old Indian woman, grateful for shelter and his protection, now trapped, hunted, and cooked for him. After an Indian half-scalped him, Tama had kept Ed alive, amputating his ruined arm, cleaning his raw skin, rubbing a foul-smelling ointment over his head and the stump. She also kept the fire burning and fed him.

In Tama's mirror, he saw how truly obscene he looked. Hair only grew on the left side of his head, his gray-streaked beard hung halfway down his chest, a white gelatinous mass instead of his left eye glared back at him, and he looked ancient, twig-thin, one-armed, and derelict. He supposed he should be grateful for his good eye and his right arm. At least he wasn't helpless.

AT CAMELANN, DOUGHNUTS and coffee did nothing to abate the growing tension. In an attempt to ease it, Hal St. Clair asked Mrs. Love to fix ham sandwiches; she packed a picnic basket adding potato salad and peach pie. He also brought along two bottles of good mountain hooch. Relieved when Daniel begged off, he took the generals and Sully fishing in the stream that fed Switchback Falls. Something had come up at the school—or at least that was Daniel's excuse.

The warm sun, the heavy lunch, the booze, and the sound of the falls put the men to sleep by mid-afternoon. General Dunn woke first and Sully stirred beside him. General Sheridan and Hal snored a little ways downstream. Dunn sat up and removed a cheroot from the silver case in his breast pocket; Sully struck a match. The general inhaled deeply and sat back, shaking his head.

"I guess I'm getting old," he said to Sully. The two had known each other for years. "I have three daughters. How does Charteris allow his sister—she's one gorgeous woman—to be that Indian's whore? Right on his own property? Living next door to him? Makes me sick."

Sully spat to the side. "Rumor is even more interesting. Seems she was captured by another Indian, an Arapaho, and that bun in the oven just might be his. Want me to do something about it?"

General Dunn took another deep drag. He shook his head. "They're a little more law abiding here in the East, and we have no war for an excuse. Just wait. When they set foot across the Missouri, we'll do something."

Sully grunted. "Maybe so, Sir, but you might be surprised at how uncivilized these parts are. I grew up not far from here, and I still have cousins on the other side of these mountains. Trust me General. Pennsylvania's wild will never be civilized."

34

NOT AS THEY SEEM

General Phil Sheridan leaned back in his chair and patted the swell of his usually flat stomach.

"Hal St. Clair, you outdid yourself again. Mrs. Love is a treasure. Can't beat a good beefsteak. And apple pie. Summer, darling, I won't be able to hook my belt for a week."

It was a glorious Indian summer evening, dry and warm. They'd dined outdoors under lantern-festooned Linden trees down by the lake. The last residue of the silver sunset reflected in the lake. The sky slowly faded into soft lavender. A family of ducks squawked as they paddled by.

Sheridan sighed. "You boys do have a piece of paradise here."

The women and Howie said goodnight and left the table while Mrs. Love's minions cleared the dishes. Hal returned to the table with a tray of brandies, cordials, and cognacs, and while he poured drinks, Sully provided lights for the men's cigars, everyone's but Will's—not a surprise to Will. He'd figured the man for a bigot right away. However, he could see Daniel was upset with the blatant snub; he quickly offered Will a light. All weekend the tension had mounted; Will remained calm; Daniel did not.

Two hours later the generals, quite soused, stumbled to bed in Hal and Fanny's house. Daniel and Will helped clear the last of the glasses, thanked Mrs. Love and walked over to their cottages, just as Summer stepped onto the porch, carrying a big vase of autumn roses.

"I didn't want to interrupt," she said, "but we received a telegram from General Grant. He and Mrs. Grant are arriving on the eight o'clock train tonight, which Lew tells me is delayed until about eleven. Seems Abbey sent the Grants an open invitation to tour the school. They're on their way to Cape May and wanted to stop for a quick visit. Mr. Graves delivered the telegram himself, and he was so excited to meet General Grant he offered to drive them out here when the train finally arrives."

She reached over and petted Will's shoulder. "Abbey and I moved her and your things into our loft. I hope you don't mind we gave the Grants the guest cottage. I think they'll only be here a night or two."

Will chuckled. "I'm honored. To think the future president of the United States will sleep in my bed." He glanced over to the cottage and spotted Abbey through the window. "Does she need some help?"

"I don't think so. We changed the sheets." She held up the vase of flowers. "Here take these over. Put them beside the bed, and make sure they have enough candles."

Two hours later, the four of them welcomed Sam and Julia Grant as they climbed from Lewis Graves' carriage.

Once Lew left, everyone said goodnight. The four of them walked the Grants to their cottage. "We left a bottle of wine and some good Kentucky bourbon on the dresser for a nightcap," said Daniel.

The general shrugged sheepishly. "Thanks. I apologize for the lateness of the hour. The trains—"

Daniel shook his head. "It's no inconvenience, Sir. The trains are always late." He explained who all was staying on the compound. "We are full up, but Generals Sheridan and Grenville Dunn are catching the early train tomorrow. They've already gone to bed, quite in their cups. You can say hello to them in the morning, if you like."

"It's a dark night," Abbey said, "but just wait until you see Camelann in the daylight, and the Indian School." She clapped her hands like a little girl. "I'm so happy you're here. I cannot believe you stopped to tour our little school!"

SULLY SAT ON Otis Dodd's front porch, drinking from Otis' jug. They were fourth cousins, had fought on opposite sides during the war. Sully eyed the huge, covered cage with a dark curiosity.

"I see you still keep the birds."

"Yep, I love 'em."

"You still …"

Otis nodded. He was a small man who always looked rumpled as if a pat on his back would produce copious amounts of dust, "I have about thirty right now. I always lose a few over the winter, but I'll get more come spring."

He reached beneath the ragged quilt which covered the cage, then wound his hand inside the door and plucked a yellow finch from its perch. He smiled broadly as the bird's feathers fluffed against his palm. Only the small head sneaked out from the cavity of his fist, the tiny eyes wild with terror. With the forefinger of his other hand, Otis petted the feathers, smoothed them, all the time sweet talking to the bird as if it were a child or a woman. "My little sweet, my beautiful precious sweet." Then he held his fist straight out and slowly squeezed the little yellow bird until blood oozed through his fingers.

Beads of sweat broke out on Sully's forehead, and he swallowed hard. "Damn. Always amazes me how you do that."

Otis grinned. "Ought to try it sometime. Their little heart must beat two hundred, maybe three hundred times a minute jist before it goes ping." He snorted like a pig upending roots. "Christ, it's better than having a woman."

He opened his fist and looked down at the tiny bloodied carcass. "You know that big heathen over where you're staying, calls that whore of his Yellow Bird? What is the world coming to? I'll tell you, Sully, I about choked when I heard him call her that. Imagine him, touching a pretty white girl like that." He tossed the dead bird over his shoulder toward the hound which waited. The dog disposed of the little body in a single crunch, and Otis wiped his hand on his trousers.

He glanced at his cousin. "What brings you around? Still working for that rich general?"

Sully chuckled and took another swig of hooch. "I don't have to ask how you feel about them Injuns living over the hill, do I?" He grunted at Otis' expression. "I guessed you wouldn't like it. Niggers and Injuns are gonna kill us all. Well, I have an idea. And I could use a couple hands."

Otis snorted, so Sully told him.

WILL JERKED INSTANTLY awake. He sniffed. Smoke. The sheets pooled around his waist and he spread the quilt over Abbey then slipped on his trousers. With rifle in hand he ducked through the window and stepped onto the roof. The night was black as a mine, so his other senses heightened. He heard the water lapping at the dock, then a distant rider. A dog barked out by the school. He climbed to the apex of the roof, his bare feet agile on the cedar shingles. He crouched, listening, looking. Because of the solid darkness his eyes picked up the pinprick of an orange glow on the far side of the woods to the north. The wind chilled the skin on his chest, raising goose bumps. He sniffed again and made out a hint of turpentine. Then he heard muffled hoof beats clomping along the road, moving toward the light.

He returned to the loft bedroom and woke Abbey. "Slip on a robe and go wake your brother and Summer Rose. Tell them someone is up to no good. I'll meet Daniel downstairs." He pulled on a dark shirt, socks, and his boots. "Don't light a candle. Not even a match."

Still sleepy, she brushed back her hair then belted her robe. She took the pistol he handed her.

"That's loaded. Keep it in your pocket." He patted her bottom. Sleepy with her hair all askew, she looked delicious. He touched her cheek. "You and Summer might want to get dressed, too. First, though, please rouse your brother. Tell him to wear dark clothes."

Careful to not wake the babies, he made his way downstairs. Daniel, still pulling on a dark shirt, met him a minute later. Summer and Abbey tiptoed behind them.

Will headed out to check the Grants, but a minute later, he returned. "They're gone. And it's obvious there was a struggle. Where in the hell are the dogs?"

The scent of smoke was thicker now. He turned to the women. "Don't light as much as a match, but sit here with a rifle and guard the children." Owen made a thumping noise as he ambled from the children's room into the living room. Will scratched the big dog's ears. "Keep him inside."

As he and Daniel made their way on foot through the woods, the tableau unfolded before them. With sickness stirring in his belly, Will saw the fire and torches, burning with a tinge of blue from the turpentine. He also saw a good number of horses and white-clad figures.

"I've heard of this," Daniel whispered. "The spineless *Secesh*, still angry about losing the war. They get themselves all liquored up and dress in bed sheets, then intimidate Yankees. We're close to Maryland here, but I had no idea they'd come this far north. Who told them the Grants were here?"

The closer they came to the fire, the more the scent of pine tar permeated the air. They made out a dozen riders dressed in white, who circled the two prisoners who were trussed up like sausages in blankets. One of the white-clad men cut the bindings on the woman, and both figures on the ground struggled. She let out a muffled scream as one of the brutes swiped pine tar over the front of her. She kicked and fought. Will smiled when she managed to land a kick in his groin.

The masked men were ruthless and rough, calling her an Injun whore. One slugged the bound man, and realization of what was happening hit him as solidly as a baseball bat. *This had nothing to do with General Grant or the war. They think that's Abbey and me. Those sons of …*

He grabbed for his tomahawk which he'd tucked in his belt at the last minute. He felt Daniel's big hand clamp over his arm and whisper. "Easy Will, this party is all for you and Abbey. They caught the wrong fish." His expression was murderous. "That's our next president and Julia. Stay smart. We don't want a political mess, and I want Grant as our leader."

Just as the words came out of his mouth, another sheet-clad rider galloped out of the dark, carrying two bulging burlap bags. The rider cut the tie and dumped the sack on Mrs.

Grant. Feathers flew through the night like snow. The poor woman struggled wildly, screaming and sobbing through her gag. The men in sheets only stood back and laughed at her distress.

Daniel loosened his grip on Will's arm. "Keep your head. Try not to kill anyone."

Will nodded. They separated and walked into the circle of light firing their rifles into the grass then holding their rifle shoulder high, they sited the leaders, Daniel shouted, "Throw down your weapons."

The man on the horse went for his pistol; Daniel fired. The horse reared, and the man thudded to the ground with a grunt. Another man went to catch the horse, but a bullet from Will's gun knocked him down. A third man lifted his pistol and Will winged him, the impact of the bullet spinning the man around as blood erupted from his arm.

The others tossed their rifles while the wounded men writhed in the dirt. Will quickly sliced the ropes binding General Grant. The smell of wet, smoldering feathers choked them. The general took the knife from Will and cut the ropes on his wife, removed her gag, then his own. He hunched over her, comforting. Will helped them both stand.

Daniel, his rifle ready, stormed toward each of the hooded men and ripped off the masks. He immediately recognized the mountain men, and Will saw him fight the urge to shoot Otis Dodd. When he unmasked Sully, he slugged him as hard as he could. The punch landed square on target, and even from where he stood, Will heard the bones of the big man's jaw crunch. Sully went down with a thud, spluttering blood and teeth.

Daniel shook out his hand as riders approached. Hearing the rifle shots and seeing the glow of the fire, Wally Saxon and Henry Evers rode up from one side. Hawk and Lobo came at a gallop from the opposite direction preceded by a small pack of familiar dogs. Even Ezra arrived in a buggy with one of his older sons, frantically flaying the reins against the trotter's back.

Ezra pulled the horse to a stop. General Grant called Daniel over and whispered something to him. Daniel nodded and turned away as Grant, supporting his wife, moved toward to the house. She was hunched into herself, covered head to toe by feathers and glistening pine tar. Fortunately, it was not petroleum tar which would have burned terribly. Daniel motioned to Ezra, who quickly pulled the buggy up beside the couple and helped them into it.

General Grant wanted the incident forgotten. But the outlaws did not go unpunished. Wally, Henry, and the Indian boys put all the tar and feathers to good use.

UNAWARE OF GENERAL and Mrs. Grant's presence, Generals Sheridan and Dunn left at daylight as planned. Sully's disappearance was noted, but was not unusual.

"He'll show up," said General Dunn as he shook hands with Daniel. The general glanced down, frowning. "You were fighting?"

Daniel quickly pulled back his hand. "Something must have stung me during the night. I better stick it in ice water. Hurts like the devil."

Hal personally escorted the generals to the train in Gettysburg rather than to the local station, thus bypassing Mr. Graves and his gossipy wife. The last thing anyone wanted was word of Mrs. Grant's humiliating experience reaching news correspondents, politicians, or army wives. Or Mrs. Graves.

Wakanda shooed General Grant over to Daniel and Summer Rose's cabin, then took Julia Grant under her wing. She removed all the feathers and tar with her concoctions of buffalo tallow, dried herbs and flowers, lava rock, sweet smelling oils, and who knew what else. To General Grant's displeasure, she was forced to cut off about six inches of Julia's beautiful dark tresses.

"At least it was only pine tar," Wakanda told the men. "It could have been worse. Pine tar doesn't burn skin like petroleum tar would have. Their intent, I believe was to frighten not kill."

After many sweet smelling baths—laced with the omnipresent sage and cedar soap—the shaman built a sweat lodge at the edge of the woods behind the cottages and administered several sweat baths over a three day period. Julia Grant, Summer Rose, Abbey, Wakanda, Mary, and even Fanny joined in the baths, giggling and carrying on like adolescents.

"I haven't seen her so relaxed since we lived in Galena," said the general. "Do you think we could install such a lodge behind the Executive Mansion?"

Daniel chuckled. "I doubt it, Sir, but you can always visit here."

35

A BAD PENNY

On the Tuesday before Thanksgiving, Lew brought more guests to Camelann. Hilda Dietrich and Georgia Gilley appeared as if by magic, both bedraggled and exhausted. Summer right away recognized Hilda Dietrich's name as the infamous Dame Dilly, and Abbey quickly whispered to her that Georgia Gilley, the sergeant's wife had been very kind to her at Ft. Laramie, helping her make the yellow checked curtains. Hilda and Georgia's husbands sent them from Ft. Laramie because of the severe unrest. The two women, on their way to stay with relatives in New Jersey and New York, brought Cricket, Abbey's pony, on the train with them. They also brought horrific stories about the happenings in Indian Territory.

Overcast, sputtering rain, and cool enough to have a fire in the fireplace, Hilda held court in Summer Rose's comfortable living room. The women gathered around the crackling fireplace. Summer Rose arranged the tray of cookies on the tea table and prepared herself; she knew from Abbey and Mary's stories how vicious this woman could be. Abbey curled up on a pillow near the fireplace as Mrs. Dietrich started.

"It all went downhill about the time you left last spring, Abbey. That's when Colonel Carrington came out and started work on Fort Phil Kearny."

"Is that the same Kearny as the one in Nebraska?" asked Abbey.

"No, no," said Dame Dilly, shaking her head. She turned over the saucer to her teacup, checking the marking on the bottom of the Flo-Blue china, and Abbey tried very hard not to roll her eyes. "Fort Phil Kearney is named for Major General Philip Kearney—I think he may be related to the Nebraska Kearney. This major general died in 1862 at the Battle of Chantilly. You know, in Virginia. Colonel Carrington picked the site for the new fort and designed it himself."

She set her teacup on the saucer again and rolled her spoon through her tea, jabbing at the lemon. "It's between Big and Little Piney Creeks, about 250 miles north of our Ft. Laramie, on the Bozeman Trail. He's also started Fort C.F. Smith further north in Montana, but he's still headquartered at Ft. Phil Kearny." She paused for a sip of tea, and then ran her finger around the smooth gold edge, frowning with disapproval. "Mary, your ankles are swollen. Put your feet up," she said in a scolding voice. "Abbey, don't you have a stool for the poor girl?"

Mary protested, but Dame Dilly insisted. As Abbey scrambled about for a footstool, Daniel and Will stepped into the room. Summer graciously made introductions all around. The men nodded to the ladies. They declined tea, but each took a Russian teacake and stood near the door. Abbey assumed they'd already heard some of this from General Sheridan.

Mrs. Dietrich jabbed her lemon slice with her spoon. "Where, pray tell, did you find a lemon? We're not used to such luxuries."

Summer smiled. "We have a greenhouse and we grow both lemons and oranges. The original trees came from my mother-in-law's home in Philadelphia."

"Goodness gracious. I must see this."

Georgia laughed. "I wonder if the Fort Kearny wives have lemon trees? They have everything else. The location is great and the place is *huge*," Georgia said. "And they've stockaded it—ten to twelve acres. Eventually the fort will contain everything, warehouses, a hospital, a sutler's store, officers' quarters, barracks, stables, laundry, a battery park for the howitzers, guardhouse, even a bandstand. Oh, and space for a croquet court." Her hand fluttered against her chest. "How jealous the Laramie wives are." She looked over to Summer. "May I have some more tea?"

Much fuss ensued with refreshing teacups and passing cookies. Dame Dilly settled again into the sofa, took a swallow of tea, and pursed her lips. "Do you realize how many trees were necessary to stockade ten acres? They send out soldiers to cut them." She took another swallow of tea and looked around the room, pointedly avoiding Will's eyes. "Almost immediately that heathen, Red Cloud stirred up the tribes with horrid consequences. Two of our men died in the first raid in mid July. Attacks, both military and civilian, have become commonplace. Stock was lost. Daily, timber parties had to travel five or six miles just to reach the ridge for the pine trees. And those wood trains are often attacked by *hordes of heathens*."

Georgia let out a little sob, and Dame Dilly petted her knee. "We became quite close to a number of the soldiers, for some stayed at Laramie. I housed two in my spare room. And dear Margaret, Colonel Carrington's wife, she knows them all." She pulled out a handkerchief and dabbed at her eyes. "Fanny Grummond knows them too."

Summer Rose's new gray kitten, Otto, strode across the room and soundlessly jumped into Summer's lap. Dame Dilly grimaced, making a face at the kitten. Summer ran her hand lovingly over the soft gray fur and smiled sweetly at Colonel Dietrich's wife.

"Henry Carrington is a good builder," Dame Dilly said snidely, "but he isn't a soldier. Never was, in my opinion. Don't you agree, Georgia?"

Georgia nodded. "My Stephen thinks Colonel Carrington is too defensive, not offensive enough. He is always sending out patrols to answer an alarm, but he never initiates anything. What he needs to do, my Stephen says, is attack those heathens in their camps. I don't know how many soldiers we lost."

Abbey felt nauseous. All the talk of heathens and hatred jabbed like small knives. From Summer Rose's raised color she realized she wasn't alone in her discomfort. When the Reverend and Mrs. Tuttle came into the room, great relief washed over her for the small distraction. While Abbey made introductions, Summer passed a plate of cookies and refreshed teacups.

The colonel's wife wasn't finished. "The ladies came to the conclusion—and our men affirmed it—that the Laramie treaty was *wau-nee-chee*, no good!"

"Of course not," Daniel said dryly. "Red Cloud's one demand was that no forts were to be built along the Bozeman. Before the ink is even dry on the treaty, two forts are being built."

Daniel and Will watched Dame Dilley stand and walk to the window. She blew her nose then turned back to the room.

"I must tell you, talk of Colonel Carrington is not kind. Some call him a coward, and no one believes him competent to fight Indians. For heaven's sake, the man was a *lawyer*. He never really led men in battle. Even *I* know you have to go on the offensive with these heathen, go right into their camps and destroy them. Georgia, tell them about Captain Fetterman and poor Fanny Grummond's husband."

Georgia reddened to the collar of her scarf and glared at the colonel's wife. "Quit protecting Bill Fetterman. He and that Colonel Custer act like teenagers. Mark my words Mrs. Dietrich, they'll get us all killed. They haven't the sense they were born with."

Dame Dilly spluttered like a chicken about to be beheaded. "Why Georgia, I never … remember your place."

Summer Rose glanced at Abbey, who made a motion as if she were about to vomit. Hiding a smile, Summer Rose stood, depositing Otto on the floor.

"You both look exhausted," she said. "Daniel and Will have taken your valises to Jack's cabin, just two houses down. I'll walk with you. Would you like a bath? I'll send over the Amish girls to heat water and help. We won't have dinner until seven tonight. Maybe you can take a nap."

ON THE WALK over to Jack's cabin, Summer Rose suggested to both women that they be careful not to offend Will, Wakanda, or the Indian children. They must not have heard her for both women continued to call Red Cloud a fiend, and the Indians heathens or savages—or worse. When Dame Dilly spoke of wanting Red Cloud's head on a pole, Summer Rose couldn't stand any more such talk. She told Daniel.

He winked at his wife. "Calling in the heavy guns, are we? I know just what to say." Daniel spoke to Mrs. Dietrich and Georgia, and whatever he said worked. Later, Summer asked him about their conversation, and he chuckled.

"I told them to pay no attention to Will's threats about cutting out their tongues. I said he was just blowing off steam at the Indians being badmouthed. I told them I didn't think he'd ever really done anything like that."

"Will didn't say that."

Summer Rose's eyes widened. "He wouldn't. Would he?"

Daniel shook his head. "No, but it works." He told her about Will's threat to Mary and how it had shut her up. "I was so grateful. You know, sweetheart, some women talk way too much, and many have a propensity of saying the wrong thing."

Summer Rose didn't argue, but she smiled to herself. Did her husband honestly think that trait was restricted to women?

WINTER ROARED HELL bent into Camelann. Through stinging sleet, Abbey and Summer Rose led Cricket to an empty stall in the cozy new horse barn. It smelled of horse, hay, and fresh cut lumber. The twenty stalls, which faced twenty more, were almost fully occupied. Two mares had foaled, so the herd now totaled thirty-four sacred ponies, plus Cricket, Chester, Rabbit (the horse), and two Percheron draft horses, huge black beauties standing at least seventeen hands high, which the little children wanted to name Hansel and Gretel. The teenagers pushed for Romeo and Juliette, which was winning. They were of the age of romance and studied Shakespeare's plays at school.

"You know why Dame Dilly's really here, don't you?" Abbey asked with a smirk.

Summer Rose frowned.

"You can bet your last dime she's here to check out the eye color of Mary's baby," said Abbey.

"No. That can't be true, Abbey. All the wives were sent east. She's just returning Cricket. No one is *that* scheming. Besides, Mary's baby isn't due for another three weeks. That woman will be long gone by then."

Abbey looked at her sideways. "You, Summer Rose, are a saint. Just wait. She'll figure a way to stay here."

That evening Dame Dilly slipped on an icy patch and sprained her ankle. By the following morning, it ballooned and turned ghastly shades of purple. Emily and Tilley, who had both just arrived for the Thanksgiving holiday, examined the ankle and insisted she stay off her feet.

"Sometimes a sprain can be worse than a break," Emily said. "I had a patient just last week with a bad sprain who fell down her stairs and broke her other leg."

As Abbey fixed a tray for the invalid's lunch—sliced chicken breast on brown bread with dill mayonnaise—she narrowed her eyes at Summer Rose. "See? I told you."

Summer Rose propped one fist on her hip. "That was an accident. She wouldn't hurt herself, on purpose, would she?"

"You are such an innocent." Abbey cut the sandwich into four triangles, then suddenly turned a pasty white. She stood straight, holding her stomach, and raced to the back door. She had just reached the porch railing when her stomach erupted, and she vomited into the laurel bushes.

"Sorry about that," she said after washing out her mouth and throwing a bucket of water on the laurels. "I was never this sick with my first pregnancy. The smell of the mayonnaise … It's just all this talk of killing Indians has me upset."

Summer didn't say a word. Mrs. Dietrich was close to upsetting her.

THEY USED THE school's sizeable kitchen to cook Thanksgiving dinner, then served it in the large dining room. Mrs. Love and Wakanda supervised, but all the women collaborated to make it an American feast with Indian and Amish touches: turkey and stuffing, but also cornbread and apple butter. They'd gone to some trouble with the carriage, too, bringing the lame Mrs. Dietrich to the school. The Indian boys fashioned a chair out of their arms and carried her into the school's dining room. Since she was thin as string bean, lifting her was easy.

The joy and abundance of the holiday affected everyone, but Thanksgiving 1866 still reverberated with the echoes of cannons. The nation still mourned the loss of three-quarters of a million dead in the war.

Children's artwork decorated the dining room walls, and surprisingly, most of the pictures were of scenes from the plains: buffalo, antelope, coyotes, wolves, the rolling hills of grass, the big sky. The pictures reminded the adults of what they were attempting, and it was showing some success. One picture was a lovely view of Lake Camelann with buffalo grazing on the shoreline. Another reminded Summer of their Open House last fall. The picture showed the tipis down by the lakeshore with both Amish quilts and Indian buffalo robes hanging side-by-side on clotheslines. Perhaps the two cultures could merge.

MARY'S LABOR BEGAN that night. Again Abbey and Will gave up the guest cottage and moved to the loft, giving Mary privacy and space. The following day, in an effort to speed up the birth process, Abbey and Summer Rose walked around the exterior of the cottage with Mary.

"Oh Summer." Mary moaned, clutching her belly. "Did you feel about to be ripped apart?"

Summer Rose squeezed her hand. "Definitely, but you will heal. It's truly a miracle."

"Just keep that woman out of here." Everyone knew who she meant.

Abbey giggled. "She's a little helpless, now that Georgia left for home and worse since she has that sprained ankle. But if she manages to get here, I'll bring Will in to scare her. Ever notice how her mouth just snaps shut of its own accord when he steps into a room?"

"He has the same effect on me," Mary said then gasped. Her eyes popped open wide. "Oh my God. I think I have to push."

"Good," said Summer Rose. "Abbey, please find Dr. Dupree."

Late that afternoon, Mary's daughter was born. While Tilley cleaned up and examined the baby, the new mother washed and slipped into a fresh gown, Summer Rose and Abbey changed the sheets then finally managed to dress the baby in a tiny flowered flannel nightshirt. They topped her little head with an eyelet cap trimmed with blue satin ribbons.

Big, fat soft flakes started right after the birth. Abbey moved to the window. The room was warm and filled with happiness. The snow was a sharp, refreshing contrast. Suddenly she squeaked with surprise.

"Look!" she cried, pointing out the window.

Dame Dilly, hobbling with two canes, made her way to their cottage.

"You have to give her an 'A' for determination. Pray she doesn't break a leg," muttered Dr. Tilley Dupree as she rushed out the door to help her.

"What color are the baby's eyes?" whispered Abbey.

Mary giggled, holding the baby closer to her chest. "Blue as deep water. But even if her eyes were peridot green, there's no denying the paternity of this little girl."

Thumps and heavy breathing approached through the living room to Mary's door, then loud rapping from what only could be a cane resounded through the room.

Abbey opened the door. "Hilda! How brave of you to come through the snow."

Dame Dilly's purple face puffed with fury. "Brave? Harrumph! No one will tell me anything, and I'm starving. It's a wonder I didn't kill myself in the snow. Well? Tell me. Girl or boy?" She thumped the cane for effect.

"Come in, Hilda. The baby's a darling girl," said Mary.

Dilly set down her canes and moved toward the baby, her fingers wiggling with anticipation, but Mary pulled the baby close, hugging the little bundle. "No, no, Hilda. Wait until you're steadier on your feet. But do come near. Isn't she beautiful?" Mary let slide the little eyelet cap, revealing a full head of carrot-colored hair, just like Emmett's. "I've named her Laramie Rose."

Mrs. Dietrich wobbled, her face contorted. Tilley steered her into a chair.

Daniel with Will right behind him tapped on the door. After oohs and ahhs, Tilley scooted everyone but the new mother and baby toward a tray of sandwiches in the living room. Before they could all go, Mary called out. "Summer, please stay for a minute."

Summer sat on the edge of the bed, smiling. "She really is beautiful."

"Thank you. But I wanted to ask … I hope you don't mind about the baby's name."

"Mind? I'm honored. I love it. So does Daniel." She grinned. "He's going to ride into Morgan's Corners before the snow gets too deep and send a telegram out to Emmett." She pulled a snippet of paper from her apron pocket. I hope this is okay: RED-HAIRED BLUE-EYED SEVEN POUND GIRL BORN AT FOUR THIS PM STOP COME HOME SOON TO ME AND YOUR LARAMIE ROSE STOP LOVE MARY."

Mary's voice cracked. "Do you have one of those big white handkerchiefs with you? I'm going to cry. Oh, I hope my little girl's as sweet as you."

Summer Rose whipped a huge handkerchief out of her sleeve and handed it to the new mother. "Be warned, Mary. I may be sweet now, but I'm pregnant again, and I turn into a witch after the sixth month!"

36

Fort Phil Kearney

Laramie Rose's new father focused his binoculars on the woodcutter's detail. Since he received Danny's telegram, he was having difficulty thinking about anything but the joys and worries of his new role as a father. He'd left his gloves in the barracks, and his fingers felt numb. The wind blew so furiously the light snow fell almost laterally, clinging to the tall dried grasses and dusting the ground. He'd ridden two hundred and fifty miles with a company of mounted infantrymen, travelling from Fort Laramie to the new Fort Phil Kearney, stopping at Ft. Reno overnight. He'd come to train his replacement on the powerful howitzers, but poor Lt. Simms had come down with the runs. Emmett stood, waiting, behind the parapet of the new stockade, patting the telegram announcing Laramie Rose's birth. He carried the piece of paper in his breast pocket all the way from Fort Laramie and decided he wasn't parting with the flimsy until he could hold his baby in his arms.

In less than a week he planned to meet Mary and their new daughter at Camelann. Daniel and Summer Rose had sent a telegram right behind this one, graciously inviting their little family to stay for Christmas and as long as they needed. Emmett patted the piece of paper again and puffed up like a chickadee in winter. He couldn't wait to take Laramie Rose east to Chestnut Hill to show his parents. Of course, *I'll wait until after Christmas, make sure Mary feels well enough to travel.* He loved the baby's name and tried to imagine his daughter's tiny features. He wanted to kiss her nose, feel the soft skin, sniff her hair. *Red-haired! Mom will be so pleased. She always said red hair has its own special scent and Bird, the old blind woman in Red Cloud's camp told me the same thing. No one believes me.* He chuckled. *I can't very well shove my hair under their nose, but I can do that with sweet Laramie Rose.* A voice startled him from his reverie. "Lt. Hathaway?"

"Yes?"

"I'm Captain James Powell. We met years ago in Washington. During the war."

Emmett pulled his right hand out of his pocket. "I remember you, Sir. I believe we met after President Lincoln's first Inauguration or was it the second?"

Emmett had a good memory. He remembered having heard Captain Powell had enlisted long before the war and had risen through the ranks, even been brevetted twice for gallantry. His reputation was one of cautiousness, but he was known as a good man. He looked older now, grayer, but also wiser. He'd lost some of his hair and a lot of his bluster.

As the two officers shook hands a bugler sounded, and the northern gate to the fort opened. In unison, they raised their binoculars and studied the trail toward Montana. Captain Bill Fetterman and Lieutenant Horatio Bingham both led forty cavalrymen out to rescue the woodcutters where a small band of Sioux had them pinned down.

Earlier today Emmett had overheard Captain Fetterman bragging to some troopers, "Give me eighty good men and I'll cut a swath through the Sioux Nation, be rid of those heathen devils for good. Show Old Mother Carrington how a real soldier fights."

Well, thought Emmett, Captain Fetterman, you are about eighty strong right now.

JUST BEHIND CAPTAIN Fetterman, Colonel Carrington and Lt. George Washington Grummond led another thirty-some mounted infantrymen. Emmett had met Lt. Grummond and his young wife this morning. They were expecting a baby, too. With a burst of paternal pride Emmett had shown them his telegram.

Emmett and Jim Powell watched the soldiers move north. When they looked beyond, they could see the entire canvas unfold like a map: Fetterman, the Indians, Carrington. The tactics were obvious. Fetterman planned to flank the Indians.

They watched Captain Fetterman take the cavalrymen straight to the wood train, then forcing the attacking Indians to withdraw, then driving them toward Colonel Carrington and the mounted infantrymen. Lt. Bingham and his cavalrymen pursued, but the timing was off. Carrington and Grummond had not yet arrived at the rendezvous. The Indians immediately realized what happened and turned on Bingham's cavalrymen who panicked. Bingham took off toward the ridge, perhaps in a futile attempt to draw the Indians to him and away from his men.

Jim Powell, observing Bingham, muttered. "What is that fool doing?"

Emmett and Jim Powell watched in horror. From the height of the stockade, they could see the entire drama unfold. "Christ," Emmett said. "They're cutting Bingham off. He's surrounded."

Emmett put down his binoculars, reluctant to watch any more. But even without glasses he saw more than he wanted. Feeling disloyal, he picked up his glasses again just as a dozen or more arrows raced toward Lt. Bingham. Emmett could make out the arrows protruding from the man's chest, and though Bingham held his seat for what seemed an eternity, he eventually simply keeled over.

"Looks like Sergeant Bowers is down as well. Good God. They're all over him," said Powell, who looked excessively pale. "God, I hate this."

Further north of Lodge Trail Ridge they heard gunshots. The Indians had attacked Colonel Carrington before he could meet up with Captain Fetterman. Lt. Grummond, like Bingham, veered off during the skirmish, and Emmett and Jim Powell watched helplessly, their hearts in their throats. Both breathed a sigh when the young officer slashed his way through the Indians.

It was a brutal end to a brutal day. The troops brought Lt. Bingham and Sergeant Bower's bodies back to the guard room. Five wounded men were taken straight to the hospital. Everyone was disheartened by the losses. Everyone realized the Indians would only take heart from their victory. The attacks would not cease.

ON DECEMBER 12TH Emmett returned to Ft. Laramie. The following day he rode east and boarded the train. Each mile closer to the Missouri River eased the band of tension around his chest. He loved chugging across Nebraska, drinking whiskey as the sun slid into the marshes. His Laramie Rose would never know the hardship of crossing the plains by wagon; she'd never smell the brackish water, the acrid smell of buffalo chip fires. By God, trains made it so much easier.

They had a little delay in Indiana, but on the 17th Will and Daniel waited for him at Morgan's Corner with a fast horse. Lew promised to bring his trunk out by either buckboard or sled the next day. The four of them stopped in the saloon—a new addition to the growing crossroads—and had a couple celebratory shots of whiskey. Morgan's Corner didn't have a church or a school, but the distillery worked overtime.

"Wait until you see that baby girl," said Daniel. He had planned to tease Emmett by saying Laramie Rose looking like a drowned rabbit or some other nonsense, but, seeing Emmett's joy, he just couldn't do it. "She's gorgeous."

He also planned to tease him about the baby's name, but Emmett put a stop to that. "I love the name. Are you sure Summer doesn't mind?"

Daniel smiled. "All of us love it. What's happening on the Bozeman? The papers have been full of rumors, opinions, and misinformation."

"What do you think of Colonel Carrington?" asked Will. "The papers are crucifying him."

"He's a good commander. Cautious. He is a bit of an old lady. He's always issuing silly orders. Things like keeping off the grass or how many logs per night per family. Now Fetterman, he hasn't changed. He's still as headstrong and brash as Custer. If Carrington can hold him back, we'll be okay. I've been out there a while. I know how to fight Indians. I'm glad the colonel's cautious."

Daniel leaned against the bar. "Everyone underestimates the Indians. They're the best fighters in the world. What do you think, Will?"

Will nodded and tossed back his whiskey. He flashed his blue eyes. "Of course, I'm biased. I know they are the best fighters and the best horsemen, but none of it matters. A tide of white men is rolling toward them. They might win a battle, but they cannot win the war."

37

HEARTH AND HOME

At Camelann, Emmett and Mary reveled in being together. When Mary wasn't nursing or Laramie Rose sleeping, Emmett held the baby, talked to her, sniffed her hair. When he wasn't holding Laramie Rose, he was kissing his wife.

"You have no idea how happy I am, and how proud. She's gorgeous." He smoothed her bright red hair and planted another kiss on Mary's cheek.

"It doesn't smell a bit different than anyone else's hair," said Mary when he sniffed the baby's hair again. She didn't give his claim any credibility, so Emmett dragged her and Laramie Rose to Will who was sitting with Daniel in the kitchen of the main house. He held Laramie Rose out for Will's inspection. With his long French-Indian nose, he sniffed the hair and agreed with Emmett.

"I can sniff out redheads around bends. They are distinctive. In my younger days, I was infatuated by redheads." He pulled his blonde wife close and buried his nose in her hair. "Now I only like blondes. My real talent is finding this curly-haired minx in the dark."

Abbey laughed. "Darling husband, I never hide from you."

Will rolled his big blue eyes.

Summer Rose, picking up the tail end of the conversation, entered the room with Johnnie on her hip. "I suggest you use those noses to sniff out a couple of Christmas trees. I'd like a decent-sized one for the school and a small one to sit on a table here in the living room, out of reach of little fingers. I'm planning on a quiet supper tonight for Christmas Eve—oyster stew, bread, and apple pie. We'll have a huge roast beef feast with Yorkshire Pudding and all the trimmings for everyone tomorrow at the school."

She smoothed her apron and hoisted the baby higher on her hip, smiling. "The children have been working on a Christmas program, a play and carols, with Daniel's mother and Howie. They're presenting it tomorrow before dinner."

When Daniel sat, she adroitly settled Johnnie on her husband's lap, then automatically wiped the faces of Gus and Mac, lifted a limp Otto from the worktable, and placed him on a shelf near the stove, then collected dirty dishes.

"Will, your family sent several boxes of things for the children at the school. New moccasins and sweaters, lovely carved wooden animals. Someone made beautiful beaded amulets for each child. The priest sent a newsy note. They'll have a nice Christmas."

"What about our children? What do you have for them?" asked Daniel, lifting an obviously damp baby off his lap.

Summer Rose shrugged as Mercy removed Johnnie from Daniel's outstretched arms and herded the boys into the living room. "They're just babies, Daniel, they won't notice. The tree is plenty for this year. My McAllister ancestors would spin in their graves if they knew I wasted money on wee babes. Next year we'll spend what we can spare on toys."

DANIEL HARNESSED ROMEO and Juliette while Emmett and Will fitted sled runners on a wagon and gathered saws and axes. He didn't need these enormous horses—they were used largely for plowing and hauling, but Daniel knew they liked the snow and needed the exercise, plus the children loved them. Mercy and the twins all bundled and mittened, ran to the big sleigh and at the last minute Hal with Hank joined the Christmas tree party. At the Indian Village, Rabbit, Lobo, and Hawk hopped on board as the big sleigh made its way to the pine grove near Switchback Falls. The sleigh bells jingled, the children's eyes grew big and bright.

The falls roared and threw out lacy sprays of ice. The men, really just big little boys, started a snowball fight, Will and Emmett against Daniel and Hal. Mercy with the help of Hawk and Rabbit kept the little ones out of the fray by diverting their attention to a hillside where they made snow angels.

Hawk tackled Mercy and laughingly shoved a snowball down the back of her coat. She feigned outrage and stuffed one in the neck of his shirt. He tackled her again, rolling in the snow then held her down for a long minute. Mercy didn't struggle, and the men, supposedly adults, continued their little war and didn't notice. Just as his lips brushed hers, Mac, Gus, and Hank jumped on them.

When the men settled down and went to work, they quickly felled four trees and loaded them on the sled. All five dogs cavorted around them, sniffing their way further up the mountain. Will whistled, but Owen didn't immediately return so Will climbed to where the big dog waited. There he found the remains of several fires tucked behind a boulder. He motioned to the other men, and when they arrived, he pointed to the fire pit then the view. Through the bare trees the Camelann Valley sparkled below: the slate pewter-colored lake, the marsh grasses, the pines, the roofs of the houses and the school, the tipis, and the big horse barn all appeared as if dusted with powdered sugar. And they all stood there like targets.

Hal fingered the ashes. "Whoever is spying on us has been up here several times." He and Daniel had hunted and walked every inch of this land. They knew this patch like the back of their hands.

Hal handed Hawk his rifle and instructed him to return to the wagon with the children and stand watch. He then quickly led Will and Emmett higher on the mountain, walking along the cliffs, showing them the sheer wall at the far side of the ridge. Daniel knelt and found pick marks where the spies had attached cleats.

Daniel stood. "I guess we should feel honored. We're important enough to be spied on." He walked a few feet away, stood, and surveyed the valley. In the foreground of his vision, the children played with Mercy, Hawk stood guard, but beyond the children all of Camelann spread before him.

Near the bridge, Howie and Daniel's mother, the last woman on earth he would have guessed to be religious, were building a chapel. Howie expected it to be finished enough for a service by Groundhog Day, and Pat Whittaker had dug a foundation for his house on the far side of the road. Pat had been a gardener for Summer's grandfather. Pat lost his wife to tuberculosis and his sons to the war. Summer convinced him to come here and start a new life. Camelann needed a competent gardener. Making the most of the life dealt him, when he met Maudie Simpson, a local widow, he wasted no time in proposing to her. They planned a wedding come spring.

Camelann was growing, and Daniel and Hal had mixed feeling about that growth. This land, pristine and undiscovered was a paradise when they first came upon it. Regardless, Daniel felt, and he was sure Hal felt the same, an overwhelming need to protect this paradise.

Will came over and stood beside him. He must have read his thoughts. "You have seven mares pregnant."

Daniel chuckled "Pregnancy seems to be contagious around here. Summer Rose, your wife, and Hal's wife are all expecting." Summer and Fanny had already announced their conditions, but Abbey had not said a word. "When are you planning to tell us?"

Will stood with his hands in his pockets; the toe of his boot shuffled some snow. "She hasn't told me yet. Women are funny. You and I are horse breeders. Don't they think we can tell?"

In an obvious attempt to change the subject, he pointed to a thick copse of black spruce off to the left. "What do you think about building a blind there? We'll keep a guard there every night. Hawk and Lobo would be good choices."

Daniel nodded. "For now, instruct them to just watch and report what they see to us."

38

CHRISTMAS GIFTS

At the school, Wakanda waylaid her son and asked him to help Howie build a stand for the tree then help with the decorations. Daniel left Emmett to watch over Mary and Summer Rose.

"I'm going into town to buy a few gifts for the kiddoes," he said. "Do you want anything?"

Emmett dug in his pocket for a couple of dollars. "Pick up a pretty doll for Laramie Rose. Something for under the tree."

Daniel nodded, frowning. "You'd think their mothers would think of this."

DANIEL WENT A little wild at the store, buying taffies, licorice, and chocolates, two dolls and two boxes of wooden blocks. He also picked up three bags of toy soldiers, a wooden train set with tracks, boxcars, a locomotive and caboose—even a miniature railroad station. He added several cloth-covered animals: a big soft monkey, a golden lion, a spotted giraffe with a limp neck, and some windup toys. From another part of the store he picked up a boxed set of colored pencils, some little pots of paints with brushes and paper, and little chests for the boys and a music box for Laramie Rose. At the last minute, he threw in more chocolates just in case he'd forgotten anyone, and a big tin of hard candy. Weeks ago he'd sent for a gold locket on a long golden chain for Summer Rose. It was well hidden in the barn at Camelann. He'd also bought her a lovely white silk nightgown and robe.

He refrained from cringing when Mrs. Graves flashed him a coy smile and popped another Turkish taffy into her mouth. She jiggled all over and her bear-sized jowls puffed in and out like blacksmith bellows. As always, she wore an excess of powder and rouge; black lines around her eyes. She grinned appreciatively as she loaded his purchases into gunnysacks so he could haul everything out to Camelann.

"You and General St. Clair are my best customers," she said. "How's that pretty little wife of yours? Heard she's expecting again. Now you don't want to wear her out." She wiggled her eyebrows. "Merry Christmas to everyone out at your place."

The bell over the door rang, and her husband walked in with a stack of newspapers. Despite only having one arm, he dropped the stack neatly in the newspaper rack and handed one to Daniel, then one to his wife.

"Take a look at that," he said.

Daniel checked out the headline and first paragraph, then sat on an upended empty nail keg and read the entire article. As he read, his stomach sank to somewhere around his knees.

Massacre at Fort Phil Kearney

Ft. Phil Kearney—Friday, Dec. 21—Eighty American soldiers rode out of Fort Phil Kearney and didn't return. Their body parts and their insides were found splattered all over the rocks four miles from the fort. Not one man or horse survived. Not only were these brave cavalrymen and infantrymen slaughtered by the savage Sioux—led by Red Cloud—every man was brutally mutilated.

One of the burial crew reported: "A lot of boys were huddled together on a small hill under some trees. They had terrible cuts left by the Indians, and we could not tell cavalry from the infantry, as all the dead bodies were stripped naked, their skulls crushed with war clubs, ears and noses and legs had been cut off, scalps torn away, and the bodies pierced with bullets and arrows, leaving each wrist, foot and ankle attached only by a tendon.

Captain Fetterman, Captain Brown, and Bugler Footer were all together near the rocks. Footer's skull was crushed, his body left on top of the officers. Colonel Fetterman's and Captain Brown's bodies had a lot of arrows sticking in them, they'd both been scalped, and Colonel Fetterman's breast had been cut open. Lieutenant Grummond, who was also scalped, had his head nearly cut off, a lot of fingers cut off, and had many arrows and balls in him.

Some of the soldiers had crosses cut on their breasts, faces to the sky, some crosses on the back, face to the ground.

It is believed as many as 2,000 Indians, mostly Sioux, but some Cheyenne and Arapahos, waited in ambush on the far side of Lodge Trail Ridge, not far from where Fetterman's men had skirmished with warriors back on December 6. Red Cloud was most likely among the ambush force, but the man behind the plan was said to be High-Back-Bone of the Minneconjou Sioux. Crazy Horse, a young warrior, led a second decoy party. The entire fight was estimated to have lasted forty minutes.

Daniel folded his newspaper and stood, not quite trusting his legs. From the war, he remembered Captain Fetterman as an aggressive fighter, a competent leader. He'd met Lt. Grummond at Ft. Laramie and he knew most of the other officers.

He looked up and met the dark eyes of Martha Graves. Gone was her pleasant demeanor. A vulgar, unhappy woman almost as big as he, glared over the paper with such intensity he felt the heat of her ire clear across the room.

"And you," she spat, rattling the paper at him. "A *hero* of our war. You have dared to bring those filthy heathen devils into our midst. That squaw living on your land is Red Cloud's *sister*. And everyone knows she's your private whore." Hate gushed out of her like molten lava from the maw of a volcano. "And that big blue-eyed Indian sleeping with your sister is that butcher's nephew." She slapped the paper with her index finger. "How can you allow such a thing? Those soldiers are our American boys. Those heathens cut off their private parts and shoved them in their mouths." She threw down the newspaper. "I'll put this on your account, Sir. But I advise you to keep those little savages on your land. Tell that blue-eyed half-breed and his mother not to come to town. They'll end up face down in the cemetery."

Hit by the unexpected tinderbox of emotions, Daniel stood absolutely still for a moment, gathering his self-control before he blew. He'd never liked Martha Graves, now he wanted to throttle her. Instead, he grabbed the sacks and willed his hands not to wrap around her fat, jiggling neck.

But he wasn't about to let her have the last word. His eyes narrowed and turned to glints of pale green ice. "I am as sick as you are about this slaughter. I served with some of those men. Recently I met several others, but I have to say I'm shocked at what you just insinuated. To even voice such a thing about the gracious Indian woman living on our land just shows your ignorance, Martha. And to smear my name is just plain mean." His words hissed. "I advise you to not repeat what you just said. If my wife is insulted with any of your lies, I'll make sure you answer for it." He knew she was aware his influence stretched deep into the Pennsylvania Railroad, and he was capable of having her husband fired.

Lew knew, too. His blood red face quickly molted to feather white. He moved to help Daniel with the gunnysacks, but his wife bellowed, "Lewis Graves, I hear the 4:15. You'd better get your skinny ass up to the station then come right back here. I need to move some boxes."

Daniel took his gunnysacks and tied them on Chester's back. At the last minute he stepped back inside and scooped up a handful of newspapers and fit them in his saddlebag. His right hand shook. Every cell in his body wanted to smack Martha Graves, send her sailing into next week, but he knew any reaction would only add fuel to her fire. He'd heard rumors himself about Wakanda being his "squaw," and he'd ignored them. He refused to insult the mother of his new friend by making a scene about a ridiculous rumor. His wife—thank God for her—refused to listen to hateful gossip and called such, the wishful thinking of unhappy women.

All the way back to Camelann, a sick knot filled his stomach. What should he do? Withhold the newspapers until after Christmas? Or tell them tonight? What a horrid Christmas Eve present. Good Lord, Emmett and Mary knew most of the names mentioned in the paper. They'd be devastated. Wakanda and Will would worry about their people. Christ, he thought, whoever said war was hell was so right.

His indecision lasted through the ride home, settling Chester, and stowing the gunnysacks of gifts on the porch. Not until he stepped into the house did he decide to tell them tonight after dinner. Safety trumped all other factors. After the tar and feather party last fall, he knew what prejudice and ignorance existed in the area. At least the adults could be on alert. Who knew what venom Martha would spread? He definitely wanted Hal to know tonight.

During Summer's simple supper of oyster stew, he mentally made a list of guns and gunmen. In his head he counted: his new Winchester, five Henry rifles, four five-shot Spencers, several pistols, three shotguns, and ammunition, plus Hal's collection of at least four more repeaters. He tallied his manpower: himself, Hal, Will, Abbey, the two Indian boys, Wakanda, Emmett, and Summer. Would Henry and Wally stick with him?

After the children were tucked in bed, he pulled out the extra papers and let everyone read them. It was as bad as he expected.

CHRISTMAS AFTERNOON, DANIEL, carrying Johnny and leading the twins into the school, almost forgot the horrid news. A medley of aromas: roast beef, vegetables, and fig pudding and pecan pie, mixed with pine and candle wax. Mercy playing carols on the piano, mixed with children's laughter.

He settled the children in the front row, their eyes as big as cookies. Daniel waved to Hal and Fanny St. Clair who just entered the school. Hank, their son, such a good-looking child, ran toward him. Powerful feeling filled Daniel's chest as he swooped Hal's son to his shoulder. And Hal, his best friend, stepped forward and embraced him. "I'm with you Danny." Daniel bent and hugged Fanny and gave her his seat. He was very pleased they decided to stay here in the mountains for the holidays. Fanny kissed his cheek. The horrid news brought them all closer together.

The back of the dining room, the part by the windows, had been made into a stage for the pageant, a fenced manger with straw, a live colt, calf, and lamb sat in a corner. Cut out stars and a crescent moon hung from the ceiling. Candles glowed from every surface.

Summer came out of the kitchen and greeted Hal and Fanny, too

Reverend Tuttle stepped onto the stage, dressed as a shepherd, and read the Christmas Story from the Gospel of St. Matthew. Happy Moonbeam with a blue shawl covering her red ribbons, was Mary and Rabbit was Joseph; together they placed the baby Jesus in the crèche, it was perfect. Every Indian child had a role. Mercy played soft carols on the piano. Hal's son Hank, and Daniel's boys, Gus and Mac, and Johnnie's eyes sparkled like stars. Every adult possessed a reason to smile until a rider galloped by and threw a rock through the downstairs window. Glass shards sprayed all the way to the manager. The children screamed.

Frightened but unhurt, the children settled. Flora reacted with admirable speed to calm the pageant's live animals. The note tied around the stone simply read: GET OUT. The women rushed to the children, holding them close for a few minutes, then set about cleaning up the glass. Howie boarded up the small windowpane with cardboard from the back of a tablet. Hal and Will immediately mounted their horses, giving chase to the perpetrators, who disappeared into the trees. Daniel and Emmett stayed back to protect the women and children. They all stayed at the school that night.

EACH MORNING FOR the next week, Daniel made a point of riding into Morgan's Corner and bringing home papers. All the adults

read them. Yellow journalism or not, the tales from Colorado were ghastly. Mutilations, survivors huddled at the gates of the fort, the soldiers not daring to open the gates, further tales of wives and children of the soldiers huddled inside the fort within a circle of wagons around the magazine.

On the 27th a light snow again dusted Camelann; after midnight the men in white sheets visited again, waking all the children. This time they raised and ignited a fifteen foot turpentine-soaked cross, right in front of the school. Will smelled it immediately. He and Daniel, within minutes, galloped to the school. Hal must have heard them for he followed. It took a long time to burn then left its ugly ash imprinted on the snow. The children were terrified, the adults, furious and frightened.

ON NEW YEAR'S Eve more snow fell, enough to cover the ugliness of the burned cross, but nothing hid the animosity. The national newspapers were in a feeding frenzy which would make a hog pen look benign. It turned ugly. Retribution was demanded.

Tracks in the snow told tales of spies watching Camelann from the mountains.

Soon thirty inches of snow accumulated. The powerful Percherons proved their value by pulling the plows to keep the roads clear. Hawk and Lobo made it their duty to keep the roads clear and the Percherons healthy. Will and Wakanda offered to take the Indian children home to the Dakotas.

Daniel shook his head. "Red Cloud predicted this. War is about to erupt. They are safer here. You're all safer here."

39

CABIN FEVER

Would spring ever get here? Mercy sprawled on her cot in the nursery, her red wool jumper tucked under her knees. Carefully she lined up toy soldiers with Gussie and Mac. Johnnie napped in his crib. Stuck in the house because of the snow, Mercy felt as if she might go crazy if she didn't get outside soon. Most days she lived out-of-doors with the twins and Johnnie. Daniel and Summer, great believers in the merits of fresh air, bought a cart which possessed runners to fit over the wheels and she hauled the little boys all over Camelann. Right now, however, the roads needed to be cleared before anyone, unless they were riding a big horse, ventured anywhere.

Mercy cocked an ear. Was that the Percherons with the snowplow? She loved those gentle giants. She stood on her knees and opened the sash. Mac and Gus scrambled up beside her. They too were desperate to go outside. She gripped each boy in a tight hug, not because they might hurl themselves out the window—it was only a two foot drop and the snow was almost to the sill, but because she loved them so much. These darling little boys had brought her back to life when her parents and brothers were murdered during the war. Now these boys were her family. The brightness outside her window momentarily hurt her eyes. They waved to Hawk.

Hawk stopped the big horses in the middle of the cleared road and knelt in the snow beside their window. He'd worked most of the night and all morning clearing roads. Now, he looked over and smiled as he fashioned a small snowman. She told herself he made the little snowman for the boys, but she knew in her heart he made it for her. She liked his smile and the attention, and she blushed all over with a strange happiness that she didn't understand.

"Bring the boys outside. I found a sled in the barn."

She looked down at her charges who nodded vigorously.

Their response was to be expected. She stuck her head out the window again. Her thick hair blew in a golden flurry around her face. She nodded and smiled. "Give us twenty minutes." It was the longest string of words anyone had heard from her.

TWENTY MINUTES LATER the boys were all bundled in their winter things, the big horses were back in their stalls. Summer Rose gave Mercy's hair a quick braid and lent her a bright red knitted scarf, mittens, and beret. "Red becomes you," said Summer as she helped them out the door. She thought, *What have I started? I should be making her unattractive, not prettier.*

Summer slipped on a heavy shawl and walked outside with them. The sun was warm, the sky a perfect blue. "Stay within sight of the house." She looked down at the big sled. Memories of flying with her older brothers down the big hills rushed through her mind. "The hill behind the barn is the best.

"When everyone is wet and cold, come in. I'll fix hot choco-late and oatmeal cookies. Do you like cookies Hawk?"

He smiled with his whole face, and Summer saw what any girl would like. He was tall, whip thin, his white teeth sparkled against his golden smooth skin, his hair, raven feather black.

"Take good care of my boys." She bent and kissed both little boys, then Mercy. "Take good care of my girl, too. She's my treasure."

EACH TEENAGER HOISTED a toddler to their shoulder and trudged up the hill, plowing a path through the fresh snow. Hawk pulled the sled. It was quite a trek. At the peak, Hawk situated them on the sled—from the front, Mercy, Mac, and Gus—then with a running push, Hawk jumped on the back, his strong legs and arms wound around all of them. Three sets of hands latched onto his legs. A spray of fine crystals arched over them as they skimmed atop the ice-glazed snow. Hawk leaned left and they all leaned the same way and missed the huge pines and soared over the road with all of them screaming. They landed in a huge heap in a deep snow bank. The giggling boys quickly plowed their way out. Hawk held onto Mercy and whispered, "I don't want to let you go."

She leaned back against him, her head on his shoulder. She laughed. "I don't want to lose my boys. They skim the top of the snow; we have to plow through it." Had she ever said so much at one time?

He bent his head and planted a quick kiss on her lips. "I won't lose any of you." He hurled himself onto the crust of the snow and slid, using perfect balance, as fast as an arrow after the twins.

They repeated the whole scenario over and over: the trek up the hill, lining up on the sled, Hawk's running push, and flying down the hill, around the giant pines, over the road, and burrowing into the snow bank, stealing kisses, each one longer and deeper than the one before it.

Darkness settled fast. As the ravens headed toward their roosts, Mercy and Hawk trudged home pulling the sled with the boys riding. Mercy and Hawk shed their mittens and held hands, warm skin to warm skin. At the barn, the boys ran ahead toward their mother who stood in the door of the cottage.

Both Hawk and Mercy hung the sled inside the barn. She leaned against the wall, feeling as if she must die with her heart beating so fast. Hawk unbuttoned her coat, slid his arms around her, and kissed her for a long time with their bodies hot and tight together. His hands on her waist put fire in her breasts and low in her belly. How did that happen? They both looked toward the sounds of the boys greeting their mother. He kissed her fiercely. "Go with them. I'll settle the horses and follow in a moment."

"I don't want to leave you."

He smiled. White teeth flashed across his bronze face. "I was hoping you'd say just that." His hand cupped her chin, and he kissed her again, this time very tenderly. "Scoot before we get in trouble."

At the house, Summer ushered Hawk into her and Daniel's bedroom and handed him some old, much too large, denim trousers and a wool shirt of Daniel's, while Mercy and the boys changed into dry things in the nursery. Summer hung all their wet outer clothes on a rack by the kitchen stove then gave Hawk a piece of rope to use as a belt.

While Summer fixed a tray of steaming cups of cocoa, topped with whipped cream, and a plate of oatmeal cookies, the boys dragged all their blocks, toy soldiers, and toy railroad equipment to the living room. By the time Daniel came home, an elaborate layout of soldiers, walls, trains, and tracks blocked his way through the house. The children, twins, Johnnie, and two teenagers, were sprawled across the living room floor, the fire crackled. Every one of them had cocoa stained upper lips.

Hawk stood and shook Daniel's hand. The boys and Mercy, so intent on the toys, just looked up and waved.

"What do we have here? You all look rosy-cheeked."

Summer entered the room. "When Hawk finished his snow plowing, he took the older boys and Mercy sledding."

Mercy looked up to Daniel, her honey-colored eyes glowing. She'd lived in his house for a couple years and rarely spoke two words at a time. "We had a wonderful time. The sled soared over the road and the fence. Gussie and Mac screamed. I did too. We must have climbed that hill a dozen times. At least that many, don't you think, Hawk?"

Hawk nodded as he watched Daniel remove his jacket and hat, then lower his tall frame to the floor. Gussie and Mac crawled into his lap. He slid the row of blocks in front of the fireplace and carefully placed the lead soldiers behind the wall of blocks. "Now this is what the center of the line looked like that third day at Gettysburg. I was right about there. Your Uncle Hal was here."

Mercy picked up one of the boys' slippers and set it behind and to the left of Daniel's lead soldier. "Is that about right for where General Hancock's cannon stood?"

Daniel looked at her. "How on earth do you know that?"

She shrugged, "I have very good ears. I might not talk a lot, but I hear a lot. You'd be surprised what I know."

He felt tears threaten behind his eyes; he looked up to his wife. Her eyes looked shiny, too. He remembered Irene telling them how they found her: curled up beside her dead mother, her blonde hair dark with her mother's blood. Her mother had been stabbed and raped by outlaws. He wanted to pick Mercy up and twirl her around, but he just reached over and squeezed her shoulder. "I bet I would."

⚜

WHEN HAWK LEFT, it was well after dark. Summer's eagle eyes picked up the lingering squeeze of Mercy and Hawk's hands.

That night as Summer snuggled up against her husband, she asked, "Did you notice how Mercy and Hawk looked at each other?"

He pulled her close to him and nuzzled her neck. "I did. I planned to suggest you talk to her. I'll talk to Hawk. How old is she?"

"I've never been quite sure. Somewhere between fourteen and seventeen. How old is he?"

"I'm not sure either, but he's old enough. Don't postpone talking to her. Now is not the time for a white girl to become pregnant by an Indian boy. They'd no doubt lynch him and who knows what they might do to her."

Summer turned in his arms and her hands massaged his chest and shoulders, running her fingers through the down on his torso. She loved touching him. There wasn't an extra inch of fat anywhere. "I don't think they've done much beyond kissing, but she's talking. Can you believe that? Maybe, the kisses started her talking?"

He placed his big hands on her shoulders. "Trust me, Summer. Kisses are dangerous. Remember how you told me that my kisses opened a new part of you?"

"Good heavens, I did. I wrote that in my first letter." She rolled toward him, snuggling into his warmth. "You were very wise to insist we get married right away. If I knew then, Daniel, what I know now, I'd have never stayed alone in the same room with you. I was wild about you."

She snuggled into him, stretching and wiggling into a comfortable position. "And I still am."

THE NEXT DAY Hawk arrived around three o'clock and took the twins and Mercy sledding again. To ease their climb, he attached a rope from a tree at the bottom of the hill to one at the top. Now they climbed faster, and more opportunities for kisses occurred, but didn't happen. As the crows cawed and flew to their roosts, Mercy spotted Summer and Johnny at the bottom of the slope. At the pines, when she knew it was a straight shot down to Summer, she purposefully fell from the sled. Hawk immediately flew to her rescue as the boys and the sled sailed down the hill toward their mother.

Mercy and Hawk lay together, the line of their bodies— even through all the layers of clothing—touching from toes to noses. Happy voices of the twins meeting their mother drifted up to them. They looked up through the fringe of pines as the stars winked alive in the sky. Hawk leaned over her, his lips just brushed hers; his heat threatened to melt her.

He whispered. "Daniel warned me not to fall in love with you. It would be dangerous for us, he said, because you're white and I'm Indian. I didn't tell him I was already in love with you. I cannot undo it, Mercy. I fell in love with you the minute I first saw you. How I feel has nothing to do with you being white." He pulled her closer. "I want to marry you. Will you be my wife, Mercy? If you say yes, I'll talk to Daniel."

She nodded and touched his face, her voice came out thick and throaty, and her fingers stroked his cheek." I like the color of your skin, and, oh, Hawk, I love you and I want to be with you forever, but they'll say we're too young."

NOW THE DARK descended like a thick curtain, and they heard Summer holler for them as they came together in their first wildly passionate kiss. Nothing more than this chaste kiss happened except the moon, huge and brilliant, popped over the mountains, the snow beneath them melted, and they knew two things: they wanted to be one being, one soul, one heart, and they knew nothing, no one would keep them apart. Ever.

40

DREAMS AND DRUMS

Deep cold locked into Pennsylvania's South Mountains. Cabin fever affected even Will Dupree who awoke in the predawn stillness listening to the wind whistle through the chimney. Outside, in the frigid winter, cold even by Pennsyl-vania standards, a few stars winked in the dark patch of sky.

Will Thunder Cloud, naked, for he never wore bedclothes, lifted the covers and quickly poked the embers and added three logs to the fireplace. Immediately, golden light flared through the room, exposing logs walls chocked with white batting, Isinglass windows with white ruffled curtains, and a low white ceiling. Abbey lifted her head from beneath a bright down quilt, holding it open. He dashed back to the bed and submerged beneath the covers, shivering for just a moment, his cheek against her breasts. He'd planned to fall asleep again but Abbey nestled closer to him, and kissed the top of his head. Ever since she'd returned from captivity, she never denied his touch. When he asked her about this, she only murmured, "You almost lost me. I want to make sure you never forget me."

He wasn't about to forget her. The evenings were so long during this time of year, he usually made love to her twice a night. He remembered how Rain, Rabbit's mother, made him beg to touch her. He'd hated that.

Now, he stretched against Abbey, the silky softness of her thighs against his waist. He felt the heat of her and the growing mound of the baby. He wondered why she hadn't told him yet. *There is no way I can't know. Is she so upset about the baby she's playing ostrich, burying her head in the sand? Was she in some strange way protecting him? Knowledge of the pregnancy, and the reason he suspected she didn't speak of it, was heartbreaking. Didn't she remember? I told her when Five Stone took her, to stay alive. I knew how captive girls were treated; usually they were passed around the tribe.* He didn't like admitting it, but, as a callous teenager, he had experienced a few captive women. No thought was given to the girl or woman. It was not right or wrong. It was a rite of passage.

As his body covered hers, she sighed. He felt her smile.

"You're so warm," she whispered.

He ran his strong hands over her, skimming from breasts to waist and hips, lingering on the baby. He wiggled down and pressed his lips over the swell of her belly. "*Mon dieu*, you're a little stove. We'd better be careful or we'll set the house on fire. I love your skin, the smell of it, the feel of it. It makes me dizzy. I love you, ZiZi, my Yellow Bird. And I know you carry a child. You know, don't you, that even if Five Stone raped you and gave you a baby, the child by law is mine?"

She sucked in a quick breath and sat up leaning against the headboard. "The child is yours, really yours, Will. Five Stone didn't molest me. I haven't told you because no one believes me. I was afraid you wouldn't either."

He sensed her seriousness and pulled his body up beside hers, the quilt draped about them. He took her hand. "Tell me, tell me what happened."

Her eyes dampened and she leaned against his shoulder. "I slept for two days. He was kind to me, fed me. He insisted I clean myself, and he watched me wash every inch. I thought that's when it would happen, but..." Her voice faltered.

Will squeezed her hand.

"Then he rubbed bear grease on himself, made sure I saw the size of his t-thing." Her eyes grew huge. "Good Lord, Will, he was as big as a horse." She loosened a nervous laugh. "He might have ripped me apart. Instead, he rubbed foul-smelling bear grease all over me, insisted it would keep me warm. Then he told me to get dressed and sent me to you. She blinked and touched his cheek. "This baby is yours, Will Thunder Cloud. Please believe me."

The fire flared and danced shadows across the ceiling. "This child will have a difficult enough time with most people believing his or her father is a rogue Indian. I pray the baby is born with your blue eyes. At the very least, I want you to know the baby is yours."

Will clasped both her hands and whispered, "I believe you. Thank you for telling me." He bent and tenderly cupped her belly and kissed it. The planes of his handsome face melted.

"Come here, ZIZI, my Yellow Bird, the mother of my child."

ED KINCAID SAT in the morning sunlight; he relaxed and communed with the spirits. His cave looked down on the valley of the Yellowstone, all frosted and frozen, so beautiful it filled him with joy. At the sound of horses, he scrambled out of the light and quickly threw ashes over his fire. He rolled flat on his belly, his cheek pressed against the gritty stone. When his remaining eye adjusted, he spotted Crazy Horse.

No Indian he'd ever encountered set his bones to rattling like just the sight of Crazy Horse did. Fear ripped through him. It took at least five long minutes for his heart to quit hammering.

He peeked out the entrance and checked for Tama. Earlier she'd climbed down by the river to gather buffalo berries and new greens for her soup. Yesterday she snared two grouse. Now, he spotted her crouched in the tall grasses. He knew she saw Crazy Horse and his men and would sit still all day for she'd used great patience to catch the grouse. He carefully dropped handfuls of ashes onto the fire and patted it down before sliding deeper into the shadows.

There were five of them plus the white man in the bright purple vest. The white man's arms were arched over a thick stick and tied behind his back. They'd blindfolded him, and he looked both pathetic and weak. They prodded him into a cave like a reluctant dog. After they unloaded their supplies, Crazy Horse and two others left. One man carefully brushed off their trail with a prairie clover broom.

Tama came up after dark, and she and Ed relit the fire deep inside the cave. While the grouse soup simmered, he stroked his long beard and watched Tama add wild rice, chopped up shoots of new onions, and finally the buffalo berries. When the soup was ready, he toasted cornbread and floated it in the broth. They seldom dined so well. He smiled at Tama. She certainly was not the beauty Abbey had been, but losing his arm and eye had changed how he evaluated many things, including women. Tama was a good woman.

While they ate, he considered shaving and cutting his hair, perhaps fashioning a leather patch for his grotesque eye. Later, he dug in his bag and found his West Point ring.

ED QUICKLY REALIZED the wealth of opportunities presented to him. He killed the Indian guards and the white man easily and without remorse. He figured the white man for a gambler. Who else would wear a purple satin vest? He took the Stetson and boots, too. The boots fit Ed adequately. However, they weren't the boots Abbey'd thrown in the fire back at Ft. Laramie. Even now, he regretted losing those boots. *Why in the hell had she done that?*

While holed up here in this valley of the Yellowstone, Ed spent a great amount of time thinking. Losing his eye and his arm had hardened him. He blamed Abbey. *What good was she? She never should have allowed Crazy Horse to take him, and when she kissed that big blue-eyed Indian, why that was just mean.*

Who did she think she was burning his things? Jake had been right about one thing. Debutantes were trouble.

He watched Tama take care of the bodies, rolling them into a deep fissure. She kept one horse for him, a brown and white paint, then shooed the others down to the river. She also kept the guns, ammunition, and packs, which produced a good bit of money and a few treasures. The best proved to be a cake of French soap and a good razor, so Ed managed a wash and a shave. Tama cut his hair; he trimmed his nails.

From the gambler's belt he fashioned a dark leather eye patch. When he checked himself out in her sliver of mirror, he didn't look one bit like his former military self. He didn't look too bad either. After all, he was a West Point graduate. His posture was excellent, his shave close, and, even in civilian clothes, he knew how to fit himself out. Tama had done a decent polish on the gambler's boots, and the purple satin vest was just the look he wanted. Having a little ready cash in his pocket made him feel like a man.

41

BACK INTO THE WORLD

E d examined the paint and nodded to Tama. She was good that way, choosing horses, caring for wounds, providing food, necessities. He tucked a couple of dollars in the neck of her shirt. She'd been a good squaw.

At the Wyoming-Nebraska border he waited with a couple dozen other legless, armless veterans. The price of war still showed. He felt lucky in his shiny boots, bright vest, and the Stetson. A Texan with all his limbs offered him good money for the hat, but Ed shook his head. *No way will I part with this hat,* he thought. *That I only have one eye and one good arm is bad enough. Former soldiers—most with some disability—wandered the tracks. I don't want to be lumped with their ilk.* He ran his fingers over the bright purple vest. It and the Stetson lent him a new identity, far from that of a beaten up army officer.

He berthed the horse and checked out the passenger car. It was fit out with velvet chairs and brocade wallpaper, all the bells and whistles, but he decided to ride in the boxcar with the animals. It was cheaper and warmer there than in the fancy cars. Ferocious ice storms, some even with thunder and lightning, lined up, one after another, and now tore across the prairie. Ed hated lightning. He missed Tama.

He grabbed the horse's buffalo robe and slept warm all night. In the morning he picked the straw out of what hair he possessed and wandered into the dining car. After a sumptuous breakfast, he read the newspaper. The waiter brought him more coffee. Within fifteen minutes, the vest did its magic, and swept him into a poker game. By noon he acquired a decent stake and knew where he was headed. Those men in the know spoke of a gamblers' *Mecca*, a boomtown in the wilds of Pennsylvania where some colonel discovered rock oil. Supposedly more million-aires lived on a certain street in Titusville, a Podunk little town in western Pennsylvania just south of Lake Erie, than any other mile in the world.

ALL OF CAMELANN collectively breathed easier when Alice Fire Cloud Dupree was born. She made her entrance into the world during the Moon of Popping Branches, three weeks later than expected. Her eyes were sky blue and her dark hair glittered with hints of copper and gold. Everyone thought her beautiful and definitely agreed she was a great mix of Abbey and Will.

Lilly Charlotte Charteris was born a month early. Dark haired, promising to look like her mother, all of Camelann rejoiced. After three boy babies in two years, Summer now had a daughter. "Perhaps now," she told her husband, "we can slow down, producing babies."

The three of them, Daniel, Summer, and Lilly sat before their bedroom fireplace on the blue velvet loveseat. The fire threw out waves of heat and golden light. Daniel held Lilly. He kissed his wife's temple and winked at the baby. "Ray tells me your mother is made for motherhood, and you'd like a couple of sisters, wouldn't you, Lilly?"

"I had no sisters, Daniel Charteris. My brothers were fine playmates." Summer walked across the room in her new white silk gown and robe he'd given her for Christmas. Her long dark hair curled damp from a bath; she shook her head and combed her hair with her fingers. "Of course, I don't want to quit having babies, but four in three years is …"

The scent of rosewater trailed behind her while the light from the fire silhouetted her figure, which a month after Lilly's birth looked remarkable. He looked her up and down and released a long sigh. "I'll try, sweetheart, but good Lord, Summer, let's be honest. Neither of us shows much restraint, and you look just too damn good. Perhaps it would help if you wore burlap bags?"

HAL AND FANNY'S second son, Charles Anthony St. Clair, was born a week after Lilly. Fanny's labor was an ordeal; she almost died. A very distraught Hal asked, "Oh, Honey, how does tiny you produce such big babies?"

"Well Hal, it wasn't easy, and we'll not concern ourselves with such things in the future. Charlie's the last child to come from my body. Ray said another baby might kill me." She threw a scowl to her husband. "You'll just have to find another way to manage your …"

WHEN FIVE STONE sent Abbey to Will, he walked leading Drum, first through Saskatchewan, then along the south shoreline of Lake Superior, and across the Upper Peninsula of Michigan and down to the Christian School near Detroit. It was there he'd learned

English as a boy and taken on the name of Five Stone. He felt a great need to reinvent himself and remembered it as a lucky place.

The journey took a few years. He stayed a season in one town then moved on. Minnesota didn't appeal to him, but he liked Michigan, staying in Rudyard on the Upper Peninsula for almost a year. He arrived in Detroit wearing white men's clothing, and his hair reached his shoulders. Neat, clean, always closely shaved, even with his great size he fit in with the local population. He took good care of the horse and the rifle, earning what little money he needed by odd jobs, itinerant farm work, or loading ships at the docks.

Memories of Abbey remained with him every step of the way. He looked at plenty of women along the trek and in Detroit, but not one interested him. Abbey was his bench-mark.

At the school one old priest remembered and welcomed him. In exchange for room and board, he became the resident handyman and guard. The parishioners liked him so much they paid him extra with hay and grain for Drum, good woolen shirts and corduroy trousers for him, and a set of false teeth fashioned by a dentist, a member of their parish.

Five Stone provided a lot of venison, fish, and wild fowl for the orphanage. In turn he received ammunition and haircuts. He read every book and periodical he could get his hands on, and every evening he started but never finished a letter to Abbey.

Five Stone, from a short story in one of the magazines, learned of the name, Quentin. The minute he learned Quentin meant five, he took the name of Quentin Stone. He wrote all about his new name to Abbey and ended up putting it in his chest with the others unfinished letters.

One morning, he overheard a traveling Jesuit priest speak of Abbey and Will Dupree and their school in Pine Ridge in the Indian Territory. He arranged with the brothers to store his belongings and took Drum and his rifle and left.

Part Three

RED CLOUD COMES EAST

"They made us many promises,
more than I can remember,
but they kept only one.
They promised to take our land, and they did."
RED CLOUD, CA 1822-1909

42

RED CLOUD COMES EAST

The transcontinental railroad happened gradually. Although not completed coast to coast until 1869, freight and passenger service gradually picked up as the tracks were laid, and once the ticket prices became reasonable, the aisles quickly filled. It was not unusual to see emigrants and Indians stretched out on the roof.

Not Red Cloud, though. The Office of Indian Affairs paid for his and other important, Indian leaders, not just the train tickets but also the cost of the hotels, meals, and gifts. The justification for these expenses was to improve relations.

Change ran rampant through America. Carlisle Indian School, near Harrisburg, opened and hundreds of Indian children were taught how to be white. Camelann and other schools grew. That year, Wakanda brought sixteen more native children to Camelann. Fourteen gorgeous sacred baby ponies were born. The ponies came in all colors, from black through shades of tan, to white with a generous peppering of spotted and painted coats. Will claimed the black male which was definitely out of Drum. He delighted in all the sacred ponies, but his heart now belonged to Alice Fire Cloud. When Daniel asked Will to travel west to escort Red Cloud east, he left with great reluctance. At least, he told himself, the train makes the trip easy.

America was changing fast. Oil in Pennsylvania swelled Titusville, a 250 person village on the Alleghany River, into a city of 25,000. Rumors of gold in the Black Hills of the Dakotas filled many trains, and almost overnight Cheyenne, Wyoming, became a boomtown, populated by the type of men who agreed that the best Indian was a dead Indian. And they worked to make that happen.

Red Cloud burned the forts along the Bozeman Trail, but still wouldn't come into the reservation. He felt he'd been tricked and wanted to speak with President Grant directly about allowing his people to freely roam the plains. Members of The Humanitarian Party suggested Red Cloud, Spotted Tail, and other headmen come east, and with Will Thunder Cloud's help, arrangements were made.

They took a route avoiding Cheyenne, Wyoming; half afraid the twenty-some Indians leaders headed to meet the Great White Father would be lynched. Red Cloud's party of politicians and Indians boarded the train forty miles east at Pine Bluff.

A flurry of telegrams between Will Thunder Cloud and Camelann sizzled along the wires. Hal and Daniel sent an equal number to Washington, attempting to arrange for the Indian leaders to visit Camelann. They had no idea how difficult such a request was.

Many of these Indians were wild men from the far north and west. Many had never seen a train or a city, but they quickly acclimated to ordering meals on the train. The trip across the country proved an eye-opener for all of them. Omaha, with its many-storied buildings and bustling harbor full of paddle-wheel steamers and ferries, had them murmuring among themselves, shaking their heads. By the time they reached Chicago most of the Indians looked overwhelmed by the number of non-Indians and by the sophistication of the white civilization.

"I welcome the opportunity to speak with the President," Red Cloud told Will, "and tell him face to face that my people do not want reservation life. We want to live on the traditional lands in the traditional manner." Red Cloud picked up Will's newspaper and pointed to a picture. "I also would like to meet Ely Parker, the Indian Commissioner. I want to see with my own eyes that he's a full-blooded Indian man—a Seneca—who can not only speak the white man's language, but read and write it as well."

"I speak, read, and write their language," said Will.

Red Cloud waved a dismissive hand. "You do not count. You have white blood."

All went well until Red Cloud and his group entered the Washington hotel and saw Spotted Tail and his followers sitting in the lobby. Immediately Red Cloud and Spotted Tail started bickering about precedence. They were about to fight it out right there in front of the desk clerks, when Will took both upstairs and locked them in a hotel room.

"Let them decide," he said, pocketing the key. "I just hope they only break furniture and not kill each other."

Red Cloud and Spotted Tail came to some sort of agreement without breaking anything or each other, and they might have settled their differences if some well-meaning admirer hadn't given Spotted Tail and his contingent each a horse with a fine American saddle. Horses gave Spotted Tail and the Brulés the freedom to cavort around Washington. Red Cloud and his followers, green with envy, were forced to ride in the despised shiny black carriages.

"You are behaving like a goat again," said Will.

Red Cloud smiled. It was not a pleasant expression. "I'd like to butt a couple of heads, starting with yours. If you want me to quit acting like a goat, get us horses. It's embarrassing for the leader of Lakota Sioux to be riding around in shiny black wagons."

Of course, procuring the actual horses and saddles took time. Until that could be accomplished, Red Cloud's contingent rode in the shiny black carriages and refused to enter any of the buildings in Washington or partake of the fine luncheon prepared by Admiral Dahlgren's wife.

"We are here on business," Red Cloud, fluttering his hands, told the Admiral's wife. "No time for fluffery."

The firing of the fifteen-inch Rodman gun did grab his attention. Red Cloud measured the bore with one of his eagle feathers and watched the huge ball skip like a smooth stone five miles down the Potomac. Will even talked him into attending Buffalo Bill's Wild West Show at Ford's Theater, which he loved.

DANIEL AND HAL had no luck whatsoever in contacting anyone who could schedule the Indian Leader's return train to stop at Morgan's Corners or Gettysburg. The Indian leaders—especially Red Cloud—were immensely popular and controversial. Loved or hated, Red Cloud drew a crowd wherever he went. Police in every city, town, and village worried about lynch mobs.

Daniel and Hal took the local into Philadelphia and stopped at Oscar's Seafood House on Front Street. They sat in the dark bar, ordered drinks and a lunch in hope of contacting someone to change the route. Oscar's Seafood House, always noisy and rowdy, buzzed with talk centering on Red Cloud, in particular. "He fascinated the public," said Daniel.

"He's ruthless, "said Hal. "He's the only Indian to win a war against us."

Daniel motioned to the men sitting at the bar. "Love him or hate him, he brings controversy."

"It's that crazy little grin of his," said Hal. "He's just so damn confident."

The authorities, fearful of riots, sent his train roaring straight through Philly and on to New York. Will informed Daniel and Hal by telegraph that Red Cloud was scheduled to speak in the Grand Hall of the prestigious Cooper Institute in New York City. From there they would be whisked by rail across upper New York State to Buffalo and Chicago, then hopefully to Omaha where lavish gifts—including horses and American saddles—would be presented to them.

"How is it that a man who has never read a book," asked Hal as he doctored his oysters with fresh lemon juice, horseradish, and tomato sauce, "has no idea who Alexander the Great is, cannot solve a complex equation—or for that matter eat an oyster, be so damn sure of himself?" He made short order of the oysters then set down his napkin. "I'm going over to the telegraph office. Why don't you check the train schedules to New York? Meet back here at two o'clock."

Hal returned with a dozen telegram flimsies stuck in his vest and jacket pockets. He ordered a beer and a bowl of clam chowder then placed his hat on the counter. One at a time he pulled a flimsy out of his pocket, read it, squashed it into a ball, then deposited it in his hat.

"Do you remember that Greek sailor who jumped ship? He was one of our first clients. We defended him. And won."

"You mean that little sailor who never paid us? What was his name? His lovely mother kept inviting us to dinner."

Hal continued reading the flimsies, crushing them then throwing the small wads of paper into his hat. Finally he held up one and smiled. "Christos Stamatelopoulos. He owes us a boatload of money. All we have to do is get to New York. He'll be waiting at the 7th Street Wharf."

Daniel looked skeptical. "I'll believe that when I see him. How on earth did you find him?"

"I kept in touch with his mother," Hal said, flushing slightly. "The lovely Sophia is an excellent cook."

Daniel shook his head, smiling. "I should have guessed."

When Daniel and Hal arrived at the Cooper Institute, Will immediately suggested they become bodyguards. "We expected just a few people, and it's already a standing room only crowd. Load your pistols and fold your arms over your chest. Don't smile." His attention moved to their boots. "You're dressed perfect for the part. I'm on the stage and will be translating." He grinned. "Red Cloud will be happy to see familiar faces. I know I am."

Red Cloud, wearing a starched white shirt and a new black frock coat opened with a prayer in Lakota invoking the Great Spirit. He stood, lifted his elegant hands to heaven then bowed at the waist in supplication. His resonant voice poured like molasses through the audience in the Great Hall, reaching the farthest corner of the Cooper Institute. Daniel felt chills all the way to his toes even before Will translated. This prestigious institute had been founded to promote science, art, architecture, engineering, and truth. This was quite a coup for the Indian Peace Party and a great accomplishment for Red Cloud.

Will filled his part, too. He delivered the translation with eloquence. He spoke for twenty minutes then closed with Red Cloud's final words. "You have children, and so have we. We want to rear our children well, and we ask you to help us in doing so. It seems to us that this is not an unreasonable request—even if it comes from a savage."

A few other men from the Indian Nation were to speak, but Daniel, Hal, and Will, immediately following his speech, whisked

Red Cloud from the Great Hall. Red Cloud, who had enjoyed the applause and congratulations, seemed miffed until they reached the 7th Street Wharf and boarded Christos' little sloop. As the sails fluffed, Red Cloud looked intrigued. He carefully studied Christos as he maneuvered the sails and lines. "I watched these canoes on the river in Washington," he said. His eyes twinkled. "So this is how it works?"

Although Christos couldn't speak a word of Lakota, Red Cloud didn't understand Greek, and neither knew more than minimal English, they communicated. Red Cloud soon sailed the sloop, slick as a whistle, across the bay and into Perth Amboy. The lovely Sophia waited with horses, and all debts were forgiven.

The following evening Red Cloud rode into Camelann on horseback. Wakanda with the sixteen new children had arrived via train two days earlier. Everyone rejoiced in the reunion. Introductions, as well as tours of the school, the stable, and pastures, were made. Red Cloud hugged Summer Rose.

"I understand why Daniel's always hurrying home," he told her. "You are so beautiful you steal my breath."

She didn't blush, just kissed his cheek and said, "Thank you."

Will told him. "Abbey and I have decided to start a new school on the reservation. I'll go back with you in a few days then I'll return for Abbey and Alice Fire Cloud in the spring. The transcontinental railroad makes our lives so much easier."

With a broad smile, Red Cloud opened his arms to Abbey. He liked very much to tease her. He rubbed his stomach. "Do you still have that fat puppy, Owen?"

He stayed for three days, enjoying the school, loving the proliferation of sacred ponies. Neighbors came to meet him, and Mrs. Love made a special batch of apple cider doughnuts on a Wednesday in his honor. The children hung all over him. As he left, he shook hands with the men.

"Visit," he said. "Write to me, Daniel. I am determined to learn your language." He kissed all the women, proclaiming, "I have never seen such a bounty of beautiful women."

Then he turned to Will, and the lines of his face relaxed. He smiled at his nephew with undisguised love and admiration. "Come Will Thunder Cloud, we will ride the train west. I've been wondering, what could I teach at this new school?"

Will's blue eyes sparkled. "Goat. How to act like a stubborn old goat."

Red Cloud's face stayed smooth. "We will also discuss respect for your elders."

43

RED CLOUD RETURNS

Before Will and Red Cloud left Camelann, Summer and Daniel received a scathing note from Martha Graves. Names were not mentioned and the note came unsigned wrapped around a rock, but they knew who wrote it. She did not mince words.

"We warned you. We will not tolerate mixing the races. Stop those little heathens before they fornicate. We will shave her head and paint her with hot tar and feathers. If she lives, no man will want her. Ever. Him? There's a big oak tree in town waiting for him. Before we string him up, we'll make sure he never fathers a child".

Howie Tuttle came up with a solution. After Red Cloud's farewell dinner at Summer's house, Daniel and Summer sent Hawk and Mercy on a mission to teach all the boys proper stone skipping. The rest of the guests gathered over coffee around Summer's dining room table.

Howie spoke. "Does anyone suggest we separate them? I truly believe it would ruin their lives, break their hearts. Shakespeare knew this. Allow them to marry. I'll perform the ceremony and they can take the train with Will and Red Cloud." He looked about the group. "With two lawyers, an ordained minister, and an Indian chief we should be able to fix up any necessary papers.

He nodded to Red Cloud. "They'll be safe with your people, won't they?"

Red Cloud shrugged. "I cannot guarantee their safety, but I believe they'll be better with us than here." He rolled his eyes. "That woman at the station, she's evil…"

Summer patted her chest. "Mercy's too young."

"She's seventeen, Summer," said Flora as she wrapped her daughter-in-law in a hug. "You weren't much older when you married my Danny, were you?" She turned to her daughter and pulled Abbey into the hug. "You went out there in a wagon. You were very brave, and I must have been crazy to let you go. Just think, they can ride in a fancy car. As a wedding gift Howie and I will pay for a private compartment."

Summer wiped her eyes. "Could they board in Gettysburg away from prying eyes?"

Abbey and Flora nodded. "Much safer," Tears flowed from all the women. When Mercy and Hawk returned with the children Flora motioned to Mercy. "Come here, darling." She brought the girl into the hug. "You want to marry Hawk, don't you? How would you feel about moving out to the Indian Nation? Hawk's home?"

Will came up and knelt beside her. "Red Cloud and I will travel with you and Hawk on the train, and in a couple months Abbey is coming west. We're starting a school. You can teach there. Help her with the baby. We know you're good with children."

Mercy was not crying. She was nodding vigorously, hugging Hawk, Summer, and Daniel. "Oh yes. Would someone send a fast rider for Irene? We must tell Irene."

Daniel hugged her. "I'll send your boyfriend and Lobo tonight with a letter from me inviting her to the wedding. She'd never forgive us if we didn't."

At the last minute Hal and Daniel rode with the boys. The times were dangerous. Two Indian boys alone on dark roads might draw trouble.

༒

THE WEDDING TOOK place the following evening in Camelann's new chapel which still smelled of fresh cut lumber. It took a full day to get all the details together, and Mercy was by no means complacent.

She knew what she wanted. She loved the Indian dress which Wakanda provided. Made of pale suede and decorated with purple glass beads and silver studs with fringed sleeves, it fit her slim figure like a sleek pelt. However, she crossed her arms over her chest and balked as adamantly as a mule over Irene's insistence of darkening her golden hair with walnut oil.

Irene, who also possessed mulish tendencies, crossed her arms over her chest. "Sweetheart, the times are crazy. Either we dye it or I'll cut it all off or you won't go west. You are not entering an Indian Reservation with that head of hair." She softened her voice. "They'd kill you for it."

Mercy hunched her shoulders and shook her head and glared at Irene. Abbey, Summer, Wakanda, and Mrs. Love held their breath.

Irene dug in her purse. "I asked Red Cloud, Hawk, Lobo, and Will. They all agree with me." She held up a thin gold ring. "I've saved this for you, Mercy. What would your mother want you to do?"

Silence louder than thunder hung in the air.

Abbey stepped forward and hugged the girl. "Stay alive, Mercy. She would have wanted you to stay alive."

෴

MRS. LOVE AND Margie Zimmerman prepared the cake, a three-tiered angel food with creamy frosting and decorated with sprigs of evergreen and purple violets made from sugar.

Wakanda and the Indian children supervised the decoration of the chapel. Using purple and lavender ribbons, they tied bunches of sage and cedar on every pew, and a huge wreath of it on the altar. Lobo, with great patience, took Gussie, Mac, Johnnie, Hal's son Hank, and a number of Indian children into the woods where they gathered laurel leaves, red berries, and fern shoots. Together with Wakanda they fashioned a bouquet for Mercy.

A hundred candles flickered as Daniel and Red Cloud walked Mercy down the aisle where Hawk waited with Howie and Will. Hawk grinned ear to ear when he saw her hair now a rich brown. The ceremony was short, Protestant, and legal. Finger sandwiches, tea, and cake were served. The women cried, and under a huge moon, Summer, Daniel, Irene, Abbey, Wakanda, and Lobo escorted Red Cloud, Will, and the newlyweds, through the mountains on horseback. The party boarded the last car of the 11:15 out of Gettysburg and well out of the sight of Martha.

44

FROM FIRE COMES NEW LIFE

Will Thunder Cloud leaned on the fence, his strong arms folded against the wood. The fence was new, like so many other things around this place. The house they'd built, well, it was a few years old now, and while the floor didn't yet show wear, a lot of feet had passed over it. Abbey loved the house, except the back door didn't have that squawk like the kitchen door in Camelann. Funny, how the sound appealed to Abbey. She wondered if there was a way to build one of those sounds into her own door's hinges.

She approached him from behind, moving quietly through the lush prairie grass, but she never could fool him. Will turned, his warm smile just for her.

"Hey, Yellow Bird," he said. "You have flour on your nose."

She snuggled in against his chest, inhaling his scent, and rubbed her nose on his shirt. "Now it's on your shirt," she said with a giggle.

She felt the low rumble of his chuckle against her ear and smiled. After a moment he squeezed her again, then they both turned to the fence, looking beyond at the life they'd built. Autumn had painted the trees until they were vivid as flames, and by the river a few tired leaves circled slowly down with every breeze.

The schoolhouse, its solid white walls shining in the sun, stood fifty yards or so from them. Its contrast to the fall color was breathtaking. Outside its doors played eighteen black-haired children, including their own children, Alice Fire Cloud, and little Emil Running Cloud. Their children were very easy to spot: Alice was the tallest, boy or girl, and Emil, being the youngest, was the smallest.

"Mmhmm," she said, letting the mid-afternoon sun lull her, caress her cheeks. It was nice not having anything or anyone to worry about—at least not for the moment. All the guests had left. They'd caught the eastbound train this morning and headed back to their respective homes in Camelann and Philadelphia. She already missed Danny and Summer Rose, but it was calming to have their home to themselves at last.

Will took her hand and turned it over. "How's that sliver?"

"All gone. Tilley took it out before she left." She unconsciously rubbed the small x on her wrist, the scar where he'd cut her wrist and mingled their blood.

Will noticed what she was doing and matched his x to hers. "These," he said, kissing her forehead, "will never go away."

His gaze drifted to the dozen sacred ponies, walking slowly in the grass. Two of them were only a couple of months old, and they still clung mostly to their mothers' sides. Ruby and Remy walked behind the herd, always alert, keeping the group together.

"Our lives have not been dull, have they?" Will said. "We have our scars, but we have all this too. When I see what we have built, I think every scar has been worth it."

Her mind drifted through the memories; briefly latching to some, letting others float away then focused on the land before her. Emil saw them and waved frantically, wanting their attention. Both his parents waved back, and he amazed them both by standing on his hands—for a short moment, before tumbling onto his head. Abbey and Will laughed and clapped, and his bright smile—so like his father's—flashed all the way to them. Alice, their beautiful daughter, ran to him and helped him stand. Mercy, from the doorway of the school waved and walked toward their son.

Will was right. Yes, there were moments she wished had never happened, but if they hadn't, where would she be? Still married to Ed? Never having met Will Thunder Cloud?

Abbey laced her fingers through Will's, and he squeezed. She knew he was thinking the same as she was. Like he had said so long before, with some people words just weren't needed. The feel of his arms winding around her meant more than any words ever could.

IN A THICK copse of golden aspen, their leaves trembling in the afternoon sun, Five Stone now reinvented as Quentin Stone, sat on a log and aimed his powerful binoculars at Alice Fire Cloud Dupree. Tall and athletic like her father she also showed the promise of her mother's grace and great beauty. Every time he passed by this corner of the Dakota Territory, he stopped to secretly visit them. Abbey and Will in addition to the devotion they showered on the Indian children were good parents to their own children.

He moved the binoculars to Abbey, immediately noticing her shoulder press into Will's chest. Her husband's arms wrapped around her; he kissed the top of her head. For a moment, a pang of razor-sharp jealousy, cut through Quent. Will Thunder Cloud was living the life Quent wanted. She was one lovely woman. Never had he met anyone like her. He willed his heart to smile. She was happy. What more could he ask?

Acknowledgements

I owe special thanks to Jan Clark, a friend who died several years ago. At one time Jan worked as nurse at Columbia Presbyterian Hospital in New York City where she cared for Marilyn Monroe™. Jan told a group of us that Miss Monroe was even lovelier in person than on film or in photos, and while Miss Monroe was hospitalized a constant stream of visitors and the press hounded her. Thinking back on the comment it brought the concept of this novel from the darkness of my subconscious to the focus of my attention.

From Jan's comment came the idea that, of course, gorgeous women like the movie stars of the twentieth century existed in the mid-1800s. How would a nineteenth century Miss Monroe have fared? Times were certainly different, but were people? From Jan's comment evolved the character of Abbey Charteris Kincaid Dupree.

I must also send out thanks to my friends, family members, and fans of Summer Rose who encouraged me. I also thank my editors: Genevieve Graham, Cheryl Wilder Krass, and Kathy Tall. They caught major errors. By major errors, I mean truly humiliating mistakes. Special thanks also go to Jeanne Klaver, a daughter of the southern Comanches, who told me of the Birthing of the Drum Ritual. Thank you, ladies.

Brad Wind, who created *Summer Rose's* beautiful cover, did his magic again with the cover *for Sacred Ponies*. He also created the updated map. The Indian children featured in the background of the cover were from a photograph of the Carlisle Indian School.

Two Indian Wars followed on the heels of the Civil War: Red Cloud's War and The Great Sioux War, both took place on the Northern Plains. This story covers Red Cloud's War. The Native Americans won that one. The history is authentic. I reviewed dozens of history books and relied on newspaper accounts for much of the details. Human nature did not disappoint us. Greed for Black Hills gold and land and ugly politics ruled. Once in a while sanity made a statement. This period following American's Civil War not only opened up America with the railroads, it opened up ways of life and ways of thinking, not always good.

Thank you for reading *Sacred Ponies*. I'd love to hear from you.

Caroline Hartman
Carolinehartman5@gmail.com
www.carolinehartman

Made in the USA
Charleston, SC
25 February 2015